BOAB

Carl Leonard Groves

Paperback: 978-1-959224-50-1
eBook: 978-1-959224-51-8
Library of Congress Control Number: 2023901572

Ordering Information:

Prime Seven Media
518 Landmann St.
Tomah City, WI 54660

Printed in the United States of America

TABLE OF CONTENTS

INTERLUDES

CHAPTERS

Can't get started chemical heart

Every time I get started you pull me apart

Can't get started chemical heart

Every time I get started you pull me apart

Forgotten

Maybe they are right on the other side Undone

Better of wishing for the stars to kill the sun

Like black rose if no body can hold no one

No one

Grinspoon

Chemical heart.

Little Boxes

Little Boxes on the hillside

Little Boxes made of Ticky Tacky

Little Boxes on the hillside

Little boxes all the same

There's a green on and a pink one

And a blue one and a yellow one

And they're all made out of Ticky Tacky

And they all look just the same

Malvina Reynolds

THE FIRST INTERLUDE

MICHAEL LONGSTREET

To describe "The house" in a single word, ah, would be Gothic.

But that would not be enough, no, it simply would not do!

To describe it as Gothic would only make the obvious, well obvious.

The thing about the house, if you think you know, hold that thought!

So how else could you explain "The house"?

Well, it's not a House per se, but a stately Home.

It's big!

Huge actually, I have heard of thirty-six rooms, a grand Ballroom, not to mention the Grand Staircase.

Some of "The rooms" in that thirty-six, hold stories of legend.

But I digress I was actually asking to describe "The house" from the outside, as I said it looks Gothic, but it is more than that, an eighteenth century mansion, with a huge Bull work verandah encircling its whole front garden, but that's up too close, looking up to "The house" built on its hill it is Gothic for sure, the reason for the look was its foundation stones, no home was built here before 1890, with foundations this big.

The house was built originally, in a little town in southern U.S.A. Polk County, and this house built for the Mayor was started from a root cellar, built with local quarried basalt sandstone that had lined the cellar walls up to the foundation, which went up another twelve feet, to the first level of the "The house" this first level continued up in stone, to the second level that was wood, milled Hardwood, which was supplied locally, but what gave it the eerily Gothic name "The house"

are the two tower like turrets, that would not look out of place in a medieval story resplendent with flowing flags from their semaphore!

Those two turrets must give a view over the whole town.

And the stone that was lifted from the old home numbered and palleted and placed on a sailing ship to make the journey to Australia.

Where it was re constructed, with the stone lined cellar, the first level leading up to the second story, then the turrets, Ghostly Gothic things, jutting into the sky.

They were an addition, Joshua had added them when the house was reconstructed.

When you really look at "The house" from where I am standing, it looks just like the mouth of Luna Park, waiting to take you in and gobble you up.

From where I am standing, I can tell you three of my friends are in there now, abandoned they say, it will be an adventure they say.

But against MY better judgement they went in, it has been two days since any news from them.

I haven't yet reported into the police.

I still haven't told their loved ones.

As I said I tried to tell them that we're taking their own lives into their own hands and placing themselves in danger, on that I could not been any clearer!

I will need to call someone soon, it's been too long, maybe I should give it another half hour.

I could tell you a little more about the inside of "the house" I've recently spent some time there myself, prior to them going in there.

As you walk in through the main entrance directly in front of you is the Grand Staircase, softly winding its way up to the second floor where myriad of guest rooms began, but where you are you could go to the left which would take you through the cloakroom into the Grand Ballroom.

You could go to the right, but you would end up in the WC or the library, that is not a pun, the toilets were in the same wing as the rather large and sprawling library.

Oh, did I tell you, if it is not bleeding obvious to you now, "The house" is haunted, ghosts have and continue to roam that house, I warned them about going in there. I really did.

I don't hold much hope for them I am sorry to say, they made me wait too long, I wanted to call after twelve hours, but they had insisted on three days, in the middle now time to call them, the police….

Six P.M News

A man was arrested today and held on suspicion of a triple homicide in Shrives Island.

He will be held pending further questioning.

Late this evening Michael Longstreet has been charged with three murders that occurred in the abandoned mansion of the Late Desmond Brown, in a search of Longstreet's unit officers uncovered a huge amount of evidence that puts Longstreet at the scene of the crime, at the time the murders occurred including video images along with photographic evidence, all purportedly shot by Longstreet.

It appears Longstreet lured the trio into the Mansion with the promise to "Make a video" but the movie Longstreet had in mind was much different to the Video the prey, had thought they would be making, oh they did get ghosts, and they had wanted them for the scares, but the one Longstreet wanted to shoot, well he had been in there for days setting the Boob Be Traps, and that was the one he got in the can so to speak, the police had had the pleasure of seeing his film, well the first thirty minutes is his count so far.

Longstreet will be transferred to the Shrives Island hospital, while awaiting his court orders to be held at the state's request, where he will be moved to a permanent location.

In the van he was gabbling and hooting, that they will still be there, in the shadows.

He had been in there, and he had shot his film, and they would see them if they looked for the sixty-three-minute mark that is when they would see the ghosts.

But they never looked more than Fifty minutes into the video, why did they NOT LOOK at the ENTIRE video, would that question ever be asked or answered.

While Michael was sitting in the chair, he had been cuffed until he was bought into the ward, he was waiting for them to assign him a room, it should have been done an hour ago, but it was while he was waiting, he had a moment of clarity, it was but a moment.

He had clearly seen or clearly dreamed in his own clear mind, or as much clarity as was to be expected with Longstreet at that moment, the Library of the Desmond Brown Mansion, it was him, it was him as the Joshua Brown thing sitting opposite him at a desk, both had fat cigars sticking from their lips, puffing the acrid dry smoke into the air.

Said Joshua Brown in his distinct monotone voice that was in fact Longstreet's own voice but as well it was the voice of Joshua Brown.

"She will not be found, she is gone from the face of the planet, she is dead"

The answer had come in a cloud of cigar smoke and a nod of the head.

In that moment had come the clarity with which he saw it, the spell that was released, if it was witchcraft, was all powerful, "The house" had needed the sustenance, it had required the blood of three to hold it over.

He was counting now.

"One two three four five six seveneightnine TEN"

Michael bounced up from his seat and went for the guard's service revolver that was not clipped.

He pulls it easily, softly from its holster inverts it and pulls the trigger, the bullet smashes into Michael's chin, its trajectory places it on a course to obliterate his nose, and smashing out through the back of the cranium, he stood for a moment before collapsing dead on the ground, the leftovers from the gunshot were making their way down the wall.

The blood tumbled down the wall, bits of grey matter clotting in the mess, there was nothing anyone could have done, he was lightning fast, super lighting fast, he had the gun and just blew his head off.

As he went over, he was laughing, free from his constraints and as he joined his ghostly friends, the curse was kept alive.

CHAPTER ONE

NICK AND JESS. (TOWNSFOLK)

Nick had been looking forward to this part of the drive.

His father would take these mountain roads at a speed that was dangerous but fun.

He hadn't been on Old Town Road one for what had been twenty years, last memory of this road was on the Firefly, while heading to the big smoke to make his fortune, cliche I know but in actual truth that was how it had happened.

It was just him and his wife of twelve years, no kids, but not for the lack of trying.

Nick had turned out to be a pretty good little earner at the word processor, Nick's second book had become a global bestseller, and that had caused a resurgence in the sales of his first novel "Catcher in the Pines"

And with his literature selling as it did, he could pen any number of subjects, all would end up with a good readership.

He owed his childhood or did his childhood owe him; he would answer these questions on his return home.

Jessie came awake as he shifted the little M.G down a gear and let the little car have it, through a section of S bends that wound down through the Great Dividing Range.

"We will be there in half an hour, I'm glad you woke up, I would have shaken you soon, you don't want to miss what I have to show you"

Jessie straitened her posture, it had been a long drive, and M.G.s didn't lend much for sleeping comfort, her seat all the way back she barely had much room at all, her dress had ridden up giving Nick a glimpse of her bottom panty line, she straightened her clothing, looking out the side window the Mountains had really closed in on them, for a lady just shy of Forty she was still a looker, her strong smile danced off her lips with the blaze of red hair, the only trace of her Irish ancestry, she wore a spattering of freckles across her nose, and with piercing blue eyes, well she was wonderful to look at her, she kept herself in shape, she ate healthy, but still indulged, she was a great partner for any man, or woman, but Nick had her snagged.

She rubbed her eyes and yawned an answer.

"Aww, and what is it you want to show me"

He was shifting up into fourth from third, taking the winding S bend filled section of mountain Highway, and as the little car rounded the curve, open in front of them was a viewing area, wide and sandy carpark, a huge place for cars to "park".

"This is what I wanted you to see" As he pulled the car up to the viewing fence, which they could look out and down onto the township that is his home, Shrives Island.

"Well, what do you think" "It's, like wow"

She looked down onto the town, on one side the mighty Odistgeeg flowed down into what was the Spencer River on the opposite side of the town.

The two rivers came together at the Southernmost tip of the town where they roared into the Pine forest, and over a one hundred and twenty foot waterfall, another reason why the town had a reputation. "Wow that explains it, but if you look down to the East of the town, from the football Ground, the street running away from the Ground, that was my old street, and if you count, from the left four houses down, that was where I grew up"

She looked down studying the street that had been Honeysuckle Avenue, counted the four homes.

"So, the one with the green color bond roof"

"Yes, but it used to be red, oh well you can't stop progress" Jessie scanned around and looked directly to the West.

"Oh, I see it, and that is ours"

Nick averted his gaze into the direction Jessie was pointing.

"That the place, that's our home.

"Yes, that's it, the Desmond Brown Mansion, but now it will be known as The Lester Home, what do you think" "Ugg the two Turrets out the front, they really need to go"

"Na just the right color shade"

As they made the rest of the journey down into Shrives Island, that was when she finally asked.

"How did it get the name Shrives Island, there aint no sea anywhere around here"

"Well, no, there isn't any sea, but if you take into account the Spencer River on the West and in the East the Odistgeeg and right there in Shrives Island they both come together, that in fact is an island, an island in the ford of two rivers, do you get it" "I see an argument there, Shrives Island well OK, I get it, I think"

It was the Jewell in the Central Highlands; Gold was the first rush.

Gold has just kept coming still today, the mine began so many years ago, by a coalition of the men folk along with the woman have forged Island Gold to be among one of the finest producers of 100% pure gold.

But then there are the mills, one for cutting the lumber down, and then onto the Yard where it is cut again, stacked and stored.

Pine mostly, fed the housing boom in three states, and continue today, that operation has steadfastly remained in Joshua Browns control, on his death it was given to the people of Shrives Island.

Jason Dougherty, who had been the closest thing Joshua had to a relative, was all but running Browns Timber Products, when Joshua was killed by a Lawman, with no family, it was left up to Jason as how things should run, and he had taken control of the company, in the first quarter there had been a fifteen percent gain.

There is no way on god's green earth because Shrives Island would cease to be a town.

They came down from the hills and across the bridge that was the town limits, she was in awe at the place, it was like she was snapped back, snatched by the "Old Police" she had been taken back in time.

Everything was as modern as you could afford, and affordability in this town was not a problem, the streets were spotlessly clean, everything even the twenty-year-old Ford was clean.

"You chose to move away from this place when you were eighteen, and you haven't been back" He didn't say anything but looked over to her and smiled, pulling into the Main Street parking, one thing they had chosen not to go with in Shrives Island was any Multi Nationals, no Safeway or Woolworths, no Coles or Target, every shop in the Main strip did well, as there was no competition, and every one lived just fine and dandy.

"Why are we stopping here" "Ice cream"

He points up, she looks out to see "Uncle Pete's Ice Cream"

Beneath this in the same script is another sign "Grange Soft Drinks"

"All his recipes, you will never had tried ice cream like it"

"OK, let's do some calorie damage"

As she got out of the car, she looked up the hill at the House, she shook her head.

"What now" She turned to face him.

"It looks haunted, and if we have to habituate with ghosts Mr., they better know how to play nicely, its Gothic that's what it is, eerie "

"Ya wanna go in"

He said while looking excited by the promise of the treat in store. She shook her head.

"Comon, you little boy, sheesh, I haven't had anyone excited by ice cream since Gerald"

"Yea well Gerald's not here, and if he was, he is too short to reach the counter, any way let him get his own ice cream, why are we talking about our three-year-old nephew"

"I suppose since I mentioned him, about the ice cream"

He pulled the door in where the air conditioning greeted them in its cooling fold.

"This ice cream will blow your mind"

The bell overhead tinkled as they walked through the door to a milk bar the likes only ever seen in movies, to the left was a bar that ran the whole length of the shop, at one end was the soft drink dispenser, where the drink comes from a fountain, in your desired flavor, and it come from a tap, Uncle Pete had to Draw your drink with the help of a lever, on your right was the expanse of the dining room everything cleared in chrome, Jessie remembered "Johnny Rockets" a themed American Burger Joint where you ordered your burgers and fries, then the waitress's, joined the waiters and did a Rock and Roll dance number.

The place was scrubbed to a mirror finish, napkins in place, water jugs, back over to the counter where you could sit, at the bar, burgers, hot dogs, chicken wings, the nachos were new to the menu, as were the enchiladas.

But at the bottom of the menu was supplementary, with a list of six pies, apple, apple and raspberry, apple and blackberries then there were the peach pies, peach with raspberries, peach with blackberries, and one apple and peach, those six pies sold out no matter how many she would be cooking on any particular day, she, Sissy Green, Sissy short for Elizabeth and the Green as in Green and Morecambe, she had once been a Watkins, and a great baker, when she went from the Watkins to the Morecambe, the baking had remained, and along with a scoop of Pete's Ice Cream there was not a better dessert in town.

Green and Morecambe had been the company for which her husband was a Partner, the Real Estate in town was there business.

From the counter came the excited squeal.

"Hi Nick"

Nick looked over to see Rosalee Watkins standing there, she was Uncle Pete's daughter, she was Twenty years old, but her excitement was unmistakable, he had remembered her being born in the month he had left town, but along with the photographs shared between them, and later the phone calls home he would chat with her, and the constant media attention it was destined that the relationship would carry on regardless.

"Hi Rose, this is my wife Jessica"

Jessie holds out her hand for Rose

"Please just Jessie"

"Hi Jessie, I am glad to meet you, so you decided to bring back the deserter"

"Well, he has been wanting to get me here for years, and with our purchase, it's time to come home"

Rose chuckled, and stopped as quickly as she had begun, putting her hands to her lips, as she drew her hand away, she had a serious look on her face.

"Can I please say something about that house, The Desmond Brown Mansion"

Jessie answered her immediately.

"Of course, what is it" "Do you know it has Ghosts"

"Yes, in fact, I have no fear of ghosts, and they have no fear of me, simple" Nick was looking at the flavors available, the tried and tested Vanilla, chocolate, strawberry, then there were Uncle Pete's Special Mix.

"So, you are not scared to move in when you know what happened to those three up there, they were murdered by a crazy with the name of Michael Longstreet, after he had been apprehended and charged, he offed himself down at Shrives Island hospital, he grabbed a guard's gun from its holster and shot himself in the face, NOW they say HIS ghost roams the halls of The Brown Mansion"

Nick was getting frustrated and spoke up. "Now Rose, I Don't buy into that, so I am saying no more trying to scare her" That was when Jessie stepped in.

"Oh don't worry about it, you didn't scare me anyway, I have heard all the stories, and that includes some that you have never heard, I'm getting off light"

Rose said. "I wasn't trying to scare her I wanted to warn Jessie, that was all, and if I did scare her, I am sorry"

Jessie offered. "No its fine, Nick why do you overreact like this, nerves about being home or what"?

Nick answered.

"I'm sorry, I don't like hearing the stories about hauntings, we bought the place we will find out about ghosts Rose"

Rose answered.

"As I said I wasn't trying to get a rise out of her or scare her, how about we talk about why you are here"

Nicks mind swam around trying to remember why they had come into the shop; was it to see Uncle Pete, was it to show her the shopping precinct, it was the first one and to see Uncle Pete, and to get an ice cream?

Nick was finally able to speak.

"Hey BTW, where is your old man"

Jessie was looking at the flavors.

"He's at home resting up, heart attack you know, just this week, but he won't slow down, you know how he is" Jessie made an exclamation when she spotted the flavor she wanted.

Peach and coconut.

Rose went on.

"The Doctor released him yesterday, he was getting up to come in this morning, until mum set on with the broom handle" "Ouch" Said Nick

"So, Jessie what will it be"

"The peach apricot and coconut thanks two scoops in a waffle cone" "Ah that's one of dads latest, some say it's a cross between a Pina colada and a peach Melba, I've never had tolerance for coconut, Ahh"

Nick requested

"And I will have a scoop of the vanilla sorbet with the blood orange on top, but can I get it in a cup please" Rose went into the case to begin constructing Nicks ice cream, and as she looked up toward the front door, she shook her head and exclaimed.

"What are you doing here" The bell jingled its musical note as the doorway is filled by the shadow of a rather big man, dressed in blue overalls normally there would be an apron as part of his attire, he stood in the doorway not moving.

"It isn't, Nicolas Lester, well, the old Mansion is looking good Nick, welcome back son"

He went toward Nick hand outstretched, but then pulled his hand back and went in for the hug, Nick welcomed the hug giving back as hard as he got.

Rose spoke up. "Daddy this is Jessie, Nicks wife" They came out of there hug and Pete looked over to Jessie, she had a knowing the hugging would be happening, the big man surprised her by putting his hand out to take her hand where he kissed it gently.

"Welcome to Shrives Island I'm uncle Pete, Jessie, you will enjoy your time here, and I am so looking forward to your next art show"

"Thank you, Uncle Pete, everyone is so welcoming, and this town, it's so clean" "Yup that's partly my responsibilities, but I've got the council on that job, no getting out of cleanliness is next to Godliness"

Rose chimes in. "And may I ask what you are doing out and about, I was sure the doctor said rest, and you aint resting"

"I am relaxing, or resting, I heard a whisper that there was new delivery of pies due today I want an Apple and Raspberry" Nick added.

"Talking of pie, what do you have I would kill for a piece of Sissy's Apple at the moment"

Rose replies

"Sorry I have four slices of pie left I do have two slices apple and peach, and two slices of Peach and Raspberry"

Nick answers.

"I will have a piece of apple and peach, and Jessie, will have the peach and raspberry, right hon" "You got me, not a fan of Apple"

Nicks says "Although I will get you to try the apple one day, you may be surprised, in fact you will be

surprised" Rose plated up the pie and placed it along with a napkin and cutlery, after which she produced a cream dispenser.

She said "On it or beside it" "Beside it"

She looks over to Jessie.

"On it or beside it"

"On top"

Rose squirts a generous amount of cream.

"Enjoy" While they ate, Pete started up a conversation.

"Well, your books have bought you a lot of wealth, you need to make sure you have it working correctly, do you have a good investor, no, no, let me begin again, who do you have to manage your funds" Nick flashed his finger toward Jessie, now getting into an in-depth conversation with Rose.

"I want to say thank you Uncle Pete, but Jessie has that all under control"

"Well, that's good then, so you are cleaning up the old house and moving in, I hope you are going to pen something, I know what you write up there will be your most honest writing Nick, I can say that with no hesitation"

Nick was shoveling pie into his face he wanted the old man to go on.

"They have been up at that house every day for the last month, saw Bobby take up a load of hardwoods, said to him they for the floor, and he spouted back how these were for the staircase, sounds like a lot of work up their Nick"

Nick had known he had been waiting for an invitation and as he placed the last morsel of pie into his mouth, he turned to Uncle Pete.

"You know what uncle Pete, you come over this evening, we can have a couple of drinks and you can try some of my roast beef, got a good piece of meat ordered from Steve's, headed there next to pick that baby up"

He then turned to Rose.

"In fact, bring your wife and Rose with you, sate her curiosity" Rose looks up from where she was standing.

"What, we are going over there tonight"

Nick rocks his head up and down and a smile beams across her face.

"That's great, and we get to see if Nick can poison us" Jessie spat the rest of her pie onto the plate and laughed.

"Yea ha-ha, you will miss out if you're not careful"

Then Jessie chimed in about a time, they had ten minutes to get to Steve's before he shut up shop.

Rose came from behind the counter, but Nick protested that Steve would not be happy if Nick did not present himself, he got up from his stool, and went out the door.

"Thank you Rose this one I need to do" He wandered down the strip past the grocery store, it was open late then there was the fruit and veg market, which was the neighbor of "Steve's Butchery" as

Nick went in a bell tickled above his head, almost identical to the one that installed at Uncle Pete's.

Steve came out from the boning room with a paper package tied with butcher's string plonks it in the counter and embraces Nick which he returns, they were very happy to see each other.

"I had the freezer and the fridge installed up there in the house yesterday, working beautifully"

"Thank you, Steve,"

Steve replied.

"So, I spoke to Craig, he said he would be back early next week, just tied up some loose ends"

"That's great, join us this evening, some nice roast beef a bottle of red, it will be just like the old days" "What Time"

"I'm going home with my wife so any time soon" "I will lock up here, go home and get a clean pair of duds and be over"

They shook gripping each other by the inner arm.

"It's so good to see you Nick, after reading your first book, I was blown. Away" "Well we can discuss them tonight, as the evening grows" Steve had the distinction of "Knowing" that part of that line, he had remembered "as the evening grows to night".

And then he was gone.

On his return to Uncle Pete's, he had found that Rose would be Going to the house with Jessie and himself, she was out the back getting changed right now, she could close up early Uncle Pete had muttered the phrase.

"Aint that regular you get a star that lands in town"

As the little M.G made it way up the drive to the house, it loomed out at them, first the turrets in their cold grey stone, as they drew nearer the verandah came into view, taking the frightful gothic view of the stones, the verandah ran around the circumference of the Garden with bull nose brick work used to fence in the wonderfully covered verandah that had been in the past the site of many afternoon teas.

They all got out of the car workmen were dashing to finish last minute jobs that was when he ran headlong into the carpenter coming through the huge front doors open to flush the dust out of the hallway, following the carpenter was a huge plume of choking dust.

"We will be back tomorrow to Finnish off, your living quarters and your kitchen and dining is spotless, so enjoy your first night here Nick"

They shook hands.

"Oh, he will be done in a minute" And a huge plume of dust was blown out through the door, as the man came through, he shut off the blower.

Jessie and Rose had their shirts pulled up to their faces protecting them from the dust.

"You can go in now, most of the dust is out here"

Jessie and Rose disappeared into the house, Nick was standing there, his package down at his side as he said farewell to the last of tradesmen and went into the house leaving the doors open.

He found the girls hidden behind the plastic curtain that had contained their kitchen.

It was all pristine, and new appliances throughout, Nick went to the fridge and opened it to find it stocked, Steve, he had thought to himself, and he pulled a bottle of white from the fridge, and checked the freezer, fully stocked, the girls had found a larder full in the pantry.

They couldn't have known that below them, in the cellar, something was coming alive, and as Nick and Jessie along with Rose, discovered the house, the roots were coming back to life.

They had begun on the first story, the stone story, all the rooms had been decorated in the same colonial furniture, of the six bedrooms on this floor some had been left as day rooms and others were left decorated to sleep in.,

There had been an office on this floor currently devoid of any furniture, apart for the desk, that sat mute, just in front of that spot it was obvious two chairs had lived there for a long time.

They were on a visit back to the kitchen to freshen up their drinks, when Pete and Dianne Watkins showed up, not long after Steve Gnik pronounced Nik, the G, first letter in his surname was silent funny that, turned up with his date, he had bought his girlfriend with him, Her name was Rhonda Spelling, and she could tell you the history of the town backwards, she was also the local librarian, and to look at her you would instantly say Amy Winehouse, Nick remembers as a kid, she had been turning ten when he left, she was the same age as Steve, and with twenty years growing completed they were turning out just fine, Steve and Rhonda were very happy.

When she had hugged Jessie and then Nick she had felt as a part of the furniture, and she was.

Nick and Jessie welcomed everyone in, Jessie was excited by the way she was just accepted into the fold, a fold with lots of history, lots of water under the bridge, and some pretty fine secrets.

Jessie and the ladies split from the boys, and continued the tour, the boys found themselves on the porch discussing the food.

Nick got beers from the fridge, distributing them around, and spoke.

"Steve I should have known I had you put the appliances in, but you filled the pantry as well"

"The fridge and freezer were my idea; Rhonda fixed the pantry"

"Well, we have supplies for a week, including Bar B Q for tonight, that beef can go in slow cooker, and burgers steaks and snags on the Barb b" Pete was going to the old cooker sitting at the edge of the verandah, the Bar B Q was sitting with its cover over it.

Pete said.

"Wallah"

As he pulled the cover from it.

"It won't even need a clean, look its spotless" He leaned over and began to open the gas bottle and turned the nobs that controlled the flame to high, the Bar B Q roared to life.

Uncle Pete did a little dance move as the Bar B Q came to life.

Steve and Nick left Pete to his dance act as they went to get supplies, Nick had a lot to say to Steve.

"Its good I am looking forward to seeing Craig, eight years it will have been this Saturday, I'm glad he we be in next week'

"When I told him you had bought the Desmond Brown place, first he was rather quite, and then he was full of questions" "Oh, what kind of curiosity was it" "The old Craig, you know the one I mean, with questions like do you know what you are getting yourself into, why couldn't you have bought your old parents place, down on Honeysuckle Avenue, he showed concern that's all, he gets freaked out by this place, I mean the triple Homicide up here sent him away again, but he refuses to talk about what happened, hell he refuses to remember"

"So where did he disappear to?" "He went out to South Australia, Opal hunting at Coober Pedy, took a house underground and hid, he got some nice Opal, with all that digging he was doing" They pulled meat from the fridge, Nick grabbed stuff from the pantry, spices sauces etc., and for good measure grabbed beers on the way back out.

"This place is huge Nick; you will get lost in here"

They had planned to use the house for a Writing and Artists retreat, and with the improvements coming along so well, they would move that plan forward.

"I know I have planned a few games of hide and seek for Jessie, that will be fun" The boys were back with Pete.

"What have you got Uncle Pete to cook"

Nick put the plate down.

"There, steaks snags chops, spices, sauces, go at it"

Nick moved to the slow cooker.

"Now to put this one on"

He slavered it with a mustard rub and oil before placing it in the broiler, set it six hours and forgot it.

The girls had made their way the second floor, and it was very interesting, on this level the rooms were much larger, the master bedroom was huge, and sat on the opposite side of bedrooms two three and four, all completely furnished this was the floor where the tragedy had happened just recently, it happened in the turret room, as well bedroom two three and four.

There had been a games room on this level, it had been furnished with a full-size billiard table and three video games, as well the bar, which still needed to be stocked.

The aroma of the cooking food attracted the woman, the smell from the steaks and snags had their mouths watering.

Rose is the first back downstairs, and out the front door, only to be swatted away by her old man.

"You just wait, they're not done yet" They were joined by the remaining woman and took their seats at the outside table setting and raised their glasses to the new house, and ate their Bar B Q.

And long into the evening after much talk and lots more drinking it was decided that no one was driving home, there were plenty of bedrooms, they could all stay the night.

Rhonda became musical as the night wore on and to every one's delight, she sang and played guitar, singing mostly folk songs and joined in by everyone eventually, Dianne sat with her daughter, sitting on her lap, Rose was never too big for a hug from her mother, she sat and spoke of how she had disrespected this house earlier in the day.

Steve was happy, and as the night wore on, he found himself alone with Nick again, he had to ask.

"Nick what was it he can't talk about, what has he forgotten"

"We have all forgotten, I cannot remember, even writing about it in the book, a lot of what I wrote was simply not true, I wrote it as a novel, only loosely based on events" "Well Nick, its bringing the tourists to town, with the success of the novel, they Come here looking for the legend, and with the murders recently that has caused a twofold rate of tourists, and I don't know why they call it Tourist season, you can't shoot em"

The Grandfather clock in the downstairs vestibule chimed out for two o'clock in the morning.

Nick rolled over, he could not sleep, he went to the hallway and peered down the stairs, the lights were on down there, all the lights were out when he had gone to bed, the last one to do so.

He walked down the stairs, looking toward the front door, the hallway light was on.

He went to the light switch and was about to thumb it off, when he noticed down the hall the library, light was spilling from beneath the door, he went to it, put his ear against it, there was no sound.

He opened the door suddenly.

Rhonda was sitting at the desk, in her right hand was a high ball glass, it was either a screwdriver or just juice she had in that tall glass, but it was what she had sticking from her lips that took Nick by surprise, she had a Stogie in her mouth.

"Found these in your desk, genuine Cubans, the humidor was installed in the lower drawer come take a look" He went to the drawer still not saying anything, he looked into the drawer, it was there, a humidor, it was hard wired to the electricity and that was its home.

Nick finally spoke.

"So, what are they like"

"As peachy as the day they were packed" Nick took a Stogie out of the drawer.

"So what are you doing up" "Couldn't sleep, Steve's hogging the blankets, I thought I would discover the library, they left full volumes here, it needs to be catalogued, I will do it for you and Jess" That had been quick, the shortened name, Jess now, that had never occurred until Jessie had thought it appropriate for the friendship to evolve to the shortest name possible, Jess, and inside of twenty four hours, that had to been a new record.

"How messy is it" Nick asked.

"It will need a full reworking, Jess said there will be boxes of books here next week, I will start it then, I'm doing it on the side, love job"

There were some books scattered around on the library's shelves, some were in volumes with more than one missing, others were novels along with history texts.

Nick bought out a box of matches, offering it to Rhonda first then lighting his own.

They drew in, big puffs of the acrid smelling smoke, Nick was the first to cough after drawing in hard.

"Oh, come on they aren't that bad Nick"

Nick asked. "

So you have discussed the library with Jessie" "She showed me this room earlier last night, I am amazed by the volumes still here, there is a whole volume on this Town its whole history, we can look up our ancestors" "Some of those ancestors need to be left alone, don't bring up some of the dead"

Said Nick. He drew in, not as much to choke, and enjoyed the cigar, Rhonda sat their twirling her cigar in her mouth between puffs.

He continued

"You do know, she has taken a likening to you, you will be in her inner circle, that's kind of cool, she is getting a gang together" Rhonda chuckled at this.

"I remember when you left here I was ten, you were on that Firefly so quick, I remember that song by the B52s was playing as I saw the bus leave town, you on it, Rock Lobster was playing on my Walkman, when you think of those Lyrics it was probably a fitting send off, you heading to Sydney heading to the harbor, well that was a ten year old take on that, you know I never understood that band their lyrics their dancing"

Nick said.

"B52s I loved that band so much when I was growing up "FUN" was how I would describe them, and you heard Rock Lobster as you saw me leaving town, wow, there was never anything to understand about that band Fred Schneider, Kate Pierson and Cindy Wilson, you know they took their name from the Hair dos, those Bee Hive hairdos were instrumental in their success, the B52 Bomber had a nose cone, the hair dos were based on those nose cones, a lot of hair"

"You do know, everyone thinks I Look like Amy Winehouse, god bless her soul, I have tried so hard NOT to look like her, I just gave up in the end"

And she had tried, she colored her hair, she would be in Jeans most of the time, but one time in a bar, in Sydney, the first time she had appeared in the bar, her singing as well as her looks she was likened to Amy, that was when she had known she was not going to have a career as a singer, she gave it up for the books, and Steve Gnik, as well as the relative quiet of Shrives Island.

The cigars went on burning, Nick was getting up to refresh his drink.

'I'll come; I need to top up my screwdriver"

Said Rhonda.

"So, it has alcohol" "Oh it has alcohol, the orange is just for the color"

They walked the short distance to the kitchen, topped up her screwdriver and Nick got himself a tall bourbon over ice, they went back to the library, this time Nick sat in the chair behind the desk, Rhonda sat in at the front, still they puffed on the cigars.

The two sat there chatting and drinking, the cigars extinguished, three drinks later, the suns first Knives of light had begun to pierce the darkness of the night.

"Look out there"

Nick motioned out the window Rhonda looked and spoke.

"We have been here talking like this for four hours, lost track"

"I am headed up, at least to get three hours"

"That will take you up to nine o'clock, I need to be at the library by Eight, that is less than two hours away, besides Steve has to open at Eight thirty, time for me to get him out of bed" They went upstairs together, Nick going into his room and Rhonda going in to rouse Steve, the first night in their haunted house with not so much as scratch.

The weeks rolled on Craig had returned to town, so the Fab Four were two, the four of them would be together by the end of next month, Ian Luther and Mark Harris the other half of the Fab Four would be home and they would be complete.

The floors in the house were awaiting their final two coats of 7008 glass finish, which had meant no one in the house for Twenty-four hours.

Jessie had booked them into the river motel on Main Street.

The first thing that Jessie had picked up, was to look out their window gave out onto the perfect view of the Mansion, the other widow to the side of the room gave out onto a view of his old street, Honeysuckle Avenue, you didn't have to look hard to see the old single story ranch house that he had shared with his parents so long ago, his parents who had survived two years after he flew the coop, his parents the ones he had loved as they had loved him, his parents killed in a Nasty crash, the Timber hauler had been in the wrong lane, and coming to the top of the rise in the road, he couldn't do anything but hit the Falcon square on the front, the Timber truck, fully laden, had crushed that V8 Falcon, his old man had done nothing wrong, nor had the Motor Bike rider who had been traveling behind Jack Lester, his wife, Estelle, and mother to their only successful born, Nick, they didn't even see it coming having her head down in the latest "House Magazine"

Jack on the other hand had two seconds to register the truck and say shit, and that was all.

The bike rider died from massive head injuries caused by getting tangled up in the mess, they now lay at rest at Shrives Island cemetery.

From the River Hotel on this fine Saturday, was a walk around the town, with Nick, to see how well she remembered everything she had learned in four weeks.

They began their walk down Honeysuckle Avenue, stopping outside the house, looking down the long driveway, it was the same, except the coat of paint, scary spooky, Nick had commented about how depressing the house had looked Jessie had to agree.

They walked back across to the Motel, along Ash street, onto the park along Forrest Drive, Opposite adjacent the Oval, well-manicured and green and lush as ever, the sprinklers were watering the grounds.

They then wandered to the north, along Fir Street the school was in their path, the Primary school was attached to the High school, at any one time you were lucky to have a dozen and a half students, from prep through to university age.

The school yards were empty, devoid of life.

Just adjacent to the school was the library, closed on Saturdays.

From the library was breezeway, that ran directly to Main Street, the breezeway leads out to one side of Uncle Pete's.

It was here that Jessie had said.

"I like the fact the streets are all named after trees, as well as plants, its pleasant"

Nick said.

"They named them after trees because the Millers were the first here, I don't know if you could say if it was in their honor"

That was where they took break, still had the rest of the afternoon, they sat in a window, and ordered, pie, ice cream, and for Jessie a pineapple and coconut milk shake, Nick was plain old boring chocolate.

They timed it just right because after they had ordered a flood of people arrived, kids wanting ice creams, (Tourists) kids wanting pie, (Tourists) kids wanting milk shakes, (Tourists) then there was Bobby Cursack came in, saw Nick sitting with Jessie and made a beeline to them.

He stood there, his International Harvester cap sat squarely in his hands.

"Ah Nick, Jessie, I don't want to disturb you, but I'm done up at the house, you need to stay off the floors another eighteen or so hours, ah here are the keys" Bobby produced a key fob containing the keys to the mansion, he passes them to Jessie.

Nick says.

"Thank you, Bobby, we will call you for any maintenance issues if that's ok" "That'll be fine Nick, you know that is one spooky house, I got the hebe gibes in there, but you two have never heard or seen a thing, it's weird, goodness yes I will help you maintain the old house, nothing like history hey Jessie"

Jessie looked him in the eyes, she saw an honesty in them.

"That's right Bobby, and that house has oodles of that" "Well I have taken too much of your time"

But Nick had felt different, he pulled over another seat, patting it on its pad.

"Bobby, come here take a seat, you know my wife likes her history"

"Oh yes, I read everything about her that I can, I will own a piece of your art one day Jessie, I will know the piece when it is done, and in the Evening Post just recently they did a piece on you, about your Global success, that was where it mentioned Jessie's love of history, Janice read it first, she always gets to it before me"

Janice was his long-time wife of twenty years, still arm in arm walking down the street when they have the opportunity of being together.

"And you say you have felt a presence in the house"

"I haven't seen anything, but I heard kids in there, little kids laughing, giggling, sometimes I can hear them behind me, I mean right there, and when I turn around nothing"

Jessie was sitting nodding her head.

Nick was thinking of what to say next.

That was when Jessie offered.

"I hope we get to hear, or see something, that is amazing, they have manifested only to some" Rose was there with her check pad.

"What can I get you Bobby apple and raspberry, with coffee ice cream?" "That's what I normally get, but today I will have the apple and raspberry, and I will have a huge scoop of the peach and coconut ice cream thank you"

"Coming right up, and how is your fare, Nick, Jessie"

Nick was putting the last of his pie into his mouth, Jessie was in no hurry and had half her pie still to go, Nick looked at her and chewed, and nodded.

Rose went on.

"You know, you have been sitting in her for say twenty minutes"

Nick had finished his pie and shook his head at her.

"And"

"Well not one person has recognized you" "That's because not many pics of myself or Jessie are published, that's why, if we get recognized we will deal with it, thank you"

"I'll be back in a jiffy with yours Bobby" "Can I please have another chocolate malt thanks"

"I'll bring it back with Bobby's" "Right you are, do you want anything else babe"

Looking at Jessie.

"No, I'm fine thanks Rose"

Rose went to the counter and put her order across.

Nick started to talk to Bobby again.

"So, kids hey, and sometimes they are behind you" "Yes that's right, but there is never anything there" "Well I've had a haunting" Said Nick, throwing his hands up, the crowd at the counter turn around and look in their direction.

Nick brings his arms down, looks at the crowd and solely says.

"Sorry folks"

That is when he is recognized, the kid was about fourteen, a girl her hair up in braids wearing shorts at least one size too small for her, she waved and smiled a broad toothy grin at him.

Rose who was standing at the counter loading her tray, said.

"Please Miss it is preferable that don't disturb our guests, thank you" The girl turned back around and continued to eat her carrot cake.

Nick offers.

"I've been hearing these kids, not from as close as Bobby, but I heard them this morning just before Bobby got there, I have always put it down to the wind, but that makes complete sense"

Bobby says.

"I knew I was not going mad; I knew I had heard them; they were directly behind me"

Rose arrived with the Pie and ice cream for Bobby and the chocolate malted for Nick, that was when Bobby decided he needed a drink, he ordered a caramel milk shake when she had the time.

"I've got all the time in the world for you Bobby, don't you worry, be back before you can say Jack Rabbit Slims" He smiled up at her everyone loved Bobby, he was succinct, he had a couple of sayings, "Say what you mean, and mean what you say" was one of them, another was "Do what you know well, or don't even begin a job" he had a defined way of speaking, he had learned there was no need for a nonsense.

Bobby went on.

"They are making themselves known Nick, Jessie, they are making it known of their presence" "But not to Jessie, and not to me, completely"

"You two have until tomorrow before you can go in there, please be careful"

Jessie said.

"We will Bobby, we are not moving in without a knowledge of the history, good thing you like what I like, we will have to compare notes one day soon"

"We will, and some stories about the house and Old Desmond Brown, are the best, the scariest I suppose, but the thing is they have all been proven to have happened, and with the murders, just recently, we didn't think any one was going to purchase it, but it's part of our history, heck this towns history, and you only co own that place at the moment, the national trust is who you own that old place with"

"The National trust are the people giving me the money to pay you, and speaking of which, I have the final Grand for you at the house, so make your way over any time" Jessie adds.

"And I am going back to work tomorrow, Sunday is the start of my working week and after four weeks lay away, I am ready to get into it"

Rose was back with Bobby's milk shake.

"So, what excited you before Nick"

"Ah nothing"

"I distinctly remember you saying that you had a haunting, spill it, what have you seen" "I haven't seen anything, it is what I have heard, and I am not discussing this any further at this time"

"Oh wow, Nick is taking his bat and ball and is heading home" Nick picked up the lunch tab, Bobby was thankful, Nick and Jessica, both thanked him for his discretion regarding the house, he told them they had nothing to worry about.

Rose remained on Nick until he was ready to leave, much to the chagrin of Jessie.

As Nick exited the shop rose had a final parting shot.

"I hear ya Nick, I hear ya"

Jessie turned to Rose, giving her the thumbs up.

By the Sunday afternoon, they were back at the mansion, they were almost knocked out by the odor, they would need to air it out for an hour once they had opened it up, he was not wrong, and for that hour Nick and Jessie got into the garden at the side of the house, all along the lower level with its ornamental Shrubs, overgrown.

They managed to move a lot of overgrowth, the Gardner's would be here on the Monday, the painters back again Wednesday to begin the fret work.

It was looking more like the house that was re built in this spot one hundred odd years before, hell it looked better, it looked like the house of the Novelist, suited down to his gothic horror novels.

He was headed to the top of the literary world, where he will become household name, but he knew he had one more book to write, this one, set a long way from Shrives Island.

Jessie was looking forward to beginning a new work, and as soon as she was able to get back into the house, she went to retrieve her painting kit.

It was in the garage where she left it but it was strewn among the tools, her magenta and deep red acrylics had been opened and oozed out all over the garage, the canvas she had bought for this very purpose, was thrown to the corner laying lankily, on its corner like a diamond, trying to sparkle, and offer some light, but there was no light, just magentas and deep reds, looking like they had been thrown at the canvas, a mess, she would need to set a new canvas, in the end she stood there and yelled.

"NICK" He came to the garage door and saw Jessie standing there, he didn't see the chaos, not at first, all he saw was his wife, the look of complete shock on her face, after averting his gaze in the direction she was looking he saw the canvas first, and then the tubes, their blue labels, lids missing the paint spilling onto the tools, and anything in the way.

He went to her and embraced her.

"Well, I remember you told me, if we were dealing with ghosts, nothing nasty, what's this, nefarious children, little imp ghosts" "Be serious for a minute Nick, they are telling us something, this is an opportunity for us"

Nick quipped. "Yea well if you say this is opportunity"

Jessie nodded her head and said with no hesitation.

"Let's go inside I think I have earned a drink, a long, tall one"

"What about cleaning up this mess" "You will be better tackling this when its tacking dry, believe me, leave it lets go get that drink" "After you madam"

"Why thank you sir" They went in to the pungent scent that was now not unpleasant, in fact they had been a little high, for some time they had felt a high until the alcohol had taken over, it was eight that night, a litter of Chinese take-out containers along with the napkins from the local Chinese restaurant, The Corner Of Chow and Main, and it was on the corner of Main Street, no sign of Chow street, the restaurant was now owned by the Chows, Zing the eldest son, had married a Main.

Main Street was named after, Harold Holding Main, Main street led on to Old Town Road as well the Mill road, he was the man who founded this town and Cheryl was his great granddaughter.

Zing had dumped the name his parents had, they had owned the Star of The Orient for forty years in this town, but there was no mistaking the dumplings, still the same, Zing changed the menu regularly, but he always had the freshest sea food bought in on his own trucks from the city fish markets, he also helped the fish shop with its fresh supply, but Zing's recipe for mud crab was secret and it was flavorsome, Jessie had agreed it was the best crab she had ever eaten.

"That was some crab and rice"

Jessie sat heir nodding; she was placing another morsel of crab in her mouth.

"It was fine"

She said as she swallowed her last mouthful, she got up from the table getting the whisky decanter from the bench and bottle of red and went back topping Nicks Bourbon and topping her glass with wine.

"Carpets, for the bedrooms tomorrow" Nick says excitedly, and Jessie says.

"Clean up tomorrow"

"Oh yes I had forgotten, I will help you"

That was when Jessie said shh.

They sat silently.

From above them, Jessie had it figured, from directly above them in the second story kitchen, it was the distinct sound of children laughter.

"You do hear that; you hear kids laughing don't you Jess"

"Shh" She said, and he fell silent with her, then it came again, a burst of laughter and this time they heard it, both of them heard the distinction between a boy's and a girl's laughter.

"Yes, I hear it, it's a boy and a girl, maybe two girls, stop listen again, we want to hear conversation"

They listened, and amongst it heard muffled voices in conversation, but the laughter was always crystal clear.

Then very distinctly, they did hear a voice, a girl's voice.

"If they decide to stay, they will come back"

That was all they heard, after that even the laughter had stopped, nothing more happened, not for a couple of days.

And on the afternoon of the third day, Nick came in through the front door, he was in the vestibule when the green ball bounced off the top landing in front of him, the ball had come from above, based on the velocity of the fall Nick had figured from the third floor, it came down on a step, three down from the landing, bounced high and continued to bounce down the stairs, and along the hall way, Nick grabbed the ball as it was about to bounce past him on its journey out through the front door, it was bouncing at his hip he just reached out and "Plucked it" out of thin air, he went to the stairway and looked up, nothing to see there, he stood their perplexed, looked up again, all the way to third floor, where had this come from? a kids bouncy ball, he held the ball in his hand, looking at it, and in a faded hand the name Tim, scribbled on it.

It had been scribbled on long ago, a very long time ago, Tim, in the hand of a ten year old, this is the property of Tim, he threw the ball up in the air a couple of times and it came down into his hand with a thud, he went to the Library and opened the top drawer, he put Tim's ball in and closed the drawer, turning the key in its hole, then he went to the drawer below that, the one with the Cubans in the humidor, that had come back into commission when the power went back on, he took one of the fine cigars, and looking how many were left.

He cut the end of it, he looked around for matches but there was nothing, all he had was his Zippo, he thumbed the wheel on the lighter, and waited for the purest flame at the tip, and touched it to the tip of the stogie, and pulled it away, he drew in deep, but puffed his first drag out, he prepared himself for his next pull and took the hit, the acrid smoke wrecking his lungs, you are never to draw in the smoke like that, he exhaled a deep plume of smoke, coughs once and pulls again on the cigar, this time he held the smoke in his mouth for five second before exhaling, the aftertaste was fruits and berries, and the district taste of whisky, the stogies had been soaked in fine Kentucky red eye.

He had the Stogie when he went to the garage to tell Jessie what had happened to him.

"Hi Babe, how's the clean going" "It's happening very slowly sweetheart"

He puffed on his Stogie. "Oh I just had a ghosting, a green rubber ball just came bouncing down the main staircase, and I caught it"

He puffed again. "Where is it" "Locked in the library desk drawer, I figure if Tim wants it back, he will come looking for it"

"Tim, what, how do you know a name" "It was etched across the top of the ball, Tim"

"I want to see it, I'll leave this mess for now, please show it to me, and that thing stinks" "It may have slight pong factor, but I'm not giving these up in a hurry, taste like fine old whisky" Then they were standing over the desk, peering into the drawer, down at the green bouncing ball now sitting idle, just staring up at them.

"If I keep it locked in here, he has to see me for it"

He closed the drawer and turned the little key in its lock, removed the key and placed it neatly in his chinos pocket.

She regarded him for a moment.

"What if we are dealing with malevolence, disguised as innocent rambunctious children"

She thought for another second before adding.

"I think you have an idea here, see if the owner will claim his ball" Nick was still puffing on his cigar.

There was knock at the open front door, followed by a

"Hello"

They went out of the library finding Bobby Cursack come to pick up the final payment.

"Hi Nick, hi Jessie, I hope I haven't disturbed you"

Nick offers.

"No were just doing some cleaning, still lots to do, just when you think you have it by the nuts, something else comes up"

Jessie pipes in.

"What would you like to drink" "A soft drink would be fine, thank you"

Jessie goes to the kitchen to fetch the drink, Nick motions for Nick to follow him.

"The floors were well dry by the time you came home" "Yes but the odor was rather strong for the first few hours, Jessie and I were stoned while eating Chinese take-out"

They were at the desk where Nick retrieved the envelope from the middle desk drawer handing it to Bobby who absently stuffs the envelope containing the money into his jean's pants.

"What not counting" "You've never been short before; you never will be in the future Nick Lester"

The two men left the library and went out find Jessie back with a tray containing San Pellegrino Orange, along with a Chinnoto, and Lemon and three glasses where she led them out into the front Patio, they all sat together in the late morning sunshine, sipping on their drinks.

"The place is looking mighty nice from down in the town, and up close the old house has come back to life" Both Nick and Jessie looked at each other when he made the final statement.

Nick was about to open his mouth, Jessie stopped him, it wasn't the right time to bring this up.

She spoke over him.

"So, Bobby I bought up with Janice yesterday, ask her how Thursday sounds for dinner please and let me know" "Well yes for sure, and thank you for the refreshment, nice on a morning like today"

Their glasses came together, and they cheered the day on.

ROSE

Hi, my name is Rosalee Watkins, we've met, I am the waitress at my dad's ice cream shop, it's a good place to work, and my old man is not hard to work for, besides it will belong to me when mum and dad are gone, retired at least and besides they say "No pain no gain" right.

My years here in Shrives Island, I have lived here all my life, I've been out to Sydney, Mum and Dad insisted I needed to see and learn of the off the boat history of the city, so when I turned eleven, they shipped me off to a Boarding School in Potts Point.

Sydney I can do without you can have that place, Melbourne, yea maybe.

But Shrives Island, this town is where I live, where my family live, this is where we have settled, made money, built homes, family.

I have some tales about the inhabitants, tales about infidelity, tales of family breakdown, some stories about drug abuse, dependency, there are tales about other things as well, things that live but they don't breathe, they have lived here, but their time ended, and like all those gone before them for some reason, these beings think they can "Miss the bus" so to speak.

I'm considered good looking, I have no problem attracting a date, and I am a bit sweet over the new English teacher as he is for me, he has recently moved here from Melbourne, he has already bought here in town.

I have blonde hair, I'm not dumb, I completed High School, played Netball, and walked into my family business, my girlish good looks made me lazy I Suppose.

I have always had an interest in things that go bump in the night, my interest in Nicks first book was of local amazement, and the "Familiarity" I had felt growing up with parents who had referred to the popular artist just how it was, they had known Nick personally.

My Favorite film maker was Rob Zombie, not the remake of "Halloween" I could have missed that and not missed out, I am talking about the films where he featured people such as Sheri Moon, Sid Haig, Bill Moseley and Richard Blake, you know "House of A thousand corpses" "Three from Hell.

Reading which I do a lot, I grew up with King Steven, all the stuff written years, heck decades before I was born, The Shining, Carrie, Cujo all had an effect on me, I was seasoned younger King fan, but he was only one author, I have read Jayne Austin "Sense and Sensibility" I have read Brett Easton Ellis, "American Psycho", I have read Tolkien "The Hobbit" during my twenty years I have read prolifically, I just completed a Historical novel, set in Rome in 80 AD, it was interesting.

Am I getting off track, maybe I am maybe not, but this is my take on the whole situation, and to know my story you really need to know me, why, I can't explain it just like that, I will go on, if I am getting ahead of you slow me down, I will be patient?

Shrives Island, from the mountains on all sides of the town, to the Twin Rivers that come together at the south of the town, to the waterfall park, from the shops on Main Street, to the homes in the residential conclaves, Shrives Island was blessed, with the riches that came from the abundant gold mines, right down to the fish smoker who had a very good supply of trout out of the river, from the Mills, the timber products that were produced, to the individual shops in the town, even dads ice cream shop we all get along in Shrives Island.

As I said before, I have all sorts of stories, and the one I will tell you is what I had known about Michael Longstreet, I had known him, not on any personal level, but as a regular client, he was regularly in here to purchase pie and ice cream, and he would chat to me, Longstreet shared information with me that was to do directly with the deaths, I didn't know, but after the murders were discovered, and the news was out, I had instantly known that the police would like to speak to me.

I told them what I knew, the information that I had, was included in the brief that Nick and Jessie were given.

Now, what he told me, and when he told me was cryptic, and it was in riddles a lot of the time, but I do remember the day it began, he came in, sat in the chair at the counter directly in front of me, he said.

"They will take her out and hang her high" When I pushed for more information, work out what he was saying he looked at me blankly, and had no idea what I was talking about, he walked out the next minute, so that conversation went waiting.

Then on the afternoon of the of the killings he had come into the shop, and he had lots to say, he was going back over historical information, saying that they would burn the witch, they would hang her and burn her, I had questioned him, and he went further, telling me that they would hang her first.

I rang the police at that moment, and waited for them to turn up, but when he had left the cops we're nowhere to be seen.

When I heard the news the next morning, I rang the police again, I had known who the culprit was.

The Police captain came down with Senior Sargent along with a couple of constables, why so many I have no idea, the Senior Sargent would have been sufficient.

So, the Captain sat at the counter and listened while I spoke, one constable was instructed to take notes of what I had to say the, the other constable was a third wheel.

And based on my statement alone, they had enough to at least bring him in for a question-and-answer session and based on the fact of my earlier call to the local constabulary and with naught happening about that initial report, it had got out and into the media that I was a wealth of information, next thing Dad's out the front, holding off reporters with a loaded shotgun, no one was getting to me.

Things pretty much settled down later the same day, after reports of Michael Longstreet shooting at the Hospital.

We had expected the media involvement, but Dad wasn't having it.

I was considered the first port of call regarding information on Longstreet, although my knowledge was retained to what he had told me I just put it all together, wasn't that hard, I had figured he was falling of his perch when I rang the police the first time.

He had managed to lure three people up from Melbourne on the chance of filming a documentary, the documentary was of Michael Longstreet murdering them.

Yep, always something interesting, or spooky, or just plain stupid to occupy the minds of the people in this town, but as I said earlier, no pain no gain, but yes currently tourism is up.

CHAPTER TWO

TIM AND MIRANDA

She opened her eyes, she was laying straight, arms by her side, head to the ceiling, she listened, then she had heard it, it was distinct, it was the sound off a bouncing ball, it would come in three bounces and pause, but it had woken her up, she sat bolt upright and looked across to her husband who was blissfully asleep, she shook him, he opened his eyes rubbing them.

"what's up?"

"Shh"

Said Jessie.

"You woke me"

"Listen"

She said to him.

He was quiet.

BOUNCE, BOUNCE, BOUNCE.

He looked toward her,

Then came the chuckles of a boy and girl, there was a short pause then the BOUNCE, BOUNCE, BOUNCE.

Again followed by the chuckling together.

They were sitting in bed looking directly at each other but did not see each other, they were both down the stairs, not physically, but in their minds, Jessica was the first to break the gaze.

"Nick"

She had to say it twice.

"NICK"

He snapped out if the trance he was in, he was thinking that they were wanting to interact, communicate, he got up from the bed grabbing his dressing gown and throwing it over his shoulder as he began to leave the bedroom.

"Hey, where are you going without me"

"Well, obviously no where, come on, get out of bed" He grabbed for her Bed Coat and threw it to her she caught it on the fly.

"Good catch"

He said to her with surprise.

She was pulling it on and tying it off.

"Lets just do this" She said to him.

He started out of the room a second time with Jess in tow close behind him, he didn't need the lights on the stairs because the upward glow from downstairs was perfectly lighting their way.

They had turned the downstairs lights on.

They went down the stairs one at a time it was on the mid landing where they spotted them, standing on the ground floor level, from the mezzanine where they were standing the two children looked verry much alive, then it came again BOUNCE, BOUNCE, BOUNCE, the two children looked at each other and giggled.

"Hello, I'm Tim"

"I am Miranda"

They looked at each other again and giggled.

Nick and Jessica looked at each other not saying a word, then Nick turned to the children.

"Hi my name is Nick"

He let Jessie have her say.

"Hello, my name is Jessie"

Jessie paused for a moment before continuing on.

"How long have you been here Timmy, Miranda"

The two children looked at each other, then back to Nick and Jessie, Tim bounced the ball again.

Bounce, Bounce, Bounce.

Forever, they both spoke the word together.

"Tim was here first, I came after Tim, you see I was faster than Tim"

"Yes that's right I was too slow, he managed to catch me first"

"And we have been here ever since, they keep us here together" They both answered again in unison.

Jess looked toward Nick, not knowing what to say.

"Who was responsible for my wife's art supply's being strewn all over the garage, lids removed and contents emptied over her completed works"

The children looked again at each other perplexed.

"It took me some time to clean up that mess"

Said Jess.

Miranda looked back toward Nick and Jess, her eyes were wide, and she was holding back tears.

"We did not do that, Tim or me would never do that, Longstreet was the one, it was Longstreet that did that to your paintings"

Jess's look on her face chanced, as did Nicks, Jess questioned the two children

"Longstreet"?

She had remembered that name from the ice cream shop, Rose had mentioned a Longstreet in her recent tirade about the murders most recent in the house.

"He was the last to join us"

Said Tim

Miranda added.

"He is a troublemaker, he likes to prank everyone, that is what he did to you he pranked you"

Jess turned back to Nick.

"What now, they are talking about ghosts pranking us"

"What do you mean, ghosts, they are ghosts, look at them"

Jess turned back to the children.

"So, can you call on this Longstreet"?

"He comes when he wants, but whenever he is around, we prefer not to be in the same place, I find him offensive"

Miranda placed her thumb and finger to her nose and pinched.

"Phew"

She said and continued.

"We have been in this house for a verry long time, Longstreet has only recently come along, he is a trickster"

Jessie stood and asked

"A trickster, what is meant by that?"

Miranda said

"Yes, I think he was placed here by Desmond to cause mischief"

Jess turned to Nick.

"Desmond Brown, did he bring this house out from the U.S.A"

Nick spoke.

"No Desmond Brown built this house originally; he was dead by the time they pulled it apart and bought it here, it is said the ghost of Desmond Brown travelled with the house, continuing to haunt the place, his son Joshua, looked after the move"

Tim stood looking at Nick, then he said.

"The tree, that was here first, the Desmond Brown Mansion was why the tree was removed"

Nick turned to Tim who said.

"Look around you, you see timbers rare timbers, never before seen in a house"

They all looked at the timbers, and some panels were finished in the most a lustrous wood grain.

Nick went back to his conversation with Tim

"Hey Tim, how did you get your ball back?"

"I retrieved it from your draw, thank you for keeping it for me"

"I locked that draw Tim, I locked it on purpose"

"Things such as locks and doors do not create a barrier to us, is that not correct Miranda"

Miranda nodded.

He disappeared and repapered right beside Nick startling Jessie almost as much as he did Nick, Miranda giggled.

"See"

Tim stopped and looked toward Miranda, she returned his stare with the fright that Tim had shown.

Tim spoke, urgency in his voice.

"Miranda it is time for us to go"

Miranda stood there only nodding her head again.

Then they were gone.

Nick stood their looking at Jess when the room began swirl with wind first, and then the sensation of rain, coming down heavy, soaking them in the few seconds the torrent had come, the wind had returned and with it came an entity.

It was Desmond Brown.

He stood there, his waxy pale skin stood out, but from the tip of his top hat down, he was dressed immaculately to the tips of his toes, from his riding boots, shining brightly, to the well-fitting jodhpurs, tucked with his well-fed body, his paunch stuck out but was sinched at the waist by a coat its buttons all five of them pinched at his gut, the fine silk cravat that covered his neck, pillowing the platinum beard that was full, his features were framed by the beard, devoid of mustache hair, his bulbous nose bridged the fine hairless lips beneath it, his bespectacled eyes shone red.

His gloved hand reached up and removed the hat allowing a river of platinum brown hair to flow down, around his face, it was then he addressed them.

"Ah we finally reunited"

Nick stood forward shielding Jess, he said calmly.

"And who may you be and how are we reunited?"

"Such a memory Nick, NOT ah ha,, you should speak to Craig, he will remind you"

"Craig what do you know about Craig"

"I know all of you, oh sorry Jess, my name is Desmond Brown, I am pleased to meet you this nonce has no memory of what transpired, Nick maybe you should talk to Ian Luther, or Mark Harris, but really the one who has retained most of what happened was Craig, best you ask him"

Nick stood forward as Desmond Brown come to him, he didn't walk, Nick or Jess did not see his feet move, he moved on the either, or was so quick that they missed it, his fat pudgy face sat coldly inches from Nicks, his frosty breath struck Nicks face.

"Ah Nick"

He whispered.

"Nick, you need to remember why you made a purchase such as this" Nick drew away from him back to the sanctuary of his wife, Desmond remained where he stood, looking directly at Jess, Nick moved into his sight blocking Jessie.

"Jessie"

Whispered Desmond.

Jess peered out from behind Nick, she looked at Desmond, then she stood from behind Nick.

"Thank you Jess, that is exactly what I was thinking, you are rude Nick, now Jess, if I may call you Jess"

Jess could only nod, she turned to Nick who stood there, he was starring off into space, he was trance like.

"Take no note of him, he is somewhere else, I need to address you"

He remained where he was, Jessie was moving in his direction, she was getting closer to him but she had not registered, it was Desmond coming toward her, gliding slowly toward her, unlike when he approached Nick it was lightning speed Jess felt his frosty breath upon her cheek when he spoke.

"You will paint for me, and the girl she will paint for me, I will "consign" both of you"

Jess didn't, couldn't say anything, she just Nodded.

Desmond moved to where he first appeared to them, Nick came out of his trance first, he saw where Desmond Brown was standing and saw that Jess was now standing beside him, Nick reacted. "JESS"

"Calm down Nick, you and I need to talk alone"

"What have you done to her you bastard"

"SSHHH, Nick Now, listen to me"

Nick turned back toward Jess, still trance like and back to Brown, and listened.

"Now, this is what I want from you, look into the paintings, look to find the answers"

Then he was gone.

Nick and Jess were back where they started, it was in that moment, Miranda and Tim returned, they were standing right where Desmond Brown had stood.

"He had you both within his power"

Said Miranda, Tim added.

"Do either of you have any idea of what just happened"

Nick and Jessica looked at each other.

"We met Desmond Brown"

Said Nick.

Jess added.

"And he had a secret for us, one each, I can't remember what it was"

"I have to look at something, I know that"

Miranda looked at Tim, she looked back to them as did Tim the two spoke in unison.

"Jess you have to paint with the girl, Nick you have to look"

Nick and Jess looked at each other and back to the children.

Nick spoke.

"Does he know about you two kids"

No said Miranda, Timmy stood there shaking his head and said.

"He has no idea about us, he cannot see the forest for the trees"

Jess turned to Nick.

"We could use this to our advantage"

It all come flooding back to them, it come to them succinctly, how Desmond had told them that Nick had to remember, he was playing a game with them, this games conclusion would ultimately end with murder.

Tim and Miranda stood and watched as the information of what had recently transpired was coming back to them.

Jess spoke to them.

"Hey kids, how would you like to get even with Desmond"

They stood there and Nodded.

It was in the afternoon, as twilight came to the house, the silence of the afternoon was deafening. The Ghosts of the departed, now absent and quiet, Jessie was napping in the sun room, after beginning a new peace earlier that day, Nick took time, he looked at the panels in the Library, he went up to a panel of timber, looked deeply into its tight colorful grain, the red swirls that leapt from the center of the panel appeared to Nick just like it was bleeding.

As he concentrated on the movement of the grain it was apparent to Nick, the house was bleeding to death.

It had all gone along swimmingly, Jess began her tutoring at the school, she had been given a student named Angie Bell, she had been a verry talented artist, from age three had shown a propensity for holding a paintbrush, instead of a tennis racquet, she even had one of her pieces hanging in the Shrives Island Library, from the tender age of twelve.

On a fine day the two were in the garden.

Jess was painting next to Angie.

Angie was painting the front entrance, with the huge Oak to one side Jess was working on a still life.

They had both been silent for some time it was Angie who broke the silence.

"You know I have painted this house" Jessies ears pricked up.

"Oh, have you, how interesting"

Angie replies

"Interesting, oh yea for sure, as interesting as like I have shown no one, now its out there, so I have to show you"

She put her brush on the easel and looked back toward the house.

"Every time I start it, every time it works out, I don't know wrong"

Jess was almost convinced Angie was "The girl" Desmond had mentioned.

"So do I get to see them?"

Angie stood looking back at the house.

"Of course, this afternoon"

Later, they arrived outside Angie's home, a neat brick two story house, which sat in its garden liked it belonged.

"Now we go straight through the house directly into my studio, no stopping at mum for a huge convo, you can speak later, ok" Jess just nodded.

As they opened the door Angie yelled.

"Mom, I'm home"

From the kitchen just off the hall they were traversing the voice came, "Ok sweet heart"

They continued to the back of the house, to a door painted bright red.

"This red door makes mom and dad stay on this side, you know artists privacy" She pushed the door open welcoming Jessie into the inner sanctum, the studio appeared to be a lot older than it was, it was big, two rooms a wall removed, canvases were laying against the wall in stacks, there were piles of canvases on the benches which were full, Jess looked out the window at the back of the studio, it led out onto the park, where netball and football were played, Angie never took note of sport, she enjoyed the nature, just adjacent the window was Angie's easel, it had a canvas laid on it with a blue hue painted into it.

The walls were hung with many of her works, a family pet cat, the waterfall was in many, the main street with Uncle Pete's front and center, there was a portrait of her parents, and lots and lots of landscapes, from rolling hills to the mountains that surrounded Shrives Island.

"Wow you have a huge body of work, you are so prolific"

"Look over here"

Said Angie as she went to the huge wardrobe on the north wall of the room, she took a key from her pocket, it was an old pipe key, in one motion she put the key in and turned it.

"Now before you see these, it is between you and me, no one else needs to know, ok" "Ah yes for sure"

Jess crossed herself.

"Cross my heart" "Well ok then here goes"

She swung the door open, the wardrobe was full of paintings.

Angie pulled two from the heap that was in there, they seemed to be all the same apart from color and shade, the turrets were the features, but the windows had seemed to be blacked out, Jessie looked at the two she had pulled out, there was nothing there, Angie pulled out another, Jessie studied it, there was nothing, and then the fifth painting gave up a small secret, in one of the higher windows was a figure, she couldn't make it out, by the tenth canvas, it was obvious to Jessie who it was.

It was Desmond.

Jessie looked into the wardrobe a final time, there was a larger canvas laying painted side down, Jess was curious, she went to the painting pulling it out.

The painting was of a Boab tree, the canvas was full of color, wispy blues bled down the canvas until they became green, the Boab was full of life, its foliage as green as green could be, the brown of the bottle of the Boab, the bottle being the main body of the painting, was rather large, and the white flowers with their bright red fronds bounced off the canvas.

Jessie was curious.

"This is good, why is it shoved in the back of the wardrobe, from what I can gather, only your worst renditions, or those that spook you go in here" Angie thought for a moment, then said.

"It is scary that one, I painted that one in two hours on a Saturday afternoon, I have no memory of doing it's like I blanked out, and when I came too again, two hours later, that was the result"

Jessie looked at the painting, noticing something she thought was very strange, there was a hill, and the Boab was at the top of it"

"So you have no recollection of painting this"

"No, I know I did, but I have no memory of it, put it back please Jess it freaks me out" Jess placed the canvas back into the wardrobe, painting side down so Angie didn't need to look at it, it was forgotten, for now.

While Jess was finding more at Angie's house, Nick was visiting with Craig, he had come in the evening before, and it was time for a visit.

Nick drove into the Motel, Craig had insisted he was staying at the motel, he would not stay at the Gnik house, and although he was sorry, he was not staying at Nicks place.

He pulled up outside Craig's room, got out and as he got to the door, it opened.

"Hey, I'm just going to Uncle Pete's for a bite, good timing Nick"

The two men embraced for a long time, craig pulled back and looked Nick up and down.

"Looking good Nick, and how is Jessie?" "She is good and looking forward to seeing you"

The men began toward the crossing that would lead them to Uncle Pete's Nick continued.

"I don't know why you are so apprehensive about coming to the house"

"I still have nightmares about that place"

He paused and looked up at the house.

"But you have done a great job on it, it looks stunning"

Nick paused and looked off in the direction Craig was starring.

"You want to see the inside, it came up spectacular, all the carpets are gone apart from the rooms, and there is 7008 all over the floors, new paint throughout, its not the house you would remember"

"Oh, I would remember it alright"

They walked on.

"I've been looking forward to this for some time I can tell you, the last time I was here, he was closed so I missed out"

Nick got the door, the bell tinkled overhead, Rose was at the counter, Craig approached, but Nick stayed just in the background.

"Ah Craig"

Squealed Rose as she came around the counter to hug him, she looked up and waved at Nick, but continued to hold Craig.

"It is so good to see you, last time you were here you took off in such a hurry "

"So how about a table for Nick and me?"

She released him from her hold still smiling.

"Sure, how about over by the front window"

Nick and Craig settled into their seats, Craig picked up the menu and was amazed at the additions.

"Wow, he added a bit since last time" "Well it has been a year"

Craig nodded as he looked around the Café, he noted new tables and chairs, new décor throughout, and the paint was relatively fresh, same color as always, but freshened up recently.

"Each time I stay away, I come back to same old town, I mean some things have grown up"

He motioned toward Rose.

"Some things are renewed, like this place, its still the same old Uncle Pete's but its different, its changed"

Nick quipped.

"Shit Craig, you've changed, I've changed, hell Look at Rose, she has blossomed since the last time I were here, things change Craig, time heals old wounds" Craig cut in.

"So tell me Nick, when are my old wounds going to start to feel better, when will I begin to be "Normal" again, you have done well for yourself, Ian has had a good career with "Tin Soldiers" and Mark nailed it, he is doing what he loves and making shit loads of money,

I couldn't believe it when he won the Melbourne Cup with a hack he bought in the country, you all have wonderful wives and the career to match, and you really landed the big one Nick, how much have you made from publishing, and to land the wife you did as talented as she is, you got it all, and I'm not at all jealous of any one of you, I'm seriously not, besides since Marlii there has been no one else, yes when I fall I manage to land in shit loads of money, but I am still the one having the dreams and nightmares, daymares even, I just want it to stop Nick"

It was then Nick asked him.

"Craig if I asked you about Desmond Brown, what would you say"

"Desmond Brown, who is Desmond Brown?"

Rose came over to them breaking the conversation, Rose looked directly at Craig.

"What will it be boys" Nick looked up at Rose.

"So, we are the Boys now" "You have always been the boys, just missing Mark and Ian, remember Nick I hear all the old tales of yesteryear, directly from the source, Uncle Pete tells me everything"

"I think she got you their Nick" Craig began to chuckle, and was joined by Nick, then Rose joined them.

Reunion

The day of the reunion rolled around like a marble in a glass dish, the Sunday morning had arrived with a thud.

The night previous had been a full one, after their visit to Uncle Pete's where there was no sign of the old man, it had been decided to go to the mountain.

As they rolled into the old man's driveway they found him under the bonnet of his old Ford Cortina, it was a love job, he was doing it up for Rose's twentieth birthday, it was almost done, now to the paint shop for its new color.

Craig was first out of the car; he went to Pete embracing him in a long hug.

"It's great to finally see you again"

"Yup, great to see you Craig, it's really good"

Nick stood and waited for the men to separate, going to Uncle Pete and shaking his hand, Pete pulled him into an embrace.

"So, nick that reunion is fast approaching, are you all set" "All set Pete, but this one is refusing to come to the house, I've explained its inanimate and" Craig Interrupted.

"Oh alright, I will not set foot in the house, I will remain in the garden, is that a deal" Pete spoke for the two of them.

"DEAL"

On the Sunday morning Jess got out of bed and left Nick where he lay, knowing the state he had made it in last night, he needed a little longer and made her way down to the kitchen where she sat the coffee pot on the stove along with Bacon, she had put toast in the toaster, and was grabbing the eggs from the fridge when from behind her she was grabbed around the waist, she turned to see Angie standing behind her.

"Surprise" "W what are you doing here so early, its seven thirty, I know I told you ten" "Couldn't sleep, I want to know as much as you do, what he thinks of the painting, did you show him yet?"

"No, the state he came in last night he would have not remembered a thing'

"So where is he, get him up if he is asleep"

"No, no, he needs more sleep, any way you are here now, I can keep you busy with the preparations for the reunion" "And pray tell what that would involve?" "Setting the tables in the Marquees, easy stuff we will do it together take our time, chat catch up a bit more, you tell a great history of the town"

Angie was taking the toast and buttering it, Jess was placing eggs in the pan, and the bacon out placing it on the plates.

As the pot of coffee came to life Nick wandered in from upstairs.

"Oh, my head" Jess was chipper

"Good morning drunk" Angie sniggered at the remark.

"Hey that's not fair, I got a little tipsy"

"You got a whole lot of drunk"

He sat, head in hands and squawked.

"Coffee for me, maybe some toast, but can't eat a thing"

Angie got excited.

"Show him, show him the canvas" Jess came to the table with two plates of food, place them down and left the kitchen.

Angie excitedly exclaimed.

"Wait till you see this"

Jess was gone for only a minute; she was holding the canvas art side in as she approached Nick she asked.

"I will turn this painting in a minute, study it, and point out to me anything out of the ordinary"

Jessie spins the canvas around, Nick looks at it, he makes no comment about it but stares at it intently, he gets in close, he even squints, he then looks at Jess and then over to Angie.

"I like your work, and this one of the house, swirling colors its quite attractive, however" He turns to Jess.

"Is that Desmond brown in the top window?"

Jess answered. "That is Desmond, I would say that meeting this particular student was no coincidence"

Angie adds.

"I agree with you both, when Jess first explained to me about this man, it freaked me out" Nick then pipes in.

"And the thing is when I asked Craig about Desmond Brown yesterday there was no knowledge, he seemed to just shrug it off, it's just weird" They sat at the table eating breakfast and drinking coffee, talking about the strange goings on, they spoke of Angie's strange occurrence's with her paintings, how those particular paintings never really issued any strong attractions of ownership, that was why she had kept them in the wardrobe, Jess had bought up Nick's latest work, and how he had changed mid-stream to now write a book about Shrives Island and the occurrence's at the house surrounded by the fact that Rose had so much on Michael Longstreet, now wasn't the time to say anything, this little riddle just got a whole lot more interesting.

The guests began arriving on time, Uncle Pete and Dianne were first to arrive, followed closely by Rose along with her squeeze the new teacher Burt Ward Steve Gnik and Rhonda Spelling were five minutes later, Ian and Cathy Luther arrived with Mark and Cindy Harris, Bobby and Janice Cursack were next to last arrive, but Craig was a no show.

As the lunch hour crept up on them, they weren't about to start without Craig, as the drinks flowed it was Steve that came to Nick'

"I'm sorry Nick"

"No don't be, I heard him commit yesterday afternoon to Pete, and me I had him on a promise" "Well I'm heading down to his motel, scare him up" Nick said.

"I will go, I need to speak to him about something" Nick made the announcement he would attempt to track down the lost guest of honor, they were to keep the party traveling along.

He pulled into the car park, and went to the car park adjacent Craig's F200, he knocked, he waited for a bit and knocked harder.

"Craig" there was no answer, he knocked again, banged on the door this time calling again, his hand went to the handle, it turned easily in his hand he swung the door open, it hit the door stop and began to close, Nick stopped it with the palm of his hand, he opened the door completely and called in.

"Craig"

He walked into the room, and stopped at the light switch, he thumbed it on.

The room was empty, Craigs bags were still on the floor beside the bed, the bed looked as if it hadn't been slept in, on the side table was a bottle of J.D with a finger left in it.

Nick turned and left the room going to the manager's office, a buzzer went off as he entered into a large room with a huge desk splitting it in half, a huge couch took up the whole wall opposite, Nick went to the desk and hit the bell.

TING.

A lanky man came through the curtain that separated the man's living quarters, his pock marked face was split with a huge smile, a goofy grin.

"Hey how can I help you Mr."

"The guest in room thirteen, Mr. Gnik do you know where he may have gone?"

"I seen him this morning, he was headed down to the waterfall park early this morning, haven't seen him since" "Thank you"

Nick turned to walk out when the goof spoke.

"Hey, you that writer, that bought the Desmond Brown place" "Yes and its now known as the Lester House" "Well ya doin a good job at it" Nick pushed the door open and let it close on its pneumatic arm, but the goof was there to stop it, he had sprung through the hatch as he had thought of something to tell him.

"Hey Mr. Lester, you know they are rather scary, the ghosts that I have heard of in that place, it must be at least a bit scary"

Nick had remembered then, the almost empty bottle on the bedside table, he stopped and took a step back toward the Lanky goofy dude.

"Who have you spoken to about the house, did you happen to have a drink last night with Craig?" "Why yep, he bought a bottle of Jack Black, he asked me if I wanted to partake, I never give up the opportunity for a drink" Nick turned and walked away.

He made his way down to the track that led to the car park for the waterfall park, as he crossed the car park to the viewing area there were little collections of people on picnic blankets, kids running here and there, the Bar B Qs were all occupied, there were a couple Weber's set up along the banks being tended by tubby beer swilling grandpa's happy to be hauled up to Shrives Island by their sons, and daughter's not having the drive in front of them they were pleased to go along to Shrives Island for the day, besides looking after the grandkids for the day would be fun.

The thundering waterfall made up of the Mighty Odistgeeg on the east and the Spencer on the west, came together and fell over as one.

Nick scanned the people looking for Craig, to no avail he turned to go back the way he came, and had noticed two of tourist's had noted Nick, looking a little frantic, he kept heading up the track, away from the car park, he had made it to the safety of the trees, as he came over into the car park he spied Craig walking into the motel, he had his good duds on.

"Craig"

Nick called getting his attention Craig waved the men came together in an embrace.

"What are you doing, the parties on hold man" "You know what today is, it is Marlii's birthday, you know how she had that religious streak through her, I went to the Church Of England to light a candle for her, besides, I find strength in that"

"I forgot, heck I hadn't even thought, I am so sorry Craig, why I chose this date I have no idea, what was I thinking"

Nick stood there looking down incredulous.

"You know what Nick, I think we are late enough, I think we should get to our reunion"

Nick looked up he looked into Craig's eyes Craig was sure he saw a tear.

Later that afternoon, the Bar B Q done, sweets served and plenty to drink, they had all gathered in the large Marquee, when they had taken their seats, Steve addressed them all.

"Please if I can have your attention"

Everyone sat eyes forward.

"Thank you all, we are here today because it is the first time four men have come back, to be together again, all have had different journeys same destination, I have a feeling two will be back with their lovely wives before too long"

This elicited laughing through those assembled.

"So Nick would you like to come up and talk"

Nick went to the head of the crowd.

"It's nice to have you all here, for our reunion, it is great all to be together again, I am sure that the four of us will enjoy our time together, I am pleased that Craig finally made it"

Craig tipped his glass.

"We have a load of catching up to do, Mark, Craig, Ian" Nick held his glass up, they saluted him back.

"Any way I am pleased to have us all together, it is wonderful that you all came"

Later into the evening the four of the men had been sitting, talking about the past, they had been catching up on the fun of being teenagers.

They had been talking about the summer of 1974, they had all been of differing ages by a year, how they had managed to get into the powder room down at the Main Mine 5, there had been explosives in there, the boys had known a secret, there was more explosives there that had been accounted for, the four of them all broke in and evened up the ledger.

It was in the newspaper, the four of them with broad smiles on their faces in the custody of the local laws.

With the headline "Four Local boys cause security scare at local mine" For the next few days they ended up becoming the hero's to the local boys including the older boys, the day after the event, after the punishments had been handed out they hung out at Uncle Pete's, the boys counted five milkshakes bought for them by the peeps of the town, two were from the mine managers wives, they smiled when they saw the boys, asking them if they wanted a milkshake, it was decided by the older boys that the younger boys had managed to High light the security problems at the mine, heads would roll, all caused by boys between thirteen and seventeen, almost.

They spoke of the time all being employed by the sawmill, and the experience in life they all received working under the Boss, who was known as a hard task master.

As the night drifted later and later, goodbyes were had, Craig was the last leave, along with Steve and Rhonda.

Nick and Jessie were preparing for bed.

Nick spoke.

"He was, ahh distant, he didn't get involved with the conversation, and he kept looking at the house, it was like he was waiting for the house to do something, waiting for it to come to life"

Jess was curious and poked Nick for details.

"So what is the go with Marlii?" "Well we don't talk about Marlii, unless he brings her up, they were in love, Craig being the eldest of us hooked up with Marlii when they were fifteen, I think if she had not been killed, he would have been a different Craig, it was a bitterly confronting death, Craig spiraled down into oblivion he was seventeen when she died" "How did it happen?" "She drowned in the Odistgeeg river"

"Oh no, shit Nick how did you bring him back from the brink?" "I don't know that we ever have, her death rocked him, for the first twelve months he was on a suicide watch, the for the next twelve months, he was a sad sack, I was thirteen, I was the only one of us four who was patient with him, Mark and Ian would get the shits with him when he was feeling maudlin, and that was most of the time"

Jess repeated Nick

"He was so serious tonight, and you are right he was tense for most of his visit and he didn't go near the house he stayed in that Marquee, and didn't move" They climbed into bed, Nick picked up the novel he was reading, it was an old American printed version of Brett Easton Ellis American Psycho, he was enjoying it but distractions of late were making the reading "Hard" but perseverance was the key, Jess grabbed her sketch pad and began to doodle.

"Well we are here together now, I will see if we can get him over later today, considering its tomorrow already"

"Well the way he was tonight, I don't like your chances Nick"

"We will see, we will see"

CHAPTER THREE
CRAIG

It was a little after twelve midnight when Steve pulled into the motel, pulled up outside Craig's room.

"You want to come in for a drink"

"We've had enough, I shouldn't even be driving, no I will see you in the morning"

After they had said their goodbyes and Craig watched the lights disappear into the distance, he went to his room, he placed his key in the door, it was unlocked.

He tried to remember locking it, and remembered finding Nick in the car park, maybe he left it unlocked, but then he remembered as he was leaving to go to the church with the flowers, he was locking the door when the manager had come to him, maybe he had distracted him, and he had forgotten to lock it.

He went into the room, the lights were on, he remembered he had turned them off for sure, water was running in the bathroom, it was the shower, had he lost time again?

Then he heard her from the shower.

"Craig"

He stood there waiting for the sounds to stop.

Running water, and it came again.

"Craig" It was her voice soft and sweet, beckoning for him, calling for him to go to her.

"Craig"

He moved forward slowly, out of the small hallway into the bedroom, the lights in the bathroom were on, and the water was flowing.

"Craig"

He took another tentative step toward the bathroom; he could see the lights flickering in the bathroom.

"Craig" The lights flickered once in the bedroom, and then in quick succession went off in the bathroom and were followed by the rest of the lights in the room plunging him into darkness.

And from the now cold bathroom it came again.

"Craig"

Now deeper, not in her voice, it was a man's voice, not her sweet soft voice.

He remembered what Doc Pratt had told him, close his eyes and block his ears.

As he placed his fingers in his ears, he heard "Cra" in a low rumbling growl, he closed his eyes, and there was silence, he waited for the minute to pass and waited another full minute before opening his eyes, he saw that the lights were on in his bedroom, but the bathroom was still dark, when he pulled one of the fingers from his ears he heard nothing, even the sound of the water was gone, he removed his finger from his other ear stood there for a time, he went to the end of his bed and sat down heavily, confusion swept over him, why did he come back here, there were so many nightmares here in this town, tragedy that he thought would have faded beyond what his memory would let him remember, but coming back here was a bad situation, however while he was here he would make things right, remembering the explosives store fiasco tonight had set in his mind a plan, he would right things if it was the last thing he would do.

He laid down on the bed in his cloths, he wandered toward sleep.

As sleep took him he uttered her name "Marlii" in a quiet whisper.

Angie had come over early the next day for the discussion of the paintings, Nick had decided that Angie's paintings with Desmond included in the window were a strange, but he wasn't jumping to any conclusion, as she had not dreamed of him and he had not appeared to her, that was when Jess had put her opinion in that if this entity is the beginning of the hauntings as well as the deaths, they should really look into the deaths here in the house, the most recent deaths, the one that Longstreet was responsible for she went on.

"I don't get any connection with Desmond Brown or Michael Longstreet" Nick added.

"But there has to be a connection" Angie added.

"He was a video producer, Michael Longstreet, look for the clues there must be something he left behind"

Later that morning while Nick did the rounds to see how they were recovering, Jess went with Angie to the local police station, the senior sergeant was in attendance with two constables.

The young constable a female came to the desk.

"What can I do for you" Jess speaks up.

"My name is Jess Lester this is Angie Bell; we would like to speak to the most senior officer please"

"Just a minute" She turned and went to the office opposite where the girls were, spoke to the Snr Sargent and came back to the desk, lifting the middle of the counter up to expose a walk through.

"Snr Sargent Little will see you right now if you like"

The girls went through divided desk and were ushered over to the office of the Snr Sergeant.

"Sarge, Mrs. Lester and Miss Bell" "Thanks Sandy, will you please put the kettle on, make our guests a cuppa"

She walked away toward the kitchen.

"Well it is a pleasure to meet you finally, we have been speculating how long it would be before you came in"

Snr sarge Little was a skinny man, and with his long face, held the red beard of hair well, that was his nickname "Red".

"You've been speculating on what exactly?"

Jess asked.

"Ah um, just about the Desmond Mansion, the hauntings"

"Oh the hauntings"

She turned to Angie.

"Did you hear that Angie, they are speculating on the hauntings, do you think they can let us know of them"

They both looked back at the Sarge he was squirming in his seat, Jess had known exactly how to handle this small town cop.

"Look I am so sorry Mrs. Lester I didn't mean to show you any disrespect, let me begin again, we were instructed by the investigators of the Longstreet crimes that we were not to bother you, we were not to approach you or Mr. Lester, I assumed you may have been having problems, you know" "It is known as the Lester house from here on in, if we remove the stigma, maybe the "ghosts" will go away, and it is the Longstreet case we are here about, not about the house" "Oh well, what is it you need to know" "The evidence from the case, how much do you have, how much do you know?"

"We have some of the evidence here, locked up in the evidence, cupboard, the remainder of the evidence is being kept in Melbourne"

"Could we possibly look at it?" "Why yes, the case has been closed for a time now, actually maybe time to log that stuff into Melbourne"

It had Occurred to Jessie, that the laziness of these police just may yield some results.

The Sarge got up and went out into the office, at that moment Sandy popped her head in.

"Coffee or tea ladies?" Angie and Jess answered her making their orders white and two, standard.

She turned and left as the Sarge came back into his Office carrying a box from the cupboard, the size in total of four shoe boxes, he dropped it on the desk.

"A lot of written stuff, rantings and ramblings of a mad man, its all here, and here"

He reached into the box, and pulled from the bottom, micro video tapes.

"And these"

He placed the video tapes down on the desk.

"These are very interesting, we began to view them in the beginning of the investigation, but there was nothing in them, well as far as we viewed them"

Both girls had thought it odd, they had not viewed the whole tapes.

He reached in and pulled out a doll and plonked the doll down on the table.

It was fine porcelain, it was dressed in fine cloths from his boots to his top hat, his pudgy body sticking out, his facial features were perfect, it was Desmond Brown.

Angie was the first to exclaim, she turned to look at Jess, who was dumbfounded.

"Is that Des"

Jess broke in.

"It's a voodoo doll, I have seen these before"

"This was in his possessions along with the tapes and the paperwork, mostly scripts and screenplays, and those tapes have a lot of interesting stuff on them"

Jessie had surmised that the tapes were from Michael Longstreet's filming days.

"Can we possibly loan some of this?" "You can take the whole box if you want, as I said there is nothing in there that is important, evidence wise all the stuff was taken to Melbourne for the case"

"Well thank you sergeant "

"Please call me Tom"

Sandy came back with the coffee, placing one down in front of each of them as she left the office she had told them to enjoy.

It was then Jess had pinched Angie getting her attention, and as the sarge was distracted had whispered to her.

"Shh, it's a voodoo doll"

The sergeant looked back to Jessie and said.

"Not wanting to harp bout the house, you have done a great job, it hasn't looked that splendid since the seventies, however tourism is up in town, people coming from the big city's coming up here to sticky beak, so if you ever need my help, just call, there is always a constable hear to take your call if I'm out"

"Thank you Tom, I will keep that in mind"

Mark Harris had been up since three A.M, he was sitting in the kitchen of his sisters house, four

doors down from where Nick's family had once resided.

A neat single story ranch house, it had moved to his sister's possession, she had kept the maintenance up on the place, it had the neatest of gardens, with topiary dotting the small driveway, and along the garden path to the verandah which run the total length of the front of the house.

He had a coffee in front of himself and the weekend paper spread over the table, he was looking at the times the horses had run at Caulfield, he was waiting for his phone to ring when the front door bell rang, he turned the radio that was rambling on in the background down, and went to the door expecting it to be Nick, or Ian, but not Craig, he had been distant to Mark, he had observed him when he first arrived, he was scary, that's what Mark had first thought.

He opened the door to see Nick, Ian's car pulled into the driveway behind Nick's.

Mark greeted him.

"Nick how are you" They both turned and waved to Ian as he came toward them.

Coffees made, relaxed, the men began to discuss Craig's problems.

"I haven't seen this non honcus bonckus, Steve had warned me when we came back to town, but he is frying his wires, that's for sure" Ian added.

"Last time I spoke to him was twelve months ago, since then he has really been hard to handle, when I heard he was heading back here I was pleased to think that coming home would help him, but I think he is becoming more explosive every day" Mark joins in.

"I just found him really creepy, last night he freaked me out a bit, Cindy knows him more than just an acquaintance, last night she was scared by him"

It was decided to take things slowly with him, they were determined to make sure he left here in better shape than he was currently.

It was the Craig from years back they wanted, not the one who spoke of Ghosts, and hauntings, not the one who spoke of long dead girlfriends like they were here in the present, how would they find him?

They had a four-week period to try and sort him out, as this break was the first for all of them since separating all those years before.

The three men piled into Mark's Falcon and headed over to the motel, when they arrived Craig's F200 was there.

Mark spoke.

"Nick, Ian, which of you is going?"

Ian was taking his seat belt off and opening his door, getting out he looked back to the other men, he was emanating a look that told you, he was nervous, he knocked.

The call came from inside for whomever was there to go in, Ian turned to them and said.

"Here goes" He went in closing the door behind him, he was in there for a short time when the door opened and Craig came out followed closely by Ian, who closed the door behind him.

Craig spoke.

"Hi boys, what are we up to today, I think we should start at Uncle Pete's, you know gas up before we head out"

Nick added. "Well OK, I was planning to get out to the timber mill today, so yep brunch it is at Uncle Pete's"

They arrived at Uncle Pete's taking up four of the stools that sat at the counter, Uncle Pete was finishing up an order.

"Hey boys I will be with you in a minute"

He took a plate of pie along with a milkshake and took it out to the client sitting by the window.

"Well boys what will it be"

Craig was looking over the menu, Nick ordered a coffee with a corn beef sandwich, Ian ordered a simple fare of chips and a coke, Mark was looking over Craigs shoulder spying the menu, he ordered a hot dog with a chocolate milkshake, Craig placed his order.

"I'll have a coffee, bottomless, a three stack of pancakes with whipped butter, and then two eggs sunny side up with sausages and Bacon, that'll do me for now" Nick spoke up.

"Craig you are really fueling up"

"Well I'm famished, woke up this morning ravenous, and the weirdest thing is I have had song lyrics spinning around in my head today, Grinspoon, Chemical Heart, but most of all was the lyric, you can't seem to see the forest for the trees, and then Cant get started, Chemical heart, every time I get started you pull me apart, its weird, but I dreamed of Marlii last night, a nice dream"

They had all heard him, they were taking in exactly what he was saying. Nick turned to Pete.

"Drop the corned beef, I'll have eggs over easy with sausage and bacon"

Uncle Pete stood on the other side of the pass and said with question in his face.

"Hey, you all gonna leave space for my Ice Cream and Pie?

Craig answered for them.

"There is always room for your Ice Cream and Pie Uncle Pete"

They all sat chatting to Pete as he worked through the pass cooking for the boys, the topic of the day was Craig's turn around, Nick sat there thinking he had made a three hundred and sixty degree flip in eight hours, it perplexed him, we was curious as to where the Craig who arrived had gone, as they sat chatting, Nick allowed the thoughts to slip to the back of his mind, for the first time since Craig had arrived he felt he could relax, and enjoy the moments with his friends.

Back at the house, Jess and Angie were rifling through the box that was stamped "EVIDENCE"

"So, there are seven micro videos, and all these scripts, you know Nick has a camera we will be able to play these tapes through the T.V."

Angie grabbed a handful of scripts and pulled them from the box.

"Look at these, complete screenplays, Michael Longstreet was an artist by the looks of these"

She held up the scripts and fanned them over her head, then bringing them to her eyes began reading.

"Here listen, "The wind in the night" as I sit here wondering the breeze has skipped up to a fair Knott of winds, I can hear the calling, it is loud, so loud that I cannot ignore it much longer, I looked out of the window earlier and I saw the watchers from the bramble at the edge of the garden where it meets the front gate, when they decide to come into the garden, the calling will be at its zenith and I will go out to them and seal my fate" Angie placed the script down and picked up another.

"This is heavy shit, that introduction was horrid, wow, and this one reads the same, and this one"

She pointed to the third manuscript sitting on the coffee table now out of the box.

"They all read the same intro, so when can we start to view the tapes?"

"The Video camcorder could still be packed away, I will give him a call"

Nick was standing outside the lunchroom at the sawmill, looking out from the verandah high above the timber yard, all the boys had gone in, and were making a ruckus, his phone buzzed, it was Jess asking where the camcorder was.

"Ah the camcorder, I was considering getting that out of storage, but I didn't need to bother, its in the red suitcase in our walk-in closet, but what do you need it for" Jess explained what they had been able to recover from the local police station, they had wanted to view them.

"Well go get it, the cords attached are self explanatory, I would love to know what is on them"

"I'm on it, enjoy your time with the boys"

"I will"

They ended the call.

"Come with me I know where it is" She led Angie upstairs to their bedroom where she went directly to the walk in, grabbing down from the top shelf the red suitcase, she found the camera resting amongst Nicks collection of scarves.

"These cords are supposed to be self-explanatory; we will see how that theory works out" She held the camera in her hand, he had left the cord in the camera for easy use, Angie picked up the cords hanging from the camera looking at the color coded whips of cord.

"This is easy, color coded, red to red and so on" They went down to the study adjacent the library, the T.V. was on the opposite wall of a large leather couch, Jess went to the T.V. in the side panel was small door that sprung open when pushed, inside were the Jacks for the cords, after connecting the cords they both went to the couch and sat, Jess placed the first tape into the recorder and pressed play.

The T.V. came to life, Michael Longstreet was front and center.

At the Mill the boys were finishing up in the lunchroom, pies, sandwiches as well as Ice cream, kept in Uncle Pete's waxed Ice Cream containers, that stayed in the Mills freezer until it was time for the fruit pies to come out, all put together by Uncle Pete himself, on the house.

Bobby Cursack had called for the workers to get back to it, one by one they filed out shaking each of the four men's hand's who had "Come Home" after their success, Bobby had begun to clean up the table, gathering the paper plates, cups, and empty ice cream containers, Cherry Ripple, Peach Pavlova and Double Choc the three flavors of the day.

The Millers had gone back to work.

That is when things went to shit.

Craig had been fine during lunch, and this morning there was a chipper than ever before Craig, he had followed the men back down to the main barn, where he was regaling them with stories of his mining exploits, the men broke off into their work crews and went to their stations, Craig had managed to be right along Ethan Swab, who was controlling the huge cutting bench that fed the men out in the yard.

The logs, which were trees, after being stripped of their limbs, are then fed on a chain conveyer, down to the cutting bench, where it is driven through the huge saw, he would pass each "Tree" Log over the saw half a dozen times, producing huge planks, that would produce everything from weather boards to decking, pergolas to sheds, framing for houses, even floor boards, just the same ones that Bobby Cursack had delivered out to the old house just a little while ago.

When Desmond realized his opportunity he took it, he was able to go into Craigs body, and control him he had continued the conversation perfectly, Ethan was none the wiser he was no longer talking to Craig, while Ethan was bending down to switch the safety bar into place, Desmond spotted the emergency axe, he went to it taking the it he swung the axe up and over in a huge arc, bringing the axe down full force on the back of Ethan's head, it split and exploded like a watermelon dropped from a height.

"Woops sorry Ethan, Ill deal with the mess after I am done" He dropped the axe and went to the body, he had died instantly, but his fate was still not there yet, Desmond grabbed the body by the feet and dragged the corpse to the cutting bench, where he flicks the switch and fires up the saw, he then picks Ethan up and drops him on the table, setting his body to be split down the center, he sets the table in motion watching and waiting, for him to disappear into the body of the cutter, the blood drenched anything around it, after the body had completed its run, it was an unrecognizable mess.

Jane, the secretary was the one who had walked in on the blood splattered Craig, at first she had thought he was covered in tree sap, but as she had gotten close enough to see, Craig had blood all over him, what accident had taken place here?

She approached Desmond but decided not to get too close.

"Craig, what happened here?"

Craig stood looking at the smashed and sliced body of Ethan.

Again Jane asked.

"Craig did Ethan have an accident?" Desmond looked over in her direction, and she had known that Craig had become Murderous.

It was not just in his eyes, that bloodied face, the scowl, it wasn't Craig, he began toward her she was able to turn and flee back to the office, racing inside and bolting the door shut.

Mark and Ian were the first to react, hearing Jane fleeing across the yard toward the office.

"Holey fuck" Was all that Mark could manage.

Ian stood there shaking his head.

Nick and Bobby joined them outside.

Looking down from where they stood, it was obvious that Craig had fried some wires, he had followed Jane into the yard when he was mid-way across the yard and he stopped,

Nick was first down the steps and into the yard, as Nick approached him, he broke down.

"Nick what just happened, I've got this blood all over me"

He was holding out his blood-spattered hands.

"I'm not sure Craig, come lets go inside and sit down, talk about it" "Talk about what, what just happened Nick, why and who's blood is this?" "Craig lets go inside get you a drink" Craig ambled toward Nick, his face down, he looked absolutely exhausted, as Nick led Craig up the stairs Ian, Mark and Bobby headed down to the cutting shed, Jane who had decided it was safe to return outside ran to join the men.

They were treated to the horror that was Ethan's blood-soaked corpse it was Jane who spoke.

"When he turned around the look in his eyes, it was not Craig, I can't explain it any other way"

"It's not the Craig any of us know"

Ian said.

Mark just stood there in silence; Ethan had not just been a friend he had been Mark's cousin.

Jess and Angie had been sitting and watching the first two videos, they had persevered with the first one which was just a montage of shots, there were many different angles and positions which where the lenses pointed, there were so many test shots, they gave that video an hour, and switched to the second video, this was more interesting, Michael Longstreet in his not so crazy days, shots from CenterPoint tower, Luna Park, the beach at Manly, he was touring around Sydney, taking in the sights, at the thirty five minute mark Longstreet sets up the camera to shoot himself, he is a rather swanky motel, a Penthouse from not just the view but the furnishing as well, the camera is set looking out onto Sydney Harbor, with a chair at front.

Michael comes to the chair and sits down, crosses his legs and begins his monologue.

"I have shown you interest in the town, shown you the sights, but now its time to get you lot started on your videos, I will pick the first three judged as the most professional, and based on this you will be chosen to partake in the verry important filming that is about to take place, the scariest, chilling video you can muster, then simply place it in a file and email it to the address here on You Tube, good luck you lot, I look forward to seeing your work" The Video ended.

Jessica's phone began to buzz.

Snow on T.V. she pushed the pause button and thumbed her phone to answer it was Nick, he sounded rather frantic.

"Jess, its me, I need you to come out to the Mill there has been an accident, can you bring the Range Rover" "What has happened"

"I will explain when you get here, just get moving" The call ended.

Angie stood their mouth open waiting for Jess to fill her in.

"We have to go to the Mill, pronto"

Jess went through the kitchen grabbing the keys from the hook Angie trailed behind her.

"What has happened, what's wrong?"

"There has been an accident I don't know anything more, its sounds bad, something is off"

They climbed into the four-wheel drive, and Jessie gunned it down the long sweeping driveway and out onto the Old Town Road, hitting the city limits and flooring the Range Rover, toward the Mill.

Although, she was upon the speed limit quickly, an ambulance came up on her outside and overtook her.

"Wow, they are in a hurry"

Said Jess.

Angie added.

"Stick with them"

Jess urged the Range Rover up to one hundred and ten, leaving enough room behind the flashing blazing lights of the ambulance as it threw up a trail of road dirt from the blacktop.

Jess spied in her rear-view mirror red and blue lights, the police were on their way to the Mill, as she backed off enough to let the cop car overtake her, Jessie reduced her speed back to sixty and pulled over toward the soft shoulder, and then rejoined the chase getting back up to speed in no time, they travelled in a convoy the last ten kilometers.

The Mill was a hive activity, the workers had shut down the machinery and were gathering at the mustering point, some looking dazed and confused.

Jess and Angie found Nick, with Ian, consoling Mark they all looked rather shocked, the police, were out of their car and headed down to the cutting shed with the ambulance men quickly grabbing the dolly from ambulance following them down.

Mark was sitting at the foot of the steps, he had been crying, Ian was sitting on the step beside him.

Mark spoke in a solemn tone.

"The ambulance was a mistake, Ethan's going to need a body bag" Jess almost yells.

"What the fuck happened here" Nick speaks up.

"We are still trying to piece it all together, when they went back to work, Craig followed them down there, when Jane went down to give Ethan a message she found Craig standing over the saw, with Ethan's body, well let's just say, he was split in two, Jane says that Craig had looked at her, and it was a different person, that was when we saw her headed back to the office to lock herself in" Jess managed.

"Holly shit"

"She is up there now with Craig and Bobby Cursack, he doesn't know who he is, when we collected him this morning he was as chipper as we remembered him, and now this"

The police were headed back up the hill, to the lunchroom.

Senior Sargent Tom Little, told the officers to wait downstairs, he started up the well-maintained timber stairway that had led up to the landing which led into the lunchroom, Jess and Angie followed him up the stairs leaving Nick and Ian to console Mark.

Craig was sitting at the table, in his hands was a bloody dish cloth he had used to wipe down his face and was now rubbing his hands with it., Bobby was making coffee and Jane was sitting with Craig, she had her hand on his shoulder consoling him.

Tom spoke.

"Hi Bobby, Jane, Craig"

He paused but began again.

"We need to work out what happened here, there is one hell of a mess down there in that cutting shed, I am going to ask you a series of questions, think about your answer, before saying anything" Craig lifted his head and looked up at the Sergeant, a blank look on his face.

"Ok Tom, but I can't remember anything" "Well explain in your words what you do remember"

"I was walking down with Ethan, Will Short, and Neville Smith, and a couple of the new kids, telling them of my success in Coober Pedy, the boys went their separate ways, I ended up in the shed with Ethan, I remember him going to the safety guard, and that is all I remember, then I woke up like this" Craig was disgusted as he bought his hands up as witness to the gore still on him.

"You woke up, what do you mean woke up"

"When I came too, I was standing well away from the machine, and I first saw Jane, she was weirded out by me, she turned tail and ran, that is it, get Jane to tell you, but that is the limit of my knowledge"

"Jane what can you add" "Well I went down to the cutting shed, with a new order, I was surprised when I heard the saw running, he hadn't been in there long enough to start it up, but when I got there, I saw Craig, he looked confused, but really angry"

Tom said

"There is the point of the axe on the ground out of its mount and covered in blood, its being bagged up, as we speak, I will need to await on forensics, but for the time being Craig I will be required to take you into custody"

Jess spoke up.

"Whoa sheriff Little, let's not jump the gun here, you are talking about arresting him, are you sure?"

"What other alternative do we have"

Angie speaks up.

"Maybe not incarcerate him, wait for the evidence to come back"

"I am afraid we can't do that, I'm sorry Craig, but it is the only option"

Jess began again.

"Bu"

She was cut off by Craig.

"No Jess, I will go, until I have answers myself maybe I am not that safe to be around" "I am taking you into custody, and you will be held at Shrives Island hospital, in the psyche ward, until we know what happened here, there will be no charges laid until things are sorted" Nick came into the lunchroom, Craig was being consoled by Jane, Jess and Angie were standing together on one side of the room, with the Bobby and the Sergeant, but he had felt it as plain as day,

There was another there, he could feel the presence.

While Jane was talking to Officer Little, Desmond appeared standing to her left, he had a Locke of her auburn hair, he was twisting it.

"Ssshh"

Said Desmond.

"You are the only one who can see me at this particular time"

He snapped his fingers, and the room was still, everyone was frozen in that instant, all life ceased to exist.

"See I can do as I please and control all and anyone"

Nick was stuck to the spot he was standing, he looked over at Jane, she looked just like a goldfish in a bowl, mouth frozen open, it looked comical.

Desmond went from Jane to Jess in an instant, he wasn't walking as much as floating.

Nick tried to go to Jess but was rooted to the spot.

"Oh Nick you jest with me, you cannot move, why would I go to all the trouble of doing all this"

He held out his arms waving them in the direction of everything that was taking place.

"You need to realize, you are not in control here I am, or do you not know this, why are you ignoring me Nick, my instructions, Jess has not started to paint yet with the girl, not good enough Nick, they are getting distracted with daily dalliances, when can I expect them to begin?"

Nick stood there stuck as if he cemented where he stood, but a thought had occurred.

"Desmond, they have been painting"

Desmond snapped his look from Jess back to Nick.

"What are you saying, I have not witnessed this" "They have been painting, in the garden, Angie started work on huge oak in the driveway, Jess has been painting Angie" "No, I haven't seen them"

"But they are, they have been, you have been taken with other things, you cannot be in more than one spot"

"I can, I can be in multiple of places, I see everything, as it happens" Nick tried to move his feet, but nothing happened.

"Oh yes, that's right, you made this mess haven't you, you torment Craig, you cause him to do this, he has no memory of what he done or why he has done it, shit, he doesn't even realize he has done anything, but why, why Craig, you have not come to anyone but Craig?"

Nick tried to lift his left foot; it came up of the ground.

"I have made myself known to you and Jess, the girl is slightly aware, Craig is completely aware of me" "No, you have manifested to myself and Jess, you are tormenting Craig"

He lifted his right foot"

Desmond chuckled.

"Tormenting him, I am using him, to get you and your wife to act, for me" Nick lunged at the ghost sweeping him away from Jess and Angie, forcing the ghost down to the ground, Nick was surprised by his force, finding they had landed in the corner, Nick on top of the ghost who was shocked by the sudden force that had been within Nick.

Nick looked into Desmond's eyes, did he see fear there could he have possibly bought the fear out in him, Nick grabbed the Ghost by the lapels of his over coat and pulled the ghosts face up to his own, Nick spoke.

"You don't control me, my wife, or anyone else, you have come here to horrify us, well you have succeeded, now it is time for you to go" From behind him he heard his name "Nick"

He stopped strangling the coat he was holding, turned, and he had seen everyone in the room staring at him all mouths wide opened, including Craig.

Jess said.

"What are you doing?"

Nick scrambled up to his feet, he had been on his knees wrestling with a huge overcoat he had taken from the rack, he stood there with the coat hooked over his right hand, he shook it free.

Jess went to him.

"Are you OK" "Is anything OK at the moment"

CHAPTER FOUR

THE MESS

That evening when the mess had been sorted as much as it could, Craig was now in custody, Bobby had closed the mill for the next week, Angie had been dropped at home earlier, Jess finding she had to explain to Jill and Graeme the day's events.

Angie had gone instantly to her studio and started work on a painting she had begun earlier that week.

"They have Craig in custody, it was Jane who found Craig in the cutting shed with what was left of Ethan" Graham spoke up.

"Oh um, I knew I should have spoken up about Ethan, he had been sharing his thoughts with me recently, obviously with no one else, shit, Ethan had been suicidal, I had talked him out of it, or I thought I had, seems I hadn't done enough" Jill Spoke up.

"You need to speak to the cops"

Graham began to walk out.

"I am right now; I need to share this with them"

Graham grabbed his keys from the hook as he went out the side door leaving the two women to their thoughts and made his way to town.

Graham pulled up outside the police station, it was manned so he got out and went up the steps and in, approaching the desk, he could see sergeant Little in his office, on the phone, Graham went through the desk partition that was already in its up position, telling Graham that Little was only one there.

Little got up from his chair and went out to greet his visitor, he had trying to get time to go and visit Graham, all those not at the timber mill were all called and informed of the death, Graham was next call on his list.

"Hello Graham, I was about to call you" "Well saved you the trouble, it's about Ethan, and what happened down there today I have information you may be interested in, Ethan was suicidal"

"What"

"He had been telling me how he planned to kill himself, ah nothing like what happened, he was going to do it by going over the waterfall, I thought I had talked him down talked him out of it, I last had a shift with him on Tuesday, there was no talk of hurting himself, in fact he was supposed to be going out with Wendy tomorrow night, that was the problem, he had broken up with her, when he started this bullshit about ending it, I was sure he had patched things up, I was sure" "Well there in lay the problem Graham, The forensics are back from the emergency axe, that we found out of its cradle, on the ground, away from the machine, the blood on the axe belonged to Ethan, I'm sure they will find his cause of death at the autopsy, was a strike from the axe, delivered by Craig"

Graham stood their solemn look on his face.

"I'm so sorry Graham, to be the bringer of bad tidings, but its open and shut, Craig killed him, why I have no idea, but the evidence is there"

The news rippled its way through the town, the next morning as the sun broke its warm slivery fingers into the death of the morning, bringing the first light.

Jess stirred, rolled, and went back to sleep, beside her Nick slept.

At his sister's house, Mark and Cindy Harris slept soundlessly.

Ian lay in dream, his wife Cathy, was beginning to open her eyes.

Angie slept silently while upstairs her mother slept in dream, her father, hadn't slept all night, had tossed, and turned.

Bobby Cursack and Janice were awaking at the same time.

Pete and Diane were sleeping restfully.

Steve Gnik along with Rhonda Spelling, were dressed, in the car, and headed out to the hospital, they had to be there when the doors opened.

Steve says.

"He sees ghosts, he is paranoid about Nick and Jessies place, he won't go near the house, at the reunion, I was amazed that he sat in the Marquee, that close to the house, he is frightened by it, I know what you are going to say, Nick and Jess have had instances, I have heard the stories, but my concern at the moment is for Craig"

"I really think the place is haunted, I've had an instance"

"Please Rhonda, not now, for fuck's sake" "But I have, I was working in the library cataloging, I heard the sounds of children, clearly, when I went to Jess, she laughed it off, told me not to be concerned"

Steve locked up the wheels on the Jeep, spun the car around in a tight arc, and blasted back away from the hospital.

"Where are we going" Said Rhonda

"To Nick's I need to know, what's going on" He pulled the jeep into the turnaround at the house, he got out followed by Rhonda to the front door, he wrapped on the door with his knuckles.

He started to knock a second time.

"Gee Steve, let them get downstairs"

They waited, and the door opened by Jess in her dressing gown.

"Hi Jess is Nick awake, we need to talk" "You woke him, with your banging, hi, Rhonda, come in" They followed jess into the Kitchen where she put the coffee on without saying a word, she broke the silence.

"So I suppose this is about Craig, we were talking about it last night"

"We were on our way to the hospital, Rhonda told me about the ghosts in this place, I've never seen anything here, I hear everyone talking, but now Rhonda tells me she has had a moment, so I would like to know from you and Nick, what the fuck is going on" Nick joined them in the Kitchen.

"What the fuck is going on, how about sleep"

Said Nick

Jess was placing four cups on the table, pouring coffee while Rhonda went round with sugar.

Steve broke the silence.

"Nick what has happened, what the hell is going on with Craig"

"I would say we are still dealing with a Craig who is flipping out, seeing dead people, and now he is being held in suspicion of murder"

"You know don't you, tell me Nick, what has happened since he got back" Jess spoke up.

"Have you not heard Rhonda, how she has had a visitation"

Steve turned to Jess.

"Just now, we were on our way to see Craig, that was when she had told me"

"So you have had nothing, no voices, no little kids, no De"

Jessie cut Nick off.

"Steve you have been here how many times, half a dozen?"

"Maybe up to a dozen, maybe more, just keeping my eye on the renovations"

"And you haven't seen a thing" "Never, not a single haunting"

"So you see what our dilemma is don't you, if we go to the authorities stating that this house is haunted, all we will get is negative media, just having the people out there talking about it keeps the whole charade alive"

Says Steve

"Its not a charade is it, you are living in a haunted house" Jess looked over to Nick.

"Nick what do you think that is about, the manifestations, the Kids, Desmond, we have been exposed to both, Rhonda and come to think of it Bobby Cursack heard kids, bur Steve hasn't heard a thing and then there is Craig he has obviously met Desmond Brown" Nick sat and contemplated.

"Steve do you believe in ghosts?" "Yes, but I have never been involved but I have met many good friends and family, for fuck sake, I do know of Craig's Battle after Marlii"

Jess spoke up.

"They don't see him, they can't see him, he is immune or something, its like Miranda, and Tim, they can avoid other ghosts, they are separate to Michael Longstreet, and Desmond Brown, but, in Steve's case they cannot see him, watch" She called for Miranda.

"Hey Miranda are you around, if you are can you please come" She turned to Rhonda.

"Nothing like manners"

At first there was laughing, singular then she was there, and for the first time Steve was seeing a ghost it was Jess's suggestion, he was sure.

Steve was stunned, perplexed all at once, in front of him stood a girl of eleven, from the top of her bonnet to the bowed shoes on her feet she was Victorian, her clothes consisted of a ankle length dress, over it she wore a red woolen stole, her face ever so slightly shaded by the brim of her bonnet was innocent, he could see her features clearly, her blue eyes shone through, her curly blonde lockets hung down the side of her face in a waterfall.

"Hello Miranda"

"Hi Jess, I hope you are well"

"I am Miranda, may I ask you how many of us are present" "Three, you and Nick, as well Rhonda, hello Rhonda" Rhonda said nothing but waved.

Miranda waved back to her in a mimic.

"Three hey, well I am afraid to tell you there is four of us, Tim if you are here will you please come"

Tim appeared.

Like the Girl he was the same age, twins even, and just like the girl he was dressed in Victorian garb.

"Tim how many are here" "Five, you three and Miranda and myself" Miranda spoke.

"There are four of them, one we cannot see"

Steve spoke.

"I'm over here"

He waved.

The children heard him but they could not see him.

Then the children were gone.

"That's the secret, you are exactly what they are to us, you are a ghost, do you get it?"

Nick Rhonda and Jess looked at him.

"She is right you know, you scared those children off"

Said Rhonda.

"What are you saying Jess?" "I don't know exactly, but I am learning, that side, where the dead walk, it is the same as us, whenever we have dealt with the children it has been pleasant, from the beginning, on the other hand Desmond has been the opposite to deal with, I need a little time" "Well, if you need time how about I leave Rhonda here, I will take Nick with me" Rhonda turned to Jess and nodded.

They arrived at the hospital as visiting hours had begun going straight to the psych ward.

Nick spoke.

"Now nothing of the ghosts, go along with what Craig says, I think he is a screw enough loose to be kept in the psyche ward"

They were stopped at the reception.

"Good morning gentlemen how can I be of assistance" Said the nurse.

"Hi I am Steve Gnik and this is Nick Lester, we are here to visit Craig Gnik" "Oh Mr. Lester" She gushed.

"Would you please sign my book" She lifted a volume of Nicks prose, it was older, a hardcover of his novel "Abandonment" handing it to him along with a pen, he turned the book to see an old photo of himself fifteen years younger.

"Yes sure, who do you want it written for" "Oh for me if that's alright, my name is Tammy"

"This is an older title, I didn't think someone your age would enjoy it" "I have read all that you have written, I have started again" Nick turned the book back the dust jacket was still almost new, the blood red ink on the lower quarter of the dustjacket bled out into the word Abandonment on a white background, this was the book that had launched his career, as well the first film in a franchise of Nick's films that were slated, he opened the front cover and wrote in his fine hand "Tammy, read read read, Love Nick Lester.

He handed the book back.

"So now I signed your book, could you let us in to visit Mr. Gnik?" "Certainly" She pushed and held on a button and the door buzzed, the men went into the ward.

The door swished silently behind them, they were in a long corridor, striking blue tiles, were spattered along the doorless and windowless walls into a sterile white, but that was the only part of "Hospital" in this wing they approached the desk, which the corridor ended at, this time the guard was on the other side of the locked door.

Steve went to the window panel and spoke into the intercom.

"Hi my name is Steve Gnik" "Yes Mr. Gnik, please I will let you in"

The doors opened inward, and closed as soon as they were in, the nurse/ watchman came the door and said.

"You will find him in the common room, down the end of that hall, he is waiting for you"

He directed them down a short hallway, they walked past a kitchen, meeting rooms and came to the end of the hallway and the common room, it was well equipped table tennis, billiards, or you could do puzzles or just sit and watch T.V, that was where they found Craig, he bounced up from the couch he was comfortable in.

"You know what happened last night don't you?" "No what happened last night?"

Asked Steve.

"The forensics came back from the lab, that axe they took in had Ethan's blood on it, there were prints on the axe not mine, but they are going to charge me today, however my lawyer sees it that I have frizzed out, I have no memory of the moments after we got to the shed" Nick added.

"They won't be able to convict you, with no prints"

"Not my prints on the evidence, or not discernible" Steve cuts in.

"Not yours or not discernible, what is it?"

"Well they aren't mine, well I don't think they are, any way I am here for the interim, my Psyche doctor says there is no better place for me than in here" Nick looked at Steve with a knowing in his face, and Steve got it.

Steve changed the subject quickly.

"Is there anywhere in here I can get you toiletries, shaving stuff?"

"You don't need to, they supply everything in here, Ill get by" Nick offered.

"Jess will be in later today, to visit, along with Rhonda, they will bring you some cloths, and odds and ends" Nick had meant odds and ends to mean, chocolates, pies, and ice cream.

Steve then added.

"So you are safe in here" Craig looked at Steve, perplexed.

"Safe, from what, I think you have it wrong, they have me in here to keep others safe"

"You have no memory, no idea what has transpired, I mean when it happened, that's why they are keeping you here, believe me when I say You are safe in here"

Nick broke the conversation.

"Well, where do I get a coffee around here?"

Jess and Rhonda were in the library, looking through the evidence box together.

Rhonda was taken with one of the screenplays, she had been reading it silently, but couldn't help but read out what she was reading right at that time.

"Listen, "The water fall fell, at the junction of two rivers, where the most powerful of these rivers, crashed into the smaller tributary consuming it.

As she stood in the fall of the water beneath, she had been naked and had been praying, she had been repeating again and again, the same words, "Cleanse and consecrate me, in the watchtowers of the quarters"

The ritual had begun earlier that day when the men of the town had begun to hunt her down, she had come to this place and had begun her ritual".

"This is about shrives island, "Where the water fell, at the junction of two rivers, that's a coincidence" "Think about it, Michael Longstreet was a long time casual resident of Shrives Island, his last visit was his longest here, a bit over twelve months, so he knew the history, he worked locally so writing about the town, not at all unusual" Rhonda shook the manuscript she was holding in her hand.

"But this is dark it talks of ritual and hunts, what else could it contain?" "Well, read them, we will find a connection here, I'm sure we will, and there are the videos to view"

RHONDA SPELLING

Hello my name is Rhonda, my surname is currently Spelling, however, it will soon be changed to Gnik, I know he is popping the question on my birthday which is weeks away.

How do I fit into the picture?

I happen to know the history of Shrives Island, the working history, the gold mines, the mills.

But I have an understanding, that there are forces that move in and around the town, Shrives Island has been made rich by its abundant natural wealth that is a boom, but the one thing that dominates Shrives Island is "the house".

"Well I am getting ahead of myself there, when I start, if there is no one to stop me I will rattle on.

I was telling you about my impending name change, Steve and I met when I was going through high school, at the end, and we met at the local when I was old enough to drink, Steve is older than me by almost a decade, but I was at the pub with friends and came in and sat right next to me, popped a Gin and Tonic down in front of me, then he gave me a line, one of those you are a thief, that I stole the stars, or some such, but I laughed so hard I almost wet myself, he had me from that moment on.

I will be happy when he asks me to marry him, verry happy.

I completed high school, and I was employed at the Library almost straight away, the head librarian at that time was a Matron, she taught me early lessons in life, she taught me that conservatism may not be a bad thing, Shrives Island for me was Uncle Pete's where you go to fill up on pie and ice cream, my mum and dad had sent me to Melbourne when I was sixteen, to a boarding school, I lasted a term, then I was back here, they had resigned themselves.

So I was hired by the Matron, where I learned that books were a lot of work, but I learned pretty quickly that having so many volumes of literature through my fingers, was a way to learn, I have read volumes about my own heritage, I can trace my family back generations upon generation, I have read everyone from Plato to Steven King, I am a fan of Art Nuovo films, in the vein of "Emilie" they never take themselves to seriously, music, don't mention it I gave up my musical career years ago, but I do have a soft spot for any Aussie band, but my historical knowledge is rather extensive as I said earlier, but it is this town that I know you are here to hear about.

Shrives Island, I could talk about the success of the town its gold, but no I am here to talk of a different history that begun in this town over a century ago, "The House", The Desmond Brown Mansion.

It has been a place of over a century of history, but its history goes back much further than that.

Desmond Brown had that house built for him in Polk County U.S.A. in 1885.

In 1899 the house was pulled down brick by brick, down to the foundations, it was numbered, frame, bricks, clay roof tiles, it was packed and Palletized, and made its way by sea aboard the Mandy-Jane, A forty gun carrack bound for Melbourne, from Melbourne it made its way by rail to Bairnsdale, where it made its destination by Horse and Cart, the long trip to Shrives Island, or as it was known "The Crossing" a fledging town at the time.

The hill was the only site for the stately home, so that was where they set the cellar and rebuilt the house, for twelve months men toiled away overseen by Joshua Brown, it was Joshua who had decided to add the two monstrosity's that are the towers.

But from the beginning the house attracted "Bad" things.

In its early days in its Polk County days, it had a fire that killed twelve, it is said to have had a witch burned at the stake, as well a flood in 1880 had taken another six lives, that was before it was moved to Shrives Island, that poor horrid history followed the house here.

It has been the site of many deaths, and accidents, but it is the town and its inhabitants who from the beginning have had the best of luck and fortune, and worst.

The drownings in this town have been prolific, in 1901 a team of 12 loggers disappeared from the Pine forest, they had been out felling the left ridge, and didn't come back to town, when the authorities went out to check, there was no sign of any of the men, the gear, the horses and carts were there along with their gear, further into the forest they found the individual cutting tools of the men, but no men, when they had completed a search of the forest there was nothing.

The miners haven't got off Scot free, there was one mine collapse, but there was one casualty out of that, again it was disappearance, when contact was lost with the team of three men, they sent a mine manager down with two men and all they found were the men's lunch pails along with their helmets so they had no light, an entire search of the mine bought nothing, the men were lost.

There were the nineteen fifty bush fires, nature you can't help, but these were winter fires, contained mostly to the homes and dwellings, of Shrives Island.

But moving forward.

What I have found in the last few days, recent history is verry interesting, in 1910 Joshua Brown was killed by lawmen and Michael Longstreet had known his history.

With the most recent murders perpetrated by Michael Longstreet, all the evidence has become evident within his writings, his knowledge of Joshua is so intricate that we cannot discount that Joshua is a huge part of what is happening.

Desmond Brown is a huge part of what is happening.

That house, the Desmond Brown Mansion is, has been a mysterious place, in fact it has been downright nasty.

However, it turns out, along with Nick, that house has put Shrives Island on the map.

CHAPTER FIVE

IT'S THE PIPES

It was later that week, Craig had been incarcerated, Mark had been attending to the funeral for Ethan, Ian had been to the bus station to see Cathy buzz back to Melbourne on the Firefly to continue business, she was negotiating a deal with a soft drink manufacture for the Tin soldiers to drink their softies whenever they drank soft drinks, that suited Ian down to the ground, he had abstained from the alcohol and drugs while on the road, it wasn't Grange's but he could live with that, he could never hope his band members would follow his suit, to them he was a Square.

They had been in the upstairs lounge room, the box marked "Evidence" was sitting on the floor between Angie and Jess.

Nick had been listening to Jess and Angie, how they had completed the paintings they were working on, then Jess came out in the open and discussed the ghosts.

"So, if Desmond wants us painting and you looking, what are you looking for, or at?" Angie adds.

"He has been here for some time; my paintings are proof of that"

Jess says. "Just the other day Rhonda came up with a theory, Desmond is a front, an entertainment tool, there is a more important piece of the puzzle, his name is Joshua, the son of the late great Desmond"

Nick pipes in.

"So where do the kids fit in, we have to sort this stuff out, we have my best friend, well one of them in a mental ward, for I don't know exactly, we are weeks away from getting our first guests, I am sure they would enjoy the ghosting's, heck some are writers, talk about writers block, I'm not doing any writing at the moment, to many distractions"

Angie picks up one of the manuscripts.

"He was a half decent writer, until his mind began to slip" Jess adds.

"It's time we started looking at these tapes, there has to be something on them, since we had this box of evidence, we haven't seen anything of Desmond, I have no idea what these ghosts are up to?" At that moment Tim appeared to the trio, he looked frightened, he was terrified, and he was drenched.

Jess spoke up.

"Tim what is it, where is Miranda?" Tim just stood there looking at the three, droplets of water hung from his hair suspended for a moment before continuing their journey with gravity.

"Help us" That was all that Tim could manage.

"He is soaked through Nick, where is Miranda?" Nick spoke.

"Tim why are you wet?" "I was trying to save Miranda, he has her in water, she can't get out and I can't reach her"

"Who has her in water, where does he have her?" "It is not Desmond, he wants to place me in there as well, please help me get my sister back"

"How, what do you want us to do?" "Nick please come to me"

Nick followed his instructions, Tim held out his hand for Nick to grasp, Nick held Tim's hand, as he took it he felt a charge rip through his body, it was then Tim said to him.

"She is in the pipe, lots of pipes around, we have no idea of where we are, but the waterfall is close" then he was ensconced in water, his visibility was not good, but he saw Tim above him, swimming, he followed, swimming up, he breached the surface and pulled in a huge gulping breath, they were in what Nick had thought was a pipe, Tim was beside him treading water.

Only this was not the ghost Tim, this was the real living person Tim.

"Tim, we are in the storm water, where is Miranda?

"I know to get to Miranda we need to get over to the next pipe" He was managing better than Nick had expected.

"What is going on Timmy?" "I don't know, we woke up today in these stormwater drains, when I came to you and asked for your help, this is how I was, alive, I don't know, we have been visiting ever since he killed us, hey we gotta go, we need to help Miranda out, I will follow you" Nick takes a huge breath and duck dives down to where the pipe intersected with the main pipe, he went along the main pipe until he was up to the next junction finding the upright pipe and swam up, when he broke the surface Miranda was there hanging on to a ladder that went up to the top of the pipe.

She had been to the top, there was a hatch there, it was locked up tight.

"Oh Nick"

She squealed and let go of the ladder jumping toward him, he felt her pressure going under at first but resurfaced with Miranda coughing and spluttering, she was a child not a ghost, just as her brother was, not a ghost.

Tim broke the surface next to them.

"Right, you two are OK, well you aren't ghosts"

"I don't know why, we woke up this morning in the drains we were still ghosts, I felt myself change, when Tim went for help, how do we get out of here?"

"Tim can hold his breath, can you hold yours for a minute?" "I think I can"

Nick pulls his belt from his pants.

"I want you to hold onto this belt with all your might, when I start swimming do you think you can do that?"

"Yes, but what about Tim?"

"I will be fine, I am a stronger swimmer than you, you just hold on to that belt" "I will" Nick dived again, Miranda held fast with one hand and swam with the other kicking her feet to help Nick along, Tim was right behind them, there was another junction in the pipe, where they were forced into the wider opening, this larger pipe fed out onto the river, at the base of the waterfall, in the rush of water, that a second ago they were ensconced, was now a flood tide, it settled spitting them out underneath the waterfall, one, two, three.

All Jess and Angie could do was to stand there, mouths open, Nick was becoming transparent in front of them, Nick was disappearing, he was holding Tim's hand and he was conversing with Nick, he was looked directly at Jess, he yelled, she didn't hear him, but she had seen his mouth move, she could make out "the fall" she had to go to the fall, they stood there mouths wide open, and as Tim and Nick disappeared there was an audible pop, Jess turned to Angie, stunned, and finally said "Shit"

They both went to where they had been standing noticing a wet patch where Tim had stood, he really had been wet, the physical told them that.

"He is gone, they are both gone" Angie stood in silence.

"The fall, come on lets go" She roared into the carpark pulling up suddenly close to the barrier, they both jumped from the car looking around the park, it was devoid of life, the sound from the fall was deafening in the silence.

Jess yelled for Angie.

"Follow me" Jess ran the length of the barrier and down the stairs to the observation platform, the spray from the falls had soaked her thorough.

"NICK"

Angie joined in.

"NICK" She spied out of the corner of her eye Nick he was on the lower part of the Falls, he had Tim firmly clutched, and on his other side she saw Miranda, he pulled himself through the curtain of water followed by the children.

The children, who had recently scared them, the children whom had recently given Bobby Cursack a fright, and the same ones who had tried desperately to help their mortal friends, were once again mortal.

Angie and Jess had made their way down to the river, along a thin escarpment that took them to where Nick stood, with Tim and Miranda, once out of the water, they quickly made there way to the car and headed home, up the hill, as the car approached the house Tim and Miranda could only stare out at the house, neither one uttered a word.

Once inside, Angie was in the kitchen preparing hot drinks for everyone, Nick was in the downstairs Lounge room with Jess, Miranda was sitting in close to the flames taking in the heat, covered in a blanket just as Tim now was, he was sitting in a big armchair, Nick was beside him, Jess sat with Miranda.

Their cloths in the dryer now they waited.

"I like being this close to the fire, I could never get really warm in that other place" Jess had thought to herself a mono world where everything is the same and never changed.

"I am not going to bombard you with so many questions, you have just as many to ask me I would bet" "Yes I do have questions, but they can wait, I am rather hungry" Jess hadn't even put any thought of hunger.

Tim tuned his head toward his sister.

"Hey sis I could eat the Horse and follow with the rider" Angie was just about to start out with the tray when she was joined by the others, Jess pulled out stools for Tim and Miranda.

She went to work at the stove, started with cheesy scrambled eggs and Bacon, then she followed up with three stacks of pancakes topped with whipped butter and oodles of maple syrup, all washed down with the best cocoa they had ever had, with little marshmallows floating on top.

Tim sat back in his stool, holding his stomach, he belched, Miranda held her stomach, and belched twice as long and loud, then she began to laugh, Angie joined in, as did Jess, before long they were all laughing harder than they ever had before.

Everyone had arrived at the house by late afternoon on the day that Nick had gone and retrieved the children from the waterfall, a huge storm had moved in and across the district the worse summer storms for years, buildings were damaged some almost irretrievably, homes were flooded in the lower town, some of the lower shops were unindicted.

Everyone meant those who had been exposed to the hauntings, or the events of the last month, Steve and Rhonda, Mark and Ian, Bobby Cursack, Pete and Diane Watkins with Rose, Angie along with her parents, Jill and Graham.

Every one met in the huge downstairs lounge room, a T.V. room was adjacent the lounge, where the children were being entertained by the Wiggles, they were up, doing "Cold Spaghetti" while it played on the television, earlier, when Nick was showing them how to turn it on adjust the volume, etc Tim was gob smacked with the T.V. Miranda went up to it trying to touch the people, they both sat there for half an hour mouths open while they watched "Barney and Friends"

Now they were up bopping away.

Once assembled, they discussed the children in the next room.

It was decided that they would meet the children, listen to them, their story, and possibly bolt together the missing bits of this weird jig saw puzzle.

Nick went into the room, the children were sitting, and watching Wags the Dog and Dorothy the dinosaur playing.

"Miranda and Tim myself and Jess would like you to meet some people, some you know others I am not sure of, but I promise that none of them are here to harm you" The children now back in the cloths they had arrived in, they had scrubbed up fine, but the children would need to wait, Jess would take them shopping in the morning, oh what an adventure that will be, they turned to look at each other, didn't say anything, turned back to Nick and nodded.

When Nick led them out into the lounge, all the people there had made themselves comfortable.

Steve and Rhonda sat with Pete and Diane on one sofa, Bobby Cursack sat with Mark and Ian, on the other, Jill and Graham sat together on a Chase, while Jess, Angie, and Rose sat in armchairs.

"Miranda Tim, these are the people we wanted you to meet"

He introduced the children and stood back while they said hello.

"Now, it's time for Coffee and cake" He went into the kitchen coming back a few minutes later with a trolley with tea and coffee, and a Hummingbird cake, as the afternoon sunk into night Nick stood and made a request.

"Would you like to tell us your story" Jess said.

"Tell us in your words, where you were born and when, tell us your history as much as you can remember before you D"

She stopped short.

Rose said it for her.

"Before you died, that was what she meant to say" Jess kept her eyes on the two children.

"And then what you can tell us about your time as Ghosts"

Tim Began.

"We were born paternal twins in 1891, in Melbourne, our father who was twenty two when we were born had done verry well in the Victorian goldfields, and our mother was eighteen when we were born, our father had come to Melbourne where he was enjoying the social life when he met our mum, she had been a scullery maid for the Mayor, I remember our father telling us of how he met her, do you remember that Miranda?"

"Yes I do Remember, keep telling it, I am remembering as well" "So dad had been served by her one evening, and when she leant in to serve him some roast beef, he had gotten a sniff of her, he had complimented her on her perfume, she told him she wasn't wearing any perfume, suffice to say he had fallen for her there and then, dad built a huge house in St Kilda, and that was where we came into the world, apparently we were fit children, and we grew up in a time when you could be one day from poverty, when gold and the economy collapsed in the early 1890s, both mum and dad were cushioned from that, good investments, he used the money he made in his prospecting days and parlayed that into his mining equipment company, he had known that a crash was coming, and saw the need to branch out, that was when he started Granges Cordials, and we all know successful that little venture went"

He turned to Uncle Pete and said.

"Isn't that right Uncle Pete" Pete fidgeted and farted and finally said yes, Dianne took his hands in hers.

"So Granges Cordials were a huge overnight success, through word of mouth etc. but the product spoke for itself" It was now that Miranda took up the story.

"We were well and truly privileged, make no mistake, privileged but not brats, we hadn't seen poverty, well from our point of view, but we saw extreme poverty when we came to Shrives Island, we had just turned nine, it was 1900, a year before our deaths, the Miners and the millers came from the very poor, their children were so impoverished, there was so much gold, but no way to get to it, that was what my dad had told me, my father had announced that we would all be moving to Shrives Island, he was preparing to move a large amount of machinery here to assist in the mine, he was rather exited by the fact that his gear would be used, it gave him leverage to get the best deal for all of us, we travelled by train to Morwell, and from there was the rather long journey by horse and Carriage, the roads were rough in those days, and in winter most years there was no way in or out, but we were arriving in the height of summer"

Tim took over again.

"The summer of 1900 was long and hot, but here in the valley between the rivers the weather had seemed milder, the town was known as The Crossing back then, it had attracted that name because it was the only river crossing in the valley, people would come from everywhere for the opportunity of trade, and many had come to trade gold, a mini gold rush had begun in 1896, causing the town to go through a extra boon time, I suppose dad had heard and thought it a good idea to get involved with the mine from day dot, we had come from Morwell, traveling north east, mum and Miranda in the covered wagon, me and dad on horseback, I can never forget the first time I saw the town from the ridge, do you remember Miranda, how the town looked" Miranda brow turned up.

"Yes I do remember seeing it for the first time the building that was taking place, this small town named The Crossing, had grown out of the landscape, a lush rich fertile valley, rich with minerals and abundant life in the forests, a Jewell dropped by a Goddess lost to be found, discovered, I do remember coming across the final ridge, down across the river, and into the Main street, the town pretty much the way it is today, the residences where Nicks house is today, the old house down in the town were mostly wattle and daub, using their tents as roofs, they were mainly prospectors, just like our dad was, then you found on main street, the businesses, those same businesses that take up the town are all ancestral, Uncle Pete, you are one of those ancestors, Bobby Cursack, Ian Luther and Mark Harris, you all have ancestral connections, Steve Gnik, you Nick, and Craig especially have those ties to this town, sorry I have gotten of track, will you take the story up please Tim"

"So you need to remember where we are, the town when we arrived was well under construction, the Main street was full of building materials going into the pub, the bath house, the Café, even the Butcher and the Blacksmith had shops here in the main street, the Mines head office was complete and open for business, and on the hill was the house, it had been completed and Joshua Brown and his family were moving in we were his guests, so we moved into the house, for the first month we settled in, we had begun at the local school, it had attracted a teacher up from the city, our class numbered sixteen, rather a large school for a district so small, dad had been working out at the mine installing pumps, and motors, and all things steam driven, and mum and Mrs. Desmond kept house and socialized, for the first eight months everything was uneventful, dad had begun to build our own house, we were happy to be there, but we were much happier when we moved into our rather modest compared to the Brown Mansion house"

Miranda broke in.

"I was just happy to be a family again, life was going back to a familiarity to all of us but that was when things started to go wonky, I mean things went bad, he got to Tim first, and then a couple of days later he got me, mum and dad were already dead by then, but both Tim and I found ourselves, dead and together in the Cellar of this house, and so far that is where we are, where we were left, if you went down into the cellar, and dug in the middle, you will find our remains, you see, no one knows we were even killed, murdered by Joshua Brown, all in a plot to take over the Mining Rights along with the Equipment, the Cordials were a bonus, he got to us first, but mum and dad were a close second, how he killed them was terrible, made it look like transients robbed murdered them, taking us children with them, it is in the paper, it was crazy how he did it, he had my father write him a note, giving Joshua control of any of his interests on his demise, he signed it thinking that he would save us all, but we were already dead and cold in our earthen beds in his cellar, dad strangled and bludgeoned mum was raped a number of times before being run through with a huge carving knife, and we had a breakthrough we are now alive, I believe, no we believe we have been bought back to right the wrongs, put a stop to the accidents and deaths in this town"

Tim said.

"We know what we have to do, we know we need to bring the others out, we need to bring Desmond Brown, along with Joshua Brown, and Michael Longstreet, we need to destroy them, bring them out and Kill them"

They all sat there in silence, thinking about the whole condensed story, but the questions were many, finally Rose was the one to speak breaking it.

"Wow, freaky shit"

When all had settled, the kids were back to the television, with Rose, enjoying the Wiggles along with Captain Feather sword and Wags the Dog, dancing in the waves at the beach, and Jess along with Rhonda were in the kitchen making fresh coffee while the others sat in their groups chatting amongst each other, Jess spoke.

"You know, Miranda said that her dad had built a house, a house that Joshua laid claim too, we need to find where the house was, you have the history of Shrives Island, lets do some real detective work"

Later at the library, Rhonda went directly to a row of books right behind the desk, she leafed through the volumes, coming back down with the volume she was searching for.

"Here it is, this is the family history for the two decades, 1890 to 1910, hopefully we will find them in here" She opened the book at the index looking down the names alphabeting as she went.

"Bell, Brown, Cursack, Dougherty, Gnik, Grange here it is page 450" She opened to the page and read until she got to the paragraph that pertained to the Grange's they had been listed in the year 1900, Jack had been listed as an investor of the town, his wife as a homemaker, and their two children Timothy and Miranda, it listed two addresses for them.

"It says here there were two addresses, the first was Joshua Brown's address and the second address is a place out on Old Town Road, I think that is the pub, "The Red Wallaby" it was a house, in the early days, it became the local watering hole around 1904, and has been there ever since" Jess then said.

"Lets go, lets talk to Tim and Miranda, see what they know, can remember"

They found the children holding court, talking about the late 1880s regaling the older people with stories of what the last century was like, they did a great job together Tim giving the male side and Miranda the female side.

Rhonda went to the children with the book she was leafing through the pages looking for a photo of the "The Red Wallaby" stopping at a page much closer to the front of the book.

"I want you to look at this picture and tell me what you know of it ok?" Tim was confident.

"For sure"

Miranda was more apprehensive.

"Maybe" Rhonda showed them the page, instantly Miranda's eyes lit up, shortly there after Tim had a realization and in unison said.

"That's our house" Tim went on.

"Its bigger, but I would never forget the original plans, I helped dad design the house, Miranda also helped with the decorating inside, but that's our house for sure" Jess thought for a moment and then said.

"Would you like to see it?" Miranda turned to Tim a wide smile on her face.

"Tim, what do you think?" "Lets do it" Jess addressed the adults.

"We are taking the Kids to The Red Wallaby, it was once their home, we may get some answers, hell we need something, so make yourselves at home, Nick will look after you, Rhonda and I will take them"

As she ran the range rover up to the speed limit, out on Old Town Rd, the children sat in the back marveling at the speed Jessie was doing, watching the trees Wizz by in the twilight of the evening, the orange and pink hues of the late afternoon sun branched down through the trees, shining there golden luminance over them all.

She bought the land rover to a halt in the car park red screenings shifting under the big wheels bringing them to a scrunchy halt.

Tim and Miranda got out excited, Miranda stood on the spot dancing up and down.

Jess spoke to the two of them.

"Kids now listen to me, I don't know what to expect, but you both need to calm down, you can't be overexcited like you are" Miranda and Tim stood still, and nodded to jess, Miranda saying.

"Sorry, we can't help it, this is where Mum and Dad, and we were together last" "Don't apologize, no need just keep it cool ok?" They both said in unison.

"We will be on our best behavior"

The four of them stood there and looked at the building, it was red mud clay brick, set into the house along the whole frontage, were windows, that were ordered specific, for one person each, the windows had been manufactured by a British glass maker, the first one had a scene set into it of a drover on his horse stained into it for Tim, the second window had a English lavender for Elizabeth, another a fishing scene for Jack, the last one had cats that was set for Miranda.

The windows had been polished and cleaned regularly, the owners up to now wanting them preserved, the colors in the window looked as crisp today as they did in 1900.

They pushed through the doors into the main lounge, it was a long room with a bar running the full length, at one end was a sign that read "Under New Ownership and Under Construction, watch your head" and just below that in big bold letters were the words "You are welcome here" the sign was set up next to construction taking place, currently a wall had been removed and new lentils were being hung prior to the brickwork being completed, and would open the area up quite considerably.

Miranda stood in the middle of the room, she turned, and stopped.

"This was the dining, entertaining room"

She came back to where the three were standing, the bar attendant was at the bar.

"Hi ladies, kids, are you here for a meal?" Jess approaches him.

"Ah no, my kids are doing a history of the town, they want to do a bit about the hotel, is there any chance we could wander and look?" "No, problem, if you need to know this place started as a single story ranch house, they built up when the hotel came along around 1900, I don't know the history that well, I only came to town two weeks ago, I've been flat out, this is the first quiet day I have had since I took over"

Jess had thought to herself that she had the history teacher with her, Rhonda would help them.

The bartender put his hand out.

"I'm the new owner of this establishment, Brett Hamond pleased to meet you"

"My name is Jessica Lester, that over there is Rhonda Spelling, with Tim and Miranda" "Oh it is you, Jessica Lester, I am pleased to meet you, and just the person I would like to talk to, but not now you have children with you"

Brett grabs a card from his wallet, passes it to Jess.

"Give me a call, I would like to purchase some paintings, brighten the place up a bit, but feel free to wander where you want, if you like I can set some drinks up on the house for you four"

"Do you have Grange's cordials" He points to the Grange's taps set into the bar, there was a green tap, an orange tap, and a Brown tap, and a tan one that meant he had Lime, Orange, Sarsaparilla, and Creamy Soda, four of the most popular of the flavors.

"Right kids what flavor"

Miranda and Tim looked at each other and in unison said.

"Grange's" Miranda was the first with her order.

"I will have Sars" Tim added.

"Make mine lime" "We will have the Creamy Soda"

"Coming up" Jess took the Kids aside and explained to them that they were doing a project, and this hotel was the focal point, most important was to keep their cover, that was when Rhonda offered.

"Don't you think they may look just a little oddly attired?"

"Oh shit" It was at this point Brett called from the bar.

"Come get it" The four of them moved back to the bar.

"Brett, the children's clothing is a part of the project" "Yes, I thought they were in a period play, when you explained the project, I got the cloths" "Oh well I thought as much"

Jess was wandering how long she could stretch this lie before she heard the snap of it breaking.

Tim and Miranda climbed up onto a barstool each, that was when Rhonda and Jess took a stool and sat down.

They sipped their drinks, Brett then said.

"The drinks will be safe, you can start your wandering"

Miranda who had first taken a sip and looked at Tim,

"Not as good as when Dad made and mixed it"

Timothy shook his head in agreement. They got off their stools looking around.

"Start out there" Brett was pointing to Batwing doors that led out into a huge kitchen.

They pushed through the doors, the room was a large oblong room, which had once been the four main rooms of the house, Miranda went a corner of the room and Tim went to the opposite side of the room.

"Do you remember Tim, this was where our rooms were" "Yes I know, this was where my room was, your room is where you are standing now" He points to the third section.

"That was Dad and Mums room and that was the parlor"

"What are you both feeling, what are you remembering, your parents what happened, who harmed them" Rhonda adds.

"Try to remember when you were here last together" Miranda's mind went back, to a long ago afternoon, she was remembering her mother and herself at their last time together, they had been folding linen, using fresh lavender through the folds, to fragrance them, they had been talking of plans her father was putting in place to secure their futures, the man who daddy was working with, was the same man they had been living with the last months and they had planned investments for the whole family.

Tim's mind went back to a time many years before, it was himself and his father they were down at the Odistgeeg, they both had their lines in the water, they had been chatting about what he was about to do, he was making an investment that would see them all cared for, Tim's line went taught, he set the hook into the trout's mouth and begun reeling it in, it was a huge Brown.

"I only have pleasant memories; I don't know who would harm"

She stopped Tim's mouth dropped open, but he managed.

"Joshua Brown, that's who it was, it was Joshua, he had everything to gain by being rid of us all"

Miranda walked away from her spot, she stopped at her parents' bedroom.

"It didn't happen here, they would have left a stain, a human stain" Tim joined her in their parents' room he didn't say anything for a long moment then he offered.

"It didn't happen here, they were dragged out of here bound, and gaged"

Rhonda spoke up.

"No that's right, your father's body was hanged after he was bludgeoned to death, he was hung from a tree, not far from here, your mum was found further away from the house, it was terrible" "I am feeling that dad is trying to communicate with me, something is trying to come through, can you feel it Miranda?" "I think I can, mum, slightly but its not clear" Jess asked.

"Is this the first time either of you have had this feeling?" "Yes" Said Miranda.

Tim stood there nodding.

"Well don't force it, let it come naturally"

"Can I go back to my drink, please?"

Asks Tim.

Jessie thinks to herself that they are possibly sapped of strength.

"Alright, lets go" They returned to the bar, the drinks were still there but there was no sign of Brett.

They grabbed their drinks and retired to a table on the opposite side of the room, it was then that Brett made a re appearance.

"I didn't see you in the public bar, why not" "The kids are bushed, we are going to finish our drinks and head off" "Before you go I have something I need to share with you, I could not think of the more perfect person to speak to about this, wait here"

Brett toddled off and came back a couple of minutes later, he was carrying a wad of tissue paper, he was unwrapping a trinket as he came toward them, he placed onto the table a perfectly preserved Cameo, splendid with its oil painting.

"Just today I found this, I was removing a wall as a part of the extension, this was down between the wall panels, goodness knows how it got there, but you know oil paintings what do you think?" Tim and Miranda stood there looking down at a painting of Elizabeth, Tim held in all he could, Miranda could not keep the breath in and she sighed heavily, Jess looked at both Tim and Miranda, they had remembered to keep their secret, but it was difficult, Rhonda picked up on Miranda's look, one of happiness but complete dread was written across her brow.

"Jess what do you think?" "I think it needs to be appraised, I could get back to you when I call you about the paintings, I will have news of it for sure" Miranda and Tim's faces changed they now had muted smiles there.

"Why yes, get an appraisal for me, and when you call me up to negotiate the paintings we will discuss the Cameo, fine" Brett picks up the Cameo, re wraps it and hand it to Jessica, all the time the kid's eyes were on the item.

"I'm sure it's safe in your hands"

They finished their drinks and couldn't wait to get out of there.

As soon as Jess and Rhonda and the kids were in the car, she handed the tissue wrapped Cameo to Miranda, she began to quickly unravel it, they were soon staring into the eyes of their mother, a century on.

Back at the house they were all waiting on the return and were enthralled by the Cameo that Miranda had to show them.

The woman who had once been Victoria Grange, was beautiful.

Blonde hair cascaded down her face just like her daughter, her son's blue eyes shining out of the orbs, a small nose, and defined lips, made the Cameo a pleasant one to look at.

A conference had begun in the library, the coincidence just now was uncanny, they had gone there thinking they would pick up on vibes or sum such but having to owner of the pub present them with a Cameo of their mother.

Coincidence was it coincidence, it was just good timing, it was a factor of all these things.

Rhonda was leafing through the history books in her possession, looking for a hint or a clue, but coming up empty.

"This is not getting any easier, I can't find what we need to know in these, I need to get to the Library, there are books there that cover the history better than these volumes as well as ledgers, you know purchases and financial Accounts, that's where we need to go to follow the money trail" Jess had taken the doll out of the evidence box, she was looking at it intently.

"How much power do you think this doll has in it?" "As much power as the beholder of the item I suppose, these things are a mystery, deep and dark voodoo is something not to get involved with unless you know exactly what you are doing" "When you go to the Library let me know, I will bring Angie, for the research you can't go through all those Ledgers on your own" "No your right, lets plan it for tomorrow morning, no use putting it off"

The following Monday was a rather hectic one for Nick and Jessie, Nick was supposed to be at the hospital to see Craig, but Steve had been running late, Jess on the other hand had the Kids to organize, she wanted to cloth them properly, she had to be prepared for any eventuality.

"I have to go, I need to stop and get the kids new cloths, before I go to pick up Angie, Rhonda has been at the Library since seven this morning, we all wanted to be there to help her" "You go, I will catch up with you later, I will call you"

They kissed, Jess then gathered up the kids and left.

She was heading down the driveway and Steve was heading up the hill, they honked at each other and waved.

Nick was coming out the door as Steve came up to the turnaround.

"What happened we were supposed to be there by 8.30"

Nick looks at his watch.

"Its now 9.15, what have you been up to?" "Slept in, no Rhonda and no work, had to organize staff for the shop, they are in place now so get in" They arrived at the Hospital a little after 9.35 seeing the Police cars front and center, making comments about how close the cops had to be to the entrance, they went through the main doors down the corridor to the mental health ward.

They found Craig in his room, he was sitting by a window, he had opened an old and tattered Hard Cover of Steven Kings "The Tommyknockers" he was a third of the way through it.

"Well" Said Steve.

"Where are the police, I thought we had a meeting with them?"

"They went out to the cafeteria to grab something to eat, always thinking of their gut" Steve sat next to Craig, Nick went and sat on the end of the bed.

"And how are you feeling, notice you are reading again, The Tommyknockers hey, fun novel that one" "Fourth time read, probably his smartest writing to date, you should try reading it"

"No thank you, there is plenty of horror in this world to keep me satisfied, sheesh why would you look to a novel for misery, I don't understand it" Nick offered from the bed.

"Its nice to know that your horror story is nowhere near as bad as what you are dealing with in everyday life, I don't have the notion to even work that point out at the moment, its kind 'a like the doctor analogy, people get sick from the round up Monsanto put out there, but the Drs. Don't say or do anything about it, they figure why upset the apple cart, keep your mouth shut, and continue to treat the people, Monsanto will pick up the pay packet in the end, mark my words"

Tom Little came back into the ward carrying a coffee cup, have a lovely day was stenciled on the side.

"Good morning gentlemen running a little late are we" Craig speaks up.

"Sergeant Little, a little respect for my brother and his friend" "Well I have been here now forty-five minutes, waiting, I am releasing Craig" Craig stood from his seat.

"What are you on about, what has happened to the evidence, there has been a change has there?" "We ran the prints through the database again, they revealed a positive I.D. to someone else, not you" Nick spoke up.

"So that's good news, you have been exonerated, you are free to go" "I don't want to leave, I don't dream in here, I have stabilized while in here, you take me out of here and I don't know what you will be dealing with" "There is no need for you to leave here, I am releasing you which means you are free to go home when the medical staff clear you, I thought you would be happy with the news" "I am, don't worry, but I won't be going home any time soon"

Nick asked.

"Who's prints were on the axe sergeant Little?"

"That's under wraps at the moment, I'm sorry I can't say, anyway, that concludes our business here today, have a great day gentleman"

Not long after the officer had left the doctor came onto the ward coming straight to Craig.

"So you have had the good news Craig" Dr. Ben Kahvejian was Armenian, and verry good at his job, he had known about Craig from day one and had taken his case, he had known through the evidence presented to him Craig would be charged, and to hear that the prints were not Craig's had buoyed him.

"Doc hey, boys I would like you to meet Dr. Ben Kahvejian, he is Armenian, and his surname has a reference to Coffee"

"Kahvejian means Coffee merchants, my family still trades in coffee, I took to this mantle because I knew that I could help people, now Craig good news, you have had today yes" "Yes but I don't want you to discharge me, ok" "I won't" Nick and Steve both looked directly at Dr. Kahvejian Nick spoke up.

"That's a positive"

Steve added.

"Its what you wanted"

Dr. Kahvejian then went on.

"You are not ready yet, you are still not right yet, we will see in the coming weeks, but I would like to discover more about Marlii, you have done well to remember, you need to keep remembering, tonight we will have a little celebration, here in the ward, for your innocence"

Craig, Steve, and Nick had the thought go through their minds, how innocent was he.

It was approaching ten thirty, Jess and Rhonda were working together with Angie, they each had Ledgers at around the early 1900s, the children were sitting quietly in the children's lounge, dressed more for the times Tim was wearing a pair of Levi jeans over a pair of Nike runners he was wearing a Nike sweatshirt which had the words, "Just do it" down the front, Miranda was wearing a summer dress, her hair was up, her curls set in a bun around her neck was the Cameo now hanging there on a Sterling Silver chain, she was taken up with an Enid Blyton book, the magic far away tree, Tim was being entertained with the amazing spiderman.

It was Angie who came up with the goods.

"Look here, Jess, Rhonda, I have something, there was a land purchase, in 1900, between two parties, it says it was between Joshua Brown and Jack Grange" Jess goes to the Ledger looking at the column in the center of the page.

"It states here it was for a parcel of land, right where the pub stands"

Angie filed in the missing piece of the puzzle.

"Joshua sold him that particular parcel of land knowing it would be back in his hands before long" Then Rhonda added.

"That's what Tim was enraged by back at the hotel, he was livid with the fact that Joshua Brown had taken advantage of them, how he had managed to fool his dad into going into business with this man" Jess quipped.

"So now we have evidence, providence if you like, but are any of you willing to go to the police, present the evidence, present Tim and Miranda, we'd be in the mental Psyche ward, right next to Craig" Angie offered.

"Well lets piece together more of the story, I am in the middle of a serious block at the moment, I haven't painted a thing in weeks, and anything I have attempted recently seems to go to shit, I know you are painting Jess, but I have nothing"

Jess nodded her head, she was thinking, Angie wasn't able to work, Nick had only just started to write after a serious block, and she herself hadn't really begun anything new recently, she just had a couple of works that needed nothing more than a touch up as well as a signature, she thought it best not to say anything, better leave sleeping dogs lie.

CHAPTER SIX

TRICKS

Tim and Miranda were left in the house with Angie watching over them, the adults were at the hospital celebrating, they had liked Angie, she was sweet, Tim had thought if he was ten years older.

She had been explaining to them the politics of today's school life, the study, the sports activities, Basketball, Football, athletics, the latter she had never got involved in rather wanting to splash paint around.

They had been having a real treat, a sleepover, with all the junk food and movies, they had selected there were so many "Films" to choose from, they had settled on two "Dinosaur" which was the second movie that they had to watch, they were now getting down to the end of "Gladiator"

Russel Crowe was in a huge arena, having fought his way through a hoard of beasts and men, now he was in a confrontation with the emperor, there is a standoff, which sees both men ending their lives.

Tim speaks up as the credits begin to roll.

"Wow, that was great" Miranda offers.

"A little much, gore and blood yech" "Well the next movie is a kids movie, I think you will enjoy that, lets go to the kitchen, get more popcorn and soft drink" The three of them went to the kitchen Angie sticking the popcorn into the micro wave and turning it on, Angie went to the coffee machine filling her cup, the kids went to the fridge and grabbed out cans of drink, Tim grabbed the milk from the door to save Angie the trouble, the popcorn was popping away in the micro wave.

Tim speaks.

"The Gladiator was a good film, historically correct, to a point" Miranda adds.

"I am looking forward to the Kids movie Dinosaur, it will be kinder, I hope" Angie offers.

"Its animated, it's a cartoon, you will like it" Miranda looks at Angie.

"A cartoon?" "Yes a cartoon, you will see, they make animations for kids, well mostly they are for children" The popcorn ceased its dance and was taken from the stove and placed into the huge plastic popcorn bowl.

Back in the lounge, Dinosaur was playing, the children were enthralled, watching the story of the Dinosaur, making his way across the lands to find where he belongs, finding a mate, eventually making there way to the "Promised Land", the credits had begun when they all heard the noise coming from upstairs, it was a thudding, continuous, Thump, Thump, Thump, Angie paused the recorder, they all sat there in silence, then it came again, Thump, Thump, Thump.

Miranda spoke.

"Ah that's weird" Angie turned to Miranda.

"It is weird, you want to go investigate?" Tim sat there perplexed.

"We were ghosts, we once were responsible for haunting people, we should know who is haunting, or trying to be heard, lets go and find out"

Angie led the way, following the noise, Thump, Thump, Thump, they entered onto the grand staircase making their way up to the mezzanine, below the first floor, Thump, Thump, Thump, it kept coming in that rhythmic beat, they made their way up to the first floor, Angie in front with Miranda and Tim just behind her, they were holding hands, they were feeling no fear, so was Angie but she wasn't showing it, Tim and Miranda did not see the irony, Thump, Thump, Thump, at the top of the stairs Angie stopped, the children stopped with her.

"It's coming from in there" Angie points to the tower room, the one on the left.

Thump, Thump, Thump,.

Angie walks to the doorway, Tim moves with her, Miranda stayed put.

Thump, Thump, Thump.

She opened the door.

It was Michael Longstreet, although she would not have known this, the children looked in recognizing the man, he was sitting on the chest of another, he had his head in his hands, he lifted the head, striking the ground with the bloodied dead head, Thump, Thump, Thump.

He stopped and looked up and out the door, immediately he recognized Angie, she was not scared by what she was seeing.

"Angie, I said to this person we would be filming for at least two weeks, but he didn't want to do it, now I have to punish him" He went back to his job, Thump, Thump, Thump.

"He only recognized me, he has no idea that you two are here"

Tim offered "It is Michael Longstreet, and one of his victims, watch this" Tim went into the room, he walked over to Longstreet, he grabbed a handful of hair, a huge clump of it and pulled.

Longstreet reacted to his hair being pulled.

"Hey, how did you do that?" Tim reefed on his hair a second time, again Longstreet reacted this time getting up from the body, the body disappeared into the ether, Longstreet looked at Angie.

"How did you do that" Angie was standing open mouthed; Tim was now standing beside her.

"Don't fear him, he is about to get a big scare" Miranda went over to Longstreet, she pinched him hard on the arm, then Tim returned and bit him on the opposite arm.

"Stop"

"I'm not doing anything it's the ghosts, they are doing it to you"

"wha, what ghosts, wh, I am a ghost'

Angie stands her ground.

"Ghosts, they are in this house, haunting it"

Tim spoke.

"He is getting confused, keep going, keep harassing him"

Longstreet says confused. "No, no, how can that be, am I not haunting you now?"

Angie offers.

"No, the ghosts I think are haunting you"

The ghost of Michael Longstreet began to fade in front of them but managed to say.

"What is happening to me"

Angie offers

"You are disappearing, being drawn into the ether" Angie threw her hands up and waved them around the room.

"You are being drawn back" Michael Longstreet kept dissipating until there was nothing left.

Miranda was the first to speak.

"Wow, he had no idea we were here, he only saw you, and you were able to confuse him"

Angie says.

"And that is because you two are with me, you two are amazing protection"

They began to go downstairs but were stopped on the mezzanine by a figure on the ground floor.

"Hello children, hello Angie, that was smart, what you did to Longstreet, showing his weakness, showing a propensity to acting"

It was at that moment that Nick opened the front door.

Where Angie and the kids were standing, there was a man between he and Jess and themselves.

Tim was the first to speak.

"This is Joshua Brown this is the man I want"

He started down the stairs but stopped when Nick raised his hand and spoke.

"Timmy, don't do it, please"

"That's right young whipper snapper, stay where you are, you lot are not being verry cooperative"

He looked over to Nick and Jess.

"You Jess have not been producing"

He reverts his stare toward Angie.

"Neither have you Angie, don't you think you need to begin" Nick spoke for all of them, as he came toward Joshua Jess behind him.

"We know all about you"

Nick reached out to grab Joshua, he thought he had purchase on him, but he was not there, he repapered on first floor, looking down at the three still standing on the Mezzanine.

"Looks like you don't know quite everything about me" Tim began up the stairs toward Brown.

"You killed us, you killed my father and mother you killed Miranda"

He was murderous going up the stairs, he was now three feet away from Brown.

"I will finish you"

He reached out and he had a handful of Browns surcoat, then there was a huge snap as Joshua Brown disappeared into the ether Tim standing there with his hands out and void of anything.

Nick and Jess ran to where Miranda and Angie were standing, Jess stayed with the girls as Nick went to Tim.

"I almost had him, I had his jacket in my hand, and he is gone, I will kill him, I will destroy him, I will end him"

Nick placed his hands on Tim's shoulder.

"Patience is the key, there is so much information coming forward, we need to wait until the ladies have more info" "He is frightened I know he is scared" Miranda added.

"I felt it, Michael Longstreet was so flustered, he was so confused, he thought he was doing all the hauntings, but we scared him off, and I do believe Tim put the fear into him"

Angie added.

"You did too Miranda, good on you both"

Nick was coming back down the stairs with Tim Nick says.

"Well to the Kitchen, I could do with a strong cup of coffee.

That was where they finished the evening off, the children telling Nick and Jess of the two movies they had watched, Tim acting out the last scenes from The Gladiator, Miranda explaining the ending to Dinosaur, that was when they got up to tonight's events, nick explained the celebrations at the hospital ward how Craig was pleased he had been cleared of any wrong doing, he was safe where he was, Jess had surmised that the ghosts had no way of getting to him while he was on the ward there was protective force around him.

Craig was looking more like the Craig from the Craig and Marlii days, all the "Visitors" had left, and the "Guests" of the hospital caried on the celebration, there hadn't been many people in the ward, their numbers fluctuated between six and fifteen, currently there were eight peeps in the ward, Craig had been friendly with all of them, most were voluntary, they could not live on the outside, they had felt safe in here, meals, showers, and a bed, what more do most want, they mostly avoided people, they didn't like to be around anyone even in their own company they were confused, scared, lonely, but in here they could be on their own whenever they had liked, most of them had liked that a lot.

Craig was sitting chatting to the nurse who had been on duty, his name was Max, and so he was, Max was a big boy.

"I had known they would clear you, its good news, but why stay in here, why not get out"

Craig says "Get out, are you going to kick me out, are you?" "Well no, I like having you in here, you are the most interesting patient we have had in here, I love how you have been so successful, so lucky with your prospecting"

"I have been lucky, verry lucky, but all that luck, that success I would trade it all away for my time with Marlii once more"

"I have lost someone I loved, I was twenty three, she was my age, cancer got her, it wasn't sudden it took two years to kill her, her name was Angelina, I wanted to die after she was gone, and for a time I almost did die, but I stayed, and I fell in love again, Brenda and I have been married for twenty years next week, and I have my first Grandkid about to be born, if you fight and you want to stay it will get better"

Later that night after Max had gone off duty, Craig was sitting with his copy of "The Tommyknockers" on his lap, and he sat and thought, how many times has he been reading, how many times has he had to put on hold any sense of semblance, any thought of what COULD be real, Cujo he wasn't real, was he?

He thought about King's writings, and then he thought of Nick's writing style, Nick was good, verry good, but he was not, Steven King.

Then there was The Stand, could that future ever eventuate?

But he kept the thought process going, when you remember King's prolificacy in writing, the Novella, "Different Seasons" published some time about 1988 contained four of King's best Novellas, Rita Hayworth and the Shawshank redemption, Apt Pupil, The Body and The Breathing Method, being able to suspend belief, but for the four of these there is no need to suspend belief, the first is about a prison break, the second is about a boy who discovers a Nazi, living and hiding among wide old America that maybe is where you suspend your beliefs because what that boy forces the Nazi to do, well, but The Body, that was about four boys, looking for a dead body reported on the news, then The Breathing Method, it tells the story of a woman whom by using a method of breathing during child birth, the woman whose life is ended in a decapitation, the result of a car accident, the headless body gives birth to the baby, later the bodiless head thanks the man for his help, scary, that's for sure.

But suspending belief, you need to read the collection Four Past Midnight, The Langoliers you needed to suspend belief, Secret Window Secret Garden, yes suspension of belief, that guy Mort was crazy, The Library Police, definite suspension of belief, and The Sun Dog, you need to be able to suspend belief, all have very supernatural forces surrounding the characters.

And right now, Craig had known of the supernatural surrounding him, but not in here, they could not get to him while he was safely within these walls.

Cujo was real, he was real and he was big, a St Bernard, Cujo, all two hundred fifty pounds, the dumb mutt tried slipping his head in where it didn't fit, chasing a rabbit into a hole, that contained Bats,

Rabid bats that bite him on the nose, and that's the hook folks Rabies, that big old St Bernard goes on a Rabid frenzy of killing, Gary Pervier, Joe Camber, Sheriff Bannerman, but it is the loss of young Tad Trenton, after the Trenton's Pinto breaks down in the Cambers door yard with the infected Cujo containing them to the hot car Tad died of dehydration and heatstroke, and that was how it ended, no happy ending, a dead kid to deal with.

He placed the glasses on his head and leafed through the book to his folded page, he began to read about a rouge Coke a Cola Vending machine that begins a rampage through town, spitting out cans. Suspension of belief.

Uncle Pete's was again weekend busy midweek, they were all there serving, Rose, Diane and Pete were all busy, Pete on the grill, Dianne fixing the drinks, and Rose run off her feet, Nick and Jess walk in the children were at the Library with Rhonda, they were taken with the multitude of books there were to read.

Looking around for somewhere to sit, they spied two stools over at the counter and take them, Diane greeted them and Uncle Pete from the pass waved, Rose came to them.

"You two traveling light today?" Nick speaks.

"Miranda and Tim have discovered the library, can't get them out of there"

"We are so flat out, not the holidays and not the weekend, they have all come up from the waterfall, the rain was sudden, I don't know why they are afraid of a bit of rain, but that enough of me bitching, what will you two be having" Jess was looking over the menu Nick gave his order.

"I will have two eggs sunny side up bacon with two pancakes on the side and toast and coffee"

"And Jess"

"I will have the Miners Omelet, with bacon on the side, and a coffee thank you"

"I will bring your coffee you may be waiting, so the coffees are on the house"

Nick says.

"So you have the purchase Ledgers, what have you come up with, you have had time look at it, what has it yielded?" "As you know we found the land purchase papers, and there are so many more of purchases from the Grange's, for the building of their home, but" "Oh there is a But" "But we cannot go to the police with any of it, I want to see what transpires, after Angie Miranda and Tim scared off Longstreet, and we were there to see them scare of Joshua Brown the other day I don't think they will be trying anything so soon, I am happy let's just let everything settle, let the twins settle in, and I have begun painting again"

Nick speaks up. "And the twins?"

"What about them, they are happy, what are you getting at"

"Jess honey, they are not ours" "They aren't anyone's, and what's the harm I don't see a problem it's not like any one is reporting them missing" Rose was back with their first cup.

"I have a minute or two, so how are things going?" "Verry well thank you Rose"

"So are you going to keep them?" Nick looked at Jess, it was obvious she had planned it, and she had spoken about it to others but not Nick.

"So what's this, what are you talking about Rose" "I agree with Jess on this Nick, you two are responsible for them, after all it was you who pulled them from the drains, so you two have that responsibility"

She turned and went back to the pass.

"She is right you know they are our responsibility Nick"

Nick took a gulp from his coffee.

"You know, if I had to choose children I mean, Tim would be the perfect son and Miranda the perfect daughter"

Rose returned with two plates of food, placing the omelet down followed by the plate of eggs and pancakes.

"I hope you two make the right decision here"

She turns and goes back to the pass.

Back at the Library, Miranda is helping Rhonda, they are putting away returned books to their positions, Tim was enjoying more of The Amazing Spiderman.

"So, Rhonda, what is your take on all that is happening what's your theory?"

"I have an opinion, not a theory, would you like to hear it?" "Well yes of course I want to know what you think?" "So you two have been here since the beginning, but you have never had contact with your parents, you have been in a separate realm, you have been in the "In Between" all this time, do you think if we go down to that cellar we will find your remains, no they will find lots of remains down there but not yours, I haven't shared this with anyone else yet, I wanted to share this with you first, get your opinion on it"

"I don't completely get it, in the "In Between" all these years alive but dead" "I have read so many esoteric books in my life, I understand it, I find that explanation the easiest way of explaining it, do you understand" Tim called from across the room.

"I get it, "The In Between" when he killed us, he didn't kill us, he threw us into the In Between"

"You heard that, Tim?" "You told Miranda, so you told me" He closed the comic and got up from his seat in the children's lounge and made his way over to Rhonda and Miranda.

"That is something that we found years ago, when we were separated, we could communicate, it's not a problem"

Rhonda says.

"Well that proves my telekinesis theory, you would not know what I am talking about, modern research" Miranda says.

"Telekinesis, the ability to move objects with the thought of the mind, watch" Miranda averts her gaze to the books on the trolley, and then closes her eyes, the books levitate from the trolley and fly off in every direction, filing of into their respective homes Rhonda stood there, books whizzing inches from her nose.

Miranda opens her eyes when the books are all back in place. "See, its rather simple, you think the book back where it belongs"

Tim closes his eyes, his comic levitates of the table and returns to its slot on the shelf, Tim opens his eyes.

Miranda looks at her brother and says

"Show off"

Later that evening it was a little after five PM, the doors to the library opened and in came Jess and Nick, Jess was carrying a bag, inside it contained two containers of uncle Pete's Ice Cream, one was

Peach and Coconut, the other contained plain Peach, Miranda didn't like coconut, not the taste the texture, but that was not what caught both Nick and Jess by surprise, it was the balancing act they were witnessing.

Miranda had her eyes closed, she was sitting in the OM position, but she was two feet off the chair, she was floating or hovering over the chair.

Tim on the other hand had his eyes wide open, he was also hovering off the chair, but it was what they were doing that was amazing.

Miranda had in front of her six books, and assorted items, a toy bear, blocks, and a complete train set, all were levitating in front of her, swapping positions, the train hooted its horn and a wisp of white smoke emanated from the black smoke stack, Tim also had six books as well as a toy boat, two toy bears as well as toy cars, the boat which was a Tug, was tooting its huge horn as it sailed on the make believe waves.

Jess and Nick went to Rhonda standing with her.

"They have been at it for about forty five minutes, they just started doing it as a competition, I don't know how this will end" They watched for a couple of minutes, it was then that Jess held up the bag with "Uncle Pete's"

Blazoned across the bag.

Nick says.

"Give me the bag"

Jess passes the bag to him, he stands their and shakes the bag.

"Hey"

He shakes the bag again.

Nothing.

Rhonda then takes the bag and shakes it.

Tim turns, he loses his concentration, and everything tumbles down including Tim himself.

Miranda still holding her concentration, opens hers eyes and looks down at Timothy" "This time it looks like you lose"

While the two are enjoying their ice cream the three adults get together for a chin wag, Rhonda explains how the children had reacted today, she had never seen anything like it, she was sure that Nick and jess have never witnessed behavior like she witnessed, they confirmed this fact, but no matter how hard you try, you cannot put out of your mind the way ALL the ghosts reacted to the children, both Michael Longstreet and Joshua Brown had been scared off, they were frightened, and it had been over two weeks since they had any hauntings.

The way everything had been going, there had been many questions, none of them presented answers, Craig was still in the Psyche Ward, Mark had headed back to Cranbourne that morning, and Ian was going back on tour, as for hauntings they had ceased for two weeks, and were not giving any signs of beginning again.

The children were happy, they were healthy, they weren't dead.

With the decision to be sure the children stayed safe, and with the skills they were showing now would need to be nurtured, powers with which they still had no idea about.

Nick called for the Kids.

"Miranda, Tim we have some news for the two of you"

They all gathered around the table; Jess spoke up.

"Well, we have made a decision, and we would like you stay with us" Tim and Miranda looked at each other, Tim smiled at Miranda she said.

"That is exactly what we want Tim" Tim nodded decidedly.

"Yes, that is exactly what we want"

CHAPTER SEVEN
HORSES FOR COURSES

It was a little under two months on from the events that had happened in Shrives Island.

All had gone back to normal, as much as anything has been normal in Shrives Island.

Nick was into his newest writing project that was under wraps even to Jess, "A historical piece" was all she could get out of him.

Jess was working on a new painting as was Angie, Rhonda had taken on an apprentice in Miranda, both her and her brother had come to the local school as Niece and Nephew to Jessica, it was never questioned.

The Mill after the tragedy of Ethan, had come back to life quickly, and was back to full production, and the rest of the town was ticking along just fine, finer than it had been in some time, Uncle Pete's was the place to be for out of towners when the weather turned sour.

Sometimes it was to get a look at the house on the hill as it was fast earning a reputation for scary Hauntings.

Ian was on tour with Tin Soldiers, Craig on the other hand remained in the Psyche ward, he had been given a private room, and the room after two months looked like the bedroom from hell, well not from hell, it was neat and relatively tidy, but it was cluttered with texts and books, he was ferocious reader was Craig, among the titles were many esoteric books on magic and witches, along with Bible text, he was looking for clues, and he was getting close now, verry close indeed.

Mark was back at his racing stables just outside of Cranbourne back in the east of Melbourne, he had kept his independent property, aside from his stables at the racetrack, the facilities at Cranbourne had been vastly improved into the Ninety's, and he appreciated the use of the establishment, but for his spelling horses and those out of work due to injury or illness

"The "Property was the place for them to be.

As he looked out through his office window the muted daylight giving way to night, his foreman was bringing in the last of the horses that were stabled there, he had known he would be required out there soon to help with the feed up, he looked down at the invoices on the desk, they had to go out tonight, he sat down and picked up the pen, and as he checked each invoice off, keeping a couple of the invoices out of his "Good" pile there were three that needed his attention, the first and third required vets bill to be added, the one in the middle racing day farrier.

He squared away the invoicing taking the prepared statements into Cindy for tonight's mailings, then he heads out to the barn out the back, the barn was a traditional stable built for his grandfather, who he had followed into the racing game, his grandfather had won a Sandown Cup some years ago, along with a heap of country cups.

He walked into the smells of the stables, and the shit was a distant smell, above that odor were pleasant smelling things like the saddles and gear, in the Tac room the oil mixed with molasses and grain from the feed room, which were directly beside each other the feed room being the closest to the entrance, beyond the Tac room were the stables twenty four in all, only eight were in use currently, in the first box was his prize, his gelding who had yielded him the last two Cranbourne cups, and in two weeks he was sure he could add a third to that, notwithstanding the extra half a kilo more than any other horse in the race, he had tested him, he had known what Stan was capable of, he went down to Stan's box and walked in, Stan was over by his water bubbler playing with the water, Mark had known that he was hungry, he loved that about this horse he would work harder the more you fed him, even with a gut full of food he would carry one point one kilos more than any horse fielded against him, Stans Racing name was "Anchors Aweigh"

He walked up and slapped him on the rump, he snorted and looked up at Mark for a second and went back to the water.

"OK I get it, I get it you want a feed" He left the box slamming the top bolt home and went the next box where he found his Foreman.

"He is turning out just Peachy Rusty, I think he will pull it off" "I do as well, and he is a pig at the moment he is eating everything" "I know I will give him a huge lick of Molasses and barley tonight" "I will be down to help you with the feeds in a sec" "Ok, oh and by the way that Kings Fool Filly is looking really smart so thanks" "No Problem boss"

He went into the feed room, Rusty was ahead of himself, the feed bin were out and placed into their category's age before beauty, except for a champ, the chaff and lucerne was there, then there was dry bran which on top of each bran pile were the electrolytes and vitamins.

The oats and the Molasses Barley were left for Mark.

It was when Mark reentered Stanley's box to put his feed in, he heard his name, he was sure it was Nick, but when he sighted the man who was really in the box Mark was frozen.

It was Desmond Brown, he was in colors and racing Jodhpurs, cramped into them, the stitching on the Jodhpurs were stretched to bursting, he had a riding switch in his hand, on his bulbous head was a skull cap, Mark rubbed his eyes when he opened them the misshapen Desmond Jockey thing was still standing there.

"I'm not going anywhere, I am here you Know, now you think this hack will win the cup do you" He prodded at the horse with the riding switch, the horse reacted, it turned its rump in the direction of Desmond, when the horse kicked out it was explosive, but all the horse managed to catch was fresh air, Desmond appeared at the opposite side of the box.

"See, you cannot kick me your stupid animal" Again Brown struck out at the horse, this time extending the full length of the switch to the horses rear end, it reacts with scared violence, pig rooting and bucking mixed with confined space could be dangerous, but the horse avoids Mark until he can get to the horse and settle it, now Desmond is outside the box.

"We will see, if this Nag did so well again this year, I would be verry surprised" Then there is an Audible click and Desmond is Gone.

Mark goes to the horse there is a welt mark across it flanks, where the switch came into contact.

"Rusty, did you hear any of that?"

Rusty comes out of the box he was working in laying the horses bedding down.

"Did I hear what?" "The ruckus coming from Stanley's box?" Mark came out of Stanley's box, laying on the ground was a riding switch, he looked down at it not saying anything, Rusty bent over where the switch was an picked it up.

"Ah where did this come from, its old, antique old"

"He turned it over in his hands, looking at the intricate pattern embossed in gold.

"Look here it has a name embossed into the handle?"

Rusty handed the riding switch to Mark, he looked at the fine embossed pattern on the handle, he turned it over embossed on the leather handle was the name of the owner.

"Desmond Brown" "Who is or was Desmond Brown?" "Someone who we are better of not knowing"

Mark placed the riding Crop down on a bag of feed and went back into Stanley's box, taking in his feed bin, the horse was now settled and tucked straight into his feed, Mark went to him rubbing his flank down feeling the ridge from where the switch had come down on him.

He grabbed Stan's rug hanging from his box gate, taking it down he threw it over the horse, going around the back he took the straps looping them through each other clipping them home, he then goes to the front and does up the horse's neck strap.

"I'm sorry you had to endure that my friend, I know its not fair, so don't listen to anything that thing said" Stanley kept chewing taking in his feed.

Mark pated the horse down a final time and went out into the barn, shooting both the top and bottom bolt of Stanley's box gate into place.

He moved to the feed bag and took the riding switch, looking at the old leather handle, it had been recently oiled, he could smell it, he went to Rusty telling him he would see him at dinner, fifteen minutes.

Back at the house Cindy was over the sink preparing potato mash, he went to her striking her lightly on the bottom with the switch, she reacted turning around brandishing the potato masher.

"Hey mister, stop that unless you want mashing, where did you come up with that, its old" Cindy was totally aware of past incidence's, they had spoken often, they had handled everything as well as could be expected, the death of Ethan, that whole sorry saga, of Craig not knowing anything that had transpired, when he had left town both he and Cindy went to visit Craig, it was at that meeting that Craig had spoken for the first time about that summer so long ago.

They had gone into the ward with trepidation, only to be pleasantly surprised with both his mood and demeanor, he had known he had acted creepy that night at the reunion, but he had been coming back to his full faculties as he had put it, he had said sorry to Cindy as he embraced her in a huge hug, and that was when Craig had said going back to the house, elicited some awful memory's in his head, and with the anniversary falling at the same time the breakdown and memory loss were all to be expected, that was when Craig had remembered about going into the house, and at that point in time Mark did not put two and two together.

It was in that moment when Cindy had said it was old.

Marks memory went flipping back to the day many years before, they, the four of them had gone into the abandoned Brown mansion, his memory of being in there was vague at best, but to remember at this moment, it was the riding switch, and that Desmond Brown thing, he had known he had a phone call to make, a verry important phone call.

"Its old, as Rusty said it antique old, but look at the name on the handle"

Mark passes the switch to Cindy her eyes open widely.

"Desmond Brown" "Yes Desmond Brown, so what do you think of that, I just saw Desmond out in the stables, he had my racing colors on and was bursting out of silks, he hit Stanley with it" Cindy was shocked.

"You are going to need to contact Nick, let him know what is happening" "You know this time I won't react, with all this shit going on I don't want it interfering with the preparation of the horse's, no I will just bide my time" At that moment Rusty showed up in the door yard, removed his boots and came in through the door, stopping to wash his hands at the sink in the breezeway between the covered alcove and the kitchen.

Rusty says.

"So what is with the ridding crop, and where did it come from?" Cindy speaks up.

"Its an artifact, and it is off subject right now, so take your seats and I will serve" Rusty adored Cindy's cooking, always filling and hearty.

Rusty had come to Mark five years previous, he had showed up drunk to an after cup party, he was washed up, a has been Jockey who had become a sop to the booze, the only reason he was allowed into the party was he had ridden the previous years cup winner, he was half drunk when he arrived, firstly making a complete cock of himself by falling into the table that had contained the Mornington Race Clubs Cup, it all went over, the cup coming to rest against the leg of the table, leaving a dent that would need to be repaired buffed and shined.

Mark had managed to get him out to the car park, not being able to speak any sense into him, he put him in the back of his car and told him to sleep it off, he stayed there until Mark and Cindy were home, at that time he was helped to the Jockey Quarters where he was left for the rest of the night to lay in his stupor.

The next morning he had gotten out of bed with a head sorer than he had ever had, when he had finally got a semblance of where he was he went into the main house to find Mark brewing coffee, he had three cups and began to feel normal again, that was when he said he realized how much of a dick he had made of himself, how he could never face up to the people who had relied on him for all those years as a Jockey, nicknamed the Ferret, he did have the ability to sniff out a run before it even became available, he had a uncanny ability of being in the right place, for the movement of the horses when the run started, if his horse had it he would kick them home, often a longshot.

He had won the Melbourne Jockey Premiership four years on the trot.

Mark had reminded him, that the Cup would need attention, it would need to be repaired before the trainer received it, last night he got it and gave it back again, to be repaired.

The embarrassing scenario had been playing in his head, he remembers getting a drink, and as he approached the table he was sure he had been tripped, because when he landed, he remembered it being in old Hollywood movie, someone shifted the floor on him and he fell head long onto the table his weight carried him through to the floor as the table was upended, one witness said it was it was comical, as they watched the Cup tumble to the floor only to be stopped by the table leg.

He sat there that morning and had decided, that with a little support from Mark he would get better.

Within the first month he was made Foreman.

The rest is history.

He was now a part of the furniture, it was his own decision to stay on at the property, but it was Cindy's idea to keep him fed.

Rusty took his seat, Rusty sat opposite Mark, he took the whip from its place on table, he looks over it.

"Its over one hundred years old, but it has recently been oiled" Cindy came with Rusty's plate and snatched the whip from him.

"I will take that, you don't need to worry about this, I have it now for safe keeping" Rusty looked down at his plate, potato mash with cabbage and corned beef.

"Superb again Cindy" He looked at the condiments on table, Cindy's Pickles, homemade, or Cindy's tomato relish, which one to have.

It was a little after one in the morning, Mark was up to relive himself, he spotted a light out in the barn, that was unusual, Rusty had turned them out last night before turning in, he went out into the dooryard, the strong winds buffeted him from the east disturbing his robe as he stood there looking at the barn, he listened, the wind rattled the big old barn door on its tracks, he had heard movement, he started toward the barn tentatively, as he entered, he switched on the light in the feed room illuminating the entrance a little more, Stanley got up from his sleep, snorting at the disturbance, he walked past Stanley's box, when he was midway along the stables he heard a "Psst" from the empty box on his left, he looked in, but there was nothing there, "Mark" he heard next coming from the box on the other side of the Barn, then he looks up and on the rail set high was Desmond Brown, he was in a saddle mounted there.

"Here we are Mark, at the Ledger, heading to the finish line, hands and heels all the way, you know you can't get away from the fact that you have to go back to Shrives Island, you have to go back to the house, all of you, Nick, Ian and especially Craig, all of you have to come back, we have unfinished business" Mark looked up at the Desmond Jockey thing, this time it was its full size, the Colors and the silks, hung from him in a raged mess, the skullcap not sitting at all correctly on his head begins to slide forward in its wake it leaves the face of the Desmond thing stripped of its flesh, the vibrant colors turning to a burgundy black, his silks what is left of them begin to change color, the skinless face begins again.

"So gather up "The Boys" and come back to Shrives Island, come to the house, where we will be waiting" The skullcap fell from the height, it landed at Mark's feet all bloodied and gored from the Desmond Jockey thing, he looks down at the blood seeping into the bright yellow silk covering of the cap, he looks up to see the thing all bloodied now, nothing but gore sitting high in the bleachers of the barn, bleeding all over one of Mark's best track work saddles.

"Remember Boy, get them all together and come, we will have a party, oh and bring your Missus too"

Mark says to the beast. "I know you are real; I know what you are doing, too you this is a game" "A game that ends in murder, I know how much Ethan's death affected you" Mark yells up into the barn at Desmond.

"No, he didn't die you or one of yours murdered him" "Murdered him, Mmm carved him up like a Sunday roast, he was dead before the saw got him, don't worry" The Desmond thing got up in the stirrups and jumped, it landed just beyond Mark's reach, he went forward Desmond put up a hand.

"Uh uh, stay there" Mark stopped.

"Now I have given you instruction, goodness me can't any of you take a direction, sheesh" Mark stared at the Desmond thing, its oozing and pulsating redness, did not scare him at all rather repulsed him, Mark laughed at the Desmond thing.

"Ah you think I am scared of you, your ilk, not at all, I will be there, we will all be there, my word" Mark advanced on the Desmond thing, grabbing it around the throat, he was looking into its open maw, the breath was rotten and assailed his senses causing him to gag, but then the thing stopped breathing, Mark looked down at the Desmond thing it began laughing at him cackling at him.

"Do you think you can kill me"

In his hands the Desmond thing changed, the blood and gore was gone, Desmond took Mark's hands from his own neck and placed them around Mark's neck, Desmond stood, from the tip of his hat to the cravat around his neck, to his rather tight-fitting Jodhpurs to his highly polished Riding Boots, it was Desmond Brown.

"You cannot kill me" Desmond began wringing his fingers together, Mark began to struggle for breath, he was strangling himself.

"You can die if that is what you wish but you cannot kill me" Desmond wrang his fingers a little tighter, Mark's grip around his own neck tightened he was now not getting any air at all.

"Or you can live"

Desmond released his fingers, Mark could breathe again, he was on his knees, but he could breathe.

"You and the other three, at the house, pronto" And then he was gone.

Mark remained where he was for a moment in the silence looking up at the rafter where the Desmond thing had been and the saddle was no longer there, he would find it on its tree in the tack room, he had regained his breath, he got up and went down to the feed room filling a glass with water he drunk thirstily, the back door to the house banged open and Cindy came from the house and headed to the stables at haste getting to her husband quickly.

"What happened, what are you doing out here"

The lights went on in Rusty's quarters.

"It was Desmond Brown, he was back again and verry insistent on how much he wants us back in Shrives Island, we will have to go back, I don't see any other alternative" Rusty came into the stables rubbing his eyes.

"What's the ruckus out here, you woke me up, what is it with the horses?"

"It's all OK Rusty, go back to bed" "I don't know how you want me to sleep with the all the noise" Cindy's ears pricked up.

"You heard what?" "Mark, and some dude in the stables arguing" "So you heard me arguing, how clearly?" "He was adamant that you had to go back to Shrives Island I know that, I remember him saying to bring your missus" Mark and Cindy looked each other that was when Cindy said.

"Shrives Island"

Mark nodded and said.

"Shrives Island"

CHAPTER EIGHT
MUSTANG SALLY

Ian Luther had been on a tour of the East coast of Australia, he had been relaxed for most of the tour, because this time they all had their respective partners with them.

Ian had the opportunity of driving his 1968 Mustang.

The car he had found while in the united states of wide old America for the first Tin Soldiers tour, he was at a Bar B Q at the behest of other supporting band members on a little farm in the corn belt of Nebraska, he had been enjoying the hospitality, when he spied the old car right in the middle of a blackberry bramble, the children had been around the bushes eating blackberry's, they were supposed to be picking them for a pie.

He was looking in that direction, after the call was made for the kids to stop eating the fruit.

He caught a glimpse of chrome twinkling in the midday sunlight, he got up from his seat and went to investigate that was when he saw his baby for the first time, the paint was totally wrecked and the car itself not far from that point, Ian was curious and fought his way through the bramble to try and get a closer look, it had been red a lifetime ago, and it had been a Mustang.

After fighting his way back out of the bramble much to the entertainment factor for the children who had found it rather hilarious, that he had gotten himself caught up on the prickles.

As much an amusement to the adults.

Randy Coolth, the lead singer of Sammy's seven, (There were four in the band) and the owner of the property came down to Ian.

"What you all doing, that old thing has been there since Moses was a kid, what Ya doon down there?"

Ian came up from the bramble dusting himself off.

"I like it, I think it's a 68 Mustang" "Yup it is a 68, the old man abandoned that car in 1972 when he went back to Vietnam and got himself all shot up to shit, geez he said when they flew him back to the U.S.A. the verry day we bought him home, that mustang can sit and rot for all he gave a damn, if he couldn't drive it no one would, so it still sits, if you want it its yours"

As simple as it was, the car was pulled out of the bramble, the breaks needed attention as did the engine, but within a month the car was back on the road, gleaming red and fiery, all he had to do was arrange the freight back to Australia.

With the improvements to the car that Ian had done after arriving home, it was now in show room condition, every inch of the car original, down to the plates in the engine bay, this car was exactly the same age as himself, he was born on January 18 1968, the plate was stamped with the date 1/18/1968.

As he thundered down the Pacific Highway toward Coffs Harbor with the love of his life riding in Baby, things could not get any better.

He swung into the driveway of the Coffs Motel, and pulled up outside registration, a buzzer sounded as he entered, he was soon greeted by a portly man, he was verry generous with his praise of Tin Soldiers, how happy he was that the band members chose to stay at his establishment, when Ian bent down to sign the register, a hand closed around his he looked up to see that the booking assistant was in fact Desmond Brown.

"I've got you, I wouldn't struggle if I were you, if you wanna play tonight" Ian felt the tension as he relaxed his hand.

"Good, now you bring those other three to the house, do you hear me?" Ian looked down at where his signature began, the pain in his fingers was excruciating, he looked up to Desmond, there was a humorous smile there on his lips, the pressure returned.

"Do you hear me?" Ian submitted to Desmond.

"Yes, I hear you, myself, Mark Craig and Nick to Shrives Island back to the house"

The pressure on his fingers reduced to nothing as he released his hand but retained a finger, the pinkie finger.

"You are weak Ian, weak as piss, you do know that don't you, oh and bring your lovely wife with you"

Desmond twisted the finger, shattering it. Ian closed his eyes, the pain was excruciating, when he heard a voice say.

"Mr. Luther are you OK?" Ian opened his eyes and looked down to see he had griped his own hand, he instantly put his hand down beside himself.

"I, I am so sorry" "No are you okay Mr. Luther, ah I think you broke your own pinkie finger "I think I blacked out for a moment" "You blacked out alright, you were going on about Shrives Island, isn't that where you come from Mr. Luther?" "Yes Shrives Island is where I am from, I may have been daydreaming?"

The assistant said. "Oh the grip you had on your own hand was, well it was rather tight" Cathy had come to the entrance and pushed the door open, looking in, she could see the concern on the booking managers face when Ian turned, Cathy could see Ian's expression, it was dread, he said.

"It was Desmond"

Once settled in to their motel room, Ian waited for the rest of the band members to arrive, but he did get his traveling Guitar out and strummed it a couple of times, then he finger picked strings from a High E down to a low E through all the other cords, no nothing wrong there, he put the guitar back in its traveling case, Cathy came out from the bathroom, she had been preparing for a girls night, they would go to the local picture theatre to catch up on the latest gossip.

"What was that about?" "Just checking that I will be right tonight, I have broken my pinkie finger, look" Ian held out his hand showing Cathy his broken finger, he wiggles it.

"Shit that hurts" "I will tape it up if you like, why don't you go to a doctor get it set before the show?" "No I will live with it till we get to Brisbane, only two shows between here and there including this one, I will survive as Gloria once said" There was a knock at their door, Cathy went back into the bathroom and closed the door, Ian answered it, it was the manager.

"I'm sorry for any disturbance Mr. Luther But I have a message for you, they tried to reach you on your cell phone, said it went to message, but you need to know, the bus has broken down just outside Raleigh, they said to charge your phone, they will call you about the set-up, because they will need to walk in and play, so please Mr. Luther charge your phone"

"Please call me Ian, Mr. is to formal"

"Call me Max, m, Ian"

"Max, what happened in your office earlier?"

"Well you were signing the registry and you blanked out I would say, then you griped your right hand with your left and squeezed, that was when I heard the mention of Shrives island, I figured with the tour so far you may need some rest" "I will be fine, only two gigs left, tonight is the penultimate" "Well I will be there front and center with the missus" "Thanks for letting me know what's going on and what went on, I will see you tonight at the gig, hold on a minute will you" "Sure" Ian went to a suitcase on the bed opened it and retrieved two passes to back stage he goes back to Max handing him the passes.

"Here you can come backstage tonight after the gig, enjoy the after party"

"Thank you, I will see at the Gig" "Sure I will see you later" He went back in closing the door, he stood for a moment in thought, until Cath came out of the bathroom.

"Who was that?" "Max the manager, we need to charge our cell phones, the bus broke down" Ian stood not moving and finally said.

"And I just attempted to maim myself, Max informed me that I had hold of my own hand, he is back, they are back, I need to make a phone call, oh he was rather insistent that I bring you along"

Ian organized the venue, the gear truck arrived, and he helped the roadies to set up the gear.

The venue was a smaller than the Tin Soldiers, were used to playing, it was more intimate, close, most of the crowd were to be seated at tables and chairs, the dance floor was designated at the front of the venue, Ian picked up his Guitar and began to strum a sound check, then he went to the other instruments sound checking each one, he looked at his watch as people began to file in taking their seats, it was now seven forty and the boys were ten minutes late, the promotor got up to the mike.

"Hey folks, I know you are looking forward to seeing Tin Soldiers tonight, however due a breakdown they are going to be about thirty minutes late, so I will shout the bar one drink each"

The gig had begun at the amended time, they begun the set with their latest hit, and had gone straight into one of their classics when the room stopped, Ian was left standing there looking out at the crowd, those on the dance floor frozen in all manner dance moves, people sitting at the tables raising their glasses, a drop from a glass frozen midair hanging.

From behind him the drums beat once.

He turned to see Desmond at the drums, he hit the skins again, ba doom.

"Hey Ian, good to see you again" He played a downbeat on the snare while tapping the cymbals.

"Now where are you going Ian, I mean after the gig Ian where are you going?" Ian stood looking at Desmond he was dressed just like Jimmy, there actual drummer, he had Jimmy's cap along with the Black Sabbath shirt, his fat form completely filling it.

Ian closed his eyes.

"You are not real, you are not there" Desmond again hit down on the Tom and Cymbal at the same, finishing with a "qitish"

"Oh yes I am, open your bloody eyes, look at me"

Ian opened his eyes tentatively, what he saw horrified him, Desmond began to play the drums using the toms, cymbals, High hats, and the bass, all in harmony, but he was using severed arms, they were the arms of a Timber Worker, it was the same Plaid shirt that Ethan was wearing the day he died.

He was holding the arm by the hands, blood sprayed from the amputated stumps each time he struck the drums or the high hat, the sound from the drums were perfect, he was playing their latest hit,

"I miss you when you're here"

"See, I know your numbers I have them all down pat" As he continued to hit the skins.

"So you need to bring that lovely wife with you, and come to the house"

Desmond continued to play,

"Don't you let me down Ian will you?"

Ian stayed where he was and closed his eyes, the drums beat on, the cymbals rang out, he then heard the base guitar and the keyboard, then he heard the vocalist that was when he opened his eyes.

The people on the dance floor had slowed down, they were looking directly at Ian, the people at the tables, were looking at him, the vocalist was signaling to him.

"What was he doing?" Ian had caught on, he had blacked out again, he was back standing there stunned, he began to play, as they progressed through the song, Ian settled into his guitar, and played the rest of the Gig.

Cathy had arrived with the other girls as the boys were playing their last two numbers.

As the band came off stage to applause the Keyboardist was the first to pull Ian up for his mental fugue on stage earlier.

"Did you go back on holidays out there?" "Hey, I'm sorry, I can't explain it, I just blacked out"

Cathy was curious at that comment.

"You blacked out again, did you?" "Yes, let's not make anything of it, please, it was Desmond"

CHAPTER NINE
JACK LESTER

Shrives Island had some visitors due into town.

The talk had been about how the two boys had taken the ghosts with them when they left.

The Talk, that had taken place all over town, but mainly at Uncle Pete's, and out at the Psyche ward at the hospital.

As Saturday approached, Tim and Miranda had been busy at school, Angie was feverishly working on a painting of the twins, as she saw them, Nick was taking a hiatus from writing for the moment, and Jess had been busy along with Rhonda on the evidence box and just where Mr. Michael Longstreet fit into the puzzle, it had been rumored that it was Michael Longstreet's prints that were found on the murder weapon, but that was impossible, according to Rose Watkins, she had been certain that Longstreet had blown a rather large part of his head away, the parts you need to live, which pretty much disappeared into a red cloudy mist, no it could not have been him, could it?

Craig had been adamant that the ghosts who have diminished powers at this moment, because of the twins, it seems while they're around the ghosts who had habitually haunted the people of the town stopped, started up in a whole different location, and are requesting the four meet up at the house, but why?

Craig had known, for some days now, he had finally dreamed, a good dream, Marlii was in it, she had explained to him, how she did not die the way he remembered it.

"Go to the house, the secrets are in the house, you will find out answers there"

It was a day later that Nick had a visit from his long dead father, he was carrying with him some rather nasty injuries from his car accident, although his head was relatively attached, his right eye hung just below his jowl, his good eye, the left eye had darted around in his head, he waited for the dangly eye to catch up, as on its stalk it moved at an independent pace, Nick should have been repulsed but for some reason he looked and saw his whole father standing before him.

"Son you need to go back to the house, you need to remember that summer, and what happened, you do know you can control this, with help" Nick tried to speak to his father he began to tell him how much he loved him but his father just kept telling him.

"You need to bring Jess with you, do you understand?" All Nick could do was nod his head, Jack Lester was changing in front of him, Desmond Brown was coming through, Nick saw this, he had been ahead off Desmond, and he did not let on to him that his Ghost was slipping.

Jack Lester went on.

"And don't forget Mark and Ian, and especially Craig, you can't forget him"

Nick cut in.

"Dad can you stop talking please?" The Jack Lester Desmond thing stopped talking.

Nick got up from the seat in which he was sitting and went round to the entity sitting on the opposite side of the desk, he sat beside it.

"Tell me this Desmond, are you afraid of the twins?" "Who is this Desmond you speak of, the twins, what are you talking about?" "That is why you need this disguise, isn't it, and until we are all in the house together, you lot are not safe from the twins?" Jack Lester lost all form until he was nothing but a blob on the floor oozing red, pulsating around, then form returned to it, it became the full entity that was Desmond Brown.

"I will stay for but a moment, to tell you the warnings are real, if you don't gather your friends and return to this house, we will reduce your family's one at a time, starting with someone much closer to you than Ethan was?" Desmond Brown was up on his feet, he began to float, then he was above Nick, floating, and disappearing into the ether.

"You need to follow our instructions, and come back to the house, we need to finish this" Desmond floated for a moment longer, there was an audible pop, he was gone.

They all came together at Uncle Pete's on the Sunday after Nick's visit.

Pete had put the closed sign out he would not be trading until the afternoon, if at all.

As they all arrived, at or about nine AM, Jess and Nick arrived about eight thirty the twins quickly sought out Rose who had been busy filling sugar canisters, the twins went to work, filling sugar, Steve and Rhonda were next, there was no distinct grouping of any one there, but everyone mingled, greeting each other warmly, the crowd swelled quickly with the arrival of Mark with Cindy, Ian and Cathy, Bobby and Janice, along with Angie and her parents Graham and Jill.

The crowd was bolstered by those who were privy to goings on at the mill prior to the death of Ethan Swab.

People such as Jane Reith, who had actually witnessed the direct aftermath, obviously people like Graham bell, all three of the Obrien brothers, Luke the youngest, then there was Heath, and the eldest Richard, they had all witnessed hauntings, strange goings on, that was how they had all come to the conclusion, strange, strange things, weird happenings were surrounding that house and this town, and they would root it out and destroy it, kill it.

Coffee and shakes were sorted for everyone as well cake and pies, once everyone was happy Pete spoke up.

"Ok folks we are all here for a reason, IF they are here, they have no power over us, with the twins here we no need to fear harm" Pete flipped the bird to the sky. "So if you can hear us, up yours, now with Craig in absenteeism, Jess or Nick who is first?" Nick speaks up.

"For now, while we are enjoying coffee and cake, or pie, we will keep the open forum, we can make it formal when there is something there, how does that sound to everyone?" The consensus being, he was correct.

Jess had been discussing the box of evidence that sat squarely on her table along with Janice, Diane and Jill, they had discussed the little china doll, dressed just like Desmond, even its paunch hung over its suspended trousers, it was when the children spotted the doll for the first time at Uncle Pete's, both of their curiosity's came alive, Miranda was the first.

She went to Jill asking her if she could see the doll, her facial expression told part of the story, but when Miranda turned to Tim, his face had told the second part of the story.

Tim blurted. "Where on hack's foley did you find that?"

"Jess has had it for weeks, I just found it now by chance" "Jess do you know what you have here?" "It's a doll the likes of Desmond Brown, a good likeness to be sure, some call it voodoo, I haven't really thought about it"

Tim was in awe but could manage.

"Wow, its Desmond Browns vessel" "With this we can be rid of Desmond Brown, we don't need much but we need something from him, cast him out for good"

Jess asks curiously? "What is this vessel, what does it do?" "It should not be here, it should not be in this realm, but while it is here, he can be trapped in here, imprisoned, how do I describe it, a coffin?" Tim says.

"Yes, a coffin that's it, something we never had the pleasure of"

That was when Bobby Cursack stood up.

"I got it" Everyone stopped and turned to look at him.

"Sorry, but I got it, Desmond is desperate, he is aware his doll is here, he doesn't want anyone to find it, he is desperate to stop anyone getting it, we know he avoids the kids right, and now more so that they are, um alive"

He looks over at the twins.

"You two are amazing, I wouldn't have believed it, but I heard you kids when you started coming through, and what you are capable of is truly amazing" The twins smile Miranda blushes.

Bobby continues.

"He has no idea you have this in your possession, so don't let him know, use that doll to pull the rest of them in, we need time, this is the way" Jess responds.

"Ok, so if we let him know that someone amongst us has this doll, but we are able to keep it from him, he will remain here until he has it in his possession, so we will work out a roster, as to where the doll will be at any one time" Rhonda adds.

"And we still have more to go over in the evidence box, there are still screenplays, and tapes to view, we are getting behind, because all has quieted down in the last few weeks"

Mark Chimed in.

"The four of us all back in town together, we have been instructed to go to the house in our group, apparently we will find out the secret, I say we put it off as long as we can, until we are four and, in the house, they are limited to what they have been up to, hauntings" Tim broke in.

"Murder and mayhem, that is what they are bringing to this town, Desmond Brown, Joshua, and Michael Longstreet will not stop until you have gone to the house, all four of you"

Ian then asked.

"So why us, what happened to us?" Nick chimed in.

"I know it has to do with what happened here in this town in 1974, none of us have any memory of it, except Craig, he was the eldest of us, Craig is the answer, I know he isn't aware of it yet, but Craig is the key to this, Craig and Marlii.

Craig had settled into life on the ward.

His room was now much neater than when he first arrived, he had been archiving al of his writings and reading into a catalogue.

"So how did your meeting go, what did you come up with" Ian answers.

"We came up with you" "What do you mean you came up with me?" Mark answers.

"You are the missing piece, it is your dreams that hold the key, you are the one, what happened to Ethan was proof of that, you are the eldest, so you are the familiar to Desmond Brown, you could control Desmond with this" Mark goes into the satchel he is carrying and pulls from it, the doll of Desmond Brown and presents it to him.

"It is Desmond Brown from the top of his hat to the shiny boots on his little doll feet" Craig takes the doll and study's it, looking into its deep eyes, looking for a clue" "I don't see how a Voodoo doll is going to help us out of this situation" Nick speaks.

"It's not a Voodoo doll it is something more than that"

Craig looks down at the doll again.

"So how much more could it be, it's a good likeness of him, but it's a doll"

Nick continues. "And do we question these things anymore, do we really want to ask this question of that doll, you are holding onto, Desmond's Vessel, here in this realm this is Desmond's Coffin, and if we can get a small piece of him into the doll, that will be the end of Desmond, I won't ask why, I won't ask another question, I have faith in things that are wonderful, and I have a belief in the unbelievable, you know you were an instrument on that day, they were all working on Ethan's death, Desmond Michael and Joshua, each of them had a hand in that day, and I think it is time that you gave up your room here and come back into the real world, you have your faculty's back, look around you at your reading material of late, Scriptures for God's sake, you haven't been religious since our school days"

Ian adds.

"None of us have followed a religion since our school days have we, all against our parents better judgment, we have all stayed well away from religion, and church except Marlii"

Craig looks into Desmond the dolls eyes again, he is whispering almost to the doll, it is inaudible, that is when Mark says.

"Speak up Craig, we want to be able to hear you" Craig looks up from the doll looking at each of the other three men, holding them in regard.

"We need to go back to the house, that is the only way we can get this to stop" All three men looked at each other and then back to Craig, all with questions on their faces.

Mark breaks the silence.

"Back to the house, what are you talking about" "Do any of you remember the summer of 74?" Mark says.

"Well yes, that was the year Marlii was drowned, and you spiraled out of control after that, we all had breakdowns that year, most traumatic summer of our lives" Craig holds the doll up.

"Do you remember the summer of 74, not Marlii, I know that was what sent me off the deep end, but what about you three, what was the trauma, I am remembering, the other night Marlii came to me in a dream, she told me we had to go back to the house, and if we want to know what happened because my memory is as hazy at best, but I know Marlii was right, we need to go back to the house, the four of us, on our own" Ian adds.

"But we have been told to bring our woman, in my haunting, he insisted on Cathy being with us" "That was a haunting, Marlii came to me in a dream, no we need to go on our own just the four of us"

CHAPTER TEN

BOOK TWO
1974

Craig Gnik was sitting in Uncle Pete's, he was sitting with Rusty Smith, Rusty was his nickname, his real name was Steven Smith which was his surname was shared with Marlii, Steve had been Marlii's older brother, he had only just had his twenty second birthday.

They were waiting for Marlii to arrive.

Rusty had been away to Vietnam to fight the boys in black pajama's he had been in Vietnam for some time, right up to the end, he was one of the last Aussie soldiers out of there.

He had been promoted a number of times, on the day he was rotated back home he had become a Warrant Officer.

But that was not like his first promotion, his first promotion was because a Corporal got it in the gut and had died, he went from a private to a Corporal in a second, he saw it all, saw all he could take, the death and destruction that he had been a part of.

"Hey Steve no one cares what you had to do to survive, I don't read newspapers any way, you are safe here, you are back with your family, you should not have those feelings"

Steve looked at Craig. "But I do, I haven't slept properly since being back, the doc has prescribed me sleeping pills, they are supposed to stop the dreams, but as soon as I fall asleep, I am back there, fighting my way through shit soup to get to safety, I don't think I can go on"

"You need to think about your family, forget what happened over there, it was a nightmare, but it's over now" Pete came to the boys sitting by the roadside window.

"How about it boys, coffee for you both" He was standing there with the coffee pot.

Craig says.

"Thanks Uncle Pete, top us both up, and can I please have a short stack" "Coming right up" Rusty added.

"I will have the same thanks Uncle Pete"

"Ayup, I will be back with it shortly" Pete went back to the kitchen.

"It is a nightmare, and it hasn't finished yet" "Think about Marlii, she has been on your side all this time, one of your most staunch defenders, she was at the antiwar protests for your benefit, she loves you man, understand this, she does" "On the surface she shows that but just underneath, she sees the beast of the Australian Armed Forces, I know she has questions sitting waiting to be asked" "No I have spoken to her, she asks me those questions, like how you were, what was it really like, you need to speak to her, straighten this mess out"

Marlii came into view, she waved and smiled widely when she spotted Craig.

Marlii was rather tall, like Craig, she wore her hair which was long and Auburn in a bun, which kept it out of her face but when she let it down it cascaded in a fiery red waterfall, Craig wave and smiled as Marlii came through the door.

Her face was flushed she had been running to make up time, she wore no make-up to hide the spattering of freckles she wore on her cheeks, her soft, slender nose fit perfectly on her face, her green eyes sparkled, as she held the smile on her approach to table.

"Hey you two, finally I have made it, Mum and Dad want you to come home mister"

He had been living in a flat down near the sawmill, away from it all. She goes to her brother embracing him in a tight hug, which did feel comforting, she then goes round to the third seat kissing Craig fully on the lips and sits down.

Pete was back with the two short stacks placing them on the table in front of the boys.

"Hello Marlii, would you like a cup of coffee?" "Ah no, can I please have a blue heaven milkshake thank you, I am up to here with coffee" Marlii places her hand up to her nose.

"Oh Uncle Pete can I have double flavor please" "Certainly, oh what about a short stack" "I will help Craig with his" She looks at Craig.

"If that's alright with you" Craig pushes the plate to Marlii, and Marlii looks up to Pete with a smile, then she goes back to her brother.

"Now Brother O mine when are you coming home?" Craig breaks in.

"It seems you have some "Questions" you need to ask him" "Oh, what questions?" "I think you should ask him Marlii, he is beating himself up about being there" "You were conscripted, what are you talking about, I was thirteen when you went into that war, it took you away from me for more years than was fair, my older brother was ripped away from me, heck yes I have questions, and I will ask them of you individually, but the most important question is when are you coming home?"

"I will move back this afternoon" Marlii got up excitedly again embracing her brother in a strangle hold.

Nick Lester and Ian Luther appeared at the window, they looked in to see Rusty was sitting with Marlii and Craig, they went in.

They greeted Pete with a wave as they walked over to the now crowded table, Marlii looked up and spied the larger table, gathering up what she could she moved to the big table, the boys picked up their coffees and went to the table.

Nick and Ian took up their seats, the bell overhead of the door tinkled, they looked up to see Mark Harris walking through the door, he spied where the gang was sitting and went straight over to them, he said.

"Hey, have you heard what's going on with the house?"

Mark takes the only empty chair between Nick and Ian.

They all look at Mark.

Marlii speaks up.

"Hey Mark, I thought we had all agreed not to talk of that place, I know it's not easy to miss, but you agreed as we all did, not to mention it?" "Well they are doing a TV special on it this weekend, Jack Martin the reporter from the Today show booked into the motel this morning, apparently they are going over this afternoon to begin filming" Marlii looked at Mark. "So?"

"Well I just thought you know TV, we could get our heads on the tv, that's all" Rusty got up from his seat.

"You know what I have some stuff to move, so I may leave the television up to you lot"

He went to Marlii kissing her on the cheek and tells her.

"I will be looking forward to you being home this afternoon"

He says his goodbyes and heads out the door.

"As I was saying you made the promise Mark, so don't talk about it" Mark was about to start up again but shut his mouth and instead began down another path.

"I'm going down to the clubhouse any way, I have a new cassette, I taped Benny and the Jets last night, I want to hear it on the tape deck, who's coming?"

Craig spoke up.

"You lot can go up there, we will come up later, we have some stuff to do"

Craig and Marlii had been seventeen now for a couple of months, he had outgrown the clubhouse, or both he and Marlii had somewhat outgrown it.

Nick, who was the youngest of them at 13 says.

"Stuff meaning hanky panky, I know what you two are up to"

Marlii spits.

"Nick Lester, how disgusting, stop speaking like that"

"Don't use a stupid term such as stuff, stuff is the wrong word, I still think its hanky panky" Pete was there with the Blue heaven milkshake, Marlii grabs it and sips it down through the straw, until she drawers the last bit of fluid with soft serve, she slams the glass back down on the table. "Lets go Craig, and you three can sort the bill out" Marlii began toward the door, Craig got up saying.

"Sorry fellas I got to go, Nick why do you need to be so rude" Nick shrugged, Craig turned and went out after her.

Ian turns to Nick.

"Wow man you really had it in for her" "Oh come on man, you know they are doing it, its no big secret" "Yes but you can't talk about it like that" "Well makes it cheap" Pete was there to get more orders, he left with orders for three choc malts and three pieces of apple pie.

Later that afternoon, the three of them had collected their bikes and were now out on Old Town Road, heading out in the direction of the timber mill, and to their clubhouse.

It required them to skirt the old hill out of the town where, perched up the top was the Mansion, or the house.

They pedaled their treadlys up past the house skirting the island that led up to a road that ribboned its way up the hillside.

Nick was leading Mark who had Ian just behind him, they come down from Old Town Road, from Main Street, and straight along Old Town Road the two miles out to the Pine Forest, turning of onto logging road two where the blacktop ended, leaving the boys to ride on an unmade road the four hundred meters to the clubhouse.

The Clubhouse was a well-built log and mud shack, it had begun a couple of years earlier when Craig had approached the Mill Manager asking where he could build a Cubby House, Craig had been 15 at the time, and as a testament to his skills at planning and construction, he had scavenged enough full logs to construct his walls to a height of a little over 7and and a half feet, the roof which was constructed of corrugated iron, placed over joists that went up at a rather steep angle, giving the impression of size.

The mill manager and the workers became so impressed with the construction and began dropping of supply's because in the first six months Craig had been joined by three others as well as a girl.

First to come along was an eleven-year-old Nick Lester who had been small enough framed for the scaffolding to hold, so he was considered Roof Plumber, followed in quick succession by twelve-year-old Mark Harris who was rather good at dry walling, so Plasterer, and thirteen year old Ian Luther, who had a penchant for fitting windows and doors, among other things, Marlii came along last.

Now two years on the clubhouse has been a steady solid beacon out on the edge of the pine forest.

The boys pulled up kicking the stands down on their bikes, Mark was the first to the front door of the club house, removing the lock and opening the door, the clubhouse had been divided into three sections, music, where they kept the Kenwood sound system with the tapes, then you had the kitchen, where an old gas camp stove sat on a bench, next to the table, it was mainly used for coffee and hot chocolate and on the occasion any of the boys stayed overnight they would use the stove to heat up their spaghetti, or baked beans, then you had the lounge area, an old sofa took up a large section of the lounge area, along with two easy chairs, posters hung from the walls, one was a kitten barely hanging from a tree limb, the caption underneath read Hang In There! Another A joint on its own with the caption Keep Off The Grass.

He entered and went to the back corner of the hut flicking on the light switch,

(A Mill electrician had juiced them up) going to the Kenwood Tape deck he depressed the key 'eject' and placed the tape in closing it.

"You really need to hear this, all of you, Elton singing Benny and the Jets" Ian speaks up.

"Still not as good as Yellow Brick Road and I say that spitting" Mark fires back.

"You haven't even heard it yet, so what are you talking about"

"My mum bought the album last year, the Title track off the album will always be the winner, I know that album better that you ever will"

"Yea well I have only just discovered him, I like this song any way" Benny and the Jets began to play, Nick says in a manner of fact way.

"You two haven't heard Lynyrd Skynyrd's latest have you Sweet Home Alabama, coolest thing, but this is cooler" Nick pulled a battered cigarette packet from the pocket of his jeans. "Ardith, I swiped em from the old girl's bag, she had multiple packs in there she won't even remember how many she had, besides she will think it was the old man"

He opened the packet and dolled them out one each, then he produced a box of matches, took the match striking it alight, he lit his own and then Ian going to Mark last.

"Na ha, no way, third light's bad luck man"

Nick drops the match.

"You pussy, that's superstition, it doesn't matter how many smokes you light from a single match, here" Nick strikes the match lighting Mark's smoke.

"Are you happy now?"

They lounged around listening to the end of Benny and The Jets, finishing their smokes they crushed them out.

Nick went to the tape deck switching it to the radio it came to life.

"It's a hot hot day out there, the heat will be going up because I am about to spin the platter that is giving the most, that's right folks Sweet home Alabama is up next, Lynyrd Skynyrd, all the way from the south of the USA" Nick gives a fist pump.

"Wow talk about timing, I'm getting this album when I get my allowance, I've saved for two weeks, so this week boys" As Sweet Home Alabama played on the radio, the boys had heard the approach of a motor cycle, it was Craig, they had all known that exhaust, blurting its way down the track, as he came of the road he revved the bike forcing the power band on, he pulled up suddenly forcing Marlii forward on the seat.

The front door to the clubhouse popped open, Nick was standing there, Craig held the bike for Marlii as she dis-mounted, then he kicked the stand down setting the bike down Marlii was the first to speak.

"Hey, you wanna see what is happening in town, its not just Today, there are three different networks here, they will be setting up tomorrow, the trucks that just rolled into town almost filled the library car park, its huge" Mark offers.

"Ah Marlii I thought we weren't supposed to talk about that subject" "Well I'm not talking about anything to do with that"

Nick adds.

"But the networks are here to film the house, there curiosity is getting the better of them again, you know they won't find anything up there, they never do, they just see it for what it is, Ghostly" Ian says.

"So every time there is an event they come up here, there is nothing different here is there?"

Marlii says. "No it has never been this bad before, well when I say bad you will all see what I mean when you get back to town, its just out of control" Craig chimes in.

"So a vagrant comes to our town, and goes to an abandoned house and dies, maybe they find it macabre and creepy, you know the media, they will scare the fuck out of you given the chance" Nick then tells them what he had known.

"You know I have been reading the papers, watching the news, this dude who "Died" in the house was not just a vagrant, he was a Brown, he had found his way to Shrives Island, apparently he thought he was coming here to take up his Ancestral Home, what a home coming"

Ian says.

"I'm going back to town, I've gotta check this out" He went to his Bike.

"You lot can lock up, I will see you all later" Nick offered.

"I'm going with you"

Mark went to his bike.

"You two can get up to whatever you want, hanky panky, if that's what you're into, see ya"   Craig and Marlii watched the three boys ride off, waving to them as they took to the pedals all turning around for a final look, all three of them spinning their wheels on the spot.

As the boys rode down into the town it was more like a circus than anything they had seen before, the Motel was apparently full, for the first time in twelve months, all the shops on Main Street were rather busier than in some time, Uncle Pete's was choc a block, the three boys thought better off trying to fight their way to the counter.

Mark had a suggestion.

"I reckon we go to the falls, see how busy that place is, and back to Nick's place for snacks" They peddled their bikes tentatively through the town, so many strange cars, new Honda's and even Beemer's, some reporter had driven his Ferrari, the boys couldn't help to notice it the car park of the motel, the car park to the falls was full to overflowing, seems the fans of the Today show had shown up in their droves to help support the Today show's Tabloid View.

They rode down to the main car park where they found most of the bays full, people were scattered around at their picnics and Bar B Qs, kids splashed in the shallows of the river where the waterfall's overflow formed a small beach, the area dealt with the back flow from the waterfall, where the river flowed down and to the left, the beach was on the elbow of the first turn in the river, it was an amazing feature of the town, people flooded here at all times of year, if they were the only visitors to Shrives Island that would be good, but with the influx of media sucks, the town suffered.

They peddled of toward Nick's house up the hill past the motel and on to Honeysuckle Street and down into Nick's driveway Jack's car was in the driveway, Estelle's little mini was nowhere to be seen.

Nick spoke.

"You will all have to be quite Dad may be asleep so shh" They whispered back to him.

"Ok, we will be" Nick led them through the back door into the laundry where they had to strip off their shoes, Estelle had a rule of no shoes or boots in her house, it was pleasant padding around the house in socks, and if you were ever without socks you could use a pair of fresh laundered socks that sat by the front and back door, the boys washed their hands and went into the kitchen, it was spotlessly clean and tidy, the new Kenwood Appliances sat proudly on the Formica bench, the table was laid with a floral table cloth, in the middle sat a huge fruit bowl, oranges apples and bananas, together with a few blood plumbs, Nick put the coffee pot on the gas hob and went to the pantry where he grabbed the bread along with Strawberry Jam, peanut butter and vegemite, taking it out to the table, where the boys tuck right in.

"Who's having Vegemite, who's having Jam, and who's having peanut butter" Ian says.

"I'm having Vegie" Mark adds.

"I am having peanut butter and jam" "And I am having Vegie and peanut butter" Jack comes into the kitchen, he had his suit pants on, but socked feet and his Singlet.

"Hey boys can I smell coffee, I was awake when you came down the driveway, I was just lying there thinking about getting up" "Gee dad you are putting in the hours, you need to take a break" "I will take a break when I straighten out the books at the Mill, they have been cooking them big" Jack hovered over the coffee maker until it began bubble, he took the pot and filled his cup.

"I think Bobby and Jane have it worked out with my help we know who has been responsible for it, so I can take some time off, hey what is all the excitement in town?" Ian says.

"It's a media circus" Mark adds.

"With no shortage of clowns"

Jack sits at the table besides Mark.

"So, what are you boys up to?" Nick speaks.

"Currently snacks at home, Dad could Mark and Ian stay over tonight, it is Sunday tomorrow after all"

"Check with your mother, its fine with me" "Where is Mum by the way, I thought she was staying home today to bake?" "She was, but Aunt Heidi called and needed a hand with the move"

Aunt Heidi was Estelle's younger sister who had recently acquired a larger shop in Main Street, where she would be able to almost double her inventory of baby and children's cloths.

Jack looks at his watch.

"She said she would be gone a couple of hours, so I would say by three o'clock"

Mark and Ian snatched a look at the clock on the wall which had read two twenty-five.

Mark offers.

"We could finish our snacks and ride up to the new shop, maybe offer a hand"

At that the little Mini came into the driveway, Nick couldn't wait for her to get inside but went out to meet her, racing out the front door leaving Mark Ian and Jack sitting at the table drinking their coffees and munching down on their sandwiches.

Estelle was closing the door to the mini, she had a big bag of groceries held by one hand against her breast.

"Here give me that" Estelle gives Nick the bag.

"What's in here, this is not shopping day?"

"Baking supplies, I need to make a Christmas cake, Aunty Heidi can't bake it she is busy with the new shop, I went over there today to help, and I got lumped with this cake to make"

Estelle held the screen door for Nick, they went through to the kitchen, Nick went to the bench where he put the sack of groceries"

"Hey boys"

She went to Jack and kissed him on top of the head, she went to the shopping, Nick began to unpack it, she took it from him putting it in the pantry in its correct space.

Nick asks.

"Can Mark and Ian stay over tonight, we are going into town tonight, just thought it would be convenient if they stayed overnight" "Why are you trying to justify it?" "I'm not, I was just saying" "Don't stress they can stay over if its OK with Jack" Jack put his hands into the air.

"I have already said yes if you do" "Well if your parents are alright with it, its fine with us" Mark offers.

"I will ring my mum, I'm sure it will be OK, I have my bag here I left it here last week, so I don't need to go home" Ian says.

"I need a change of duds, so I need to go home, Mum and Dad will be fine with it, I will go when I finish my coffee" Nick says.

"We will all go, I wanna go downtown on the way back sus out the mess, see if we can get into Uncle Pete's, it was packed this afternoon, wall to wall" Estelle asked.

"What is it with the networks all here at the same time, it's ridiculous, it's all about that god dammed house there on the hill" Mark pipes in.

"No, you shouldn't be talking about that place, Craig and Marlii has said that topic is off limits when we are together, someone should put a match to it, poof"

Jack adds.

"It has been the place of many a scare, this latest one involved an old family member a long-lost cousin or some such, they are playing their cards close to their chest are the police, not saying a word that's why the armchair detectives have arrived in the last couple of days"

The boys finished their sandwiches and jumped on their bikes peddling down Honeysuckle Street which fed out onto Smith Lane, four doors down on the right and you were at Mark's house, he went in to find his mother, Patty at the sink pealing vegetables.

"Hi Mum"

"Hi Sweetheart, hello boy's"

"Can I stay at Nick's tonight, please"

"Yes but can you run me an errand"

"What is it?" "I would like you to take this bag of lemons to Rhona Sheedy" "Yea ok it's right near town any way, we are going back to Nick's through town"

The boys set out on their path first stopping at the Sheedy's then heading into town which was one block away, as the boys reached the intersection of Main and Whitewood, they pulled their bikes up to assess the situation.

Main Street from the Garage at the Southern end to where they were now, at the North of the town, was so full of network vans and cars, along with reporters numbered in the hundreds, they were running cables from the vans to the closest source of power they could find, Pete had erected a barrier to keep reporters and their vans away from the shop.

As the boys pushed their bikes along the pavement, they noticed reporters going over their lines, some were still setting up, others were just sitting and waiting.

They fought the crowd until they arrived at Uncle Pete's barrier, where they were finally free from the crowd, as they went through the door, they noticed a big sign printed in big bold red letters.

"No NETWORK STAFF ALLOWED"

The bell tinkled overhead, Pete's was full of locals, Millers, Miners, Loggers.

Pete was serving at the front counter, Bobby Cursack as well four loggers, he was sitting with, on the other side of the room was Graham Bell, along with three Millers, sitting eating pancakes, and drinking coffee.

The tables at the windows were taken up by the Miners, who were all happy to sit and watch the passing parade.

The boys took an empty table and waited for Diane to come take their order.

However, the chatter in the restaurant was focused on one thing, or two things in general, the influx of the networks, and the house.

The boys sat and listened, eavesdropped on the men from the Mill, the Miners, the Loggers but mostly they listened to Uncle Pete.

"So I said this afternoon, no one from the networks in here, at ten this morning the place was packed with them, all lining up to use the phone, and I can get supply for our customers but they were eating me out of house and home, so I had to put a stop to it so the sign went up, but they are here for the next day or so, we have to deal with them" That was when Bobby Cursack added.

"Well it is the most interesting breakthrough as far as that house goes, when they found out it was a Brown, they went off their heads for a story, and they are speculating now on a treasure that is said to be buried there, Gold and silver bullion, millions of each apparently, it is said to be in the cellar, but if you ask the Local Forces they will attest to nothing being down there, rumors, lies, and inuendo, good for no one" Diane was suddenly there standing next to Mark.

"Hi boys what are you having, Apple and Rhubarb is of the menu" Mark ordered a choc malt along with a short stack, Ian ordered a tall stack and a strawberry malt Nick ordered a bacon and egg sandwich with a side order of fries, along with a Granges Sarsaparilla.

Nick broke the silence.

"So in the city they are talking about Gold and Silver in the house, they are trying to scare up excitement, pardon the pun" Ian then states.

"Ah we shouldn't be talking about this; you know Marlii's rule?" Mark adds.

"Marlii isn't here, so it's not off limits"

"Just because she isn't here it doesn't mean it should be part of the discussion, any way I am changing the subject, we want to eat and drink and be merry, not arguing" Nick adds.

"He is right you know that place has been nothing but a horror story our whole life, to actually have a known haunted house in your town, it is a bit of a joke, they won't destroy the place, it is only ever inhabited semi irregularly, and now we have these networks here, this is the worst I remember it, and its only going to get worse" Mark asks.

"So what are you proposing, I mean we are still speaking of the house?" "Well yes, but that's because it is forced down our throats by those from outside, look out there, those people out there are not invited, they are interlopers, people after a story"

Mark asks again.

"So I will ask again, what are you proposing?" "Well nothing, I don't know what to do about all these people, heck I don't think Uncle Pete has any idea apart from barring them from his store" Later that evening all normality had returned until just after dinner, they had been all sitting in the lounge watching New Faces, when the studio went to a live breaking news story, the reporter was coming live from Shrives Island, she was there to tell you how they would get to the bottom of the sorry saga that were the Browns of Shrives Island, the boys watched with a fascination at seeing Shrives Island front and center of Main Stream News, while in the background they heard the disdain in both Jack and Estelle's voices, they had been talking about the news reporters.

The boys were camped out in the lounge with blankets and pillows to suffice, Jack and Estelle headed of to bed after the Saturday night movie, it had been Duel, a story about a car driven by Dennis Weaver, who pisses a truck driver off by overtaking, the truck driver becomes hell bent on revenge, chasing Dennis through outback America.

But now time for Deadly Earnest, so the lights are turned off and the television turned up to a volume as to not disturb those trying to sleep, you waited to see the front of Deadly's coffin, who was played by Ralph Baker, and out would pop Deadly Earnest, he spoke with an old English, pommy accent.

"What a week, lashings and lashings of pian, Oh good evening ladies and gents, and may long you suffer, and the movie tonight is "The Ghost in The Invisible Bikini" oh are you kidding me if its invisible, that means you can't see it, but you can see the things that supposed to be hidden by the bikini"

He consults his hand which is nothing but a useless claw, deadly Earnest refers to it as Igor.

"Maybe we can watch a commercial, oh why should we put ourselves through this torture why, WHY, haha, maybe because we like it"

The add begins on the tv, laughs have been elicited from the boys, and they are hopeful for some titty in the movie coming up.

Ian offers.

"Deadly Earnest is so prime man, really cool" Mark nods his head, and Nick agrees.

As he comes back onto the screen the boys sit with their bottles of Grange's soft drink and Colvan chips, Ian had his pack of Cheese Fonzie's.

"Well, that will keep our sponsors happy, but now to the film I'm not saying the title again, that was stupid, but be prepared for gratuitous nudity, oh what a horrible movie, on with it"

Although the film had plenty of gore and not much on a story line the boys were rewarded with not just Titties but Bush as well.

The next morning was an orderly organized breakfast, first juice, then you can have cereal, or you could wait for the full cooked plate which consisted of eggs three ways, you had a choice of scrambled, fried or poached with bacon, and or sausage, hash browns, tomato and Black Pudding for Jack, to top it all of there were plenty of cups of Coffee or Tea, and lashings of toast made from Estelle's home baked loaves, spreads galore, jam, marmalade, vegemite.

Jack was sitting with the Sunday paper open to the third page.

He speaks.

"See how far the news story from the Mill goes, I solved that money problem, well I helped the newspaper with the front-page story, and they cannot be trusted, you have to be kidding me"

He rifles through the paper, backwards and forwards finally crimpling it all in a ball and tossing it onto the floor.

"I hope you are going to pick that up Mr."

"I will, it makes me livid, even the news is affected when those mongrels come to town"

Jack gulped his coffee.

"Well that's me, these lawn wont mow themselves" He gets up from his chair, ruffling Nicks hair.

"What plans do you three have today?" Nick answers.

"I think we should give you a hand, rake and sweep, pick up leaves and stuff, after we will go to town today, check out what the networks are going on about" "You three can go I don't need a hand, I'm big enough and ugly enough to handle it, but I will expect a report this afternoon"

Nick got up from his seat and followed Jack out into the laundry where he put his gumboots on, Nick grabbed his sneakers, following his father, Ian and Mark remained finishing of their breakfast, Jack went into the garage pulling the cover of the lawn mower.

"So, what do you think will come of this house Dad, it's a house of horrors"

"Well, I have been around a lot longer than you, so has your mother, and we have seen much more than you could imagine"

Nick wheels the mower out to the front yard.

"Nick I forgot the petrol, can you get it from the garage" Nick raced back up the driveway, to the corner where the fuels were kept, he noticed an odd shape in the garage, it was covered with a tarp, and had a distinctive look of a Dirt Bike, he went to the tarp and lifted it just a little, there was a knobby tire hidden there, connected to a spoked wheel, a Honda.

Estelle's voice came from behind him.

"Hey Mr., what are you into" Nick drops the canvas and bends over to pick up the mower fuel, he stands and turns.

"Getting this for dad" "Well stop your snooping, there's nothing for you in here but that petrol, now get" Nick went back down to his father.

"What was that about?" "I don't know mum was accusing me of snooping, I wasn't snooping"

"Well, if you were, you will spoil the surprise in there, that's for sure" "You told me to go fetch the fuel"

"That's right, and you know exactly where the fuel is kept"

"I won't be going back in there"

Ian and Mark joined Nick and Jack on the front lawn, Jack filled the tank and yanked on the start cord the machine fired up first go.

"See you all this afternoon with the report" They went back inside cleaning the kitchen of dishes, cleaned the lounge of their chip packets and empty Grange's bottles, that was when they hit the pedals arriving in town at nine forty-five, to find people running to and fro, reporters recording news feed, to cover the live feed, the boys were amazed, they had never seen the town this busy in their lives, they stopped and listened to a reporter who was blathering as Mark put it.

"The man a Lester Brown had come home to find the family's hidden fortune what he found instead was death"

Nick spat.

"They think they know the history; they know sweet fuck all" Ian adds.

"They will tell you what you want to hear" Mark says.

"Bastards" They followed one crew to the base of the hill.

Nick says.

"I wonder if they are going in, they wouldn't have come this far to get shots of the outside, would they"

Ian offers.

"They are motivated by stupidity aren't they, they will go wherever there's a chance of a story" The crew who had been from Channel 7 had an exclusive look into the lobby of the old house, as the boys watched they saw the lawyer for the family driving up to the house, as he passed them, he waved, the boys waved back.

Mark offers.

"Wow, the Brown's lawyer is going to open the house up"

The Brap, of Craigs bike could be heard coming up Whitewood Street, Marlii was riding pillion, he saw the boys at the base of the hill he went to them.

"What have you three grubs been up to?" Nick adds.

"I could ask the same question of you pair, what have you been up to?" "None of your bees wax, mind your own business" Marlii says.

"What is the interest here?" "We are just checking out the networks, what they are up to, have you heard the lies" Marlii says. "Oh the gold and silver, yes I was talking to Rusty about that this morning, he says there is nothing there, I had known that already" Craig says.

"Their rumors and lies are stupid, all that last lie was to do was beat up public sentiment, but it only attracts those from down in the city" Nick adds.

"And those big city types are getting worse, one came up in a Ferrari, they are getting paid too much" They all decided it was time for a visit to Uncle Pete's, at least they had known they would get in, Pete's ban was working a treat.

Later that evening when everyone was in their respective homes, the news sounding out from the tv, the reporters currently packing up and going back to the city with their reports, A Current Affair picked up the scoop, they were the one to get a peek at the lobby to the old place.

They were all front and center in front of their television, Nick along with Estelle and Jack, Pete and Diane, Bobby Cursack, Ian Luther was with his parents Caleb and Gina, and Mark with his mother Patty.

All watching the news, all watching A Current Affair, waiting for the big news story of the day.

The report begins, with the reporter in the alcove to the entrance of the house, the door has been unlocked by the Brown family Lawyer.

The reporter is saying how decayed the house was, it was in verry poor condition, cobwebs tangled in her hair, there was no light, only the camera lights to add to the eeriness, the power could have been turned on, but the station had decided for the effects, it would be best to leave it relatively dark.

She walked through on the lower level approached the grand stairway and made her way back to the scullery quarters, where she was saying that the house had been inhabited by nefarious ghosts, as she made her way back to where she had begun, she stopped at an alcove to the left of the entrance, where she pointed out a blood-soaked carpet, that was where Lester Brown had died.

Slowly one by one they turned their televisions off, it had no information that was helpful, and most were not interested in the Tabloid media, better to wait for the Sunday night movie.

Nick had been looking forward to tonight's movie, is "Walkabout" it was a debate if Nick should get to stay up to watch it, but he won that debate, Nick had known about the violence in the beginning, he was slightly embarrassed when Jenny Agutter got her kit off and swam nude in the billabong, he blushed when Jack made the comment.

"Oh, oh Boobies, oh no bush"

Estelle nudged him.

"Jack please, Nick is here" "I know, have I embarrassed you, Nick?" Nick turned back as the commercial came on, his cheeks were not flushed anymore, as he turned to his father.

"Lame Dad, just lame"

CHAPTER ELEVEN

CHRISTMAS 74

The Shrives Island High school had been established way back in 1898.

The original building still stood; the remainder of the school built up around it.

Nick being in his first year of high school was in the Old Building, Mark and Ian were in the same building a newer wing added to the school a decade earlier, Craig was in the senior building, along with Marlii.

It was the last week before starting the Christmas holidays.

The lunchtime bell began to ring, students let out happy to have a break, kids were running to their preferred patches of grass or picnic tables, some began to kick the football around immediately.

Craig was where they would always find him, sitting at his bench, Marlii right beside him.

They were Five again the magnificent five.

Craig had football training that same afternoon, Marlii had netball training, none of the other three went in for football, rather playing cricket was what they liked.

On the afternoon of that day the house came alive, from the school oval you could clearly see the house, no one knows how, but there was a gas explosion that blew out the interior kitchen wall, and outside stone wall, there was a fire along with the explosion, at first police had speculated that explosives from the mine were used, but after the check of the house it was realized to be the oven in the downstairs Kitchen, the electricity in the house was on for sure, but the gas the gas had been turned off.

Firefighters said the damage could only have been caused by a leak or a rupture, they were perplexed by what they had found, most of the interior wall was obliterated, and a huge chunk of the East wall.

The kids were let of class to watch the happenings from the oval.

Marlii and Craig were together, as per usual, Nick found them, followed by Ian and Mark.

"I told you all yesterday that house is haunted, don't you know that you know that explosion was in defiance, because those reporters were up there yesterday, they don't know how lucky they are"

Christmas day arrived, Nick was excitedly up as soon as it was light, he came into the lounge to see a new Honda XR 75 sitting under the tree.

He went to the bike tearing at the tinsel that was covering it, he had taken off as much as he wanted to, he climbed aboard the bike, he yelled from the lounge, not knowing if they would be awake.

"Thanks mum, Dad, I love it"

His father was the first out of bed, followed quickly by his mother they both came into the lounge and found Nick mounted on his bike"

"Look under the tree I put them out here early this morning, I saved for months, so I hope you like what I have got you both"

He got of his bike and went to his mother's gift, and then his father's giving them there package.

His mother opened hers, it was the Lhadro figurine that she had liked, she was planning to make the purchase next year, she had known exactly how much her son had saved to get her this piece" "Oh my goodness, you were listening, but I never expected this, it is wonderful, thank you sweet heart"

She embraced him in her arms and planted a kiss on his cheeks.

"Come on mum, no need to get so mushy, here Dad her is yours"

Nick handed his father gift, he opened it to find a personalized diary, embossed across the front cover in bold gold lettering was **Jack Lester: Chartered Accountant.**

"This is great son, this is the exact Diary I would have chosen myself the embossing is awesome" He went to his son, giving him a hug, he kissed him on the top of the head and shook his hand.

He sat with his parents speaking of where he would ride, that he would stick to the trails and never ride his bike on the road.

He had thought of the times Craig would drive his bike on the blacktop most days, he had said it was quicker, now they could test that theory.

He had called Ian earlier who was happy with a new push bike, Mark was happy with his new Motor Bike, same model as Nicks, they would get together this afternoon for a ride, Ian would be pillion.

Later that morning at the breakfast table, Nick was excited, he wanted to get out, on the trail and ride.

He had been dressed when he had come to the table, his mum and dad were in their Christmas jumpers, Jack had a big Santa on his Estelle had Rudolph the red nose Reindeer, Nick's had Santa's helpers on it, he had said he didn't want to get aunty Rhona's knitted jumper dirty, but he would have been embarrassed, that was solved when Mum went out of the room, and came back with another package for Nick.

"What another present after the Bike, wow" He attacked the packaging finding a Honda racing jacket, along with Motorcycle pants and boots, he had bought his helmet earlier, as his Mum insisted, he never be on a bike without his skid lid, so even as pillion he had to have his helmet.

Nick had called Ian earlier telling him he would pick him up on the way out to the clubhouse, he would meet up with Mark on the trail.

Nick took of down the parkway that led to the river track, he rode carefully, not wanting to dirty the bike up at all, he came up off the track two doors down from Ian's home he got off and pushed.

He honked his horn, Ian bounced out the front door.

"Wow man, its hot"

They went back to the track, Nick kicked the starter and it fired up, Ian got on and he gave it to it, for the first time, he had made the run to the clubhouse, in seven minutes, with a pillion, Craig has more power than the Honda, what would he say to that?

Two bikes approached one the unmistakable Blat of Craigs Yamaha, and the familiar sound of the Honda, approaching the clubhouse.

Craig was the first to speak.

"Fine Honda my man"

He was nodding.

"I said the same to Mark, you both did well" Marlii climbed off the back of Craig's bike, going to the clubhouse.

"All the adults at my place are sloshed, even Mum" Craig adds.

"Mine can't get pissed they have the three-hundred-mile trip to see my Nan and Pop"

Nick asks. "Are you going"

"No, I'm going down next week for a couple of days, but I will be back on New Year's Eve, Marlii is coming with me, we are going down on the coach, it will be fun"

They went in, Marlii went to the radio and turned it on, Mark put the kettle on and said.

"So, who is starting this meeting, Craig you are the most senior here, I think it should be you"

"Well, I know how we can get explosives, blow that joint sky high" "Nick says.

"You are talking about the mine aren't you"

"Yes, I am, we can get in and out with explosives, use it to blow that house of the face of the earth, we have enough time up our sleeves, before I go to my grandparents, but we need to do it today or tomorrow" Ian says.

"Are you talking about breaking into the mine" "Not the mine, but the mine office, I know how to get to the explosives magazine, there won't be any one there for three days, I could get in and get some dynamite"

"Marlii adds.

"We will get rid of that place Afterall"

Mark asks.

"So, professor what's the plan"

"You need to go through the main office to get to the magazine, the outer door you will find unlocked but the inner door, the one that leads through to the Magazine will be locked, I can tell you that for sure, so we get Nick he is the smallest of us here, boost him up to the eaves, he can go in through the roof, and come and open the door for us, Nick go for the Inventory as soon as you let us in, I know where the key is" "So you are going to boost me up to the roof line, I can get up there myself"

Craig continues.

"Once he lets us inside, I will get the key to the magazine and bobs your uncle" Mark asks.

"But alarms will be triggered, we won't even get in there"

"They never set the alarms, this is Shrives Island not the city, they are lazy with the security believe me" Craig adds.

"Let's do it tonight" They all agree to meet up back here at the clubhouse, at six pm, it was also decided that they should bring their bikes, they didn't want to make any more noise than was unavoidable.

It was five forty-five when Nick rode out on his pushbike, making the ride out to the clubhouse, before he hit the blacktop he was joined by both Mark and Ian, as they rode onto the logging track, they saw Craig leaning against his motorbike.

Ian protests.

"You said bikes, no motor bikes"

"That's right, I will need this after we are done, I need to move the goods"

Mark is curious.

"Where's Marlii" "At home, she doesn't need to be involved"

Marlii and Rusty were going to Marlii's Aunties for Christmas Dinner, Craig was supposed to be going with them, but he would catch up with them once they were done. Craig took his pushbike from inside the clubhouse and put his dirt bike in its place, no use leaving stuff around for people to find.

They rode the additional six miles out to the mine.

It was obvious it was quiet, the emergency lights were burning brightly, the boys went to the gate, it was an old Master padlock which took two sturdy hits with a rock, and it popped open.

They closed the gate behind them and pushed their bikes to the office, Nick tried the door, but it was locked, so he climbed up the outside of the building, pushing the eave tile out of the way and climbed through into the roof, he made his way to the air conditioning vent he removed the screen and dropped down immediately going to the door and unlocking it, he stopped, looked down to his right, there was German Shepard laying there, snoring, he shook his head in disbelief, he could not believe the security here, he opened the door, letting in Craig and Ian, he pointed to the "Watch Dog" and placed his fingers to his lips, shh.

Ian whispered.

"Which way to the dynamite?" Craig answered.

"It's this way, and why are you whispering, no one is going to hear you"

Nick moved toward the outer magazine door trying it, and it opened.

Craig was riffling through the managers desk and found one of the drawers locked, he grabbed a letter opener from the desk and prized open the drawer, sitting there was the magazine key.

He took the key turning it over in his hand, its color-coded teeth glistened in the muted light of the office.

"I have it"

Nick is going through a filling cabinet, looking for a book, he came up with it, written across the front in silver script was the word INVENTORY.

"And I have mine" Craig goes to Nick, he opens the book, checking the columns, he looks at the page where the Dynamite is listed.

"They are confused, they have more Dynamite than they think they have, look at this column, the number has been whited out and the new number put in"

Craig goes to the main door inserts the key, there is an audible buzz coming from the door, this signals that the key is being used, he turns the key, the heavy door begins to retract the automatic light blinked on above them, a soft blue light.

Nick exclaimed.

"Wow, it's like a World War two bunker"

The interior of the bunker dropped away from the door, it was sub terranean, as you walked down the ramp, and into the magazine, you would end up twenty feet below ground level, the boys entered the magazine, shelves on both sides of the magazine contained blasting caps, boxes and boxes of dynamite, plastic explosives as well as a single box of TNT, they would notice that missing in a minute, Craig had known what to look for and where to find it.

Tess Hillfort, the Mine managers daughter, was the same age as Marlii, and she shared information about the mine with her closest friend, Tess had known about an oversight her father was trying to sort at the moment, the people responsible for the logging of all explosives in and out had been lazy just of late, Marlii in conversation told Craig of the irresponsible, workers who were making Doug Hillfort's life a nightmare, he had needled her for more information, and when Marlii came back with the news's of the inventory of Dynamite, he thought he would beat them at their own game.

About halfway down on the shelf at chest height, they found it, boxes upon boxes of it.

Craig began counting.

"Ok so there forty-five boxes here and the inventory says forty-two, so this box is ours"

Craig griped the rope handles on either side of the box and tried to lift the box, it wasn't budging, Ian and Mark grabbed one side and Nick and Craig took the other, they lifted the box down off the shelve and plonked it down on the floor.

Ian speaks up.

"Careful, you want us to go sky high"

"You need a blast cap to ignite it ya ninny"

"Well, I wasn't to know that"

They removed twelve sticks leaving twenty-four sticks to do the job, placing the leftovers way back on the stacks, it made the box much more manageable, Craig could carry it on his own.

They had known they would have no doubt notice the break in, but Craig's theory would be tested, would they pick up on the missing Dynamite?

Getting the sticks onto the bike was another thing, securing it with octopus straps was not that easy, and the ride back to the clubhouse was slow.

Back at the clubhouse, Craig and the boys put the Dynamite in a corner and covered it with a tablecloth, it looked just like a table.

He then got on his dirt bike and took off in a hurry to catch up with Marlii and Rusty leaving the boys to lock up before they left.

Tuesday afternoon, Nick had visit from the local constabulary.

Jack was sitting reading the paper when he saw the officer walking up the driveway, he got up and went straight to the door opening it before the officer could knock.

"Good morning officer, may I ask you what the pleasure is?" "Good afternoon Mr. Lester, I would like to have a chat to Nick, with you present off course" "What has he done" "We suspect that Nick has broken into the magazine at the mine, we need to know what they were up to, why they broke in"

"Just kids mucking around I bet, the problem is officer, Nick s not here now, I will bring him down to the station when he gets in"

"I do need to chat with him so would appreciate it Mr. Lester" When the Officer visited Ian's house, he found three of the four boys there.

Ian see's the police officer approaching.

"Shit, it's the fuzz" Mark and Nick joined Ian at the window, he was now on the steps about to knock.

Knock Knock.

Caleb yelled from the back room.

"Someone get that please" Ian was getting excited.

"Shit, what do we do, why have they come here first, shit"

Nick says.

"Calm down, you don't know what he wants, do you?" "What else is he here for, they are onto us"

Mark adds.

"Just cool it, wait, just don't say anything, all of us clam up until we can speak to Craig"

Knock Knock.

"Someone get the bloody door, I'm busy"

Caleb was hard at work out in the back room sorting out his bookings for the next few weeks, Caleb was a classical guitarist, he was very busy at the moment, he had a gig later that night, Gina his wife was his Vocalist, she was verry good, she does covers supported by her husband songs such as "Do you know the way to San Jose" and "I say a Little Prayer, good wholesome music, she was currently out having her hair done.

Mark goes to the door and opens it.

"Is Mr. Luther here please"

Ian has calmed down a little.

"Dad it's the Police they want to talk to you"

Caleb comes in from the back room brandishing papers.

"I need to get my bookings complete, hi officer what can I do to help?" "I need to speak to Ian, and Mark as well as Nick" "What's this about?"

"A break in at the mine, we have reason to suspect the three of them" Nick whispered to Mark.

"They only want to talk to us three, shh don't say anything"

"Well, I will tell you what we will do officer" Caleb turned and glared at the boys and went on.

"I will not be available this evening, however I will contact Jack Lester and Patty Harris, the three of them will be at the station by six pm, will that suit you?" "Well yes, that is fine, and it saves me the trip to go see Patty, so fine"

"Ok then good afternoon officer"

He closed the door, when he had known the coast was clear, he yelled.

"So, what's going on Ian, Mark, Nick, what have you three been up to" The three boys stood their coyly, Nick took the lead.

"I, we did it, we broke in, it was for a gag, a joke brake in"

Nick looked at Mark, and back to Caleb.

"We had to see how easy it was to get into, we were going to make coffee, but we didn't even do that in the end" "Well you three need to get to the police station by six tonight I will ring Jack and Patty, get them to pick you lot up, Ian you can go with Jack, got it?" "Yes Dad"

He looked down sheepishly at the ground, he looked up at his father.

"I'm sorry Dad" "Just get it sorted, if they want to lay charges both myself and Jack will have something to say about that"

The boys had played in Ian's yard, Jack arrived early in the afternoon, Caleb greeted him with a cold beer, they sat under the umbrella in the back yard, the boys were keeping themselves occupied on the trampoline.

Eventually it was decided that they would meet at the police station.

Six pm rolled around, Jack along with Nick, Mark and Ian in tow.

They came into the reception and were greeted by the officer who had come their places, he opened the hatch between the reception and the offices, he ushered them all into separate offices, once separated he went to the parents.

"As I question each of the boys, you can be there to witness it, but you cannot say anything, is that ok?" Both Jack and Patty agreed.

Patty had to admit, that this was so out of character of Mark.

"Ok, we will begin with Nick"

The officer led them into the office where Nick was situated.

"Now Nick, the Mine office was broken into on Christmas night, I have evidence, I can prove you broke in there" "I know, I lost my wallet the other day, I didn't realize until I was home, I must have lost it while I was in the roof, so yes I am guilty, but you don't have a thing on anyone else" "Well that is to be determined, I would like you to sit here while I go talk to Ian and Mark" The Officer led them into Ian's room.

"So what do you have to say about the break in?"

"We did it, don't let him tell you he did it on his own, I was there"

"Well ok, let me talk to Mark" He led the parents into Mark's room.

"And what do you say about the break in?" "Nick broke in and let us in through the side door, we were all there" "Well that is determined, so wait here, I will be back in a minute" He walked out to the foyer and spoke to Patty and Jack.

"Well at the moment that is all I need, the Mine Principals would like to chat to them, maybe tomorrow, I will confirm that later tonight" Jack says.

"So, we are done here now?" "Yes, you can gather them up and take them home" That night, before bed, the phone had rung in Nicks kitchen, his father took the call, he heard his father call him.

"Nick its for you" Nick got up from his desk and went to the kitchen, he waited until the conversation ended between Craig and his Dad, they had been discussing Nick's new bike, he handed the receiver to Nick.

"It's Craig"

Nick says.

"Hey, what you up to"

Craig sounds concerned.

"So are you alright, I will hand myself in if you want, you know take the heat for you boys" "Na, don't sweat it, seriously I have it under control" "Ian told me you lost your wallet in the ceiling, drats hey" "It's alright, I got my wallet back, tomorrow we are meeting with the Mine Principle's, but what can they do to me"

Craig asks.

"So, the cops haven't laid any charges?"

"Nup, and I don't think they will, you were right about the inventory, they were all over the joint, oh and that box of TNT, wasn't on the inventory, seriously, what they are doing, it's dangerous, people could get killed, no I am going to the meeting tomorrow, and I am telling them what I know of the inventory, how there were actually forty four boxes of Dynamite that's all, we will be fine, and we all have our stories down pat, don't stress" "Well if you think you have it sorted, I will go with what you guys want to do"

"So where is it, have you moved it yet?" "No, I thought I'd better wait until we sort this mess out, it's not so much a mess any more so well done"

They chatted a bit longer, Nick would catch up with him when he gets back from Warragal, which was three days away.

The meeting was set at the town hall, the meeting time was ten O'clock, everyone was present, Nick was dressed in his Sunday best, as were Ian and Mark, Jack was in a suit more for the fact he had to be at work after this mess had been sorted, Caleb was in casual clothing as were the woman, Patty was dressed for work also, her uniform pressed, her name badge sparkled, beneath her name badge was her station, Dental Nurse.

They were ushered into a room at the end of the hall, eight chairs had been placed together, three feet away from the table that had contained the four principals from the mine.

They all took their seats and waited.

A mustached finely dressed man began.

"We have a dilemma, you boys have a dilemma, I would like to know what you found there, in the mine office?" Nick speaks up.

"I found the current inventory" He shut up.

"Oh, what did you find, what did you discover?"

Nick thinks. "People at the mine can't count"

The mine principals were slightly shocked by Nicks last comment, the man with the moustache said.

"And how did you determine this?"

Nick pauses a short time before he blurts. "Because we broke into the magazine, all we had to do were simple sums, there are explosives in there that are not accounted for"

The Matronly Mine principal sitting there her hair done earlier that morning, she had ordered it done big said.

"Who have you been speaking too?"

Would they catch him out? stay cool he said to himself.

"I haven't spoken to anyone, it is what I have heard directly from Tess Hillfort, we were out on the oval and I heard her say how much the employees were doing her father's head in, how their inventory is in such a mess, so I thought I would go in and check it out, I found out about the magazine key from Tess as well, she had let it slip where her father had kept it" With that information, the principal's put their head together for a bow wow, when they came back the three boys were excused, but told there would still be questions.

Questions for another day.

Jack and Estelle put their heads together with Caleb and Gina, and along with Mark's parent Patty, they had this mess in the palm of their hands.

CHAPTER TWELVE

NEW YEAR'S EVE 1974

On the weekend of new year, the boys went to the Firefly station to meet up with Marlii and Craig on their return, they had fun, he had been given some decent presents, Marlii got a nice dress and some perfume, she was wearing both when she arrived.

They walked the block all down to Uncle Pete's together, Nick explained how he had said he had heard all he had known from Tess, that would stop the heat from Tess toward Marlii, Ian had explained how he had nearly blown the whole gig and Mark only nodded.

They arrived at Uncle Pete's looking in through the window told them that they would have a choice of where to sit, they took the table at the back of the restaurant, the big round table with the Lazy Susan in the middle Craig sat facing the window with Marlii, Nick sat next to Marlii, Ian and Mark sat opposite them.

Nick speaks up.

"So, what did you get from your Grandparents?"

"I got a new pair of R.M. Williams boots and these Levi's I have on, but fill us in on what happened, they didn't even lay charges on you, any of you"

Ian says.

"After Nick had said what he had to say, the Mine people huddled together, and when they came back, they dismissed us, told us to wait for the next round of questions" Mark took up the story.

"But none of us have heard a thing, its Saturday, and the last time anything was said was on Tuesday" "Shit Nick, what did you say to them?" "I just told them, that their Mine employees couldn't count, and I told them that I had seen the Inventory, once you and I realized they had stuffed up completely, my little brain got working overtime, hey if this gets out, it is embarrassment city"

Pete approached the table.

"Hey, you lot, what are you all up too on this fine New Year's Eve, parties to go to, we will be at yours tonight, Nick"

"I will be there, Ian and Mark, and Marlii and Craig will be there with their folks"

"So, what will it be for you now?" Craig ordered for everyone.

"Milkshakes to every one's flavor, a big bowl of chips, and toasted corn beef for all of us"

Pete had known that Nick, Mark and Ian liked chocolate malts, Marlii was Blue Heaven and Craigs was Vanilla Malt, simple.

"Ok it will be out real soon"

Pete went to the kitchen and Craig went on.

"That's right they can't allow the media to get a hold of this news story, and they haven't told you not to say anything?"

"No, none of us have been spoken to, it's just gone really quiet, everyone has clammed up" Marlii interjects.

"Nick, you need to speak to them again, tell them you will go to the media in Melbourne if there is no action on this, this is our opportunity to get something done" Nick says sarcastically.

"Here we go, the big political pants are being put on now"
Marlii punches Nick.

"Stop it, I was being serious, you have to stop joking like that"
"Ok, I will contact them after the new year" The milkshakes arrived followed shortly by the sandwiches and chips, while they ate they talked about the plans for tonight, and how Craig would slip out of the party and transport the explosives out to the Brown Mansion, they discussed their tactics, how they would fool the elders.

The plan was afoot.

The afternoons plans went off, Mark and Nick along with Craig went out to the clubhouse, this time along Nick's route, they found this way to be five minutes faster, once there they took Craigs Bike into the clubhouse, there they loaded the Dynamite onto a luggage rack he had fitted earlier, and they used Occy strap after Occy strap to secure it, but the job was secure, all they had to do was lock up and get back to Nick's house to prepare for the party.

Craig, Mark as well as Nick arrived back a little after three Pm, Marlii had been assisting Ian with the decorations, they were greeted with tiny voices from Ian and Marlii thanks to the Helium.

The Garage tidied up, chairs set out, tables situated, and the Bar B Q front and center.

Marlii found herself in the kitchen helping Estelle prepare deserts, canapes, the trifle was her favorite, its layers of fruit, cake, custard and cream, not forgetting the walnuts and the sherry.

Streamers were left for the boys to string up.

By the early evening, Jack and Caleb were back with the Keg, the boys were there for the tapping of the Keg, for if it went badly, it would be a laugh riot.

The Tapping of the Keg was a success, Jack and Caleb were joined by Gina and Estelle to celebrate, with a frosty beer with the perfect head, the kids were disappointed NOT to see the explosion of beer that they had expected.

The guests arrived in a flurry all at once, John and Sandra Smith the first, both stopping to kiss Marlii on the head, Rusty trailed in behind his parents, also kissing Marlii on the head, the keg did it's work for the most part and the canapes went down a treat, to the pride of Marlii.

The Bar B Q was fired up, steaks snags and chops, as well as burgers were put on to cook, with Jack standing over the cooking, chopping onions with his spatula.

There were two main gatherings, those sixteen and under, and those over eighteen, the seventeen-year old's drifted between those two groups, there had been four of them, Tess Hillfort was one of them.

She had tended to hang around Marlii, more than the adults.

The others gravitated toward the adults.

The kids were by the pool, it had been a hot New Year's Day, and the evening continued into a balmy haze that cold drinks and dips in the pool were the only way to stop or live with the humidity.

It was approaching seven, Nick went to Craig.

"My push Bike is by the front fence, we know how to cover for you, good luck" He would be gone forty minutes so they would not need to cover for long.

Craig went out through the front door and was gone.

Marlii and Tess stayed together by the pool, the boys sat on the trampoline, chatting and goofing off.

Craig rode the bike as fast as he could, he had come out on Old Town Road, and pumped the pedals hard, he had made the first part of the trip to the clubhouse in record time, coming off the blacktop and hitting the dirt in a flurry of dust.

After storing Nick's bike and removing his Yamaha he left the clubhouse unlocked jumped on the bike and kicked it over.

He headed back into town, and as approached the verge at the turnoff to the Brown Mansion, he flicked his lights off, and headed up the long hill of the driveway as he got to the top gate he pulled up, and looked around, he could see the whole town from where he was right now, he had never been here before, and to look down from here was spectacular, Marlii had always said that the bottom of the hill was as close as they could ever get to the house, present company excluded because he was on a mission, but to look out over the town at this moment, it was lit up, the whole of the Main Street as well as the, library, the park was a hive of activity the men setting the fireworks were hard at it, setting charges, and down on Honeysuckle Street, the lights at Nicks place were lit up like a Christmas tree.

He refocused, he had this delivery to do, he rode into the front turn around, put the bike on its kickstand, he unstrapped the Dynamite, he took the box by the straps and went to the side window of the west tower breaking the window he cleaned up the broken glass and dropped the box onto the floor, and climbed through the window.

He grabbed the box by its rope handles and headed out of the room he was in, he turned to the left and was in the stairwell of the tower, he headed up the stairs looking into the room, not here, he had known, not here, he climbed up to the third level, this was it, here in this room, he opened up the door, the room was void, he went in, put the box on the floor and went to wood paneling that lined the walls, he found a section and prized it open, it was the perfect niche, the perfect hidey hole, he pushed the box into the spot and replaced the paneling, he looked around, everything seemed to be in place, he headed down the stairs, and out through the window, real quick, he went to his bike and jumped on rolling the bike to a start, he blurted down the hill, getting to the bottom, he flicked his lights of and roared off toward the clubhouse.

Back at the party Marlii had come to Nick and gathered Ian and Mark.

Craig had been gone for forty-five minutes; Marlii was getting excited by now, not in a happy way.

"He should have been back five minutes ago; I am starting to worry" Mark answers.

"He is a couple minutes late at the most, don't panic just breath, remember he is fine" Nick had begun to placate her as well.

"He is not late at all; he will be coming through the back gate any minute" At that moment Estelle had popped her head into the alcove where the kids were situated.

"Hello, you lot, you got separated from the rest of the kids by the pool, I'm just checking in, have you lot eaten, there is still plenty left, or deserts"

Marlii speaks up.

"We are fine thankyou Mrs. Lester; we will come get some desert soon"

"Oh ok, Fine but where did Craig get too" Marlii had to think of something.

When from behind her Craig said.

"What's up Mrs. Lester" Estelle turns to see Craig with flushed cheeks standing just behind her.

"Oh, where have you been you look a little puffed" He was standing there with a cricket bat.

"I had to run home and get this"

He held up the bat.

"I thought we would get a couple of innings in before midnight, you know get this party started"

Estelle says.

"Organize yourselves, I will warn the senior citizens, it will be on for you all, I promise you that"

She walked off.

Marlii was up from where she was seated beside Ian and went to Craig's side.

"I am on Craig's team that is a given" Nick pipes in.

"And who selected Craig as Captain" Craig put his arm around Marlii.

"I did, my seniority, that's why I am Captain" Marlii pokes her tonged out at Nick.

"Really Marlii, that is showing your seniority isn't it, and that was a brilliant get out Craig, good on you, now we have to play a couple of innings of cricket"

The night wore on, the cricket sides were selected, and the seniors being made up of the parents and the Juniors taking in the kids they played more than a couple of long innings that took them right up to eleven thirty, the Juniors skipped ahead in the first innings, but as the seniors warmed up they overtook the Juniors, in the end, winning by twelve runs, the last ball bowled got the seniors six runs, the celebrations that followed were comical, with the seniors dancing around hooting and hollering.

At Midnight they had all gathered in the street to see the fireworks.

It was not the explosives experts from the mine, the ones that couldn't count, no, this fireworks display was organized through Pete, he had friends at ACME Incendiary come up with safe explosives.

They closed the whole park off with a cyclone fence around the perimeter and had been there since dawn setting charges and trajectories.

The first two were massive Crossette's that exploded into the night, once at their height they split in two becoming four, they criss crossed each other before exploding again, into huge gold, green, red and purple Chrysanthemum, this was followed by a waterfall of color, shots were being fired now at one a second, the crackles, pops and whistles of the fireworks along with the bangs and booms were deafening.

The town was lit up completely by the dazzling light show, there was a Dahlia, a Spider a huge willow tree, and so much Time Rain, everyone was mesmerized, for the full twenty minutes.

And after the last firework sputtered out into ash, they had continued to look into to sky most of them waiting to get their eyes back.

Nick Ian and Mark were together on the opposite natursetrip to Craig and Marlii, but when they finally looked over and saw them Nick put his thumb out and up to Craig, Craig responded the same.

But then the noise had come from the hill, the mansion, everyone there stopped what they were doing, and all looked up the hill to the house, it was like a trumpet call, it was the house, everyone had heard it.

It echoed off trailing a distinct note from a trumpet as it went off into the distance, there was silence but for a second when it started again, this time stronger, it was like all the chimneys on the house were playing a tune, there had been six main chimney stacks which had vented all thirty odd rooms, this time the noise continued.

That was when the shit hit the fan, the chimneys, all six of them, exploded from the roof line at the flashing, sending bricks, and chimney parts out over the town, one of the venting caps went through a skylight at Uncle Pete's, smashing into the fryers destroying them along with electrical appliance's strewn through the kitchen, he would need to assess what to do.

However, chimneys aside, what was coming was soot from the house, it went straight up and out, the Moon light that had been adding to the festivities was blocked completely out.

Jack Lester called from somewhere in the crowd.

"Alright everyone inside, come on"

The crowd moved of the nature strips and the road, and back into Nick's house, people cramming into the kitchen spilling into the hallways and into the lounge.

Nick was in his room with Ian and Mark.

"This is bullshit man; I mean what the fuck" Ian says.

"That fireworks display was awesome but the house, after it" Mark Adds.

"It was speaking to us, warning us, I know a warning when I see one" Nick leads the boys out into the loungeroom, he sees Marlii sitting with Tess but no Craig, he goes to the back porch where he finds him, he is watching the ashen cinders fall, some whisps have painted his hair that same ashen sooty grey color.

Nick says. "I couldn't find you, what are you doing out here?" Craig answers.

"I had thought the dynamite was going up then for a moment, but what did happen, that is freaky" Nick says.

"Mark says that it was warning us, if that is a warning, well I would hate to see what it would do" Craig says.

"We can't wait, it has to be done as soon as we can get to it" Nick agrees.

They wander back inside as the ashen soot continued to fall, now dispersing into the atmosphere, it had spread out as far as the Mill, and back over the whole town and outer reaches, including waterfall park, and all the residencies.

When the new year's day dawned the ashen soot laid over everything, the boys found on their walk in the morning, that the huge grey lumps were actually cars, but it covered everything, as they arrived at the corner of Honeysuckle and Main, they looked straight up the street, Main Street was a mass of Ashy sooty grey, the petrol stations hoarding which held an advertisement for Grange's Cordials and Soft Drinks, its picture of the family down by the Waterfall enjoying a cool bottle of Grange's was nothing but a huge grey black pock marked mess.

As they crossed the street toward Uncle Pete's they noticed a work man on the roof, wondering they picked up their pace, they were curious.

The bell tinkled overhead, as they entered the shop the carnage was evident, Pete had one side of the restaurant cordoned off with yellow police do not cross tape.

Uncle Pete came out from behind the counter to greet them.

"Hi boys, as you can see you can't dine on that side, and you can't order anything hot, off the menu, plenty of pies and cake, and I can still do coffee and your milkshakes are safe and so is the Grange's, I was lucky I wasn't in the kitchen when that chimney came through, would have wiped me out, crushed me for Shure" The kids are sitting and listening to Uncle Pete intently, Pete's matter of fact way of explaining the event, they all agree with Uncle Pete, Craig nod, Ian says.

"Well, you are lucky it happened when it did then, you were safe" Mark adds.

"That chimney did some damage to the kitchen, its ripped wiring out as well, and that wall and ceiling is stuffed"

"It will be a couple of days before I get things back to normal, it is stuffed you are right, any way what are you having" Craig orders

"Can we all have chocolate malts for each of us, and Marlii will be here soon, so can I have a Blue Heaven as well" "Coming right up" Nick offers.

"Wow look at this place, it will days before Uncle Pete is cooking again, the destruction is affecting people who shouldn't be getting affected, this is not fair" Mark adds.

"They will be cleaning the town for weeks, that soot is inches thick all over the place" Marlii came through the door, signaled a hello to Uncle Pete and continued over to where the boys had settled, she kissed Craig sitting as she did she said.

"The whole town is covered in soot, there have been workers at the house since one this morning looking into the explosion, I haven't heard anything yet, so what are your thoughts?"

Craig says.

"I think as soon as the coast is clear, I go in and set the charge, BOOM" Ian adds.

"But you can't do that, there are men working up there at the moment" "As I said when the coast is clear, any way in the meantime Marlii and I are spending time at the library, looking up the history of this place, what has happened in the past to make it such bad place, we are trying to find history regarding the Browns" Marlii interjects.

"I am ready, to search, Mum filled me in this morning, basic history stuff, the disappearances at the Mill and Mine and the strange happenings around town, she laughed at the events of this morning and Dad thinks it's a joke" Nick adds.

"Well look at Uncle Pete, he is going on like all is normal, but his kitchen is devastated, my old man was out in the front yard sweeping up the mess and he was whistling a happy tune, like he was doing a chore that was set to him"

It was at that moment Diane came in through the door, here to assist Uncle Pete, she waved at the kids and went to the counter, the four chock malts were ready, Diane bought them to the Table.

"Hi you lot, interesting new year's wasn't it"

She placed the chocolate malts on the table in front of each of the boys.

"Yours is coming sweetheart, he is making it now" Marlii offers.

"Thank you, Diane, it's a shame Uncle Pete has to deal with this mess" "Oh well he has it covered, don't worry about it" The bell above the door tinkled, a man walked in with a briefcase, he went straight to Uncle Pete as Diane went back to get the final milkshake.

They all watched and listened to the man, he began to explain the explosion, they had heard him clearly.

"It was a buildup of gasses, that could not exhaust, the pressure built up until it could not be contained any longer, you lot must have had a show last night" Diane was back with Marlii's milkshake.

"That's the insurance representee, they act really quick, they have already assessed the damage here, all he had to do was confirm where the chimney had come from, obvious really, we will have this place spic n span in no time" They sat and sipped their milkshakes while listening to the conversation taking place, the insurance dude was now eating a piece of Apple and Raspberry pie and sipping on a coffee.

When they all left Uncle Pete's together, they stopped outside the shop and looked up at the house, its towers standing silently in the morning haze that Shrives Island found itself in, it now looked the most eerie it ever had, Nick's imagination took off, with him in tow.

He saw Mansion had grown a face, its towers were huge jowls that hung limply, two of the third story windows flickered open, and had become eyes, the entrance to the house opened and closed and Nick heard that trumpet note again, its entry had become a maw, the stairs became teeth ready to chew them all up.

When the house stopped moving around it was the face of Desmond Brown, Nick closed his eyes, and opened them, Desmond Brown was still there.

"Are you guys seeing this?"

Craig and Marlii stood stunned, Ian and Mark nodded confirming Nicks fears.

The house spoke to them.

"I will not wait for you much longer my patience is growing thinner by the day, you must come to me" The blood red paint around the eaves began to liquefy, it ran down the side of the house leaving a blood trail, the house was bleeding.

It spoke a single word.

"Tonight"

It then fell silent.

They all looked up to see the house, back to its normally horrid site, the damage on the roof was obvious from where they stood, the chimneys that were a focal point of the mansion, were now obliterated to nothing.

Craig said.

"It has to be tonight; we need to get it done"

Mark says.

"Half the job is done; you just need to set the cap and get out of there"

"It was easy to get the dynamite in there, I'm not sure about the blast cap, I felt a presence in there when I was there last" They gravitated to Ian's house, Patsy had the news on, it was talking about Shrives Island and the news year's eve event, Ian led them through to the kitchen, they all helped themselves to drinks and sat at the table to talk about what to do next, Marlii was insistent that they wait for a few days maybe, see if things calm down, Nick speaks up.

"What do you mean wait, we have waited long enough, haven't we?"

Craig says.

"No I'm not waiting, that place is going up tonight, you can count on that"

CHAPTER THIRTEEN

BOOM

The hot summer afternoon had led to a sultry evening.

Mark Nick and Ian were at Nicks place, Craig and Marlii were at Marlii's.

They had planned to meet up the next morning, once again the three were staying together at Nicks, to make it easier.

Their nerves had been on edge, they didn't really know the extent of damage that twenty-four sticks of Dynamite could possibly do, but they had known it would be huge.

Nick speaks up.

"You know I'm not sure we should let Craig set all twenty-four sticks of Dynamite, after all we have no idea of how big the explosion will be"

Ian offers.

"Well it's a bit late isn't it, he is setting the charges now isn't he?" Mark says.

"No, it's still light out, he wasn't going up there until dark, we could meet him up there"

It was decided on dusk they would ride up to the house, meet with Craig, and talk about what they would do.

They waited.

The evening was upon them, the three boys took their pushbikes and began toward the Mansion, Mark took the lead, out of Honeysuckle Street, and up Main Street toward the hill and the house, Mark pulls up at the bottom of the hill.

"Are you two sure you want to do this?" "Nick says.

"Of course we are, we wouldn't have ridden out here if we weren't"

Ian adds.

"Let's get up there, before anyone sees us"

The boys start up the hill, peddling as hard as they could, finally making it to the top of the hill they all look back to the town, in the muted light was eerie, it looked spooky to the boys.

They rode into the turnaround, and kick stand their bikes next to Craig's motorbike, the doors and windows had almost all been blown out, they went to the front door, there was no sign of Craig.

The three boys went in through the door Nick called.

"Hey Craig, where are you" They all waited for an answer, none came.

Ian offers.

"He must be upstairs, you know where he told us he hidden the stuff" The boys go to the right finding themselves in the tower, where Craig would be on the third floor, Nick is followed by Ian with Mark bringing up the rear, they get to the second story, and continue up to the third floor, the panel was missing from its niche, and the Dynamite gone.

Nick says.

"Shit where can he have gotten to" He calls out again to Craig, but nothing comes back.

Nick heads back downstairs, followed by Mark and Ian, when they get to the ground floor, they realize it was now dank enough for the torch, Mark takes the torch from his haversack and flicks it on, the torch beam cuts through the gloom.

Ian says.

"He must be here; his bike is still out there" Nick looks directly ahead.

"That way, the staircase, he must be on another floor, lets go" Mark leads the way to the staircase, they arrive at the first step, Mark starts up the stairs slowly, as he approaches the first-floor landing, he sees what he thinks was Craig disappearing into a room at the end of the hall.

"There he goes, he went into that room down on the left" He is joined on the top riser by Nick and Ian.

"He went into the last door on the left, let's go" |Mark starts down the hallway toward the room, he takes the handle and twists it, there is a creaking as he opens the door wide scanning the interior of the room with his torch, the room is void, apart for a desk sitting at a rakish angle.

"It was him; I'm telling you both it was Craig, I saw him go in here"

Nick interjects.

"It's the house, it knows we are here, it's been requesting us to come, quick, let's go" As they turn to run the door slams shut.

Nick grabs the door handle and pulls on it, nothing, then Mark grabs Nick at his waist and Ian grabs Mark by the waist and they pull with all their might, the door gives sending them all sprawling to the ground.

Ian is first up followed quickly by Mark and Nick, the flashlight forgotten hanging at Mark's side slashed the darkness away, they were down those stairs at lighting speed, through the front entry and out into the evening twilight, they had kept running until they had all leapt over the bull nose verandah and landed on the grass, Ian went down onto his knees and rolled, Nick and Mark were left in a tangled mess, coming together after they had leapt, hitting their heads together as they hit the ground.

They all stood dusting themselves off.

Nick says.

"I aint going back in there, I am listening to Marlii" They considered the police tape, fluttering near the entrance, Craig had obviously torn it down when he had entered the house earlier.

Ian says.

"You know Craig is in there, somewhere, we have to go find him, what if he is lost?" They all stood there looking into the house, it was not welcoming, but they then looked at each other.

Mark says.

"He is right you know, we can't leave him in there, we have to go in after him" Nick says frustratingly as he grabs the torch from Marks hand.

"Oh, give me that" As he began toward the maw of the house, Mark and Ian Followed Nick through the chasm that was the entrance.

The beam of the torch was directed into the house, the boys followed the light, once inside, Nick made his way up the main hallway past the stairway and onto the kitchen, everything from this point was covered in a fine dusting of ashy soot.

Nick scanned the torch around over the table, a litter of dinner plates, now covered with cobwebs, the corn and potatoes had shriveled to nothing, the jug, its unknown brown liquid sat squalid on the table, candles were sitting on the table, their wicks extinguished, and their wax frozen in time dripping down to the glass holder where it pooled.

Mark went to the candles taking two giving one to Ian, Mark then goes to his pocket and brings out the Zippo thumbing the wheel and setting the wick alight.

The illumination from the candles proved to light their way a little better.

Nick stopped at the door to the cellar.

"Here, this is the cellar door, and look down, those prints in the soot are his, I'm telling you go down here" Ian took the handle and turned it opening the door on the dark cellar's wooden staircase, Ian starts down.

Mark says.

"Whoa what are you doing, stop" Ian backs up.

"Why, we are going down right?" "Yes but hold your horses, we don't need to rush, go slowly man, you will get down there in plenty of time"

Ian begins down slower this time, the three boys kept one step free in front of them.

Ian feels tera firmer as he steps down onto the hardpacked earth that made up the floor of the cellar, the light from the candles and the torch making the walls visible, they were a washed blue color, furniture was stored down here most of it covered with sheets, those pieces exposed held a layer of dust.

A piano sat silently in one corner of the cellar, the sheet that had covered it hung limply over the top corner, exposing the keys to the ravishes of time.

The piano stuck an A.

The boys stopped and all looked at the instrument, it began to play again this time a tune.

Ian picked the tune "Kismet" it was playing Kismet.

Nick said.

"Its haunted"

At that moment a woman materializes out of the ether, sitting at the piano stool playing the tune.

She stops and turns and addresses the boys.

"Hello Nick, Mark, Ian, I have been waiting for you to arrive, I am glad you found me so quickly" Mark says.

"Where is Craig, we know he is down here?" "No, you are the only ones I have seen, as I said I have been waiting for you" Mark goes on.

"Who are you, why are you down here" Nick says.

"You are a ghost, aren't you?" "I am Lucinda, I am from the Neither world, I died a horrible death" As she turned to look at them her face flashed skeletal features, as she looked directly at them her complexion was perfect.

Her long auburn locks of hair hung loosely around her face, she wore a bonnet on her head, she was dressed in a simple blue ankle length dress.

"I need to explain to you as quickly as I can, before any more of you are lost, you need to come with me, to The Neither world if you want to save them" Ian says excitedly.

"Save who?" Lucinda replies.

"All of them" She goes back to the piano keys and begins to play Kismet.

Nick asks.

"How are we going to get to this Neither world" Ian grabs him by his sleeve.

"What are you doing, are you really considering this?" "Yes, shh, be quiet" Nick goes on.

"So, as I ask how we get there?"

She stops playing.

"You follow me through here" She raises her hand, the whole cellar lights up a brilliant white glow, the rear wall of the cellar is a doorway carved out of the light.

And as the boys followed Lucinda through the door to the Neither world.

Craig's fate was much different indeed.

He had arrived two minutes before the boys, to find Marlii waiting for him in the first tower.

She had been in the room when he had come in to collect the box of Dynamite.

"What are you doing here, how did you get here before me, I mean I left you at my house, I took my motor bike" "Yes but you had to go out and get the blast caps remember, I used my father's car, I parked it deep in the garage, there is someone here you have to meet"

She leads him out of the tower room down a long corridor, there had been rooms either side she walked him into the last room on the left, closing the door behind them, Marlii has Craig put the box down by the door, they go to the chairs sitting in front of the desk.

"Craig this is Desmond Brown, please say hello"

He managed. "Hello" "Say those friends of yours are trouble aren't they"

Craig sits quiet, Marlii nudges him in the ribs eliciting an answer.

"Ah yes they can be trouble"

"Well you need to do something about that, see that box you bought with you, you need to use it" Craig did see Mark Ian and Nick, in this verry room, but they had not seen him he signaled them as they looked around perplexed, first at the desk then at the partition, he watched as Nick tried the door, watched as Mark went to his waist, and Ian to his.

Brown said.

"They cannot see you; they are unaware if that describes it" He watched them sprawl to the floor followed by them fleeing the room.

That was when the Desmond Brown thing changed, from its top hat to its pudgy waistline, down to his highly polished riding boots, he changed in front of Craig and Marlii, all they could do was watch, as they were rooted to the ground.

Its face disappeared in a molten misshapen mess, horns now sprouted from where the man wore his hat, they continued to be drawn to his face as it slid around in a coalescing mess, when it ceased its movement, an Imp was present.

It came forward and grasped Marlii around her throat choking off any oxygen getting to her, Craig reacted by going to the Imp and attacking it, picking up the chair he had been sitting in and dropped on the Imps back, it released Marlii, she fell away from it, she watched it close in on Craig, it leant right in close to him its acrid breath stinging his nostrils.

"You think I will kill you or her, I have too much at stake to make a silly mistake such as that" He stood up, Marlii was as far away from him as she could get, she was only just getting her breath back.

He went toward Craig, it was Desmond Brown again, it went back to the desk and sat.

"Now if you two will come back to the desk we can chat" Craig got up as did Marlii, he picked up the chair he had earlier used as a weapon and righted it Marlii sat down in front of Brown.

"So they got down to the cellar, and that bitch Lucinda got to them, and now they are in the Neither world, do you know what the Neither World is, I will tell you, it's a safe haven, for those who have reason to find safe harbor, from people such as me, well they won't be there long and when they come out I will have you all in my care, just the way we all want to be, one big happy family, Marlii you have done wonderful"

Marlii sat and smiled at him, with obviously no recollection of what had transpired only minutes earlier, Craig looked at her eyes, there was more there, Craig had felt that the look she was giving Desmond was normally only reserved for him, jealousy was rearing its ugly head.

CHAPTER FOURTEEN
INTO THE ETHER

Through the Lighted doors were the Neitherworld.

It was Shrives Island (The Crossing), at the turn of the century.

The boys were standing at the bottom of Main Street, there were a few timber buildings and some

of stone, but the most noticeable piece of architecture was the big house being built up on the hill, it was having the last of the finishing touches put to it.

Nick says. "We need to get up close, get a better look, this is freaky" Mark adds.

"It sure is, it's so new" Ian then asks.

"Why were we dumped here at this time, this is weird" Nick offers.

"We had to be here, to see what it is that is evil about that place, let's go"

He begins up the dusty dirt road that will one day be paved toward the center of town, as they approached the area familiar to them as Uncle Pete's the boys couldn't believe their eyes, above them on the hoarding was Grange's sign, they looked into the shop, tables and chairs were arranged in neat blocks of four, they went into the shop, they were not out of place as when Ian looked into the Mirror behind the front counter he saw his cloths were correct period.

They approached the counter the lady behind the counter was Lucinda.

"Hello boys" Nick was surprised to find the woman here; she was now dressed as you expect a shop owner to be dressed.

Mark was the first to speak.

"So are you just going to pop up on us like this now" They each took a stool opposite Lucinda at the bar.

"You three must be thirsty!"

She began to fill three glasses with Grange's Sarsaparilla.

Mark adds.

"So, I give up, what's going on, why are you here, what is the next peace of the puzzle?" The three boys pick up their glasses at the same time take a draught and put their glasses back down.

"You lot think answers are that simple, they aren't, you have to ask questions, you all need to discover what is happening right at this moment, in another place, you are all in the Neither world at the moment but one of your number is missing, the footstep you saw earlier at the house, there is someone here in the Neither world that should not be here, you need to find that person, you and they will know what to do" Mark says.

"One of us is missing, we left Craig behind, so who is it we have to save, who is in danger?"

Lucinda offers.

"All of your loved ones, if you three don't manage to stop the Brown clan it will end in disaster for you Nick, and your wife, and you can see how it affects you Ian, and Mark, it will affect my existence also, you need to find the connecting pieces of the puzzle, I can tell you now, find the connection to me, look outside the house, look to the mighty Odistgeeg, you will find answers there" Ian asks.

"So where do we go from here, where do we stay, sleep, if that's what you do in the Neither world?"

"That depends how long this takes you, when you are done you will wake in your own beds, so the quicker you get this done, the better for all involved, but if you need to crash come back here to me, you can sleep here, if you fail, you will stay here an eternity"

The three boys all looked to each other Mark quipped.

"Well, we know what we are here to do, well I think I do"
Nick offers.

"Well, we can do the best we can" Ian adds.

"We can try our hardest"
Lucinda looks at them all sternly.

"You better get it right, do you get it, you do know how you three succeeding will affect us, well I hope you do, our futures depend on it" The three boys look at Lucinda, then back at each other, they all turn to Lucinda.

Nick says.

"We've got it, we won't let you or anyone else down"
The three boys finish their drinks and head out the door, thanking Lucinda she smiles back at them.

Outside they look up the hill, the frame of the house is huge and hulking, the boys continue to walk up the hill toward the house.

The trail up the hill was narrow; the boys are forced of the trail a couple of time to make way for horses and carts that were transporting Goods and services.

Breasting the top of the hill, the boys got to look out over the town, it was a yearling town.

Nick looked off into the distance, and where the Mill stood then was where it stood today a wisp of smoke spiraled into the sky from the Mill, and looking back across the town, it was but a skeletal town, the bones had to nurture themselves, get some skin and muscle on them, the Mighty Odistgeeg, and the softer more gentler Spencer on its right, flowed down and over the falls crashing at the bottom into a single force that forged its way South.

Nick looked back to the house, the painters were finishing up, the house was being prepared for its new owners.

Ian breaks the silence.

"Well we are here, may as well look around, ask some questions, that's what we need to do" Mark and Nick agree moving onto the work site.

They make their way to the Mason working on the stonework, the walls of the cellar were finished in quarried rock that had been transported from the U.S.A. the timbers and hard woods came from the local Mill, one of the Mason's was working on the Bullwork verandah at the front of the house he was finishing the finer work of one of the piers to the brick arbor, that would end up an ornament in time.

"Hey, one of you kids crab me that raking tool please, I don't want to get down" Nick went to the bag of tools and peered in, a raking tool, Nick picked out a long narrow piece of wood with two small wheels at one end, between the wheels was a Adjustable nail, Nick held it up to the man.

"That's it, that's my raker, pass it up please" Nick handed the Mason the tool he went to work, running the wheels along the mortice, the nail gouging out the excess mortar leaving a clean mortice joint.

Mark says.

"It's nice stonework Mr. this stone is not from around here, is it?"

"It is nice stone all the way from somewhere in the South of U.S.A. it's a mix of basalt and granite, strong, but it weighs nothing, easy to handle"

Mark continues.

"Where in America did it come from?" "Polk County, the Mayor was Desmond Brown, he planned the move but died before they could complete it, his son Joshua took over the planned move, and this house is the result, some of the locals are not happy with it being built here on this hill, they say it is cursed, it is said to already be haunted, they say it's a bad omen, being built up here, and its cellar stinks already, they went down to far for the foundations, they were warned not to dig it so far down, but he insisted, so it's a bad omen that's all"

The boys looked away from the Mason toward the stone walls of the Mansion, the walls were looking at the boys, the three of them had seen them move, it was a fleeting moment but they saw the stone blocks move.

"You know we were in there earlier today"

Mark agrees and Nick says

"Lucinda said the Odistgeeg we have to go to the river, she said we will find answers there"

Ian then says.

"So, we know this place is rotten to the core, even that brickie said so" Nick cut in.

"Stonemason, he is a stonemason"

Ian continues.

"The stonemason said it, this place is cursed, we all know it, but what is the connection, why was Lucinda so cryptic, I'm confused"

Mark yells up to the man.

"Hey mister" The stonemason stops what he is doing and looks down.

"Yes son, what is it" "You seem to know a lot about it, what more can you tell us?" "Not much, the little I know about it the better, my brother warned me when he heard I was coming up here to help them complete the house, he only told me the basics, but he knows much more" Mark asks.

"Where can we find your brother Mr., I would like to know the history a little bit better?" "His name Dougherty, Jason Dougherty, he works at the Mill, you can find him there through the day, or tonight at the local, it's a hike out to the Mill, on a hot day like today, don't want to punish yourselves more than necessary"

"Thank you, we will be fine" Nick says.

"Dougherty, that would be Kevin Dougherty's grandfather"

Ian agrees

"Yea I think its his great grandfather, I have heard him talking about him all the time, doesn't shut up about him, sheesh who would've known"

Mark says.

"Well, let's go, we will walk by the Odistgeeg, along it until we reach the Mill"

The three boys walked from the old house, down to Main Street and up along The Old Town Road, and walk along the road, about half a mile out of town was the first of the twin bridges that spanned the Odistgeeg and the Spencer Rivers, the Odistgeeg was flowing at a fast current, the boys watching the water skip over the rocks, leaving eddies behind them.

The track that ran the length of the river, was well worn, it had been established with the gold miners who had made this section of the river their camp spots, close to a bend in the river where they expected a little protection.

The boys travelled quickly, stopping often to wet their shirts, and to take a drink.

When they approached that would become the number six logging road, they found a narrow foot trail that led them up and away from the river, over a verge, that bought them down into the Mill.

They were astounded at the size of the operation, they saw and milling machines were run by steam, the huge saw that was running screamed as it cut its way through the hardwood gum that was destined to become floorboards, in a home at the Crossing, soon to be renamed Shrives Island.

They continued down the hill toward the site shed, currently an old shack which sat at the front gate, as the boys approached, a bullock train with six beasts pulling a logging cart, were coming back through the fence to pick up another load of timber for the burgeoning town.

They waited for the bullocks to move further into the yard before continuing, Ian saw who they had to approach he said.

"That's him he is so much younger, he may be my age, or maybe he is as old as Craig, but there isn't that much in it" They began to approach him Nick was first to speak.

"Hey, are you Jason Dougherty?" "That's me, are you three here to fill the jobs?" "No no we would like to talk to you about the house, where your brother is working, he said you know its history"

Jason began walking toward a larger shed.

"Follow me, I need to chase up where those hands are, yes, you don't want that house up there, its cursed" Mark asks.

"So what else can you tell us about it?"

"I can say with no hesitation, that Joshua Brown is not nice man, yes he looks after me, but you can't help honesty" Ian says.

"Oh, and how is that?"

"Ok, so it is said that Desmond Brown, Joshua's father, had killed a girl a young woman, but it was an inconclusive case and Desmond walked, it seems that Joshua has done the same thing here, killed a woman who was an inconvenience, and he got away with it, I say, angry ghosts are wicked they never found her, the woman just disappeared into thin air, rumor was she was pregnant"

They had made their way to a larger covered shed, where the men ate and slept, and generally socialized, Joshua went to a stove and placed the kettle over the flame.

"It seems that they are a mad bunch, it just goes to show you how far money will get you, would you like a cupper?"

The three boys spoke in unison.

"No thanks" Joshua looked up at them.

Ian explained.

"We need to keep moving that's all" "Well Ok, I hope I have been enough information" Nick answered.

"Oh don't worry you have"

The boys said their goodbyes and left Jason with his staffing dilemma, making their way back to the Odistgeeg, once back to where they had started, they had walked across Main Street, and into Uncle Pete's, Lucinda was there, a cigarette hung limply from her lips.

"You boys look beat, come, sit up here I will sort you out"

Mark, Ian and Nick took their stools at the bar, Lucinda began to pour three glasses of Grange's Sarsaparilla, placing the glasses once again in front of the boys.

"Say you three look famished, wait here just a minute" Lucinda went back into the kitchen, she returned a couple of minutes later with chips, as well as chicken sandwiches she had prepared earlier, on the fact the boys would be back to see her one final time.

The boys ate heartily and drank a lot Lucinda filling their glasses more than once.

"So what have you been able to find out?" Nick spoke for them.

"Well we found out that Joshua is a killer, Jason Dougherty who works at the Mill told us, that a woman went missing and Joshua was suspect but without a body they had nothing, but we still need to find where in the Odistgeeg we will find that final clue?" "Finish your lunch, go to the Odistgeeg, find the final piece of the puzzle"   The boys finished their sandwiches and drinks and said their goodbyes to Lucinda heading out the door.

Once in Main Street the boys sat and pondered what way to go next, they had known they would end up somewhere on the Odistgeeg, but where?

Nick said.

"I think we should go to where the waterfall park is today, I mean from our time, where the bar b qs are today, sorry from our time" Ian and Mark agree, and they set off toward the waterfall park, they find their way to the waterfall, the whole site is different, overgrown, but a small clearing was evident.

They made their way to the river, the waterfall was raging, the torrent coming over the breach, and tumbling down was immense, the boys had known this area well.

Nick says.

"The waterfall, under the waterfall"

Ian questions.

"What do you mean under the waterfall?" "That's where we need to look, we need to look under the waterfall"

Nick starts towards where the falls end, a curtain of water, running so fast its noise was deafening.

Mark yells.

"Look, over there, if we can get out on the ledge, we could make our way over to where the water fall ends, you know it's there don't you Ian, Nick, you do know it's there don't you?"

They both nodded.

Nick makes his way to where the track stops, and the ledge jutted out of the side of the cliff, he shimmied along the wall, his back hard against it, Mark followed closely by Ian.

He kept his back flush with the wall, when he got to what seemed like the end of the ledge, it went at right angle to where the other two boys were, he disappeared around the corner, Mark and Ian had first thought he had disappeared into the waterfall, and that is exactly what happened, as he approached the curtain of water, he slipped in behind the waterfall, Mark and Ian joined him.

Ian said.

"Wow, I never knew this existed"

None of them had.

They were in a cave system, two caverns separated by a dividing wall, the stone had been left smooth, by the river that had once flown here, prior to the waterfall coursing its way through the valleys to end up here.

It was dark, they had no torch with them, but they had all thought she was in here.

She appeared to them; it was Lucinda she was a part of the ether, suspended over them,

"You have done well so far"

Her dress trailed out behind her as she motioned for them to come forward, Nick was the first followed by Ian and closely by Mark.

Nick tripped; Ian almost fell on top of him.

His hand landed in something mushy and soft, he pulled his hand away.

They were struck by an odor so fowl, they all gaged back their sandwiches Lucinda had given them.

Nick cry's in disgust.

"It stinks, oh shit"

Nick bounced up from where he was, he waited for his eyes to adjust to the poor light, a figure slowly transformed in front of him he was able to make out it was a decomposing body.

Nick backed away forcing Ian and Mark back.

Nick said.

"It's a dead body, its rotting, it has been here for a bit" Ian yells.

"It's Lucinda, that's who it is it's her Lucinda, I'm telling you" Mark exclaims.

"Shit" Nick just stood there for a moment then said.

"We need to report this, we need to go to the police"

Ian and Mark stood there in stunned silence.

Lucinda was now on the ground, standing just behind the boys, as she came out of the shadows, the boys all jumped, reacted with fright Lucinda spoke to them.

"Boys, I didn't mean to startle you, I'm sorry" Nick said.

"But you are over there, it is you isn't it, you are over there" Lucinda says as the boys are panicking with each other.

"Calm down Nick Ian Mark, yes it's me I'm dead, but I have to be found and reported to the authorities"

Mark Ian and Nick began to calm down Lucinda said to them.

"Do you remember what I told you all you only need to find out where they hid me, the rest will look after itself, so now go, find the authorities and report it, please" It was then Lucinda dispersed into the ether.

The boys left the cave, heading back into town, when they were standing out the front of the shop that Uncle Pete would one day own, they walked in, it was different, the counter ran in the opposite direction, behind the counter was older woman, she was eager to serve them, they all ordered Grange's sarsaparilla.

Nick speaks up to their server.

"Excuse me, I was wondering where I could find the local constabulary, the Police, you know the Traps?" She replies.

"If you would like to wait here, my boy will be in soon, he is as close to anything the law would look like, finish your drinks, on the house, he will be here soon" The boys thanked the lady, Nick says.

"The coincidences are amazing, and this place, our Uncle Pete's, it's a focal point, like I don't know a magnet, to the happenings" Mark says.

"Don't read too much into it, you are over thinking it" The door opened and in walked a man in a finely tailored suit, he goes behind the counter and kisses the woman on the cheek, the boys are watching as the woman tells him something, he looks over to them, Nick looks away but Mark and Ian, hold his gaze.

He comes from behind he counter, he is dressed in a fine black vested suit, on his head at a rakish angle wore a Trilby hat, his fine but strong face beamed out to the boys as he came across to them.

"Hello boys, my name is Burt Watkins, I am the custodian of the town how can I help you?" Nick spat out.

"We know where the body of Lucinda is" Burt's facial expression changed from a friendly face to one of neutrality, and in that moment he was shocked, but finally he would have evidence.

CHAPTER FIFTEEN

MARLII AND CRAIG

Craig and Marlii were thrown into a pit, it wasn't the cellar, this was away from the cellar, it was exactly that a pit.

The pit was dark only the light of a single torch which was situated outside it, flickered the thin finger of light that filtered through to the pit was sullied.

Marlii went to bars at the front of the cell, the walls to the sides were solid concrete, she put her arm through the bars.

"Craig" She waited for an answer, it came, craig was startled, he had no idea Marlii was this close.

"Marlii, you are down here as well"

"Yes, I am sorry I lead you here, I don't know how he did it?" Craig answered.

"He has been manipulating us, probably since not long after we were born" Marlii put her arm around through the bar and gripped Craig by his hand, Craig Said.

"It's alright, none of us have been able to resist him, them actually, its not just Desmond Brown it is Joshua Brown as well, and there is another one her too, we need to get out of here" Marlii pleaded.

"How, we are locked up, how do you propose to get out of here?" Craig answers.

"They have us locked up, we don't know what's in front of us when, if, we get out of here" He went to the lock on his cell door, it was a new lock, a huge silver Master lock he grabbed it flicking it out of his hand.

"Shit, he has us in his grip"

Marlii squints, looks out of her cell.

Marlii yells.

"On the table look, right on the corner, the keys"

Craig looked hard, he could see the keys sitting just on the corner of the table, the table was three feet from Marlii's cell.

"Take your belt off, use it to catch them, do you think you can do it?" "I think I can,?" She unbuckled her belt, removing it, she was wearing it as a fashion statement, not to hold her pedal pushers up, she took aim, she flicked the buckle toward the table it landed directly on the keys, she pulled the keys off the table, they landed on the floor, Marlii pulled the belt back, and flicked the buckle toward the keys again, she found the belt buckle landed short by inches.

"I moved the keys away from the cell, my belt isn't long enough" Craig began to strip his belt off.

"Here, take mine, this should be long enough"

Craig passed his belt through the bars on his cell.

"Wish me luck"

She held the belt by its tongue, she flicked the buckle it landed to the left of the keys, she sighed" Craig said.

"Take your time breath"

Marlii lined them up again and as she flicked the belt buckle, she closed her eyes, but heard the audible click of the brass buckle against the keys she pulled the belt slowly, inching them toward herself, bit by bit she pulled the keys toward her cell, she put her hand out and grabbed them.

"I've got them" She stood up going through the keys she saw the Master key and unlocked her cell, she pushed the bars open going to Craig's cell unlocking him and letting him out, as he opened his cell, she went to him embracing him smothering with kisses.

"Marlii please, we need to get out of here" He was trying to thread his belt, Marlii picked up her own belt threading her belt back onto her pedal pushers.

Craig went to the torch that was burning on the wall, lighting their way down the narrow corridor, the only path in out of the cell, he came to a heavy metal door, he gave the torch to Marlii, he found the key placing it in he turned it unlocking their escape route, he grabbed the handle and turned it, he pulled the door open onto a hallway, that led them into the laundry just down the hall from the kitchen, Marlii followed Craig down the hallway slowly.

"The place is empty" Craig went to the staircase, he called.

"Desmond" Marlii shrunk.

"What are you doing, Craig let's get out of here"

"Shh"

He calls out again.

"Desmond, where are you?" Nothing comes back to him.

"I told you this the place is empty"

He heads up the stairs to the second floor, down to where he and Marlii had visited with Desmond, the Dynamite was still there in the dark, he gripped the rope handles and hauled the box out of the room, he headed back to the stairs, Marlii was waiting for him at the bottom, he came down them two at a time when he got to the bottom, he gathered up Marlii and kept going toward the front door.

When he got there, he opened the door, they were not in the Desmond Brown Mansion, not in the Desmond Brown Mansion that the kids had known.

The front yard was a graveyard, the trees hung dead over the old grey gravestones.

Craig began to move out onto the verandah, the dark of the night split by the torch.

He heard the screech of what he could only remember as a buzzard, but beside that there was an eerily deadly silence nothing moved everything was stagnant.

As they moved down off the Verandah the stones loomed out at them, the torch kept the way lit, they went to the border of the fence, and looked out over the town, it was black as night, no lights burned, no one was moving around.

"Marlii, wait here, I'm going back in just to the entrance where I left the dynamite, I need to get a couple of sticks" Marlii went to hand him the torch.

"No, you hang onto that, I will get sticks of boom and the bike, we need to get down to town" Craig heads of back up onto the verandah, she watches as he disappears in to the inky blackness, Craig goes to the entrance, grabs four sticks stuffing them into his jacket, she isn't waiting long when she hears Craig kick the bike over, he rode out to her.

"Jump on"

Marlii pitched the torch where it sat burning.

She climbed on, Craig flicked the lights on and roared down the hill.

As he drove into the town the headlight was the only sliver of light in the town, he rode down the main street, the windows were all blacked out with paint, hoardings were falling down, Uncle Pete's sign hung cock eyed, swinging from the remaining bolt that held it, the petrol station looked abandoned, like no one had been there, the houses in the residential precinct all looked abandoned, like everyone had fled the town in a single night, leaving all they were doing at that moment.

Craig continued to on to Tamarisk Drive where he made his way to his house, he pulled into the driveway, Marlii got of the bike and Craig kick stranded it.

Craig says concerned.

"It's all abandoned, it looks as if the whole town just disappeared, like in a puff of smoke"

All Marlii could do was nod in agreement, staying silent, Craig says.

"Wait here by the bike, I'm going into the garage, to get the torches, somehow I don't think the power is on" Craig goes to the garage and retrieves the torches coming straight back to Marlii, his torch swishing as he runs.

"Here take this" He switches on the Eveready Dolphin and passes it to her.

"I want to take a look around, I have no idea what is happening, but we need to find out"

He went through the front door flicking the light switch, expecting nothing to happen, it didn't.

The flashlights flashed through the gloom knives of light, everything was dusty cobb webs were everywhere, it was like no one had lived here in years.

Marlii finally says.

"This is bad, and I know that is an understatement, but where are the boys, where are your parents gone"

Craig stayed silent as he went through to the kitchen, the dust was evident that no one had been here in years, the table had been left set, Craig remembered that particular meal, the rolls had moldered and rotted to nothing, the roast beef shriveled.

"They left here a long time ago, I remember the table being set exactly the way it is right now, I was like five years old this is weird"

Marlii said.

"Everyone has gone, we are here alone, let's go to my place, I need to know" "Ok, l would like some answers as well"

They went out to the motor bike, he climbed on and kicked it over, that was when Marlii pulled on his jacket signaling him to turn the bike off, he stopped the engine.

"What was that" Marlii stood their silent she said.

"Shh, listen"

They both stood there in the nighttime darkness both listening, Craig heard a crackling slightly audible, but it was growing, he looked out focusing, his eyes on the house, the weather boards were losing their paint, it was ageing in front of them.

Craig says.

"It's this house, the paint is ageing and peeling cracking off"

The crackling began to grow louder, a low rumble was heard coming toward them, it was not felt, but the noise was becoming louder, the house began to fall, firstly boards began to lift from the frame, leaving a plume of dust behind, Marlii looked at her watch, it was spinning at a speed she had never known before.

"My watch, look"

Craig looked at his own watch, it was moving a little slower than Marlii's, but it was spinning freely.

Craig tells her.

"I have no idea what is happening, but we need to get away from here" Marlii agreed, he kicked the bike of its stand, and backed it out of the driveway Marlii by his side, he stopped at the verge of the street.

The house that he had grown up in, its timber windows now sat at odd angles, the door fallen away, the verandah hung limply to one side, it shook, just a little, the roof line collapsed in on the frame, straight through the interior wall's leaving a square box sitting on the lot, the garage that had been adjacent the house was nothing but splintered firewood.

Then the walls began to crash inward disappearing into a pile.

Craig says.

"Let's go, there is nothing we will find out here" He kicked the bike over, Marlii got on, he turned and headed down Tamarisk Drive all the houses were collapsing, disappearing, back on main street everything had gone to shit, that was when Craig turned the bike off Main Street out of Shrives Island, he crossed the twin rivers and the waterfall park, onto the Mountain Highway, he gave the bike a workout all through the bends until they arrived at the lookout, the town was laid out before them, from the same spot that Nick had stopped with Jess, in another time, and when they looked down on the decimated town, the houses, the shops, the school, and the business districts were gone, but when they looked over to the hill, that house remained, but it looked more dilapidated and unkempt than ever before.

They moved into the dark before the dawn, in that inky blackness was where they would wait for the first slivers of light.

When the first early light arrived, they looked back upon the house, it was grotesque, a massive Boab tree had sprung from the foundations of the house, setting the foundation at a verry weird angle Marlii says.

"We need to go back, we need to get closer, don't you agree?" "No not yet watch"

The tree had continued to grow, its tangly branches grew through the roof and out the windows Craig observed it for just a moment.

"That Boab is strangling the house, watch" Marlii looked at the tree, it limbs lengthened gaining more traction on the house, its limbs worked around the house like a tentacle, as they collapsed the roof inwards, the tree kept getting larger, until the Desmond Brown Mansion was completely obliterated, in its place was the largest Boab in the whole of the country, it stood immensely Marlii and Craig had surmised the thing was at least Ninety feet high, it may even tip the measurement to reach one hundred feet.

Not only was this the largest Boab Craig had seen anywhere, Marlii on the other hand, who had toured the far north of the Northern Territory with her family, she had seen many, while touring in Western Australia, she had even remembered seeing two Boab trees that had been used to house prisoners, mostly native Australian Aboriginals, they were large, but this one was definably one of the biggest she thought could exist

Marlii and Craig stood there stunned, the whole of the countryside was changing front of them, and the one thing out of the ordinary was the huge tree now sitting atop the hill.

Marlii observed.

"Look down at the Island, it's all overgrown, green again"

The Boab stood proudly surveying all around it.

Craig says.

"We need to get down there, we need to see this up close"

Marlii agreed, he got on the bike Marlii got on behind him, he kicked the bike over, it roared to life Craig steered the bike down the mountain side, avoiding trees that had sprung up where the roadway once was, as he came down and out of the Forest, and into what they had only known as Shrives Island, all that was left of there past, was timber piles covered in grass and blackberry's, the fruit was ripe, and that was it, that was all that was left.

Craig steered the bike through and up where Main Street had been, verry minimal evidence sat as proof where the road had once been, Craig had judged the distance of where Uncle Pete's used to stand, and also opposite where the service station had once stood, was where you sighted the largest grass covered mounds, he continued a little further on until he was at the foot of the hill, they had both been in awe of the Boab, and stood there staring at it, mesmerized by it, they left the bike where it stood and headed up the hill.

Marlii offers.

"It's well, a little creepy" "It makes you feel creepy because of where it's situated, I don't think its creepy, I think it is sad, I can feel it" Marlii says excitedly.

"That's it, it's not creepy, that's right I can feel it too, and it does, it feels sad" It is but isn't, the classic shape of a bottle, where a Boab normally holds the shape of a milk bottle, this tree was bigger, it was fatter, to look at it, it was sad it was scary all at the same time, the body of the tree led to its branches, that grew off the tree in all directions, its branches spilling out from the tree were full of foliage, and it was abundant with its white flowers, mostly closed and sleeping waved in the soft summer breeze.

The petals flickered to life in front of them, opening and exposing the yellow fronds that held their pollen, the Boab was a giving, bush bees were busy collecting for their Queen, and Honey was the produce, the petals flickered again then the limbs shook, shattering the relative peace of the flowers,

The bottle of the tree began to shift, the shapes that had been there before, seemed to move around, now there was no mistaking the mouth, eyes, both closed and the nose, it even had the semblance of ears.

The face moved again, first the mouth moved, opening, and closing, gnashing at the morning light, then the eyes blinked, once, and then again, it blinked a third time, they remained open on the fourth, its gaze struck Marlii and Craig, it looked down on them, it was scowling at them, Marlii said.

"I don't think he is that sad, now he feels angry, I think we need to go, don't you?" Craig responds.

"I think we should leave, real fast"

As Marlii turned on her heel Craig was a little slower, it was a branch smashed into him knocking him to the ground, as he landed on his chest, the wind knocked from him, he saw Marlii landing on her but, only a couple of feet away from him, it was loud very loud.

"Stop, where do you think you two are going' It bellowed down to them in its antique rusty man's voice, there was gravely timbre to it, Craig looked back to the tree, it was standing there looking at the two kids with a distain for them.

"You two aren't going anywhere, I have questions to ask, and you will answer them, okay, do you both have that crystal clear" Marlii was back to her feet, she was heading for the Boab, she struck out at the trunk landing a couple of right hooks and jabs, she was angry and frustrated at the Boab, but it reacted bringing two of his limbs and grabbing Marlii by her two hands she squealed as the limbs caught her hands and yelled as she struggled against the constraints.

"Now let me go you beast" "No, not until you are more controlled like Craig" Marlii stopped struggling and looked directly into the tree's eyes.

"So, you know who he is but do you know my name?" He snapped back.

"Marlii"

She was stunned by this, she continued to glare at the tree with question on her face, it was the knowing, the familiarity of this Boab to her and Craig she cried.

"Let me down, this instant"

The Boab leaned forward gently placing Marlii on the ground next to Craig who had regained his feet.

Marlii kept her gaze on the tree.

"Who are you, what are you, why have we been sent here?" The tree replied smartly.

"Who, what, why, very inquisitive of you, Craig knows, you should too"

Craig interjected.

"Hey, hey, both of you stop your argument, please I have no idea, why I am here, or where this place is, I mean I know its Shrives Island, but when I have no idea, and I have no idea of who you would be, a tree yes a Boab to be exact, no scratch that, a talking Boab, that's rare, so you think we know, we are as much in the dark as you, maybe you should take the higher road being as you are the elder here"

The Boab shook and its foliage quivered, the yellow fronds exposed to the stiffening morning air came free from their home, dancing their way across the light of the morning, Marlii spoke.

"It is frustrating, we were both angry at each other, I am sorry Boab, I am confused, you say you know us, but I and Craig have no idea, why?" The Boab shook making its leaves shudder, the soft morning breeze was beginning to warm, the sun now on the verge of the horizon, the shadows cast from the Boab were beginning to shorten in the light of the new day, the first day of the rest of their lives, the Boab spoke to them he was, sad, because it was he, who had to break the news to them.

"You are in the Neitherworld, you are here because you were attracted to me, this is my form, this is where I am now from the day, I was a seed germinating in the ground, I remained here for many, many years, I cannot say why you are here, I had thought that Craig had known" Craig looks to Marlii, she says.

"The Neitherworld, when is this place, I know where we are, but I have no idea when we are, it all started after we left the house"

Craig offers.

"Yes, we left the house"

He felt the bulge of the dynamite in his jacket, it was safe he went on.

"And when we came down the hill from the house, my home Marlii's home heck every house in town collapsed" Marlii took the story up.

"We came to the lookout more out of safety than anything, but when we saw you, when we saw how you consumed the house, well that was magical, scary but magical"

The Boab changed its expression, its skin like bark moved its mouth twisted upward into a grin, which became a smile, its foliage began to shake and shudder more than they had before, more fronds began to drift their way on the wind, down the hill landing at the feet of Craig and Marlii, the Boab spoke excitedly.

"Craig, you can't seem to see the forest for the trees"

Craig took up the next words.

"Can't get started, chemical heart, every time I get started you pull me apart, I know it's a song, those are lyrics" Marlii said.

"Not any song I know, It's not in the top forty"

The Boab spoke, addressing both.

"Yes, it is a song, you sang it to me, your older self, you sang the whole song to me"

Marlii looked at Craig and spoke.

"You need to remember; it is all important"

The Boab shook again and spoke.

"Marlii, you know the Neitherworld, you need to recognize it"

Craig went to the Boab stopping at the bottom of its bottle, Jug, like trunk.

"I don't remember but I do, I remember the song" The tree began grow a luminescence, its flowers began to open, its foliage shuddered it screamed into the distance.

"I have been here forever, from a seed, I grew, but now I no longer exist, those responsible for my destruction must be punished, you see, they didn't get all of me did they"

The Boab began to laugh firstly a little shudder, but that shudder became a shaking, its foliage rippled, and its laugh had become a long shriek that caused Craig and Marlii to put their fingers in their ears, blocking the deafening sound.

When it was safe to take their fingers from their ears Marlii spoke first.

"Well, you are angry, but what did you mean when you said, that they didn't get all of you, what are you saying?" The tree allowed its branches to relax, the foliage fell dormant around the Boab, the Boab sighed.

"Alas, when they tore me down, they left a little of me, and what they left there, was my root stock, lying dormant in the ground, you see, when they built that monstrosity, it has sapped the energy out of me, if it were not for the Neitherworld, that part of me, my root stock, would have died out a long time ago" Craig spoke in an excited tone.

"I think I am getting it, the hill, you, that hill is there because of you, your size had to have an impact on the ground, the hill is you, do you get it"

Marlii was looking a little perplexed.

"I think I understand, the growth of the Boab, caused a ripple in the earth because of its sheer size, and because"

She stopped for a moment and then went on.

"It's the house, the house is stifling you, it won't let you grow" The Boab turned from its sad sullen face to one of anger, not directed at Marlii, aside it was angry because of time it had lost, not much more than a blip on its own timeline, but a blip non the less, it said.

"No, no, the house is not aware, it doesn't know I am there, its rotten seething cellar, it has to be stopped, you can do this Craig, you have the power, look into your Jacket, Boom Sticks, I think that they will do the trick"

Craig responded.

"Boom sticks" His hand went to the bulge in his jacket.

"I will blow the place to smithereens" Marlii went to Craig taking his hand, she said.

"We need to do this" The Boab stood silently, but began to ruffle his leaves and foliage, the white flowers sprang back to life eliciting from them sunlight, the tree held time in its soul, and with the wish came the day.

Marlii and Craig stood in the shade that he was emanating, pin pricks of light shot from the blooming white flowers their silhouette's cast from them sank back down the hill, the Boab spoke.

"So you understand know what we need to do?" Marlii stood there and nodded her head, Craig was still, he didn't move, but he whispered.

"Better of wishin for the stars to kill the sun, like black rose if nobody can hold no one, no one" The Boab said.

"You have remembered, great" Craig began to shake his head violently.

"No, No you cant do that"

He went toward the Boab and screamed.

"I SAID NO" The Boab was taken back by Craigs anger, his leaves and foliage shivered slowly, it was as if the Boab had shrunk before him.

Craig stood stoically at the tree, he had known the boy was angry, but why?

Marlii came forward and spoke.

"I do get it, he wants me doesn't he, he wants me to keep him, I think I have known for a little while now" Craig spoke up.

"Marlii was never a part of the deal, I said to you to take one of us four"

The Boab changed its expression, and said.

"Marlii is one of four, you Mark and Ian, make up the four, simple arithmetic, not at all hard"

Craig asked.

"And Nick, what about Nick, what do you know?" The Boab shook and its foliage quivered, he said" "I only know of you four, Marlii is the strongest of all of you, that was the deal, and you know it, I take the strongest of you, you are a poor sod, you are the weakest of the four, you barely rate, I am sorry if the truth hurts, but it was Marlii that bought you through into the Neitherworld, without her you would have been stuck between the worlds"

The Boab shook and said.

"You are so out of control in the world, you would be freaked by your own behavior, I think you should stick to your first job, BOOM"

Craig softened his stance, relaxed, as did the Boab, Craig said.

"Wow, the truth hurts a bit, I thought I was the alpha, but it is you" He turned and looked at Marlii and spoke.

"I should have known, that is why I am here in this Neitherworld, and the boys are in the other Neitherworld, your strength pulled me through with you" Marlii was smiling at Craig and said.

"A bit unexpected hey, I had no Idea but think of the ramifications, we need to follow the path, the path set out for us, set out for us by him, I am assuming you are a male, you sound like a male, and what is it with that song"?"

The Boab sighs.

"The song, I know the words, but Craig knows what they mean"
"No I don't, I don't even know how the words came to my head, I don't know what it means"

The tree said the lyrics.

"Better off waiting for the stars to kill the sun" He stopped, Craig began to sing the next lyrics. "Like a black rose nobody can hold no one, no one" He stopped and thought for a moment then he turned to Marlii.

"You are the black rose, no one thing can contain you" Marlii looked surprised, and then she turned happy.

"It's destined"

She stood there with her hands out in front of her, then she put them on her hips, and in that moment, he saw it, he saw the magic emanating from her.

The tree shook, its foliage shuddered, its flowers came to life and he spoke.

"You all need to know, learn to remember, Craig it will be up to you, it has always been up to you, you have all gone on to making your fortunes, you did it with back breaking work, but financially you have had a moderate to verry good living"

Craig stopped the Boab and said.

"Whoa up a minute, what, how do you know that?" "Listen to me I will explain" Marlii told Craig to shh and listen the Boab went on.

"Think about it Craig, I am, I exist, and you exist, the Crossing is a verry important place, and I still live, My roots go much further and deeper than you can imagine, everything in this region is affected by me, every one of you who were born here, have my essence, when they cut me down they only cut me down to the bottle, but I have held sustenance from the Odistgeeg, from the forests and the hillside, IF THAT HOUSE WAS GONE, I would flourish once again, you need to go back to the boys, I will keep Marlii here with me, she will be safe, I give you my word"

It was at that moment that Craig went over, he went back to the Netherworld of 1974.

But as he spun away, he saw the Boab clearly take Marlii into the folds of his branches, covering her with his foliage, the last thing he remembered seeing was Marlii's face, it had begun to turn into the smooth bark of the Boab.

Chemical Heart
Grinspoon

When

Look for a ride and you need to get high my friend's

Spend all your time just walking around instead

Like black rose there's somebody to hold for them

For them

Let's

Go outside have a nothing to hide for free

Can't seem to see the forest from the tree's

Grass is always greener but how do ya know we'll see

We'll see

Can't get started chemical heart

Every time I get started you pull me apart

Can't get started chemical heart

Every time I get started you pull me apart

Forgotten

Maybe things are right on the other side undone

Better of wishin for the stars to kill the sun

Like black rose if nobody can hold no one

No one

Can't get started chemical heart

Every time I get started you pull me apart.

Can't get started Chemical heart

Every time I get started you pull me apart

Yeah

When

Look for a ride and you need to get high my friends

Spend all ya time just walking around instead

Like stack road there's somebody to hold for them

For them

Can't get started chemical heart

Every time I get started you pull me apart

Can't get started chemical heart

Every time I get started you pull me apart

Yeah

Can't get started

Chemical Heart

Every time I get started

You pull me apart

Can't get started Chemical heart

Every time I get started you pull me apart

CHAPTER SIXTEEN

TOGETHER AGAIN

It was dark, it was damp, he could hear the dripping of water close by.

Also there was the distinct sound of running water.

Craig waited for his eyes to adjust to the darkness, as his vision began to come clearer it was obvious he had woken in a cave, a network of caves, but he had now known distinctly where he was.

He was under the town.

Craig got to his feet, wondering what direction to go in, there were intersecting passages that went off in three different directions, the second of the three had a small pin prick of light emanating from within the tunnel, that was the way he would go.

As he felt his way along the cavern, using the walls that were cold, damp and rough he followed the pin prick of light, which had grown and grown until he realized, that he was heading to a rather large opening, he quickened his pace, making his way to the entrance of the cave.

The light of the day made his eyes water, he squinted, held his eyes closed for a moment and opened them, it was clearer now and he had known where he was, he was on the west of the saw mill, but he had never remembered this cave entrance, where he was, he had known the area for rather a long time, that cave had never been there before, he looked back at the entrance, it was not a new entrance, it was overgrown with brambles and Blackberries, the fruit was summer ripe, normally he would stay there and eat of the berries but not today he had a mission to complete.

He went onto the sawmill, finding it empty, all the machinery idle, and the front fence locked.

He climbed the chain link fence and went out onto Old Town Road, and hoofed his way into town, it was obvious he was back "Home" yet, he was back in Shrives island he just had to work out when, in Shrives Island's history.

He walked into main street and saw the milk bar where it should be and as he walked in, he was stopped in his tracks.

The boys were there, they were being stood over by a well-dressed man, he was standing over them as he was writing down all the evidence the boys had uncovered.

The man looked up and the boys followed his gaze, Nick was the first up and out of his chair going to Craig, Mark and Ian were close behind him, Nick yelled.

"Craig, where have you been"

The three boys engulfed their older friend, Burt Ward had to wait until the reunion was complete, it was when they begin to settle when Craig blurted out.

"You will never believe it, I'm telling you" Then he stopped and looked up toward Burt.

"But that can wait just for the moment, seems you have business here"

Burt Ward came to the crowd of boys, patting Craig on the shoulder and spoke.

"So seems like we have need of refreshment here ma, what would you like son, what do you want to drink?"

Craig turned.

"I will have Lime, thanks" The boys continued to harass Craig about what he had found out, but Craig was remaining mum on that point, instead joining with the other three to listen to what they were relaying to Burt.

As the boys told Burt of what they had found a crowd had gathered in the bar, word was out, that the body of Lucinda was about to be retrieved.

Millers and Miners had begun to form a Posy of sorts, and the boys after retelling their stories, the men had gathered to recover the body of the woman, Burt was set at arresting Joshua Brown.

The men had left the bar in a rage, the boys remained in the booth, fresh soft drinks all around, as Burt went out the door, following angry town folk, Burt said to the boys.

"Sit tight, don't leave this bar, got it?" Craig nodded, the other boys all agreed.

Nick was first to speak.

"So tell us where have you been what have you found out, and why are you here now" Ian asked.

"Where is Marlii?"

The three boys directed their gaze on Craig, he spoke in a hushed tone.

"Not here, she is with the Boab, Shh don't say anything" The boys sat and planned their next move.

Mark spoke up.

"We need to get out of here, I don't want to be around when they bring that Brown character in"

Ian protested.

"But Mr. Ward wants us to stay here, we can't just leave" Craig said.

"I will handle this, just watch and listen, follow my lead"

He got up from the booth and went to the bar, he said to the woman that they had a prior engagement, and then he began toward the door, Mark gave his apologies that he had to go, Nick just stood and walked out, it was Ian who dillies and dallied, finally, Nick put his hands through the open fly wire door and grabbed a shoulder, hauling Ian out into the street.

They went toward the hill, the house, now in the gloom of the afternoon, the house stood in a muted light, a darkness hung over it and around it, they all stood at the bottom of the hill looking up, Craig broke the silence.

"It's evil, I've got these"

He opened his jacket, the boys saw the BOOM sticks, dynamite, he went on.

"Marlii is it"

The boys all turned to Craig.

Ian managed.

"Sh, she is the one"

It had dawned on Ian as much as it had for Mark, just at that moment they remembered an integral part of the mystery, the sum.

Craig said.

"Nick you are not one of the four, I was told in no uncertain terms that I was nothing more than a passenger, I know the series of four, it is Marlii at the top, you Ian are the second, Mark you are the third, I'm the fourth, you are here Nick for your own skills, your story writing skills, you are an extension of us four" Nick stood there and finally managed.

"Where the Hell is Marlii?" "Marlii is with the Boab, they are keeping each other safe"

That was when Ian said.

"You can't do it here, you can't blow that place up, it's new, I don't mean you don't blow it up, but not in this world, we need to be away from here, we need to be in our time" They had all agreed to heed Ian, this just felt like the wrong time, their own time would be more appropriate, the house now standing high on the hill it stonework and timber facades standing over the town like the pallor that hung over it blackening everything in its sight.

The four boys continued to skirt the hill always in the shadows of the house, they headed out onto what would one day become Old Town Road, toward the mill where the boys had all known it would yield its secrets to them.

It was midafternoon as they approached the camp, that had been erected for the loggers, they ate in town, and they drank in town, but they lay their head by their saws.

There were a group of men tending a hog on a spit, others were at the tables preparing salads and buttering bread, the boys approached, Craig had seen his friends in those faces, although these were their grandparents, and Mark was familiar with at least two of them, he remembered them as old, a weird thought he had said.

They gathered at the pit fire and all shared amongst the pork, filling freshly baked bread with the meat and finishing it with coleslaw or potato salad, or sometimes both, they were to begin a Big Mill Weekend, and the food had been put on by the Mill, they spoke of the crossing and how it was forging ahead, they spoke of the house on the hill, they had known it was evil, but they did not know how evil, the Milled timber in the house came mostly from within that same Mill, but they would cut a forest in the morn, the boys stayed and sat for hours putting off the inevitable.

With belly's full the boys said there farewells to the loggers and moved into the forest, but the forest that they had entered had been an older growth forest, this was a forest that was being preserved, unlike the Pine forests this forest was a mix of scrub, and dense undergrowth, that began even before you got to what was referred to as the whipsticks, once they had fought their way into the whipsticks, the going was a little easier, this part of the forest was full of thin wiry gum trees, mostly eucalyptus, they stopped at dam just a little to the west of the Odistgeeg.

Ian complained.

"The humidity is killing me" Mark quips.

"I'm sweating up, look at my shirt"

That was when Craig cut in.

"Well we are getting there, the Odistgeeg is a little further on, were we come to it is rarely traversed, most people who go missing only to be found downstream go missing, or were last seen heading into the area, we need to be careful" Nick was dipping his shirt into the dam, keeping cool in here was difficult.

Craig had thought they had rested enough, wet their shirts and drank forever, that was when he announced.

"Time to keep moving, we want to make it by dark, look, it's almost twilight"

The boys battled their way through the Whipsticks into the forest where everything went quite, off in the distance you could hear the mighty Odistgeeg flowing strongly down the ridge, the boys found themselves on, they continued along the trail that had run very thin half a mile back, and as they peaked the rise, they had come to the top of a bluff, down in front of them the Odistgeeg, they stood there in awe of what was laid out in front of them, across the river was where the forest was at its deepest, and that was where they had to go.

The problem, that was trail ended.

Nick spoke up.

"Well there is only one way down"

And he leaped of the bluff, and dropped down five feet, into the forest, Craig went next followed by Ian and then Mark.

They had to fight their way through the underbrush, finally coming to the river, the bank was verry narrow, and that was when they realized that to cross, they would have to swim a good sixty feet.

Craig pointed up the narrow bank, where there was a sandbar over to a huge rock in the middle of the river, it was a swim against the tide but making to the center rock meant that you went downstream and were spat out onto a small beach in the elbow of the Odistgeeg.

Mark said.

"We have to do this clothed, so make allowances"

Craig said.

"Oh shit, I've got Boom sticks, Ian take off your jacket, it the only waterproof one we have" Ian gave up his jacket instantly, knowing that it was important that they maintain the dynamite, Craig took the sticks and placed them in a sleeve, then he looped the sleeve into the jacket, making it waterproof.

Mark went in first, and swam with all his might, getting to the mid rock in record time, he stood up and waved the next boy on, as Mark continued his journey Ian was followed by Nick and then Craig, at the end of the journey, reached out and plucked Ian back into the flow, that would land him on the beach as he climbed up onto the bank from the sandy atoll he quipped.

"Wow, that could have ended in tears, thanks Craig" Craig went to him and embraced him.

"That's Ok buddy what are friends for if not saving your life from time to time"

He unraveled Ian's Jacket.

"Perfect and Ian here's your jacket back" Ian takes it and slings it over his shoulder and speaks.

"Onward and upward boys we have a ways to go" Again they found the undergrowth verry difficult to penetrate and after struggling for what had seemed like hours, and now they were moving on the light of a full moon, the forest began to clear and before much longer they had entered a clearing, standing there was a Boab tree, the boys approached it, its leafy foliage flickered to life, its eyes sprung from the smooth bark, a nose and mouth came to life the white flowers bloomed, it shook, the sound of the leaves on the branches almost sounded just like a laugh.

The boys approached the Boab, Craig saying as they approached.

"It's smaller, the other tree was easily eighty feet high" The tree shook again and spoke.

"Yes, I was bigger, I did grow to one hundred feet in fact, but you need to go back further to when I was but a seedling, I grew and grew but that was when I was harvested, pulled from the ground and milled into that house, LOOK"

The four boys were spinning, around and over and into another Neitherworld, and when they landed, they were standing at the base of the hill, at its top sat the Boab that Craig had remembered, it shook and flickered to life.

"This is the day I am to be harvested, I didn't want you to witness this, but it may be the only way to win this war, shh, stay quiet and watch"

And with that the four boys watched as Joshua Brown along with six men arrived to fell the massive tree, the whole job lasted a little over eight hours, which the boys endured hours of watching the Boab fight, and it did fight.

They began with axes which elicited from the Boab verry angry branches, they struck out at the men, striking two too the floor.

But eventually the Boab was much too tired, it had been weakened, in the end it was like the tree gave up.

The Boab shook and the boys were standing again before the young Boab.

"See" Ian answered quickly

"Yes I do see, your roots are still there, you are being stopped by the house, the mansion" The Boab eyes lit up, it shook, and its radiance lit up the clearing, they boys were bathed in a luminance that was magical.

The Boab spoke.

"My roots?" Ian considered for a moment.

"They may have harvested you, but your root system, it still exists"

"I am, and I have been, and I will be again, you need to know the evil of the Father, Desmond, he had known about me growing here, how I should not have grown so strong, so huge this far south in the country, my life force has been a part of the Crossing forever, but Desmond had learned about me from a traveler, who had been through the crossing and had seen me, it was then Desmond had made it his dream, to come find me, and to cut me from the earth, I exist IN THE HOUSE, I make up the decoration he used my beauty to highlight his stature, you have all been in the house, you have witnessed my beauty"

Mark said.

"We have all seen you, all the kids in town have been touched by you, I have dreamed about you for so long, I have grown up knowing, you"

Ian agreed, and Nick remembered the dreams as well.

Craig said.

"None of us remembered, after this, this time we will remember"

The Boab began to sing.

"Little boxes on the hillside, little boxes made of ticky tacky, little boxes on the hillside, Little boxes all the same" Nick took up the lyrics singing in perfect Falsetto.

"There's a green one and a pink one, and a blue one and a yellow one, and their all made out of ticky tacky, and they all look just the same"

Craig recognized the song as "Little Boxes" it was folk song by Malvina Reynolds, his dad like to sing, he would be whistling it wherever he went, often singing the words out loud while working in the garden, Craig spoke up as soon as the chorus stopped.

"Little boxes, dad is always humming or singing the tune all the time, how do you know the words Nick, I have never heard you sing it before?" Nick stood there with his hands up, he had no idea of how those lyrics popped into his head.

The tree shook and rattled.

"Its me, you all know, you are imbued with me, your patterns mimic me, I show up in your art works, I am everywhere, I am everything, you see Craig BOOM"

Craig placed his hand on his jacket the dynamite was still safe.

"You need to set the Boom sticks and detonate them, you know where, you know exactly where" "Yes I do know, I know where we need to set these, I came out at a cave entrance I had never known of before, it is switching time around on us, no strike that not us, the ghosts, Desmond and Joshua maybe even others"

The Boab shone its radiance through the boys, a multicolored aura all in shades of blue emanated down out from the limbs, its bark moved, pulsating its power through its roots and down into the ground, it emanated up and met its power centrally from where its limbs had set the pulsating, water blue to the deepest indigo.

The boys began to rise up from the ground, the pulsating auric lite, had shifted them a foot of the ground, then two feet, it was not long before they were fifteen feet into the air they were under an umbrella of foliage, it was at that moment the flowers began to open, Craig reached and pulled the blast caps from between the white petals of the flowers, Nick reached out and plucked a pad and pen from its flower, Ian took a flower and held it in his hands, Mark had taken hold of a branch, it snaped of easily in his hand, they were suspended in the light being lowered, to two feet from the ground, at that moment the light ceased and the boys all tumbled to the ground, they all sprung to their feet, dusting themselves off, the Boab was gone, standing there in its place was an old gnarly Eucalyptus Gum tree, the moonlight struck its higher limbs splitting the moonlight into a fractured kaleidoscope, the moonlight refracted through, breaking the moonlight into a myriad of color, the gum leaves ruffled awake, the tree shook, the eyes flickered open, its lips shaded by its huge nose of bark spoke.

"Who wakes me in the dead of the night?" Craig looked at Nick, then to Ian and Mark.

"Well, a speaking Gum tree, wadaya know, we woke you up wise old gum tree?" The gum shook and rattled and ruffled its leaves Eucalypt flowers rained down on them.

"Don't be so stupid boy, your insolence will not be tolerated, now listen" Craig bowed his head and said quietly to the tree. "I apologize I didn't mean to be so rude"

"That is a better attitude, I expected that kind of attitude from Nick, he is the youngest amongst you, Now listen, you need to remember this verry important point, when you set the charges they need to set in sequence and exploded in that sequence, you need to enter the water fall, at the park, the first charge is to be set at the junction, the second charge, to be set in the dead end, the third and final charge, set midway along the long corridor, then Boom, Boom, Boom, you got it,?" Craig said.

"The junction, the dead end, and midway, yes I have it"

The tree shook, and when its foliage was still again, its eyes were closed, its nose had turned out to be a broken branch, it was slumbering.

Mark held the stick up.

"I have no idea why I took this, but you all have an item so just go with it"

They went south from the talking trees to a section of the river that was much tamer, a rope bridge had been placed there the previous summer, it made the crossing safe and fast.

During the crossing the sun breached the dawn shining the light of a brand-new day.

They all managed the crossing and sat for a moment, they had to rest.

Nick broke their silence.

"We need a solid plan, so you have three to set, I say Ian and I will place them and you and Mark come behind us and set the blast caps"

Craig said instantly.

"I was thinking the same thing, but you know more about setting the lines, they will need a percussive joint at the point of each explosion, so swap Mark for you, you ok with that Mark?" "I sure am, I want to be as far away from you Craig as I can be, you look after the boom" They moved into the Pine forest heading toward the mill, they skirted out onto Old Town Road, and headed directly toward the waterfall.

It was running relatively fast, the boys new they had to get behind the waterfall, Craig followed them up into the cavern, The flower was a light, it lit the cave almost to day, the boys were able to find their way to where they needed to be, Ian and Mark went ahead as the boys lay the cable down, they begun at the junction where the cave branched off into two corridors, the and they set the charges as they were told, by the time Craig and Nick had returned to Ian and Mark, the waterfall had slowed down quite a lot, what was not lost on the boys minds was Lucinda, her body had been recovered, and they were certain Joshua would be in custody.

Craig backed up to the curtain of water, he warned them of the blast, they all prepared by placing their fingers in their ears.

Craig's mistake was not the single shock from the percussive outfall, but rather three sticks together, was much larger than any explosion he had ever witnessed.

He connected the leads to the detonator, said.

"Ready for the Boom boys?" The other three nodded.

Craig slammed the plunger down, and the result was immediate, the blast, which was felt from the town limits all the way back to the House on the hill that rattled, out to the Mine that sat a mile up past the mill, the boys were all thrown out through the curtain of water, and into the river.

Nick was hit by the percussive force first, he was tossed into a summersault, his eardrums shattered, blood erupted from not just his ears, but his nose as well, but the thing that hurt the most was when his clothing was ripped from his body, his shirt flared and disappeared, what was left of his trousers were naught, and his Groszby Scouts were blown straight of his feet.

Nick hit the water one hundred feet from the waterfall, when he hit the water, it shocked him back to consciousness, he began to sink, turned and headed to the surface, as he broke it, his face slicked with blood and snot, and the most magnificent ringing in his head, he had to breath out, what came was smoke, he exhaled as hard as he could and then heaved in the life saving rush of air.

Ian who was standing closest to the curtain was spared what Nick had endured, because Ian had decided to take the extra cover of the cave wall, the blast blew straight over him, his eardrums broke, but with no blood he had gotten off real light.

Mark had to deal with broken eardrums he was not directly in the line of the blast, he was flicked out and landed in the waterfall pond, Craig was still holding the blast plunger, when the shockwave hit him, it was debatable who got of worse, Craigs ears shattered as bad as Nicks, the capillaries in his nose burst, blood flooded out, Craig was backflipped out of the cave, he only travelled fifty feet, but that may have been the side wall of the cave slowing him down, Craig also had a broken collarbone.

It was not Marlii, that drowned, Craig had seen himself drowning until a huge hand grabbed him from the water, then he passed out.

CHAPTER SEVENTEEN

THE BOYS ARE BACK

Ian was released from the Shrives Island hospital, the following morning, Mark a couple of hours later, Nick as well as Craig had to stay in for a couple of days, they were checking them out.

All four of them had been aware when they blew the cave out, they were blasted, tossed and flipped back into 1974.

Ian and Mark were first visitors on the next day, they were rather excited, Mark could not contain himself, the two boys had found themselves sharing a double bedroom, Mark as he and Ian went pulled the door closed it shhhd on its pneumatic arm.

Mark held court.

"You wouldn't believe if you were looking at it" Ian took over.

"The house looks like its dyeing"

Mark began again.

"Everyone is talking about the blast, or as they call it an earthquake, but what I was able to find out the tunnels have changed, the epicenter was the house, my old man reckons we were playing in or around the waterfall when the earthquake hit, I don't know how he has put your injuries, but there was no explosion as far as the people in the town are concerned" Craig sat up in his bed, his collarbone had been aching he was waiting for the nurse to come in with his pain killers, the pain now forgotten, he was ensconced as Mark took up the story again.

"They believe the "Earthquake" shook to the whole region, it was felt as far away as Moe, three sticks of dynamite could never cause movement like that, apparently on the west of the spencer there was a huge subsidence of the bank, the water coming through there has doubled, but they have checked out the house, the cellar is completely flooded, all the way to the ground level, but it isn't dead yet, we need to finish it off" Nick managed.

"Wow" Craig got out of his bed and went to Nick's bed sitting on the opposite side of Ian and Mark.

They began their pow wow when the nurse came in, they stopped, she was young not more than a trainee, but she did have the nurse's uniform, she had the hat.

"So what are you boys discussing, I've been told to keep my eyes on you lot, Marlii has still not been found, she is missing aren't you boys concerned?" Craig offered.

"Do you think they will find her?" "They are searching for her as we speak, they have searched the cave, there is no sign of her" Craig then said.

"She was with us till the end, I have no ideas, what about you boys?"

Ian shook his head, the others agreed.

Her name was Jane, Craig saw her name badge"

"Right mister back into your bed, breakfast is coming, so you two need your medications" Ian and Mark got of the bed going to the armchairs sitting against the back wall of the room.

Ian asks.

"Can we stay?" "Yes why not?" "I was just asking; they may need an injection"

He enunciated Injection like it was an evil thing.

"No injections today, just pills, and rest"

She went Nick and puffed his pillow and did the same for Craig, the breakfast cart pushed through the door, the smells coming of the cart were bacon and eggs and toast, there was cereal for those who had a shifty constitution, the boys were in for a treat this morning.

Jane distributed the boys their meds, Craig was getting more Percodan, for his broken collarbone, the pain had been a mild gnawing on Craigs nerves, he was happy to get them, soon the pain would be nothing more than a dull ache, he had to live with that for a couple of weeks.

After Jane had left them to the breakfast custodian, he was a rotund man, he was rather short as well, but he was jovial.

"Hey boys, how are we this morning, gee the celebrities of Shrives Island, you boys are all over the news, Nick your old man was saying you were thrown one hundred feet, and just to think, the mine accusing you boys of breaking into the mine office, what happened with that by the way, the Mine Custodians backed off there pretty quickly didn't they"

Nick spoke up.

"They couldn't count, we had to bring it to their attention" This elicited laughter from the server, a hearty belching fun laughter, three of the boys began to join him, his laughing went up another notch when the boys joined him, that was Nick said.

"I was serious boys, it was us that straitened that mess out" And that was it, the boys were hysterical, the jovial server had tears coming from his eyes, he was able to slow down enough to spit out.

"I w was s serious Boys" Then he went up again followed by the three, hysterical laughter could be heard around the wards.

On the boys release, they gathered at Craigs for a complete debrief, Craig had his right arm in a sling, the first round of x-rays missed the fracture that ran along the radius of his shoulder.

The pain had been controlled but the plaster was beginning to itch.

Nick sat with his note pad and pen making notes, Ian had lost the flower when they were blasted out of the cave, but, the note pad had been in his room on the bedside table, and that was where Mark found his stick, it was on his bedside table sitting and waiting for him.

The blast caps and the flower had given the boys what they were meant to do, Nick kept the pad and pen on him from the time he found it, what would be their purpose, the branch, that Mark had managed to grab, served no real purpose at all, it was a stick, and it remained on his bedside table.

Nick Ian and Mark had been by to look at the house to report to Craig what was happening Ian led with the story.

"I think that house is hanging in there, yesterday it looked finished, today the paint is restored to the east face, it looks as if painters have been there working on it"

Nick adds.

"I think we need to go back; I know we have to go back; it needs to be finished"

Mark says. "It's dangerous, we were taking our lives in our own hands, heck we have no idea of where Marlii is" That was when Ian offered suddenly and coldly.

"Maybe she is dead, you too couldn't say that you know for sure she is safe" Craig said.

"Oh, she's alive I can usure you of that, I know I can feel her, no she is safe"

Mark quips.

"Well, we won't be going back in there unless you are with us"

"That's right I will be ready in days, and you better remember to bring your stick with you"

The morning rolled around Craig still had his arm in the sling, so he rode on the back of Mark's new XR 75, Ian rode on the back of Nicks bike.

They came out of Honeysuckle street onto Main street, they stopped their bikes, immediately there gaze was averted to the house on the hill Craig said. "Wow I have never seen it like this, I mean the damage from the last explosion, and the New Year's Eve soot blast, its sick, it is hanging on for dear life, cant the adults see it, it's like they are ignoring it?" Nick says.

"No they aren't ignoring it, like us they forget" Ian was curious.

"How can they forget so much that happens and just of late, the house has been attracting its fair share of news, scarry and otherwise, they are putting everything down, until the next event, the Boab needs us to carry on, we are who he, it has chosen" Nick gave his bike a couple of revs.

"Are you boys ready?" They all nodded and with no regard for not riding on the streets, he popped the clutch and took off toward the house, Mark dropped in behind him, and soon they were riding up the long driveway.

The changing faces of the house had been many prior to this day, and this was really different, it actually did look quite sick, its Towers were slowly falling away from the house, it's eaves were rotting out, the timbers were cracked and devoid of much paint at all, where paint did exist, it was now beginning to become patchy, its widows had turned opaque, allowing no view to the town, and no way of looking in.

Ian picked up a large red piece of scoria and pitched it at the window closest to him, it shattered into the house, and for a moment nothing happened, and then a huge gust of wind struck the boys from inside the house, it was a gale, when the wind stopped the house sunk and rose before them.

Birdsong, it was coming from the house, there was fluttering of wings and the birdsong was back again.

Nick asks.

"Did anyone else here that? Ian agrees.

"Yes, I heard that"

Then the birdsong was joined by chirping, then there was the unmistakable sound of the Boab shaking.

Mark says.

"I am sure I heard that, that's for sure"

Craig speculated.

"It's the Boab, it's telling us it is there for us, remember the house is unaware of the Boab" They went toward the front door, it was closed but not locked, and when Nick slowly turned the handle and shoved the door open, the water was lapping up to the doorway.

Craig got down on his butt and took of his boots, he tied the laces linking them around his neck, then he took of his socks stuffing them into his pocket.

"No use getting wet boys" In the next moment the other three were doing the same.

They waded into the house, the water was cold, ice cold, they found the cellar door an pushed it open, the water was up and over the whole stairway.

They went back out to the kitchen.

Ian asked. "So what now, what are we going to do?" Craig squeals.

"The stairs, Boom sticks, we will fire a short wick and get out of here" Craig started for the stairs, with the three behind him, he got to the first-floor landing and stopped.

Desmond Brown was standing at the top of the hall, in his hand he was holding three sticks of Dynamite, he was twining the wicks together, he was not looking in fine shape, his shock of hair had thinned out under his greying top hat, his eyes had sunk into his skull, and his ashen cheeks had disappeared into his face, he said to them all.

"Boom sticks, three almost did the trick" The cigar hanging from the rotting black lips almost shook free, but he was able to bring the trio of Boom sticks wicks, they came to life spitting their sparks everywhere he was laughing when he yelled.

"CATCH, hahaha"

Desmond flicked the dynamite toward Craig, and when it exploded, they were hit with a Tsunami of water, flushed down all the way through the cellar, the last they remembered was the pipes, the pipes were very thin, and were spat out into the Odistgeeg River.

The four boys were fished out of the Odistgeeg River for the second time in a week, they were all placed in hospital, all boys completely recovered, the girl was presumed lost and drowned, the boys, had no memory of what had taken place.

CHAPTER EIGHTEEN

SEPTEMBER 2001

Life went back to normal, everything at the house stopped months ago, Mark was with his stable and his horses, and Cindy, he had reconciled that the horrible time he had spent at home, at Shrives Island was a little bit more of bunk, he went back to saddling up winners, he had indentured the best apprentice in Melbourne, a fifteen year old Professor, the kid could sit on anything, and get them to work, it was like he had known what to say to them, all of Roy's horses were the calmest you would have ever known, his old man had kicked him of the country property, because he was light enough to ride winners, if you were light enough to ride winners that was what you would do.

His relationship with the "Old Man" had always been a tight one, and Roy ended up in the stable of Mark Harris, well, he could not have done any better.

Mark was whistling, he whistled when he was nervous, the Cup was tomorrow, Stanley, or Anchors Away was sound, and he had a young boy up.

He walked along checking that the bottom bolts to the boxes were shut, at least one of them would be out sniffing around the feed room if that bottom lock wasn't in place, the top bolt was easy, a slick tongue and the bolt just slips out, as he approached Stanley's box all was quiet, he took a Pall Mall from the crushed pack out of his work shirt, struck a match and lit up, all the staff finishing earlier in the afternoon, it was a tradition at "The Downs" cup eave close up and get out by one PM.

Mark likes to get the cup eve feed done on his own steam, no distractions, while he smoked his cigarette, he looked out over the freshly raked yard, the day yards all raked and set for, The winner, have a roll in the sand a big feed.

He crushed the smoke with the heel of his boot, and picked up the but, putting it in the bin, he then went in and said goodnight to the horses.

He, shut of the lights and walked the short distance to the house he walked in through the laundry, Cindy was in the sitting room, she was reading a Nick Lester, he went to her leaning in for a kiss, she hugged him tightly.

"Your nerves are kicking in I can feel it" "I know, I know, Stanly won't let us down" "I know this, he never has, I think your nerves are about Roy the boy, he was a find, you know his old man, hey I spoke to Roy this afternoon, there was not a nervous muscle in that kids body, don't sweat it" "Well this is a wonderfully comfortable place to be, but I need to go finished up in the office, shut down my pc, turn off the light, and come back to this comfy position"

He kissed her and went down to his office, he walked in going to his pc, shutting down the browser, it hummed out its final tune before the audible "click" and the pc went to sleep, his gaze fell on the stick, the branch that had shown up on his bedside table so many years ago, he had known it meant something, he picked up the stick turned it in his hands like he had so many times before, the sheen that now existed over the grain, it was very fine, the more he rolled it around in his hand the more the luster came through, it was a dark brown now, the shadow from the grain giving it almost a two tone look, its gnarly end was like a handle almost, he placed the stick down where it lived, a mystery for the ages, he got up switched of the light, and left the room headed back to the welcoming arms of his wife.

The nerves that Mark had fluttering around his head were completely gone, the Cup was on, he came out of the Jockeys room with Roy, the young boy had his hands crossed his whip in his right hand he was listening intently to everything he was telling him.

"You know he can get back a long way in the beginning, but when you round the home turn, you need to be up on the leaders, looking for a run as close to the rails as you can get, don't let him drift, if he drifts you will lose this, got it?" "Got it, I think we will be right, the field is full though" "Just remember what I told you" "All good"

Roy went around to the horse and grabbed his head by the headgear, the horse lowered its head, Roy whispered something to him, the horse snorted an answer and nodded its head up and down.

Mark grabbed Roy around the shin and legged him into the saddle, the strapper began to lead the horse around as Roy adjusted his gear.

"Right Mr. Harris lets go get this Cup"

Mark saluted Roy and Stanley as they went through the gate leading out onto the straight, and watched him turn and canter away, Mark went to the stand.

Stanley was relaxed all the way to the barriers, once behind them he walked and trotted not barely breaking a sweat, Stanley was called up he walked into his gate and it was shut behind him, they were set.

Stanley waited for the gates to open, this was a walk in the park, remember what the boy had told him, jump sit and sprint, he wasn't flat footed out of the barrier but he had known there would be trouble just after the jump, his pause set him on a perfect trail, he dropped back and settled on the fence he was tracking faster than anything in the field, as they passed the eighteen hundred post he was beginning to travel, if he staid where he was, he would be stuck behind a wall of horses, there was nothing on his outside so he began to drift, he was one off the fence, now two, then three, as they rounded the turn onto the back straight Stanley was working three out, and he had eighteen horses in front of him, WAIT, he continued on along the back straight picking of horse after horse, WAIT, coming down the side he had picked of nearly everyone, seven to go, and as they came into the home stretch he said to himself, SPRINT, as fast as he could, six horses still to catch then three then two, he made it to the front of the field, and the boy told him to go harder and get to the rail, Stanley kicked down to his final gear, and shot off away from the rest of the field, crossing the finish line eight lengths in front of number two.

Anchors Away 1st	$10.00 Win	
	$2.40	Place
Brooms Folly 2nd	$2.50	
Copper Sent 3rd	.50 C	

That dividend was mighty fine, the owners cleaned up on track, and Mark had his fee.

How much did Mark and Cindy invest on the race?

That was a well held secret, and while he had many accolades, the night had belonged to Anchors Away, as well as Roy.

Mark took that excuse to leave the party early, not wanting to whoop it up in town, they had booked into the Nova, why not enjoy the night, looking over the field of his victory, the room he had booked overlooked the straight, they would sit out on the balcony and sip on margaritas.

Stanley was being looked after by those who cared for him most.

They had done it, first trainer to win the cup, two times up, Cindy was such a big part of it.

When they had met Mark had no memory of his childhood, she had heard the stories and some of them were just so far of the Richter scale they left the past behind, left Shrives Island, Mark taking a job as a foreman for the most eminent trainers of the time, Cindy plied her trade as an equine vet and together they had made a wonderful career.

But the highlights were lost, even trying Invitro Fertilization they had had no luck, and that was what they thought they had been, successful on the track, but they wanted so much to have children they wanted to be doing this for a reason, why build it if it had a use by date?

You didn't, and that was why Mark and Cindy sat there that night, at the top of the straight looking down toward the finish line, too far away, Cindy was sitting with a glass of Yellow, Mark was drinking a bourbon straight over ice Cindy said.

"You know, I would give all this up to have a baby, be dirt poor farmers, etching out a living, with kids to help, hey it would be hard, but we chose the way of the money I think it was destined that we are all to be left without children, but I know it is more than that what about Nick and Jess, Jess being the only one of us born outside Shrives Island, Ian and Cathy, and you can't forget Craig, I just cannot get around the fact the four of you, none of us can reproduce, it's not lost on me, too much of a coincidence, what did happen to you in. 74' it affected all of you, not just in the physical way you have all had your mental break downs"

Mark thought for a moment and spoke.

"I have never felt comfortable going back there whenever I am forced back there and I say forced because every time I go back there I want to leave almost immediately, Mum has been happy there, and you know the other weird thing, strange phenomena, all of us were only children, except in the case of Marlii, she had an older brother, who survived three tours of Vietnam, Cath and yourself, only children, and now you have Nick and Jess taking over the children's lives, I never felt they were doing the right thing, the correct thing to do"

Cindy said. "Well what would have you done, how do you think we would have handled the gathering of two ghost children, would we take them in, I think we would, you saw them, living breathing blood pumping human beings"

Fireworks began over the finish line, this was what they had come to see, fireworks in honor of Anchors Away, for Roy, and for the owners, but especially for Mark, it was a childish indulgence he had enjoyed all his life, they had both remembered the Fire Works put on by the Custodians of the town, and as the trace shot silver, gold blue green and red, purples magentas all exploded above them into an umbrella of multi colored lights.

Ian and Cathy had settled back in Terry Hills in Sydney's Harborside, the gigs had continued to come in a monotonous gathering.

Their last album release broke the Billboard Top 100, entering at fourteen with a bullet, and managed to take top spot and stayed there for two weeks, but the singles taken from the album stayed in the charts for months, and just recently at the local shopping center, Ian was approached by a local politician and asked for a selfie, Ian obliged, but realized he had a Pollie fan, he didn't know if he liked that.

They had loved their spot, a dock sat on a small beach, which they used to find their way around, friends, shops, he liked being on the water, but he missed his Mustang, that was being cared for by his mechanic in Pyrmont, getting a tune, it was running squeaky clean but Roger loved that Mustang maybe more than him? no, not anyone loved that Mustang more than he did

He pulled the boat up to the mooring setting the boat at rest, Cathy had tied her up and was headed up the dock with the supplies for the evening party they were to have, to celebrate the success of the last album.

Ian set up the Bar B Q and Cathy started on the salads, the first of the guests would be here in thirty minutes, and nether Ian or Cath were dressed, they came together in the bedroom, Cathy asking Ian to Zip her, he zipped her into an emerald, green dress, her hair would have to do as she passed the brush through it, then Ding Dong.

The guests had all but arrived on time all at the same time, bottles of wine were added amongst the beers and bourbon bottles who had found a home in the ice filled bath tub, deserts galore were placed in the refrigerator, the cooking had begun, the band members gathering around the cook, it was then announced that the drummer was having a kid, this announcement had led the night festivities, Ian found Cathy, sitting in the room where their dreams were not being fair to them.

They had set this room up in hope, but their hope was never realized, she was crying, sobbing, Ian went to her sitting beside her, taking her into him hugging her he said.

"Shh"

Cathy said through broken sobs.

"It's not fair, we have been trying more than anyone, I don't care about the money for IVF but I am so over the trying, Nick and Jess lucked out, those twins have been good for them, but Mark and Craig, all of us have the same problems not being able to produce, you have all had your own success, you and the band really hit it big with that last album, I have always wanted a child, now all the bandmembers have offspring, all but us" Ian offers.

"Comon come back and join the party, help them celebrate, we will give IVF another try, the doctors are confident with the new protocol, once more around the block" Cathy brightened up dried her eyes and said.

"Once more round the block"

Back at Shrives Island Life had continued on, preparations to open the Mansion to the artists of the world.

Both Miranda and Tim had been excelling at school, the town had taken the twins into its fold, the whole town of Shrives Island had been living a lie, tourism had died down, Craig had been going to the Mill daily putting in hours on behalf of Ethan, he worked the same saw that Ethan had worked oh so recently, Craig had been on a penance kick, he had still felt responsible for the meltdown, all had said at the time, the events at the Mill and the hauntings at the house had been a weird time, but, the two children in the care of Nick, and Jessica, was foul.

Nick had been working feverishly on a new novel, under wraps, Jessica had been painting, she had begun a Boab tree, just that week.

That was when she went to speak to Angie, she had painted a Boab, once, Jess had seen that painting, shoved into a cupboard where her most spooky pieces went, why was it spooky.

When Angie had visited Jess early one Saturday morning, Jess had been working on her Boab, this elicited a conversation, it was begun by Angie.

"Oh, that is wonderful"

Jess looked at Angie, she took note of the happy surprise on her face and said.

"Do you remember the painting in your wardrobe, you have a Boab in there don't you?" Angie face turned sour.

"Oh, yes, that I have no idea as I said I don't even remember painting it"

Jess went to her.

"Pull it out, look at it, there is a message there, the evidence that we have found about Michael Longstreet, I mean, I don't know, I didn't see anything evil in that painting I don't think you should either, take it out, look at it, you will be surprised how much you may remember" Angie nodded her head and spoke.

"Ok, I will get it out when I get home, and I will look at it, see what transpires"

Later she held an audience with her Mother and Father, Jill stood and looked at the painting, Angie had set it up on an easel in the lounge room, against a window that allowed the light to fall in the right direction.

Graeme stood next to Jill, his hand went to his chin, Angie asked excitedly.

"Well, what do you two think?"

Jill broke the silence.

"Its wonderful, your colors are well set, the way the blue bleeds in to the green, and the Boab is stand out, when did you do this?"

"Months ago, um I don't remember when, dad what do you think, you haven't said anything" Graeme was looking at the tree, having a connection to the Milling in town, he was mesmerized by her painting.

"You know, when I was younger, I dreamed about that tree, that particular Boab, I'm sure of it, its an amazing painting, the colors are amazing"

He fell silent but stood in the same spot, he was studying the painting, then he said.

"I can't believe it, I think this is weird, but I have no explanation" Angie said.

"I don't need and explanation dad, but it seems like I painted this from your memory" Jill spoke up.

"I dreamed of this tree, I didn't want to say anything, until he made the admission, I know I used to dream of this tree" Angie stated.

"I completely blacked out when I painted this tree, I began it one morning a little while ago, I have no memory of painting this"

THE FOURTH INTERLUDE
ANGIE

H^{i!} My name is Angie Bell, I am seventeen years old, I am
Gothic, I follow it like a religion, not like the city Goths, I don't
generally go for troop boots and black, but I have a ritual based
on the pagan arts, I have an Alter set up in the lounge both mum
nor dad have really tried to influence me to church, but you will
see me from time to time at the Baptist church, I like to listen to
the Reverends sermons, I have favorites, like when he speaks of
pride, to be proud of what you do, but to be humble, that was a
Sermon for those to be saved, he did, in every church gathering
saved someone.

Mum nor dad have ever been religious.

I Like color, it is a part of my life you see I am an artist, both of
my parents along with anyone that meets me say I am a prodigy, I'm
not, I have been painting from verry early age, I sold my first canvas
at age four, that was to a philanthropist from Queensland.

My paintings hang everywhere, they hang in many galleries, but
my personal customers, they range from timber workers to rock stars.

I know being a bit factitious there, sorry, but I am here to talk about The Island, that's what we younger generation call it, Shrives, no, just The Island, my seventeen years here have been rather interesting, just so you are aware, I went to Melbourne once, to stay with an Aunt and Uncle, dads brother who had left the Island, many years before, I didn't like the bustle there, it was all to rushed, I was Glad to get back here.

School has been interesting, never many students at the school, I always had a good education, I think what I know about Shrives Island, or The Crossing, is verry interesting, but no more interesting than Jess and Nick, taking "The Orphans" as they are becoming known in the town, I don't think it matters what I think, but I can tell you that both Jess and Nick, have taken those children on as their own, but they have a history, because they were resurrected, by Nick, they had been dead for one hundred years, don't get me wrong, without them, The Island would be a much more boring place, but I think keeping them, I mean keeping them alive is the wrong thing, I think that they should have the opportunity to return to their parents, I know it could be done, I think that they are a rather large part of the puzzle, they are the key.

After learning more about the Boab, that was an awakening, both of my parents had dreamed of that exact same tree, coincidence? I don't think so, but I am finding out about that at the moment, I have been needling both of my parents daily, extracting information, and bit by bit, I am maybe getting a handle on this.

I have been thinking about the Boab that Jess has just completed, how similar it is to mine, right down to the colors, the shading around the leaves, the flowers and there form how similar the paintings are, teacher, student, same wave length, it is more than that, the ghosts who have recently fallen verry silent, and based on that one fact, the silence for so long they are about to open the house to lots of artists, I don't know how this will end, however I believe that allow guest, they will awaken those who have fell into a slumber, The Desmond Brown Mansion has kept coming into the limelight now and again, through the hundred year history of this town, no, I think it will end badly.

There is something underneath the house that has to break free, in my opinion, if there exists a hell, that house is a doorway to another world, or worlds, the hill that it sits on, is alive.

I think I feel it whenever I am there.

I am going over to the house this afternoon, I have done as Jess had suggested as you know, I have looked at the painting.

I need to see the piece that Jess just completed, I need to really look at the color, look at the shading, and I need the opinion of Nick as well.

At least at the moment things are relatively quiet, up at the house I mean, I believe the furniture for the rooms on the second level turn up today.

That means they are less than a week away from opening.

CHAPTER NINETEEN

DOWN AMONG THE DEAD MEN

Nick had come to Jessie, he had a galley in his hand, part of the novel he was writing, he said as he placed the manuscript down in front of Jess.

"Well, here, first hundred and fifty pages" She picked it up, looking at the facing page she looked at the title, "Little Boxes" By Nick Lester. The © on the facing page had told her he was serious.

She says. "Little Boxes" what does it mean?" "Read it, just read it, I'm being truthful, why not tell the whole story, this tells the story as I remember it, with what has happened of late, I have written in a flood, it's all there, Miranda and Tim, Desmond Brown, Joshua Brown, you, me Craig, Ian as well Mark, the girls, all occurrences we have proof of, hell everyone is in the book, Steve, Rhonda, Angie, I even put a bit in there about Jill and Graeme, I think it will sell, and its good, needs an edit but the once over will be good" She leafed through it, reading the first few pages and skipped ahead, she had known the story, she had known what had happened, it was succinct, as she read through the galley, Nick made himself useful, going to the kitchen and getting them coffee, when he returned she was ensconced, he placed her coffee down on the table beside her, he then went and sat in the easy chair beside her.

"So, what do you think?"

"Its brilliant, it is succinct, but if it gets out about the kids we will have hell to pay, after the ridicule do you think either one of us will have a career, how do you think the fans would take it" "So, you have to suspend your belief, I don't know, this has happened to us, we have witnesses to back up our story and our story collaborates all the others, I think we sent it my ed, see what she thinks"

The new thermo induction arrived, Nick had to be there to see it fitted in the cellar, right in the spot the old Boiler had blown, the wall, and the infrastructure had been replaced, and repaired, they had to heat the house a room at a time when it got chilly, a small price to pay for the new thermo induction that was put through the whole house.

The induction system ran to the main vent and spread to all three floors the new aluminum ducts would be quieter than the old boiler pipes that was for sure.

The gas fitters had been down in the cellar a little over an hour, when the foreman came up the steps of the cellar, he came out to find Nick in the kitchen.

"We are all done down there Mr. Lester, please come down so I can show you how to fire it up"

Nick followed the tradesman back down the stairs, it was a rather simple process, Nick had listened as the foreman explained to close the main valve before switching the system back to start, he explained how the monitor on the wall would tell him the status of the heater and where the warm air was going.

Nick shook the men's hand's and spoke.

"Thanks for that, it is much easier than the old boiler would have been, so now it is set, great" Nick led the men up the stairs, and through the kitchen too the hallway where he said a parting goodbye, he closed the door and turned to see Jess on the stairs.

"Wow that heating is great, but I think it is up a little too much" Tim came out from the library and Miranda who had been up on the second floor, helping prepare the rooms for grand opening, she had appeared on the top landing, and had yelled down.

"Hey, the heaters are working, but maybe it's a bit high"

Nick looks at Tim.

"Sissie's, can't handle the heat" He goes to the control panel on the wall by the kitchen and thumbs down the temp, he had found the ambient point, and locked it in.

Later that night, after Jess and the Twins had gone out to catch up with Rhonda, who was helping, with putting the paperwork together that would win back for the children what they had ownership off, Nick had felt uncomfortably cold, he checked the monitor and it was saying it was a balmy twenty-one degrees, but no, he now had his dressing gown on.

He went to the cellar and hit the light switch; he went down the steps to the cellar floor.

That was when it happened, the door slammed shut, and the lights went out, he was standing at the bottom of the stairs in pitch black, and then the furnace lit up, the old furnace, the furnace that had decided to blow itself out of the cellar one day in spring, Nick remembered the blast that was not just seen from the school but the children who had been out on the oval, all got to see the blast, but here it was and it was firing up, the tongues of flame were finding themselves licking through the grate growing as they reached out to singe Nick's dressing gown, then they died.

Then from behind him

"Nick pst"

Nick spun around, and was looking at Desmond, he was dressed as he remembered, Top hat, riding breaches and a fine surcoat, but they were only remnants of how Nick had remembered him, his hat was sunken, like an accordion, under it was an emaciated Desmond brown, his eyes were translucent, the skin around the cheeks had turned green, his lips had all but rotted off, and in his pallid skeletal hand was a cigar, he bought his hand up to his rotting check, drew in a breath of smoke and said.

"You know Nick, you can really taste the old Kentucky Red Eye in these, as good as the day they were packed" Nick laughed and spoke.

"You are slipping Mr. Brown, you are losing it, nothing is original any more, and to look at you, the twins are the reason you are rotting on your feet, you will be nothing before long" The Desmond thing had thought to itself, blame the children, but I know it is the Boab, he said.

"Well Mr. Lester, Without being too forward, you need to bring the boys back here, you know unfinished business, get it over and done with, get rid of the rif raf" Nick saw a shadow behind him, it was Desmond's son Joshua, and another this time it was Michael Longstreet, he was hauling a chain along with him, attached to the chain, were more lost souls, it wasn't long before the cellar was rather full, the "Attached Ghosts" were never ending, victims were among them, but he had known the difference, because those who were harmless, never maligned him.

The lights had begun to flicker sending the beings present into a grey sullen light, but the lights finally gave up, now amongst the victims, Nick had a protective shroud around him.

Desmond and Joshua had remained front and center, and one he had a semblance of but could not place a name, was it Pricilla, Lucinda, he couldn't remember?

Little boxes.

He had remembered that song at that moment.

It was Lucinda he was sure of that now; the song words were clear; it was Lucinda vocalizing the words.

"Little boxes on the hillside

Little boxes made of ticky tacky

Little boxes on the hillside

Little boxes all the same

There's a pink one and a green one and blue one and a yellow one

And there all made out of Ticky Tacky and they all look just the same"

He looked around him those nasty ghosts were fading away and what he was left with were the spirits of the sane people that had passed at the hands of those evil ones.

Lucinda spoke to him.

"Nick, remember the song"

"I do, I remember the song, Little Boxes on the hillside, and they are made of ticky tacky"

Lucinda who was now floating on the ether above him, the dress that he remembered her in from the Neitherworld was gone, she was now in a red gown, glowed a crimson, the color began to return to all the ghosts present, Lucinda was now beside him on the floor, her long Auburn hair flowed on the breeze, her face now discernable, he looked closely at her features, her blue eyes shone brightly in the gloom, her completion, pale as alabaster pink allowed the perfect light to bounce around the cellar.

Lucinda said.

"Nick, there is more you need to know, I have some people here for you to meet, this is Elizabeth Grange" The woman who appeared in front of him was simply stunning, her blonde curls hung limply on the side of her face, and her blue eyes were as blue as sapphires.

"And this is Jack Grange" The ghost that came forward was a strong man, he wore a drover's hat, the face shaded by it was sun chiseled, his eyes, brown, burned out at him, he had a smile slightly there on his face.

Victoria came to him.

"We want our children back, we miss them, we cannot continue until they are with us"

Jack pleaded.

"Please, allow them to go, to come back to us" Nick was feeling lightheaded but managed to say.

"The twins, are your children, you are the woman in the cameo" Victoria stood there and nodded, jack had said the twins were all they existed for.

Nick passed out and went into the dark.

He was awakened an hour later when Jess and the twins had arrived home, Tim had noticed the Cellar door open, and the lights on, he went down the steps, finding Nick passed out, or asleep, he was shaking him as Jess and Miranda came down the into the cellar.

He began to come too, he looked at Jess and then to Tim and Miranda he said to all of them.

"We all need to have a discussion, it's an important one"

In the afternoon a huge thunderstorm rolled across the mountains and into the valley, destroying roofs, as well as buildings, the Lester's were safe and sound in their mansion, although on top of the hill even the towers were safe.

In the downstairs lounge the four were settling in for their conversation, Tim and Miranda, sat on the two-seater, Nick and Jess on the couch opposite the twins.

It was Nick who began.

"I know how you two kids feel about us, I have come to love the two of you, so has Jess" The twins looked at Jess, she nodded, the twins looked back to Nick he continued.

"But I know how much you miss your parents, Victoria and Jack" The twins face's lit up Nick went on.

"I feel making this choice would be simple, in different circumstances, but I am afraid we only really have one choice, and that is you two must return to nineteen hundred, back to Mum and Dad" Tim and Miranda were stunned, Miranda sat there with her mouth open, Tim was shaking his head.

Jess said.

"You are going back to where you know, back to those who love you and care for you"

Miranda said.

"Whoa stop" Everyone sat their looking at Miranda, she turned to her brother and spoke.

"The life force, that is what is surging through us, through them, it's the tree, it's the Boab" Tim broke in.

"I told you about the Boab, it was here before this house" Jess spoke.

"I have just finished painting a Boab, I was going to show you today, before the confusion, but it got forgotten"

Nick slapped himself in the face.

"This house, what do you say, this house me, and Mark, Craig, and Ian, we, ah, I remember it all, the rush in my memory is unbelievable, we need to be out of this house, we must destroy this house" Tim was sitting a smile drew across his lips.

"Yes, blow it sky high"

CHAPTER TWENTY

REMEMBERING

The clarity of their remembrance was brilliant.

Mark had taken his stick and placed it in the safe, Nick had kept the children close to himself and Jess, Ian had arrived back in Shrives Island along with Cathy the same day he fell into the clarity, his mind had opened the most, maybe that had to do with the music, he was immersed in music.

They decided to meet at Uncle Pete's Ian and Cathy were waiting when Nick Jess and the twins walked in.

They went over to where Ian and Cathy had placed themselves at the largest table, which was at the back of the restaurant, Pete wave to the four as they came in and went back to what he was doing.

Ian started up straight away.

"This place is out of control, we didn't finish it back in seventy-four, and that house you are living in is pure evil, you are living in the stomach of the beast, do you know that?" Nick offered.

"Oh we know, but we need to be there while we have the twins, they are at their weakest when the children are here, and that may have something to do with the fact that the kids are going back"

Ian was not surprised.

"When and how are we sending them back" Tim broke in.

"Back down through the cellar, our parents will be waiting for us in the Neitherworld, when?

that is up to you lot" Jess speaks up.

"I can feel it almost as much as Nick, the tree, the dreams, I mean I have seen what this house can do, I can only imagine the magic at work here, the tree, Master Boab, is through everyone in this town, his waters have nourished the people, you are all the product of it" Cathy joined in.

"The dreams, I had shared them with Ian early on, but when I witnessed Desmond's hold over both myself and Ian, my awakening was sudden"

That was when nick added.

"And if anyone knows the result of Mr. Joshua Brown being arrested for a murder he had committed earlier, he never did the deals with Grange, he never killed your parents, he never got to either of you"

Nick looked at Timothy and Miranda,

"You two have so much to return too, but we need to be rid of the entities, because as you can imagine, with the advent of Joshua's untimely hanging, for the murder, he should not have chosen a sweetheart of the town, but he has been a ghost now for that long he thinks he is invincible with the support of his father"

Pete was beside them with his order pad, the Granges logo on the pad was new, Nick had thought to himself, there were small noticeable changes in the nuance of the town, but it wasn't complete, something was missing.

Pete stood for a moment listening in for the close of the conversation then he spoke.

"I think they will keep getting thinner and Thinner until they just disappear into the either, wait and see" Nick offered.

"I think there will be a bit more noise than you think, we are going to end this" Pete held his hands up and said.

"Oh you mean, ah what are you planning?"

Ian said.

Please Uncle Pete, if you want to be a part of this conversation, please sit down" Nick reached over and grabbed the closest chair, patting it he said.

"Sit here" Pete sat down and set his ordering pad on the table, there were only a couple of other diners there on that day, Rose would care for them Uncle Pete said.

"So what do you mean end this?" Nick went on.

"You remember when we broke into the mine, we were suspected of breaking in to prove that the mine couldn't keep inventory, well they couldn't count, because we still have sticks of that stuff stashed" Pete looked rather frightened.

"How did you pull it off and where did you stash it?" Nick says.

"Well if my Spidey senses are correct, I say it is stored in the east tower of our house, I remembered just recently, I don't know how long Craig has remembered, if he has remembered at all, and that reminds me, I need to speak to Steve, he will know where he is, he just shot through, without a word to any of us"

Pete added.

"He came in and saw me when he left town, what are you talking about, he told me he had to go to Sydney, he did say he wanted to keep mum on it as long as he could, but you all know now, so he will be back in a couple of days with Root Stock, Glen Innes he said he had to go to, that was it Glenn Innes"

Craig had remembered, in a rush, and it had kept coming back, as he pushed the old ford up as far as he would allow himself, he was on the final leg to a town he had been in a number of years earlier.

He had stopped at Armidale half an hour earlier, and had just had another memory flash, it had been a waking dream, he had spoken to Marlii, she had said to him.

"Yes keep going, Glenn Innes, that is right" And with that he had remembered where he should go.

Running along the road into town he was looking for a street from his memory, "Lambeth St"

He had found it and turned and continued down to the end of the street, before it continued up and over a disused railway line, he pulled up at the last house on the right.

An old weatherboard house sat squat on the piece of land it had found itself on, the old house looked rather neat, its fresh shocking coat of white paint, made it a jewel amongst the old mining gear, four-wheel drives, and trailers all with assorted mining tools that had sat gathering the grass to grow up amongst it, the mower had left it in an island in the middle of the two acre block.

Craig looked to see the light on in the kitchen he was up, not unusual, well not for a sixty-year-old.

But Craig was here to see a man about a dog, a very old dog.

He walked up along the path, lined with gerbera's as well as posies, he opened the screen door and knocked, the door opened, the man standing there was old and decrepit, he held himself up with a cane, in his left hand he held a port sipper.

He was almost one hundred and eight years old, his name was Henry Lester.

"Come in, quickly, you are letting the heat out"

Craig obliged him stepping in through the side door into a sunroom, closing the door behind him, he kicked of his boots and followed Henry into the kitchen, clean as a pin, everything in its place.

"What do you want, Port, coffee, tea, what do you want" "I will have a coffee thank you" "So you are back, I suppose you need to pick it up, you want the root stock"

Craig nodded and spoke.

"Yes, I have had a rush of memory just in the last couple of hours, what I know horrifies me"

Henry looked over at Craig, he was stirring sugar into his coffee and says.

"Horrifies you, why do you think I have never been back since 1906, I say any one just visiting there is taking their own lives into their hands, I have always said that town would end one day, seems the heroes are coming to save it, that house I will never forget that house"

Craig responds.

"I think the real hero, has been in a living hell since 1974, Marlii, I have spoken about her to you often, I know I could get her back" Henry puts Craig's cup down heavily.

"Don't ever assume, because you are saying you know, doesn't make it so, and if you don't get her back, you can't cry about it, if you do this, you do it for the Boab" "I realize we have to do it for the Boab, all those years ago, when we first met, you had been fossicking around the old Smythdale diggings, doing real well too I must say, you knew who I was, you had known that I had been friends with Nick, I never put it together, but you had me pegged, so why did my memory not jig then, why no clarity until just recently?" "That would be the root stock, why do you think I have lived so long, good diet, no smokes, and fat, no I would have never lived this long if not for the root stock, it has memorized the whole town, in fact, I have been wondering how long I would go on once the root stock is gone"

He snaps his fingers and speaks.

"Probably just like that"

Henry grabs the port and tops up his drink, while he is up he tops up Craig's coffee.

"Let me go get it, you sit here and drink your charr"

He shuffled out of the kitchen going to his room, he returned a couple of minutes later with a box, Henry placed it down in front of him.

"You need to use it like a graft, and it has to be neat, real neat"

Craig looked at the timber, the box had been formed from, the thought was the Boab, he watched its grain swirl in front of him, on the lid, on the sides, even on the bottom, you could not escape the timber, it looked alive, the grain was bleeding in front of him.

He lifted the lid. "Whoa"

In front of him was a small piece, of the root system of the Boab, Adansonia Gregorii.

Craig was taken back by the small piece of the tree he was looking at, it was pulsating, a solid green light, but as it emanated outward the light softened, and radiated through both of the men, they had both seen the colors from the tree light were all on the spectrum, from the sheerest silver and every color in between, blues, greens, yellows, reds, into purples, it instantly stole the breath from Craig.

Henry stood there he took in a huge gulping breath of air and said.

"Sorry I should have warned you about the first blast, that one is a real breath stealer" Craig had grabbed the corner of the table, he had needed to steady himself, even though he had been sitting, Henry came over and closed the lid of the box, and again the grain in the wood continued to speak.

Craig coughed, wheezed, almost choking, the old man patting him on the back, he said.

"When you have lived through a few more of those, you know you're alive" It was not long after, he left Glenn Innes for Victoria, back to Shrives Island.

THE FIFTH INTERLUDE
HENRY LESTER.

Hey, we recently met, my name is Henry Lester and I am 110 years old.

So yes I could tell you a once a time story, but you would never believe me, I don't care, I have lived as long as I have, not through a healthy diet, or a regimen, let's just say I had a traveler with me, when I say traveler I don't mean the sly stubby down the side of the seat, I am talking a real TRAVELER.

I know, I know, you have questions to ask of me, well they can wait, and you can sit there and listen to me prattle on for a while, I have been here longer than most and what I have seen would bleach your hair without a skeric of sun.

I came to the crossing in 1905, I was just shy of fifteen, I made a lot of money early, most of the gold fields had stop yielding anything, at The Crossing they were still pulling out by the shovel full, I married, at sixteen, she was eighteen, and she had known I was a workhorse, and she managed me well, Irene was her name, and be buggered if she didn't keep me on my toes all our married life, she was my darlin from the very beginning until she up and died on me two years ago, so maybe that is it, I may only have two years left, better get my affairs in order, that two years will fly by.

But I am getting off track.

In 1905, when I arrived at The crossing, soon to be renamed Shrives Island, as I had begun, I did rather well off the Milling, they paid timbermen well, if you could cut the mustard, I had attracted my brother here by 1906, Reginald Lester, he is the one you want to follow if you want a lead into Nick Lester's line, Reginald was five years my senior, and he did some very tidy business in the town, and set up the Lester mantle there at the Island, Reginald would be, let me think, Nick's Grandad, he is still kicking, they don't talk much about him, I think they were somewhat disgusted with how he did some "Tidy Business" in the town.

But I am getting a little ahead of myself there.

However, the line had come down to when Jack had defied his father, and they ended their relationship, in a verry bitter way, when Jack and Estelle were killed in the collision, his Grandad had wanted to take care of him, but by then Nick was writing, and he sure didn't need any one taking care of his business, the rest you all know is history.

But how will he explain this away to mainstream media? He didn't think he would need to,

Me I think it was destiny that he bought that house, and I know how this is going to end, Ka Boom,

And all the others, especially that crazy bastard, I was talking to when we met, Craig, we know his destiny is tethered to Marlii, Ian and Mark, were victims because they chose to be a part of it.

But I can tell you, now, with Craig going back to The Crossing, well things are going to get crazy, oh the ghosts, they don't stand a chance in the end, with the twins being thrown into the mix, it all had the ingredients of going a really bad way, well that showed me didn't it, the kids had them by their throats from day dot, I mean the dead kids, any other time, they may have just been "Haunters" but the powers that those twins possess, are nothing short of awesome, I do remember a history of them, how they had been kidnapped, but that wasn't true, they were murdered, but you know that story.

Me I have been at The Crossing a number of times, but no matter how far I wander, with the little bit of Adansonia Gregorii that I passed on to Craig I had The Crossing in my pocket, I have mined everything from gold, the finest Black opal, I have found diamonds in the Kimberley's.

I have lived a long fruitful life, we lived in the most spectacular places, from The Crossing, to far north Queensland, across to the west, where we had the opportunity of witnessing the Boab in all its glory, The Alice, but what we saw overseas was tremendous, Italy, we were there in 1926, I was there to Garner a diamond and Opal deal, it went off very well thank you, so much so, we stayed on in Sorento, right by the jewel they call The Bay of Naples, I wouldn't want to describe it to you, but those Romans know how to throw a party, believe me, solid decadence.

But it all ended today, to be honest if I see out another week, I will be happy, more than happy death, bring it on, I promise I will not aggressively hinder you.

So coming to the end of my story really, yes we had the best of life, thirty two years ago, we bought this plot of land and we have been here ever since, when Irene and I arrived here in Glenn Innes, it had been at the height of a marked upturn in Beef, and Mutton, but all the stock was on a huge growth merge at the time, we paid a premium for our place, today Glenn Innes is pretty dried up, apart from a little stock, but what has kept this town alive so long is the rich blemishes of Sapphires scattered along the district, if you know where to look, well, you'd be filthy rich, there isn't much more to tell, but suffice to say there is going to be spectacular show back at The Crossing, or Shrives Island for you hippies.

If I stay here, do you think I would wither away and just die?

No I think I would go on, but if I did stay, those old ghosts won't stay quiet, I actually heard Irene earlier today, she was saying that I should come down to Shrives Island, but the funny thing with that, is she is buried out at the Glenn Innes Memorial Park, I know I go down to her tree almost every other day, I make sure I take a little care around the gravesite, I often take down a possie, but I am digressing again, so as I was saying, the voice is insistent, I really should go back to The Crossing.

I know that the old Mitsubishi Pajero would do the trip well I think, time to get my affairs in order, gas up the Pajero, check under the bonnet, and she will be apples, BOOM"

CHAPTER TWENTY-ONE

LITTLE BOXES
SEPTEMBER
TENTH

The sun came up on the tenth just as sure as spot was a dog.

The pall that hung over the town had a depressing effect on all the people in the town, no one was at school, and the shopping district had been void of life for days, and the waterfall park had been empty, the town was not at all welcoming.

The people rose that morning, to open the gloom in their homes, by opening the curtains, only to be met by the gloom of the town that had hung no worse than this morning.

The house stood empty, Jess, Nick and the twins had been in the Motel for the last few days

Nick had been busy up at the house, working, he had Steve Gnik with him as well as Bobby Cursack, on the morning of the tenth, Nick had taken off earlier that morning, leaving the twins snuggling one a side with Jessie, he was not disturbing them.

When he returned later that morning, he was driving Bobby Cursack's truck, the contents were the course of his work, it was full of boxes, ten in all, made from the Boab, Nick was preserving them.

He roused Jess and the children they were to have their final meal together, they would go to Uncle Pete's and order anything on the menu, Jess had a feeling that she would not be able to eat anything,

The twins were a different story, they were famished, they walked the short walk to the end of Honeysuckle turning left onto Main Street, then legged it up to Uncle Pete's, it was probably the hub of activity in the town, no tourists, just Millers Lumbermen, Miners, the usual fare, but the mutterings throughout were of the house, and its sickly look.

They took the communal table to the rear of the shop, Rose was on them just like she would say herself, white on rice, but she was curious about the health of them, genuinely concerned, but still curious for their order, she said.

"Well you are all OK, so what are you going to order"

They went around the table, Miranda was having pancakes with a strawberry malt, Tim ordered the Timberman's breakfast which had consisted of eggs, bacon, mushrooms, sausage, beans, and black pudding, Nick ordered the same as Tim, with coffee to wash it down, Jess ordered a cup of tea, and a single poached egg, on sourdough.

After finishing at Uncle Pete's, it was time to meet up with Mark and Ian, but after Nick had ordered his second coffee none other than Craig Gnik walked in to Uncle Pete's, he stands in the doorway and announces.

"Well, I'm back" He holds up the box.

"And when I show you lot what's in this little box of tricks, it will be go time" Craig went to the table where Nick, Jess and the twins were seated.

"I don't want to open this in here, and when I do open it for the first time I will warn you now, it literary will take the breath from you"

Jess was curious.

"What's in it?" "You will need to be patient a little bit longer, I want Mark and Ian with us when I open it again"

Nick prodded.

"So who did you go to see in Glenn Innes, and why not let any of us know, we were left not knowing"

Craig blurts out. "And that is exactly why I kept my mouth shut, it only took one of us to retrieve this" Craig tapped on the lid of the box, the grain was alive in front of them, Nick had known that grain, he had been working on it the last few days.

He spoke.

"That is made of Boab, I need to see this"

Craig said.

"Well lets go do it, I have the perfect place to open this box, down by the waterfall, I know that Tim and Miranda have something important to add" Tim speaks up.

"It's stock, it is a small piece of the Boab, it radiates its power through all of us" Miranda takes up the story.

"That is why, how, we can avoid those ghouls who have taken over your house, we were imbued by the Boab a long time ago, I know why Craig refuses to open the box here, because when he lifts the lid, whoever is in the vicinity is fed a huge dose of what makes us better, stronger, smarter, and a whole lot of other things" Jess gets out of her seat, and heads for the door and calls back.

"Tim, Miranda, you two stick close to Nick and Craig, I need to bring a young lady along with us, I thinks she would enjoy it"

She smiled and went out the door, the bell tinkled overhead as she went out.

Jess trapsed across the school oval in the direction of Angie's house, wondering what she would be working on, she was welcomed in by Jill, who walked with her following her up the stairs, chatting, about stuff, both herself and her husband had the confidence that Nick, Jess, and others around the town would get a handle on this thing.

She found her in her bedroom, which was rather unkempt, her hair was disheveled and her dressing gown had been well worn for a little over a week, the depression that she was feeling was bought about by her attempt to start any art project, because she would either end up doing a rendition of the Boab, or the other one subject she had in her head was Desmond Brown, she had stopped a week ago now, and had dropped in to a depression that was scary for Jess, she was sitting on her bed, her earphones jacked and the music up real loud, her face lit up when she saw Jess coming up the stairs.

She pulled the earphones out, sprung up of the bed and almost landed in Jess's arms, they embraced for a moment, then Angie pulled away.

"You need to see this, it is driving me insane, you know I have had two works in my head, now I have one, look" Angie picks up the pad she had been doodling in, she began to leaf through, boxes, drawings of little boxes, all tied with a different colored bow.

"That is all that is in my head, boxes, little boxes, no Desmond, no Boab, just these boxes" Jess stood there a small smile crept across her face, she spoke.

"Angie, you need to get tidied up, get dressed and come with me, I know, the boxes in your head, you need to come with me, now" Angie stood there.

"Why" "I think I have the Little Box, you have been looking for" Angie looked at her with question then asked.

"Where?" "The waterfall park, we will meet the rest of the crew there"

Back at the waterfall park, Nick, along with Craig and the twins were awaiting the arrival of Mark and Cindy and Ian and Cathy, Jess came across the motel car park with Angie in tow, as she breached the rise where the carpark met the park, Tim spotted her, and waved to them.

As they approached Mark drove into the carpark, Nick saw Mark and Ian in the front, the girls were in the back.

Tim and Miranda were back in the cloths that they had showed up in, they were saying their goodbyes, when the children got to Angie, they had saved that particular hug until last, Angie had told them, remember your time here, remember us.

Miranda put her finger to her lip.

"Shh" She said and went on.

"You know we will see you again" But that was all she said, she fell silent.

Angie was stunned by that cryptic sentence and whispered.

"In the Neitherworld" Craig had set up a picnic bench with the box sitting right in the middle, the gathered around the table, that was when Craig began.

"Well we don't have much time, but I think we will pull it all together from here, you all know what is required, we all just do our bit, now soon, I will lift the lid on this box, I am warning you now, it will take your breath away, but you KNOW, everything"

Then Craig stopped.

"No this is not right, where has the birdsong gone" They all looked around and up, he was right, they could all hear the Odistgeeg flowing beside them, but there was no birdsong, no sounds just the river, and they could hear themselves, then Craig grabbed to box and moved closer to mouth of the caves, where the Mighty Odistgeeg fell at their feet and continued to flow downstream in a rush, he set the box down by a mighty gum tree.

"Here should be good"

Miranda and Tim had followed Craig, they looked back to see the remainder of the crowd looking at them, the children signaled for the rest to come, it wasn't long before they were gathered together, the birdsong had returned, all was as it should seem.

"OK, everyone ready"

Craig looked up and he knelt by the box.

"I would advise you all to sit around the box, it won't be as bad a fall, I'm telling you all this is amazing, but you need to be seated"

They all gathered around the box, Jess and Miranda were joined by Tim and Nick, Ian and Cathy sat with Steve, Rhonda and Angie, Mark, Cindy and Bobby Cursack sat together made up the circle, a circle of twelve, the thirteenth was Craig.

Craig waited for them all to be seated, and he flipped the lid of the box.

They watched as the green light pulsated out of the box, it instantly snatched all the air from them, their knowing and understanding of what was about to transpire as the single most important fact in time, imbued by the Boab, the green lit mist that wandered amongst them turned into a gale, this was far more than Craig had even expected, it scattered the circle, Angie, being thrown ten feet back from where she had sat down, she had known now why she was having the difficulty she was, this was the moment that she saw and understood.

Little Boxes, she had seen the boxes made from the Boab tree, those same boxes would be instrumental in locking away each of the spirits that are in the house, those boxes and there is one for every person that had been present at the destruction of the tree, will hold them prisoner for an eternity, including the elusive Mr. Desmond Brown, Nick had parked the truck at the base of the hill earlier that morning, no use driving a huge truck up to the base of the hill, when it's all about to go down, better off keeping mum, as he had gotten out of the truck Nick looked up at the house, it was looking more weather beaten than it had looked its entire history, and that was not long after major renovations, no taking the Boab out of the house was the best thing to do.

Bobby Cursack was thrown six feet, he saw for the first time the Boab that had, has been existing for millennia at least, he understood The Crossing, he saw his grandfather, attempting to stop the destruction of the Boab, it had been full, the birds of different variety's that sung and chirped their way into the light.

Ian was thrown fifty feet, he had held the flower in his hands again, this time it was a massive ball of root stock, Mark had seen himself with his stick, the same stick that he had landed on, after he had felt like flying over one hundred and fifty feet, his habit was to keep the stick in his back pocket, and when he landed with a bone shattering slam, the stick broke, and it was only thing that did break on that day, Nick had been shunted twenty feet, and when he stopped, he had his note pad and in his right hand, was a Black Beauty no 6 pencil.

Jess was blown four feet outside the circle, the same distance that Cathy and Cindy were thrown, they had seen the Boab from the boy's perspective, and were in awe of it, it was majestic.

Craig himself was not affected at all by the blast, Tim and Miranda stood by him as the Gale of root stock had blasted past them, they watched as the mist attached itself to them, it slowed its movement with the human barrier but the more it made its way through them it sped up again, the mist changing colors many times, it was amazing to watch.

As they began to come out of the haze, it was like they were being reborn, they witnessed all of them individually take that first breath after having it snatched from them almost a minute ago, whooping great lungs of air.

Mark who had landed so far away, bounced up from where he had landed, signaling with his arms he was glowing purple, as they looked around them, greens and orange's, reds and pinks, blues to aqua.

Craig didn't need to replace the lid, instead he reached into the box picking up the root stock.

"So, which of you two want to carry this"

He held it out in the direction of Miranda and Timothy, Timothy and Miranda looked at each other, Tim said.

"It's a females Job, give it to Miranda thankyou"

Miranda glowed a brilliant silver purple as she took the root stock, she was radiating between silver purple and green.

They had all re gathered at the Gum, where Tim and Miranda stood along with Craig, and it was soon evident, that among them, they would continue to radiate all the colors of the spectrum.

The gum tree shook and came awake, the bark came to life, and as it shuddered, its dead and dying leaves fell to the ground, this gum tree was old, very old, it opened its bark eyes, and then it opened its maw and yawned, it limbs shuddered and its green foliage, it shook loose the dew it had collected overnight, it fell like rain upon the collection of people in front of it.

Those assembled stood and looked up at the tree, it said to them.

"You have the Boab root stock, good to see, Craig, be on the lookout for a gum just like me, its older, shorter, squatter, there you will find the Boom sticks, Miranda Tim, the water will come for you rapidly, swim, you must swim,

As they came out of the waterfall park and up out onto Main Street everyone stopped what they were doing and looked up in amazement at what they saw.

There was a car accident down at the corner of Takoma and Main, the driver of the car coming down Main, didn't see the lights change, he would have a witness or two, he had seen a colorful haze coming toward him, it distracted him.

Eyewitnesses had said, the colorful display, which had swirled around and enveloped everyone in the group of thirteen.

As they approached the central shopping district, all had come out of their shops and had gathered on the footpath, the customers from the shops came out with shop owners to get a decent look.

Uncle Pete was joined by Rose and their clients, some left hot meals to go outside and gawk at the lightshow, it was just like the Founding Day Parade which took place every November the Twelfth, but the crowd of rubberneckers they had attracted, almost outnumbered the Parade on its best day.

When the three broke of the group, Craig along with Miranda and Tim, from Uncle Pete's shop, it looked like small mass had broken off the larger loom of color, the smaller ball of light, continued up the hill toward the house, the remaining light stayed at the bottom of the hill, the whole town was still, watching, waiting, the pall of color that hung over the house, the town, had become a thunderhead, moving in from the south, it was almost like night, but the light of those trapped, or willingly going on a journey, as well the lightning striking leaving ribbons of electricity through the pallid dark.

Each of the ten at the bottom of the hill, had begun to move around independent of each other, each going to the back of the truck, and taking a box, when the ten had their boxes they surrounded the hill, each taking up a particular spot, when they had found their position, their color burned fiercely, now not changing but remaining a Saffron Yellow, or a Blazing Red, another burned a Magnificent Orange, Nick had remained fluorescent green.

At the entrance Craig stopped and looked back down the hill, he could see the boxes were being distributed around the house, he looked down to the twins.

"You two ready?" Miranda nodded Tim answered.

"As ready as we will ever be"

Craig turned the handle pushing the door as he did, everything in front of him was a mire, a swamp, it was not the house he had remembered, but an overgrown swamp, whipsticks and stunted bushes, along with the occasional tree, but the mud, it would easily come up to the twins knees.

"Alright so this is how it is going to be" Craig picks up a twin in each of his arms, Miranda clutching the root stock, and wades into the house swamp, it came alive almost instantly.

"You disturb me, you come here to disturb me"

Craig keeps going until he looks back and the door has disappeared into the swamp.

He puts the twins down, the mud barely covers their ankles now. The water rose in front of them, the tepid mud forming a rough outline of what could only be the Desmond Brown ghost, they could see its sickness, it was almost done.

Craig looked past it, for the tree he was told about.

Miranda spoke to the Desmond Brown thing.

"You and your ilk are finished" Craig spied the tree.

"Well kids, this is where we part ways" He gathered them up and hugged them he then waded of in the direction of the tree, the water had begun to come, it was above their knees when Tim had yelled to Miranda to swim, she had tucked the root stock into her petticoat, to allow her the power she would require.

Into the water she went, the mud now settled she had vision within a minute, above her water upon water, Tim swam past her, she followed, Tim had begun up, toward the surface, he broke, a second later Miranda breeched as well.

Miranda said

"We are back in the pipes, see" Tim pointed but then he poked it.

"No, not in the pipes, it's a root, we are in the root system" Tim looked both ways.

"This way, Comon, swim"

Miranda went back into the stream, she was just behind Tim the rush of water grew behind them,

The water rushing behind them pushing them further in to the roots of the tree.

Craig reached the tree as the water was beginning to rise, the tree was a small Boab, directly in front of him was a knob, he grabbed it opening a cupboard sitting there was the box of dynamite, he grabbed it, the box was lighter now, but he was much older, than the time they had stolen it, he was much younger when he lost Marlii.

Tim and Miranda came to a junction, Tim took hold of the corner of the bend and Miranda held on to Tim's trouser leg, he pulled and pulled until he was almost out of breath, eventually pulling himself to safety, as well pulling Miranda up behind him, saving them both from being washed away forever.

Craig had moved swiftly through the house/swamp, when he got to the cellar and opened the door he found it as dry as a bone, he looked at where the water lapped up to the door, now midway up, it was like it was trapped, behind glass, but his body walked though it and down the stairs with no interference.

Tim motioned for Miranda to follow, she now had the root stock in her hand, as she crawled behind her brother, the root stock lighting there way, it wasn't long before they came to where they should be.

Craig had made his way down to the cellar, it was rotting, there was black sludge making its way through the stone cellars mortar, he set the box in the corner, took the blast cap that was with the sticks, and set the blast cap, he had about two minutes to get out.

Tim stopped, there was a shape in the root exact as the root stock, he said.

"Here look, the root stock belongs here look at the shape and the color in the root" Miranda crawled to Tim.

Without saying a word, she placed the root stock into the root system, it fit the root system exactly, when she place it there she heard it "Click" into place.

At that moment that click, they were gone.

From outside the house the ten had been standing and waiting, watching, each with their boxes, radiating their color, their boxes radiating their grain, flowing blood red.

The crowd gathering had begun to swell, the three had been inside the house now for almost fifteen minutes, that was when they began to witness it.

The eaves began to split and fall, the towers changed to a jet black, the windows, one by one began to implode in on themselves, there was an audible burp elicited from the house, that was when the house breathed, well it took a breath and held onto it, expanding until it was about to pop.

The door opened, Craig scurried out, the house behind him now, bloated to thwart their plans, Craig was running, sprinting away from the house when it detonated.

In the first instance, the ear tearing crack that spread across the countryside, out past the Mines in the north to well past the town limits in the south, was followed rapidly by a thunderous earthquake, the house went straight up, leaving a trail of debris behind it, the vortex sucking anything not nailed down, the walls of the house tearing away from the subframe disappearing into the vortex, the roof tiles disappeared in a second in a blast of dust.

Craig was caught by the shockwave and picked up in the folds of the explosion, thrown into the air, those who had seen Craig one second, the next he was just, gone, they had feared the worst, Mark Craig and Ian who had seen him disappear, could only stand their rooted to the spot, their ears and noses bleeding from the initial shockwave, the explosion had lit up the afternoon twilight, like the birth of a new sun.

It bloomed out and up, bright orange and yellow to deep red, singing anything within a radius of eight hundred meters, but not the ten, they were immune

Their boxes came to life, the red glow of the grain was gone, the color now was green, pulsing it's fluorescence, the lids popped open and from each of the boxes a slivery tentacle of root emanated from the box, it went off in the direction of the house, the roots began to disappear into what was left of the hill, and as each of the ten roots re appeared they were each holding onto the spirits, the rotting evil spirits that had begun this whole saga.

Mark had Desmond Brown, Ian, Joshua Brown, Nick's root had hold of Michael Longstreet, the other seven had those who had been responsible for the destruction of the tree.

As the roots drew ever closer to the box, they could see them fighting to no avail to break free, Desmond Brown now nothing but a rotten corpse, he shriveled in front of Mark, he would remember the look in his eyes, or what had presented as eyes, that look, was sheer terror, Joshua Brown was tugging at his root trying to break free, he shrieked, it was cut off with lid snapping shut.

Michael Longstreet, like the other eight were resign to their fate, the snapping boxes all played a musical note as they closed.

The three men were sure that the tune was perfectly in key with the song Little Boxes.

That was when Nick turned to Mark and yelled through the din.

"Where is Craig?"

Mark stood there his box in front of him, he shook his head.

He turned to Ian who was on his opposite side, he yelled.

"Did you see what happened to Craig?" Ian yelled back to him.

"I saw him get swept up into the vortex, but I haven't seen him since" The ten came together with their boxes seeming immune to the smoke, burning bits of building along with parts of bricks, they had been continuing to rain down around them this entire time, Nick put his box down, the other nine joined him, on the driveway at the entrance to the hill, when the boxes were on the ground, the grain moved from box to box, until just like a jigsaw puzzle a picture was drawn before them, it was a Boab, the grain pulsed out at them, they began to lift of the ground forming a straight line, the boxes went straight up into the sky disappearing into the smoke haze, the debris had stopped falling but the smoke had been acrid.

The ten boxes came back down, thudding into what was left of the hill, causing another explosion that rippled along the ground, the ten shook with the mini quake, and then all was quiet, the smoke persisted for some time, and the Shrives Island hospital had never been this snowed under, calling all staff who was not in the town at the time to come to work, because there was plenty of work coming and plenty of work already there.

Mark along with Ian, went off to search for Craig, where Ian was sure he had seen Craig go.

The rest of the eight, stayed to help those who had need for it, Uncle Pete had required help, out of all the stores on Main street Uncle Pete's coped it worst, it had seemed to rain down on Uncle Pete's, concentrated on Uncle Pete's, there had been no one there when the damage was done, Pete had closed, kicking all the patrons out as the colorful show had begun, which was a good thing, by nine on that night, the death count had been three, had Uncle Pete' been trading, the death count would have been closer to fourteen or fifteen.

By ten, the search had been called off, Craig was listed as missing, Ian had thought to himself, Craig was "Boom Dust".

Cleaning of the town wound up at about four pm the next morning, it would be days before the town would be back to normal.

CHAPTER TWENTY-TWO

LITTLE BOXES 2 SEPTEMBER ELEVEN, 2001

When Nick and Jess returned to the motel room, she, Jess fell into bed and went into a deep sleep, Nick on the other hand put the kettle on and switched on the T.V.

A movie?

What he was watching was not a movie.

The world trade center was under attack.

What he was looking at was happening, this was no movie, this was happening live and in real time, he sat on the end of the bed, he picked up the phone and dialed Mark's sisters house, it rung once.

"Hey Mark, turn on the television" Mark answered immediately.

"I have, it on channel 9, is this really happening, I had thought it was a movie" Nick had stayed quiet, Mark went on.

"This is real, this is happening right now"

Both men stood there, mouths open as they watched the destruction, Mark spoke.

"Are you thinking the same as me, is this connected, to us, what has happened here?"

Nick replied.

"Connected, how do you mean, we are on the other side of the world.

Mark said.

"Desmond Brown, Joshua Brown, they were both born in the states, nothing could be more obvious, everything we have been through, everything we have witnessed, you cannot explain away with an answer, no one has an answer for what we have been through"

Nick stopped and thought, he said.

"I'm giving Ian a call, see if he is still up, ask his opinion" Mark said.

"Good, have him ring me when you're done"

They rung off, Nick went straight back to the dialer and called Ian it rang once, twice, he picked up on the third ring.

"Ian are you aware" Ian cut him off mid-sentence.

"I am aware, I put the T.V on try to unwind, there is nothing on apart from the World Trade Centre, they are under attack, this is connected with what went down here, I know it sounds silly, but do you have an answer?" Nick answered.

"Well I have no answers, I, like you want to know what is happening"

Ian says to Nick, with conviction.

"Nick, isn't Margaret's offices in the towers" Nick stopped and thought for a moment, he had remembered when he along with Jessie, had visited his publisher in New York, that was in 1990, they were finalizing the publishing of the book that would launch his career, The catcher in the pines, initially they had met at Margaret's most favorite restaurant, which just happened to be at the motel where they were staying, The Plaza, he had remembered that Luncheon like it was yesterday, he had remembered the buffet, Lobster, shellfish, splendid.

"Yes she is, but she is in the South Tower, it's the North Tower that's ablaze, hey I need to find out what has happened to her, you need to find out about your band management, they're in New York, aren't they" "Yes but they are in a building four blocks away, but I should get on, see how they are faring"

Nick and Ian rang off, Nick picked up the receiver again and dialed the international code, he was grabbing his wallet out, fumbling through receipts looking for her number, he didn't have his diary, but found the number and began dialing, it rang twice and he got a recorded message.

The number you have dialed is temporarily unavailable, please try again later.

He frantically tried the number again, this time it rung once and was picked up by Margaret.

"Hello this is Margaret, we are waiting on advice?" Nick was taken back.

"Margaret, its Nick, Nick Lester" "Oh Nick, I think we need to get out of here, we were told to sit tight, there're is talk circulating around, a plane flew into the North Tower" "Yes, yes, its time to leave, please get out of there" As Nick completed his last sentence, the South Tower was rocked by the impact of the plane, Nick's phone cut off, he dialed as quickly as he could.

All he was getting the busy tone.

Margaret was standing there with the receiver in her hand as the building continued to shake and rattle, she dropped the phone and headed out into the rather wide lobby, the elevators were off limits, fifty landings down was where she was headed, many others had the same idea, on every floor below her, there was a traffic jam, firefighters from Ladder fifteen had tried to be traffic cops, and for the most part had been very helpful.

But the crush on the twenty fifth floor had left two people dead, and five needing respiratory help, Margaret herself a number of times, had felt crushed of air, almost gasping, finally she had reached the ground floor lobby, people were scattered all among the place, most were injured and among them a few dead, Margaret kept moving out of the lobby and into the open air of the Plaza, she didn't stop, but looked over her shoulders, papers fell around her just like confetti, she made her way out of the Plaza she had run no further than three blocks and had made it to Park and West Broadway when a huge rumbling came behind her it was the south tower falling, she had begun to run as hard as she could crowds of people yelled and screamed, as they were being followed by a huge white billowing cloud, Margaret looked over and saw the Smyth Tribeca Hotel that was when Margaret was consumed by the cloud.

Her vision was gone, she bumped into someone, but was hit again, this time a lot harder, she went down with the missile that hit her, they stayed down on the ground together, Margaret had managed to get her scarf around her face, and while low to the ground, she had felt safe.

The person who had crashed into her, was coughing, Margaret helped her cover her face, and said.

"We cannot stay here, we need to get out, stay with me, I need to find the Tribeca, take my hand" She took Margaret's hand and was led by her, she managed to lead them into the lobby of the Smyth Tribeca Hotel, the lady had continued to cough, Margaret had saved her life, for now.

The first thing would be to try and contact Nick, she had known he would be frantic, they had been rudely interrupted, she went to the desk, and paid cash for a room on the lowest floor possible, and was pleased to be on the fourth floor.

Once inside she striped down to her petticoat, brushing the foul-smelling dust from her hair, she went straight to the phone, and dialed the desk for an open line, when the dial tone sounded she quickly dialed Nick's number, she was not to know his house had exploded only hours earlier, instead she dialed her own home, her daughter, Lee would be frantic by now, her daughter was frantic, answering the phone before it completed its first ring" "Mom, please tell me it's you" "Yes dear I am at the Tribeca, I am in a room on the fourth floor, don't worry I am safe"

"I thought you were dead, there is nothing left of the south tower and the north tower is still burning, put the T.V. on" She put the receiver down on the bed as she went to the television and switched it on, there it was in living color, the dust cloud had consumed a large part of the north tower, she witnessed a person stepping out of a broken window, falling to their death, she went back to the phone.

"I am having a shower, to wash of this stinking dust off me, I will have to make do with cloths I have, but I will be home as soon as I can get there" "Please don't be long, I want you home, a soon as possible"

They rung off and Margaret went back to the end of the bed where she sat and watched.

Margaret was crying when the north tower fell.

She didn't shower in the end, instead dressing in her smelly cloths, besides when she went down to the lobby, the dust outside was still a problem.

It took her three and a half hours to make the thirty-minute trip to her Park Avenue apartment, when she arrived, she was greeted by her fourteen-year-old daughter, Lee whom grabbed and hugged her mother like never before.

"When I saw the South Tower fall, I was beside myself I thought you were still in there, Mum lots of people are dead, they are saying it was a terrorist attack"

Later that night Nick had managed to catch up with Margaret, he had called her apartment earlier that day firstly to be told by Lee that she had no idea of her mother's fate, Lee was crying into the phone, Nick consoled her by telling her that she had fled the building in time, Nick was relieved when later he rung the apartment and Lee had said that her mother had called her, she was safe.

"When you rang me this morning, I was shocked to hear your voice, I had been waiting for security to get back to us with advice, if you hadn't rung when you did, I would have still been there waiting, pretty much dead, where were you calling from, the phone at the house is disconnected"

"Margaret, we have both had an event, my house is no more, it was levelled today in an explosion, my paranoid brain did flips when I switched on the television to see the North Tower on fire, I was frantic, if you could imagine, I could write a story about what I have witnessed recently, but not even you would believe it, it has been supernatural"

"With what has happened today I don't need to suspend my belief, terrorists attacked us right where it hurts"

Nick sighs and speaks.

"I think the two events are one, I really believe they are connected" "That's silly Nick, how can you make that call, it's coincidence, that's all it is"

"What if I asked you about Desmond Brown"

"Desmond Brown, how do you know that name, he is an ancestor of mine, directly, after he passed his son Joshua, moved, emigrated to a place called The Crossing in your country, good riddance to him, he was an animal, as was his father, murderers both of them, Desmond was an Uncle, Joshua was a cousin, my maiden name is Brown I thought you had known that" "I had forgotten, to me you have always been Margaret Thorn, but there is so much from my childhood that had been locked up, locked in my brain, as far as the last decade, I have often had fugues, my writing has been pretty succinct, but my memory is proving to be a big part of what has happened".

Margaret said.

"Nick, your home, it's not in the city is it?" "No I told you we have purchased the Desmond Brown Mansion in my home town of Shrives Island"

Margaret went silent.

Nick was growing impatient.

"Margaret?" "OH I'm sorry Nick, my god The Crossing is Shrives Island, oh no, I see what you are saying, I think I need to go back to Polk County, home"

Now Nick had gone silent, Margaret spoke.

"Nick, wake up" "Oh I'm sorry, how are we so connected, how did I find you as my agent, yes yes, go back to Polk County, I will give you and Lee a couple of days, you need to look into the history, your history, I have just realized something, I will need a couple of days myself"

Margaret thought for a moment, then said.

"A few days, we may have a bit more than that, the flights have been shut down over here, all flights have been grounded" "Well I think I may be getting an angle of this, I will call you tomorrow night actually, when will you get back to Polk County?"

"Amtrak, so I would say we will take the overnight Charlotte, then down to the County by hire car, so tomorrow by lunch" "Ok, I will call, when I have some news, I think with what has transpired the answers we are going to get are going to be trippy, how much more trippy than what had transpired in the previous twenty four hours, well" They said their goodbyes and finally rung off, Nick sat down in a huge sofa that sat opposite the bed where he sat for a moment and watched Jess, rolled up in a fetal position, he would let her sleep, she would deal with the news much easier in the morning, today he had thought, the house, was gone, what would today bring.

He went to the bed sitting on his side for the moment, then he lay his head down on the pillow, Jess rolled grabbing him in a sleepy hug, he turned to her, sleepily she whispered.

"Tired, so tired"

He drifted off into a haze, before he disappeared into a dreamless sleep, a long dreamless sleep.

Jess on the other hand remained on the line of dreams, and nightmares, and as she dropped down into rem sleep, she was dreaming of boxes.

When Nick awoke on the day after, he had noticed a dull throb in the back of his head, the explosion had affected all the people in different ways.

He pulled his head from the pillow, Jess was not there, he looked toward the curtains, the light outside was going down, he had slept for some time, he began to get out of bed, the door to the Motel opened Jess called in.

"Make sure your decent, unless you want shock a young lady" Jess walked down the narrow hall, looking in to see Nick, sitting on the end of the bed, he had managed to get out of his dirty jeans, and shirt, and had managed to find a t-shirt and clean jeans, he was still waking up.

The young lady was Angie, they were both holding take out bags from Uncle Pete's, Jess was also carrying drinks, she said.

"Hey sleepy head, I thought I would let you sleep, you will need it, nothing out there is the same anymore, the whole town is just different"

Nick got up.

"What do you mean, different?"

Angie held up a bag waving it in front of Nicks nose she said.

"Mmm uncle Pete's Cheeseburger"

Nicks eyes caught the bag waving in front of him, the realization that he had been ravenous as never before, he took the bag opening it and pulling out the burger, unwrapping it and taking a bite, Jess held out a chocolate thick shake, Nick took it chasing the burger with chocolate ice cream treat, he had come back to himself and said with a look of satisfaction on his face.

"Wow, you two don't know how much I needed that, but how different?" Jess went to the door opening it.

"Take a look"

Nick, burger in one hand and thick shake in the other went to the doorway, out onto the stoop, to the he looked to the West, the Odistgeeg was skirting the Motel, and when he looked to the East, as he walked up the motels driveway the Spencer river had run a new tributary, and eventually, that new tributary would eventually shear away its banks until the Spencer river would be almost three times it own size, it had taken quite a bit of old growth Malley Gum, Ghost Gum, Eucalypts as well as Pine.

The school was lost, it was directly in the path of the Spencer, as were the tract of homes on the East, the roads were split in almost every direction, there was one crossing still passable, and that was the Odistgeeg at the town end of the shire, when he looked up, to where the house had stood, it was void, along with the house half to three thirds of the hill was also gone.

From the top of the hillock, that was what he had thought of it, a hillock, water bubbled up, and flowed straight down the front, gouging a furrow through the roadway that lead down to Main street where it dropped, sixty feet, as the waterfall hit the ground it pooled out into what would become a swimming hole, the little river, as it was known, then flowed down splitting Main Street through the old Garage then down to the Odistgeeg, twenty feet in front of him, he shook his head, looked back to Jessica, and then to Angie, he shook his head, then said.

"Well, the schools gone"

She nodded, she answered.

"Yes, so has the church, so double good to me, hey"

Both Nick and Jess nodded and laughed along with her.

She got serious.

"Hey come on Jess, please tell him"

Jess, then said.

"How it all looks, that's not all that has changed, the history is all different, Browns influence over the town is no longer a part of it, but the house, well that is not as easy a history as we first thought, that house has a physical root in this town, it was put where it should never have been placed, but we need to go out to the red wallaby, well it was only a pub for short time back then, but Miranda wants to speak to you" Nick looks directly at Jess.

"Miranda?" There was a question in his face.

"We changed it all, yes Miranda, I have spoken to her today on the phone, we are meeting her in an hour, so freshen up and prepare, this little adventure is not over yet"

Angie stood behind Jessica; she spoke out.

"She wants to see me as well; I don't know why"

The turnoff for what had been in another time, another place the Red Wallaby, was a manicured farm entrance, topiary ran along the driveway, following the path that would have been a road, as they approached the turnaround at the house, it was all different, rose gardens were abundant, the porch that led up to the house had been set out with a table, a long table with place settings for a couple of dozen, roughly, as they began up the stairs the screen door was opened out walked Miranda, the three stopped, it had dawned on the three of them, it had only been a matter of hours, since the children had been sent back, they had known it had changed, but Miranda stood there in front of them, they all thought she had looked not a day over a sprightly seventy year old.

Her hair spilled around her cheeks of all the thing that had changed, that hadn't, she was tall and slim.

Miranda was only days away from her 120th birthday.

Nicks head was spinning with questions, as was Jessies, Miranda could see this, and was amused, a smile on her lips, and then laughter spilled from her mouth, Nick, Jessie, and Angie all looked at each other, they had heard that laughter, it was laughter that was wedged in the memory's forever that high chuckle with a musical note, "Mmmhhaaa", but there was something missing, it was Tim.

Nick went to her and embraced her, Jess followed as did Angie, the four of them stood there just like that for a long, long moment.

Jess was the first to speak.

"Where is Tim, what has happened to Timothy?" They all pulled away and waited for an answer.

"Oh, my parents survived, I will share this with you now, get it out of the way, we were not in the storm water or sewerage pipes, we were actually in the roots of the Boab, I carried the root stock back to where it belonged, Tim had realized, he could go back further than me, and he saved our parents, as well he had made sure that the evil of Joshua Brown had been known, a pre-teen boy gave his life up, save me, save our parents, he had known it would cost him his life but he did it anyway, that is why everything seems so changed, That is what this is for" She motioned toward the table set.

She went on.

"Come with me, I think we all need a stiff drink" as they entered the house it was obvious that the interior was Boab, it was made up from boxes, it was the same timber he had used in the boxes that had taken the ghosts from the house.

Miranda led them down a long hall, photos lined the walls, and fine paintings, she led them into a large sitting room, where there was armchair for them and many more, drinks were served Miranda spoke up.

"As we wait for the other guests, we need to de brief, the whole of Shrives Island has changed however our family's, have not, apart from certain things" Miranda went to a bookcase, she pulled a volume and held it up, it was Nicks, she passed it to him and spoke.

"I would advise you to read this"

Nick looked at the cover, it was his name but the title "Forest Green" he leafed through the book, pausing at pages throughout, it was a Novel, his latest, that he had no memory of writing.

It was the complete story of what had happened, but it had his, Marks and Ian's memories with a forward written by his father.

"Dad, how could have Dad"

He stopped, he looked at Jessie.

"Dad, Mum" Margret was prepared for this eventuality EVERYTHING had changed, she was by Nick's side, he swooned, and almost passed out.

"Yes, your mum and dad are alive, that timber truck had been replaced by a rail head, they have been taking Timber out of Shrives Island by rail since 1932, so that truck had never existed"

Angie was sitting listening to her intently.

Nick and Jessie were only becoming more and more confused, that was when Angie broke in explaining it to them, Angie went on.

"You, we have been trapped, caught up in some sort of storm, no not storm, it hasn't ended yet, that's it, we all need to see it out to its end"

Maranda spoke up.

"That's right, this hasn't ended yet, with Tim in the Neitherworld, Desmond and Joshua's ghosts now roaming around Polk County, you Nick need to go sort it out, Jessica, Angie, Rhonda, all have work to do, but first we will dine, and everyone can take a deep breath and relax"

They could, and they did, the house was built on special land, magic land, healing land.

And as the evening rolled ever so gently toward night, the rest of the guests arrived, each was shown to their rooms for the evening, Angie and Rose got to share a room, with the "changes" Rose was still single and unattached, it was subtle things that had changed that made all the difference. All were sat around the table, a special reunion went on, one in which, Nick's parents were non paused, they had been here the whole time, they hadn't gone anywhere, it was much harder for Nick, who had shed tears when he greeted his mother and father.

That night, a heavy dreaming took place all over Shrives Island, but especially, out at the Grange's property, there was a lot of magic in that one place now.

There were no nightmares, but the dreams abound.

They awoke the next morning refreshed, where they all gathered in the dining room to share to share their dreams with each other.

Angie, was perplexed of her dream, and she sat there listening to the others as they went on about their dreams, Mark and Ian were sharing how they had both inhabited the same dream, everything that had happened in that single dream, they had been young, early teens, they had out at the mill, cutting huge planks of old growth forest, that was the dream, they had sweated, working their bodies into a frenzy, ending with enough timber to build a house, and them some.

Nick had been in a room, writing a book, he had to stop and think, did he pick up that book last night and read it?

No he had written the book in his dream and his memory of the script was photographic, after all it had been Nick who had written

"Forest Green" there was no "Catcher in the pines" that book had disappeared, it had vanished into the either, so much had changed, but so little, that was when Angie joined the conversation.

"Well, my dream, I am a little confused, it must be hard, to have written a book but have no memory of it, recently Jess found me in my bedroom, earphones in, eating junk food, because of the little boxes, now I am feeling an understanding of them, because when they first appeared in my head, I was drawing them, hundreds of them, but in my dream there I was, placing box after box into the trunk of the Boab tree, those boxes hold everything in them, they hold our thoughts, they hold our memory, they even hold our futures, Little boxes, I am getting there, but I know now" She looks over to Miranda, Miranda nods her head to her, Angie goes on.

"I Know now, while we stick together, the more people my age bracket, pick up on it, it is too large to contain In my dream, I remember placing boxes into the tree that were pleasant but sometimes what I was placing into the Boab was pure evil, I think those boxes could have been left out" Miranda broke in.

"No sweat heart, ALL of those boxes were destined to go there" Angie said.

"Well I think the good boxes far outnumber the evil" Breakfast was served, Uncle Pete had made himself at home in the huge kitchen, and having a full larder it was laid on.

Uncle Pete, who had been among the "Knowing" he had remained, along with Nick's folks, who were none the wiser, Jack sat and chowed down with the same haste he had always done, Nick couldn't help but smile as his old man sat opposite guffawing at something that Ian was sharing with him, then Pete was at his side.

"Pancakes, three stack, no make that a four stack" Pete put the pancakes on Nick's Plate.

Nick looked up at Uncle Pete, he had an exuberance that built and bubbled up, Uncle Pete was spryer, fitter, not a man who was dealing with high with high cholesterol

"What, have I grown a new face or something?" Nick exclaimed.

"No, no, how are you feeling Uncle Pete, since the heart attack"

Of the people gathered around the table, some stopped and looked at Nick, Pete looked down at Nick, a pained expression on his face, he said.

"What are you talking about, hat attack, are you kidding me" Another small change, it wasn't lost on Nick.

He had known he would need to take a flight when they allowed air traffic again, there was no flights in the continental U.S.A. currently everything was grounded.

MARGARET THORN A THORN IN THEIR SIDE

Margaret Thorn alighted from the amtrac cross nation sleeper car with her daughter, they had gone to the car rental desk straight away, the car she had reserved had been a small hatch, and with a short stop in Charlotte to meet up with her husband, Gerald Thorn, who in fact was full blooded Cherokee, it showed in his strong body, his face, sun chiseled, showed high cheekbones, his hair was full and long and as black as a raven, all you had to do was look at him, he screamed Cherokee, she herself was part native blood, part Pawnee but her daughter, Lee was gifted with her father's bloodline, Margaret herself had been strong with the native eye, was beginning to think they were soon to be woken from a dream / nightmare.

Gerald had his own opinion but was keeping it to himself, he had known the white man's way, he had known how wrong it was, he did his penance working for the forestry's, he fixed what they had fucked up.

The three of them in a state of shock, with the loss in New York, news that planes had struck the twin towers, as well a plane smashed into the ground in Pennsylvania, one down at the Pentagon.

Returning to sleepy old Polk County, should be a pleasure, as much as a pleasure could be at this moment.

They were all sitting in Denny's, they had ordered and were waiting for their plates of food.

Lee had been dealing with the loss, her friends in New York, lost a parent, or an aunt, uncle, or brother, Margaret had been lucky, she hadn't lost anyone, almost her mother, but that never eventuated.

Margaret had made the statement.

"If it had not been for Nick calling her at that moment, I would be a dead duck"

Gerald smiled at his wife and daughter, he took one of their hands into each of his, placed a kiss on both and spoke.

"We are going home to Polk County, we will be back with family, friends, our losses we can look at as the days play out, we are together and we are strong" Margaret and Lee, parroted the Line 'we are together, and we are strong'

Gerald took over the wheel from Charlotte, and they coasted into Polk County almost an hour ahead of schedule, it was ten forty-five, the final ten-minute drive to their home was pleasant, the sun was out, it allowed its rays to split the leaves that were still to change color and drop from the trees.

Gerald turned the tiny hire car into their driveway pulling up at the portico, none of them had been back here in the last three months, and they had all been buoyed with the same joy.

Margaret opened the front door and was struck with pleasant aroma of home, and she breathed it in, Lee brushed passed her making the statement.

"Its home mum, it smells just like home" It was a little after midday and the house was full to overflowing.

There had been parents, aunts' uncles nieces and nephews, brothers and sisters had all come to welcome Margaret Lee and Gerald home, but mostly Margaret, all who that were gathered thought she had gone down with the tower, and were overjoyed to hear her voice, she had been saved those who possessed native blood say the bear and the eagle were watching over her, the Anglo church going people said, thank the lord.

But at this point in time Margaret was saying no thanks to anyone, she had on her mind how big this thing really was, while most were saying "TERORISTS" she was saying wait and see, just wait, she needs to be looking at Nick, she needs to be talking to Nick.

Over cold cuts, potato salad and coleslaw, with the beer flowing and the wine bottles popped, it was a celebration of sorts, while it was taking place, a grotesque and horrible monstrosity was gaining strength, and from the bowels of the earth splitting the cold autumn day the house sprouted from the ground, its first semblance of a house was twisted out of shape, out of that shape, came a single branch, it was gnarly and twisted its dark feeling fingers crawling over the back of your neck, it had actually sprouted from where it had first stood, what was now the corner of Kent and South Road, it had been a children's playground for some time, and it was now giving way to this monstrosity, in the first hour, it had gone from a seedling to the size of a sapling, and from a sapling to a full grown tree in the space of two hours, but it had kept on growing the slides and the swings were gone, gobbled up by what?

Was it a house?

Was it a tree?

Was it a tree house?

The cubby house was incorporated into it, giving of points of color throughout the tree, throughout the Desmond Brown house, if it were not for that color the thing would be devoid of any color at all.

It had been Mandy who had seen the excitement, there was a stream of people heading down to the corner of Kent, Mandy called into the party from the verandah.

"Hey someone, come take a Look at this, there is a stream of people running, headed for town, something has happened"

Mandy went down off the porch, and was soon running, glass in one hand, the leaving of a cucumber sandwich in the other.

She had been joined by a number from the party, with her when she stopped at Kent, as she rounded South, Lee was by her side, they looked at each other and back to the monstrosity sitting in front of them.

It was a house, the first level finished in stone, but from the second story it was a Boab tree, it had sprung up as the house came back to life, and it had appeared only a couple of hours ago.

As Margaret and Gerald came upon the house Margaret stopped mouth agape, she wouldn't need to really talk to Nick Lester, he was correct, the house had come back to its roots through a portal, along with its nemesis, or was that the wrong way round, the tree had found its way to where its nemesis had originated.

As the crowd swelled those at the front of the pack were moved closer to the house, tree thing, the people toward the front were encroaching on the house, and as the crowd relaxed, those moving closer to the tree could see faces, in there, transparent ghostly faces.

They were relieved when they were able to back away from it.

Gerald come to the front of the crowd he stood next to Lee and Mandy, Margaret was directly behind him.

"We need to be prepared, any one with Native Indian blood come now, come forward, any amount of native blood, be you Apache, Cheyenne, or like us folk here Cherokee, we will come together and our strength will be one"

There were many, many with half blood, there were the purebreds among them, almost as rare as hen's teeth today, as a result of massacre, the white man had known how to wipe them out, bought their pestilence with them, along with the violence, they knew no peace as far as Gerald was concerned, up until this day, what just happened?

There was an explosion, a rather huge explosion, it reverberated, it hummed and rattled itself all the way to the big old U.S.A. and plonked itself down on the world trade Centre, downing those two huge buildings, hoping to take Margaret Thorn with them, and failing, how many others Gerald could never be able to work that out, but a disaster so huge, in order to take out his wife?

She was a publisher, that was all.

Why did she have to become involved?

They had all gathered around Gerald, he was chanting in his native tongue, the words were a blessing to the trees, in his native Cherokee, along with a deep understanding of his native tonged Iroquoian, behind that you could hear the Appalachian, it was now and again punctuated by distinct English, he went.

"Ah ahetke, house hear me now, you will not win this war, askeh ahrok hah, we have your mettle, atek athsaht, all come together and protect our magic, ahetke is our strength, is in our "Eh" our strength is in Marlii, Marlii is our Eh"

The house moved, or was it the Boab tree?

And then the tree came to life, its branches with early spring foliage, very late this far north, shook, and shuddered, in the cold autumn breeze, the tree spoke.

"Gerald of the soaring eagle" He could tell it was tired, it was in pain as well but it went on.

"Your chanting is wonderful, it gives me strength, I will not let this evil win"

The house came to life, its rock foundations swelled, causing the tree's grip on it to slip for a moment, there was a huge groan, as the foundations of the house coughed up the playground equipment into the crowd.

A swing that had disappeared well over an hour ago, appeared coming out of the air to crash into a dozen people in the verry front row, most were only knocked out but there were some who needed medical attention.

The Boab's branches pulled and twisted, ripping the life from the house, that was when the Boab lamented.

"Oh Marlii, where are you, Craig, Mark, Ian and Nick, I need you, I need you all"

Margaret fought her way to the front of the crowd and yelled.

"They will find you; I promise you they will find you" The maw of the house opened wide, mimicking Margaret, the houses voice was grating on their ears.

"Oh they will find you, I promise they will find you"

Gerald began to chant again stilling the house making it quiet.

Gerald remained, chanting the house down allowing the tree to grow and grow, the news van that had been the first arrive focused on Gerald and his harmonious chanting, the crowd that had swelled around him joined in the chants, harmonies continued, Gerald bowed out going to Margaret and Lee, they gather him into a bundle, a blanket wrapped around him, and as they made their wat down Kent street, almost home, Gerald had been able to speak.

"It's evil Margaret, it is bad, I don't think this will be a pushover, I hope they arrive and soon" Margaret and Lee make Gerald comfortable; he sits in his easy chair and begins to nod off, the girls let him sleep, doze, he needed it.

It was then Lee said what was, had been on her mind for so long.

"Mum, Marlii has been in my dreams for years" Margaret stops, she has never said anything to her about Marlii, heck she had only realized in the last days that Marlii was an important part in all of this, but now her daughter is telling her that Marlii had been appearing to her for years?

Nick, who had taken a flight out to Canada, even if he had to, he could drive down from Toronto airport, but luckily didn't find the need, by the thirteenth civilian traffic had been allowed again, and he found it easy to get a connecting flight from Toronto, all the way down to Charlotte.

Once on board the Canada air services jet he had finally had the compunction to shut down, and just for a while forget everything that had transpired, but he could not shut down or off, the hostess came by his seat, checking if there was anything she could get him, would he like a drink, did he need a cushion, a young Canadian hostess had recognized him, he was sure.

When she arrived back with his whiskey, he said to her in hushed tones.

"I am sorry, I don't have a book to sign for you"

"Oh, if you are offering to sign a book one of yours, it would be splendid if you would"

She stood waiting for an answer.

"Go get it, I would be more than happy to sign it"

She returned shortly with a copy of "Forest green" along with a pen.

"Please sign it for Lori Anderson" He looked up, he always checked, and asked her.

"Are you Lori Anderson?"

"Oh no I am Jenny Anderson, Lori is my kid sister, who has raved about this book, so I loaned hers after she finished it, this will be a pleasant surprise, her book back with the authors signature"

Nick went back to the book opening it to the facing page and wrote, "To Lori, do yourself a favor, if you haven't yet go read Tolkien, with love and best wishes Nick Lester"

He passed it back and she looked at what he had written, a smile first come to her lips, and then she had burst out laughing, and through her broken laughter she had explained, that Lori, the huge Nick Lester fan had picked up the Fellowship of The Ring, just the evening before.

For the rest of the flight, he was left pretty much alone, surprisingly he is recognized more in the United States, that was because of the propensity for the pictures, mostly of Jessica, taken to hang in Galleries of New York, Chicago, as much on the west coast as much as the east coast, there had been photos of them up in many places.

He was on his third scotch, the sun was coming up over the horizon, the wing of the plane burned a bright orange, in the haze, he was dozing, the wing, shifted, it was rising up, with the shaking of a feather, the wing was gone replaced by the flapping orange and red wing of a Phoenix, Nick unbuckled his seat and leapt, going to the opposite window to look out it and see if the changes were, had been the same, and as he gazed out the small porthole window, the fuselage became the body of the beast and they had all been captured, by this thing, Nick saw the wings had both changed and were the wings of a huge bird, Nick stood there as everything around him turned to a membranous grey to a thick inky blackness as they were devoured by the Phoenix.

Nicks eyes snapped open, he looked down at where his tray was, should have been down and open, but there was no glass and the tray had been locked back up in front of him.

Nick looked out the window, the wing had taken a tinge of orange from the sun, they were descending into Charlotte Airport.

Nick had been surprised, Gerald and Lee were with Margaret at the gate, Margaret went to Nick embracing him, relieved that she could finally look at him, she introduced Gerald and lee, he shook and hugged.

Margaret spoke up.

"I say we eat here, go to the bar and get a steak; I know you could do with a decent meal before we get back to Polk County, they concurred and made their way to the bar appropriately monikered "Sky High Bar"

While they ate Gerald spoke a lot telling Nick of his own experience with house, how that with his chanting's, and with enough people chanting with him, he had seen the evil Desmond Brown, but he had also seen what had been standing behind him, it was a killer of all things, if you look at it, it will kill you.

Nick sat there, he had begun on a roast potato, he nodded at Gerald's last quote.

It would kill you.

Margaret and Lee joined Gerald, waiting for him to say something.

As they watched him putting potato into his mouth, he chewed, swallowed and spoke up.

"It will kill me? it has taken two of my friends to date, three if you take into account the Mill, it won't kill me, I have a way of beating it once and for all"

Gerald regarded him, he had known that this man across from him strong, but he was "just outside" of the magic, he had a strong aura about him, maybe that was it, maybe his strength is in his aura, he was then sitting there nodding his head, along with Margaret and Lee, and he spoke.

"We will be with you; we will raise the forest to aid you in your battle"

It was in Gerald's big blue Chevy Blazer on the way to Polk County in reflection of what Gerald had said to him, "Raise the Forest" was what he had said.

His thoughts had gone back to the forest of his childhood, and he had not realized he had been verbalizing.

"Every time I get started you pull me apart"

Margaret looked over at Nick who was getting comfortable in the back passenger seat, Lee traveling beside him, was curious about the words that were spilling from Nicks mouth.

"Wha, who is pulling you apart"

"Oh It's a song the Boab sings, it has been singing it to us since the seventy's, it is a current hit in Australia, Grinspoon, Chemical heart, it was written about a crowd crush victim, you know, the kids at rock concerts today, that's right the mosh pit, she was killed in either a mosh pit accident or a crowd surge, I don't remember exactly"

Margaret shook her head, but Gerald spoke up.

"About twelve months ago Lee was on about a concert in Charlotte they were in New York, so she missed out, missed out on being crushed to death in a crowd surge, two of her friends went, one was pulled from the crowd Mandy, but the other friend Rochelle was dead" Mandy was the same one who had told them of the excitement.

Gerald went on.

"I can tell you the news vans in town are unbelievable, wait see"

Nick offered. "Oh, I would believe anything you showed me, you could have the lord Jesus Christ off the cross and standing next to me, with Godzilla on the other side, I would believe that"

As Gerald turned on to South street, and continued down toward Kent Street, the traffic in the town had trebled, the local Sheriffs and Deputies had some control, but they were waiting on backup, the camera crews, along with the vans, had taken up any space available, one a CNN van, parked across the driveway, of the towns Coffee shop, the owner, who was about to deliver to his regulars, a big solid sixty year old, who had been perplexed by the goings on, got out of his car and went to the CNN van looked in the driver side, saw there was no one in there and spied the keys hanging in the ignition.

He stood at the side of the van and yelled.

"Alright, I am doing this for the business in Polk County" He got in and started the van, and as he drove off, with cables and bits and pieces of computer trailing behind the van, those followed by the network staff, explain this to your boss, coffee shop owner had thought to himself as he looked out the side mirror and saw the circus trailing behind him.

Nick cackled at the van; he saw the comedy in it.

Margaret asked.

"What is the joke?" Nick's laughter trailed off as he said.

"Oh, it's just Shrives Island the press and Shrives Island, they are the same here, anything for a story"

They joined Nick in his laughter which was cut of suddenly as they came to the corner of Kent.

OZ, THE GREAT AND POWERFUL

In the changed town of Shrives Island, over the last couple of days it had attracted its older name The Crossing.

The extra bridges under construction in and out of the city limits of the shire, had been appropriate, they would be needed, a new necessity, within and around the town.

Life didn't go back to normal, well not the same normal, it was a changed normal, all the new things to do with the people of the town, especially those in the older quarter, just that one change to have Jack and Estelle Lester back, a fit and trim Uncle Pete, even down to the spinster who had become known in the town, Rose.

On the day that Nick left Shrives Island, Mark had offered to drive him the long trip to Bairnsdale, where he would take a small plane to Moorabbin, and then he had an hour in a hire car out to Tullamarine.

He had arrived back at the island early in the afternoon, and had gone to Uncle Pete's, where he was told that they had all gone to a meeting out at the Grange Farm, Uncle Pete had said he wasn't needed, but he would be blown away if Mark wasn't, he said.

"I would get my but out there and, in a hurry, I reckon they would be waiting for you"

Mark sat at the front bar Uncle Pete opposite him, after he had propped himself in the seat he said.

"Uncle Pete, please don't rush me, can I have a Double Chock Malt, and a piece of apple and raspberry pie, I just want to sit and eat my pie and drink my malt, I need to think" Uncle Pete regarded him, he did look forlorn, somewhat distracted, Uncle Pete spoke up.

"Hey, what did he share with you, you look stumped, what's wrong Mark?"

He placed the pie in front of him with a serviette wrapped cutlery, and went to the milkshake mixer, not taking his eyes from Mark.

"He told you something that has you stumped, I can tell after all the years under the bridge, What has he told you"

"He said he was convinced that the explosion in this town has reverberated back to New York, it is a coincidence that the American Government has covered it up with a terrorist attack, I think he is biting of more than he can chew on his own, I just hope he is right, I just hope he has it figured"

Uncle Pete, mixed Marks malt, and had come back to the counter placing the milkshake down along with a glass, he poured Mark the first of the malt, and stuck a straw in it.

"Well, if you know him like we all do, you know it will be fine" Mark then said.

"If it is going down as Nick says, well anything could happen" Pete offered.

"You really need to get out to the Grange house; I know they had all met out there two hours ago"

Mark drove into the turnaround, he saw Ian's car along with Jessica's 4WD and that was it, he was the only one they would be waiting for.

He got out of the car and walked up the stairs, the house was quiet, he called out as he went into the hallway, as he made his way down toward the huge lounge room he heard the muttering of voices, as he turned the corner, he found the rest of "The Players"

Ian looked rather nervous, as much as Mark had felt, he spoke up as he entered the room.

"So I suppose this is it, this is what it all comes down to"

Jess who was there for the boys got up from the seat she had been sitting in, she went to Mark and embraced him in a hug and pulled back he looked at him and spoke.

"I know Nick may think he has things covered, but I went to the two-hour mark on Longstreet's tape, come take a look.

Jess went the wide screen T.V. that had been hooked up to Nicks camera she hit play.

The screen flickered to life, the darkness was muted by the poor light, water dripped in the foreground, the camera was catching the interior of a cave, a huge cave, the ceiling through the muted light you could see going up and up, it was damp and as there was a single Dolphin Eveready torch cutting through that tepid light, and then you saw, it pulsed oozing yellow puss, it crawled and slithered, slowly, the torch stopped swinging and stood still, that single beam cutting through the gloom, allowed the viewer to focus on thing that was approaching, the person placed the torch down on the rock out crop, and then you saw Michael Longstreet, he moved away from the camera and reappeared carrying something in a sheet, he placed it down and moved back behind the torch bringing up the beam so you could watch it eat, it was quick, it was fattened up obviously having a supply of corpses was a start.

It was grotesque, its body a misshapen mess, all the things of your nightmares, its head had resembled a Dragon, but it had no wings, its elongated body, covered with green scales had allowed the animal to sprout eight legs, the legs of a spider.

Its maw opened and it regur gated over the body the oozing yellow slime, a proboscises lashed out of its mouth, whipping around in the air, until it landed in the mess in front of it and sucked it up, after it had eaten it raised its head to the ceiling of the cave and wailed, it was then that Longstreet turned the camera on himself, he looked a rather bit crazy, he was gabbling into the camera, talking nonsense and gibberish, but said in perfect clarity.

"This is the eater of souls, she will soon take the world, and I will be beside her"

Miranda walked over to the T.V and switched it off.

Mark had now known why Ian had looked so nervous, and why Mark himself stood their open mouthed, Miranda was the first to speak.

"Well, Ian Mark, there is no need beating around the bush" She said just as she had less than a week ago, but the defiance and timbre in her voice had thrown all three of them Mark Ian and Jess.

Jess looked at Miranda, Miranda returned the gaze, the look in Jess's eye held an aura of confusion, Miranda went on while holding Jess's eyes.

"We now know we are not just dealing with nefarious ghosts" Jess in that instant remembered it was only nights ago she was sitting in Uncle Pete's with the pre-teen Miranda and her brother, eating their "Last Meal" and after which Tim was lost he had been thrown into the Neitherworld, lost to Miranda for a lifetime, almost, Jess had thought to herself Miranda has lived the life on her own, she should have had Tim by her side, especially over their formative years anyway, the ghosts had been real Miranda and Tim are, were proof of that to all of them.

But the ghosts of Desmond and Joshua Brown were just as real, and viewing the tape of the footage, Desmond is not even aware of the thing he had been covering for, Longstreet had been lured in as the "Human" character in the whole charade, and he had played his role to a "T", his prints on the axe at the mill was genius, kept everyone guessing.

Miranda went on.

"It has become a particular problem, and until it is done, there will be no peace, so you two need to finish this" Ian spoke.

"Are you sure you have this pegged Miranda?" She answered.

"I will show you, come" She turned and went out of the lounge room down the hallway toward the larder, she stopped at the door to the cellar, she opened the door, the dark stairway below smelt dark and dank, she said motioning down the cellar stairs.

"Down there, you two need to go now, you will know, you will be guided" Mark stuck his head into the stairway and took in a lungful of air and spoke.

"It smells, familiar, it smells ok" Ian goes to marks side and sniffed, he looked at Mark knowing on his face, he whispers.

"Uncle Pete's"

They turned to the woman with their goodbyes, Ian and Mark both asked Jessica to look after their wives and she had agreed, then they turned and started down the stairs into the darkness, there would be light enough if they needed it.

That afternoon, Miranda sat with Jessica, and talked about the danger that Nick had placed himself.

That evening it was decided that she would go to Nick, she would fly out on the first available flight,

On the hill, where once a huge house stood, the water had begun to slow down, the ground was changing around the fountainhead, the Boab, had begun to grow, it had been amazing so far how strong the tree had been, its growth so far had been double that of a sapling, almost to a Tree overnight.

Its roots had been drinking the waters from the Odistgeeg, and the Spencer rivers.

"Wake up" It was a call, but an echo rang down from the hill, into the town, Pete heard it as did Rose, Rhonda, everyone had heard it in town.

"Wake up"

It was emanating from below the tree, out of the ground, from the roots, the roots that had given this tree life, trying to come in sync with the root stock that had been added to it days prior, it grew again, tripling its size in almost an instant, Its trunk solid standing wide, tapering, where its trunk led out to limbs, branches reaching out in all directions, to gather you up, its foliage led to blooms, buzzing with life, honey bees and birds.

By now the shops were all empty and the streets were full, everyone had come out to see what was happening, Pete, was standing under his awning, he was wiping his hands with a tea towel he had in his hand, the birdsong being produced echoed down the hill in a haze of sound, confused by the multitude, Kookaburras, parrots, eagles, finches, birds of all variety's.

From the chirps to the caws and cry's, there came a melody and with the melody the tree woke up.

It shook, its leaves shuddered, the flowers fell, its bark moved, eyes opened, and a mouth appeared under a bulbous nose.

The birdsong had continued becoming clearer as the seconds ticked away, people stood in silence, listening, and then adding to the birdsong the people all begin to sing, like in a trance, "Oh Oz the great and powerful, Oz the killer of worlds,,,,,,,,,

CHAPTER TWENTY-FOUR

POLK COUNTY

Nick had heaved in a huge sigh, the news teams had been a joke but the house had taken the breath from him, Gerald pulled over and they slowly alighted from the car, Nick who was seeing for the first time, Margaret and Gerald and Lee who had been blown away by the size of it, Nick was stunned.

There was no semblance anywhere of the playground equipment, and the tree, a huge Boab, which had no business being where it was, the strong bottle trunk, knotted with a face, the eyes closed, its mouth frozen in a death grip, the face was tortured, sprouting from the tree, was a house, here was an eave, running along its branches, a window sitting at a slant, was trying to shift itself to a right, the Boab resisting it until finally, the mouth opened and screamed, a long screeching pain wrecked howl, and then it fell quite again.

Later, back at the Ranch house, it was a long house, sprawling, with rooms that opened on to courtyards, even a chapel for the many religious visitors Gerald had received, in the end they settled in Gerald's study, a collection of people, mostly tribes people, wanting to know what to do about the grotesque monstrosity growing in the main bit of town.

Gerald explained what Nick was there to do, deal with the problem, after they had been satisfied, although only just getting the confidence of the Tribal Chiefs, and had showed them out, they had come together in conference, Margaret, Gerald, Nick, with Lee listening in.

Lee sat and sat, taking the information as it came, and each time they swam around the most obvious answer, finally exasperated she shrieked.

"Hey"

The three adults turned to the teenager, sitting there with a perplexed look on her face, she turned to her mother.

"You didn't hear me the other day mom, come on, Marlii, you have forgotten all about Marlii, we are similar, Marlii and me, do you know I dream of her, I have been dreaming of her for, well, years, I told you just the other day, gee don't you remember" Margaret looked over to Nick and then to Gerald, and then back to Lee, and said. "That's it, we forget, until it shows its face we forget it" They gathered into a circle of four, each would remind another, finally it was coming at them at a speed, and the trees were a major piece of the puzzle, Marlii was the answer.

THE SIXTH INTERLUDE
"MARLII"

"So, did you think I would leave without a word?

This whole mess had begun a long time before I came along, because when I became involved with the whole mess, we were committed to go the whole way, and I know we have held up my end of the bargain.

What happened to me?

You will still need to wait a little longer to find out what had happened to me.

The house, the hauntings, the scares, the deaths, that explosion, that was the epicenter for something far more sinister than you would probably believe.

But you still must be waiting to know what happened to me in the beginning, when the Boab took me, she I found out actually nurtured me, I had been floating just above the either, I could see it happen as it did, the way it played out each time, but the power of this monolith of a tree, nowhere on the planet would you find a tree of life just like this tree.

A tree of life, mixed up in death?

Ghosts, people caught in between worlds, not being able to find their way through the either, it is confusing for some, most, but ghosts like Desmond, only fetter evil.

The Boab has educated me, as I said it has nurtured me, what can you say about a tree that will only grow in a certain place, unlike your gums and pines, as I have mentioned before, they were used to lock up Aboriginals in the early days, I know I have seen them.

I am of Yorta-Yorta clan, my Dad is full blood, my mom was a white Aussie, that doesn't diminish me, it made me aware from a verry young age, just how our people were, are being treated, the stories that I can tell you about the Boab in the dreamtime are unsurmountable, the stories that my father told me of the Boab, because when he took his walkabout, he did it properly, he went to the top end, and stayed up there for a decade, moving among family, all the while he learnt and he educated me, when I was only a baby in arms dad took me to the capital of Australia, to a protest, Dad was a part of the first tent embassy in Canberra, the Government stole my brothers youth from him, he got drafted, he was thrown into that war, that lie, he killed the enemy, but he was no baby killer, and when he came home and it was time to heal what he had done, how could he say sorry? Where was the Government then?

So I have stayed, I have taken religious instruction, that is mums fault, but she has allowed me to follow my traditional native past as much as I have wanted.

Two choices, my Methodist upbringing or am I in the Dream time?

I think it is a combination of the two, I really want to believe what the church tells me, because then the whole world will live in peace, NO, strike that, some of the world would live in peace, from my dad's side I have taken on all of the leads I could from him, our peoples are living in a prison, my father's work, he is a Forester, has been involved in Shrives Island Timber for some time he knows how to conserve the forest, where to plant, where to thin out, and where to strip the land and begin again, the balance of nature was always over the re planting of trees, I have them in my blood,

All my life, yes I am in the Dreamtime, I am a part of the Dreamtime, I am of Yorta, I am alive but I am dead, I have the oldest believes in my mind, and if you look into my mind, into my head, I can show the path, a path that goes everywhere, even to Sherwood County, the Scottish Highlands, the Jungles of the Fijian islands to Polk County, they travel deep underground deeper than anything should go, maybe that is it, Hell is supposed to be down there, from my Mom, the evil devil and his cohorts are down there waiting to eat you up, maybe, the roots of the Boab have been to Hell, have visited Hell, and some of it has hung on, travelled to our world on the roots of the Boab.

Maybe we will see each other later, but maybe we will never cross paths again, but either way, I know that we must win this war, we need to kill this evil, for this world to be safe again.

Ah so what happened to me, well, let me fill you in, Craig had known about me the whole time but was sworn to secrecy, when he left me he remembered seeing me disappear into the tree, what the Boab has taught me has been lifetimes worth, my existence has allowed me to visit the worlds outside our own, but, I have been forbidden to appear in my time, for now, I know the Boab, my life force has become stronger, many times over, maybe this was because of my knowledge of this majestic tree, I have committed myself to the battle that lay ahead, if I am asked I will give my life, my soul to overcome the evil that we have been left to deal with, the evil found itself at The Crossing, there it tried to lay its roots, but it had not considered encountering the Boab, I have seen it all, the Boab did not shield me from anything, for a while I was in my brothers head, Rusty, he had encountered a company of U.S Grunts, after they had torched a village, there had been an argument among the Aussie Command, and the Command of the U.S, they would explain this away as another Viet Cong hideout, Lance Corporal Stephen (Rusty) Smith moved the Australian contingent of Australian soldiers around the village and into the relative safety of the rice paddies,

It was late in the afternoon when they had been greeted by fire, it was a contingent of the American Grunts had flanked them to the north, shut them up, but it backfired on them hugely, and could not keep it out of the press, the Aussies massacred the Americans, leaving none of the twenty five alive with only one death, and maybe a couple of non-life threatening injuries for the Australians, first the Americans tried to say it was "Friendly Fire" incident, Warrant Officer Steven (Rusty) Smith countered that first press release with his own little packet of information, which got him drummed out, they could have just murdered him, saved themselves some effort, but the "Dreamtime Ghosts" had been looking over Rusty, so he got out unscathed, well maybe a little scarred, but then I am in the heads of infants, baby children, all ages, all ethnicity's, colors, lots of different languages lots of different tounges, I have been there to see those who offend, and are protected by the Pedophile judges, Pedophile police forces, Pedophile politicians, Pedophile's everywhere, Pedophile Priests and God forbid, Pedophile Social Workers, the woman as much as the men Pedophiles, they are the monsters not the media hyped up version of a monster, but the real monsters out there, they have a face that you know, Rusty could have been an offender, but I know the good human being he is, and I know the filth that inhabit this planet, moving anonymously just below the surface, that is the scrouge that will be cleaned from the earth.

So you see, this is it, this is I think my Granda said to me "The war to end all Wars"

I think I will take on that mantle thank you, I will go now and find who I find, what I want to seek, the tree will which are so full of life will break their restraining roots and pick them up and use them to walk on, I know of four that have that power to "DO" at the moment, and many more will come, I promise you this will be a battle to die for.

Its time to come home.

CHAPTER TWENTY-FIVE

MARK AND IAN

As they begun down into the dark that had been a damp dark place apart from the sixty-watt globe that hung low down underground, spitting out a pitiful glow, Ian and Mark slowly crept down the steps to the hardpacked earth finally at their feet, they looked into the gloom and saw nothing move, Ian spoke.

"She said we would be guided, where is the guidance?" Mark said.

"I don't know, but remember the smell, it smelt like Uncle Pete's before, now, that's changing, the Mill, I can smell the Mill" Ian sniffed, the scent of freshly cut pine cladding, huge gums that would be used as floorboards, the earthiness expunged from their solid insides danced around his head he smelt as the huge saws hacking their way through softwoods and hardwoods, the aroma that was filling their nostrils now, was the forest.

"That's the Mill alright, it smells like the main cutting yard, I can smell a hint of diesel"

The walls shimmered and shook, and then there was thunderous crash as the stones disappeared in front of them, Ian and Mark found themselves standing right and center at the Mill, it was working, flat out, but they were not seen, by anyone, Mark approached the young logger he had known, he walked through Mark as he was nonexistent, then a mist descended over the Mill and all its inhabitants, soon Ian and Mark could not see each other, for a short time they both wandered through the haze, not hearing, not seeing, deafness engulfed them, then they were spinning, both of them felt the Vertigo as it gripped them both in its safety at falling and being suspended over a bottomless cavity, boom, they were in the house, the Desmond Brown mansion, the walls were missing, all the Boab wall paneling striped to make the boxes that had failed them, and then their hearing came back to them, they had called for each other and realized they were in adjoining rooms, then the walls were gone, they were beside each other again, the wilderness stretched for an eternity, to all points of the compass and beyond was desolation, then off in the distance there was explosion so intense so huge that the epicenter of the explosion glowed white and angry and time flashed before them, the birth of the life taker, they were made to witness the atrocities thrown at the human race, the wars for oil, the wars for land, the wars to stop an economy, the wars, the wars,

The wars, they ended, Ian and Mark slept.

Mark awoke, in serene bed of the finest feathers, warm and comfortable, Mark yawned and opened his eyes, he was sharing a room with Ian, but looking around the room, he saw there was a third bed, Ian was in one, but who was in the other, then when Mark got out of his bed and went to Ian's bed he pulled the bedsheets Ian was there, that was sure, but it was Ian from the 1973.

Mark stood there a perplexed look on his face, and when he spoke he realized that he was also the younger Mark, they both looked at each other, and then to the third bed, Mark went to it followed by Ian, each grabbing a side of the blanket they threw it back and found Marlii, they both looked at each other and back to Marlii, she opened her eyes yawned, turned to the boys with a smile on her face.

"Well boys, here we are" She got up and went to the end of the bed and took her bed coat putting it on.

"So, I know what you know, and more, I know about the explosion, I know that Nick has gone to the U.S.A."

She laughed softly and went on.

"And I know where Craig is" Marlii went to the center of the "Room" where she spun around in a tight circle three times, they were outside, they were in a dale not far from The Crossing, they were all dressed, Marlii in a green dress, that shimmered with the flowers of the Boab, they danced about, throwing a luminance that should have been blinding, Mark and Ian were dressed in armour, it was made of bark, the question on both of the boys lips was, when were they, they had known that they would not be far from The Crossing, Shrives Island, but "When" were they.

The mid -morning sun blasted its radiance down on them, they all drank in its warmth, and feasted on the beautiful countryside, the lush green paddocks, like walking on plush soft carpet, the gum trees grew higher and wider than any others any of them had seen, Marlii said.

"Follow me, I have something to show you two"

They fell in behind her, Mark and Ian were dumbstruck, Radiata Pines, Ghost Gums, an old Oak, obviously verry old the Oak was massive, the birdsong was massive, birds of many types, alighted round Marlii's head, bringing flowers to decorate her hair, coifing her long tresses into a huge bun.

They were approaching a clearing, it was a meeting place, if you looked you could see where the crowd gathered.

There was a rubbish pile of sorts set up, of sorts, it was constructed with all types of what could only described as flotsam and jetsam, the pile was made with garbage, the two boys were drawn to it.

"Mark was the first to ask.

"So what is with that" He pointed to the rubbish pile, turned too Marlii, an went on.

"It's a pile of rubbish, so what is with it" Marlii smiled, and tried to explain it.

"Well, it is what it is, its rubbish from then, from 1973, and the decades before and the decades after, it washes from the river we have an Odistgeeg river here in this time it is actually a plug, keeps nasty's away from here, from me" Marlii pointed off into the near distance, the boys followed her direction, they saw, and now heard the burble that they had known as the Odistgeeg, it had a particular sound, she went on.

"And we collect it and add to the pile, the plug, we have a battle to fight, Nick has his own battle, he bought the house, so unfortunately he has his own fight"

The boys looked back toward the rubbish heap, Ian could see the cast of an old toilet he had been sure he had once sat on it, the wheel of a bike jutted out in front of the toilet, it was Ian's wheel, the card attached to the spoke was a Fleer, it was a common card of Spiderman, it was how he had remembered the card, the wheel, but why was it here?

Mark had been looking at the heap, he had spied a tabletop, it had on a tablecloth that had belonged to his mother, it was his dad who was the mystery, it was his dad who did not know anything about, but he did know, he had known his father had been a Cop, a good Cop, he died in a gunfight, and when he looked above the table he saw his Billy Cart, he had remembered barreling down Old Town Road in that chariot he turned to Marlii and asked.

"Why have these things from our childhood, these things here, why are they here" Ian added.

"Yea my bike wheel, and it is mine, and there is Nicks old dart board, the one he bought down to the clubhouse, Craigs motor bike"

Ian pointed high onto the pile, foam eskys, and a bit of an old bus, there was bits of buildings timber as well as steel girders and joists.

Marlii answered.

"It's every day stuff, the stuff that we see every day touch, drive, I cannot explain it any more than it is a plug, when we pull it, it will all come through, it will be like scraping a scab from an infected boil"

Ian nervously stood there, looking down at his bark trousers, and had wondered how much protection he could expect from them, he asked.

"Ah, so when you "Pull" the plug, you Mark and me will be here to fight those ghosts?"

Marlii smiled and went to Ian, she put an arm around his neck.

"You, me, Mark, and the forest"

Ian looked at her incredulously, a whisper escaped him.

"The forest?"

She went to Ian's ear and whispered back to him.

"The Forest"

Ian looked up and around, the Gum's and the Pine's, along with a huge Moreton Bay Fig, he actually "Looked" at the forest, the trees were in general much larger than the tree's from his time, their time, the birdsong was fabulous, all the breeds, he heard a Kookaburra laughing, and the flat drawl cry from a Crow, he heard Rosella's, Parrot's at one stage he heard the screech of a Wedge Tailed eagle, he looked deeper into the forest then he noticed a Blue Quandong, its flowers of vivid white, he had a thought to himself, those Quandongs would light the dark.

Behind the Quandongs were Acacias or Golden wattles, and further into the forest, he spotted off in the distance Mountain Ash, and Jarrah eucalypts, he had remembered he had done a project on Milling trees, and what he had learned about tree's had fascinated him so much his mother had bought him a book on Australian tree's he had read that book cover to cover, well he couldn't remember how much he had actually researched, tree's, that book, "Majestic trees of the Southern Land" was becoming tattered, that book was returning back to the earth after starting life as a tree, it was pulled down, cut and pulped, and there you go Paper, Marlii had snapped him out of his daze.

"Ian, here is someone you will want to see" He came out of gaze into the forest and turned to see Craig standing beside Mark, Marlii went on.

"Oh I forgot, this one here will help us battle them as well, but now that the three of you are here there is something we must do, sit, and watch, observe what I do"

The boys went into an embrace, they all stood there, arm linked through arm, their heads in a cluster, they stood there not a word spoken among them, but they were all thinking of Nick.

They broke away from each other and turned to Marlii, Mark asked.

"Where do you want us to sit?"

"Anywhere here in the clearing, sit on the grass tufts"

She pointed to where tufts of grass would offer them good seats for this show, she went on.

"Make yourselves comfortable, I don't know how long this will take" The boys sat close together, facing Marlii.

"Good, now you are settling here we go" Marlii took a few steps back from the boys and spread out her arms, and stood with her feet a bit apart, the boys had known that Marlii was standing in the shape of a Pentacle, she closed her eyes and branches sprouted from her arms, not out of her arm but out of her dress, they reached up into the sky, and on its highest limbs a Wedge Tail came to roost, then in a flutter, birds of every size and color came to Marlii, in the flurry it was hard to know just what bird you were looking at, once they had settled, they had made out birds the size of a Finch through to Parrot's, Magpies and Crows, there was even a flock of Seagulls, normally the loudest of any bunch, shared a limb together, they sat their quietly preening themselves.

Marlii's eyes remained closed, and she began to chant.

"Allocasuarina, Decurrens, Eucalypts" The trees had all begun to shake, their foliage danced to life.

"Serrata, Torolosa, Tessellaris, Torrelliana"

The forest was waking up, the Moreton Bay Fig had started by shaking its branches, it yawned and instantly there was a face, its eyes squinting, it shook its huge wide trunk.

"Signata, Acacia, Gregoriam"

The three boys observed this with an of wonder, they had seen tree's wake up, but the Morten Bay Fig was truly monumental, its huge wide trunk that opened out into a broad umbrella, below its foliage you felt safe, its name was Ficus Mac.

Marlii opened her eyes.

The tree spoke.

"Marlii the wonderful, you call on me to help you in your quest, but you ask for all of the forest" At that all the other trees came to life, Pines and Gums, Acacias, Yellow Box, Mountain Ash, the Blue Quandongs, and Jarrahs.

They all watched as the tree's woke up, shaking their branches, their foliage shivered dropping flowers and leaves to the ground like confetti that had been thrown into the air.

Ficus moved its limbs around like he was "Limbering up", his leaves shook furiously his body was breathing heavily the Bark was heaving, it moved just like skin, old skin, sun beaten skin, its face was a patchwork of scars, had Ficus Mac seen battles.

Its right brow furrowed as it looked down at the three boys.

"And who are these three?" "This is Craig, Ian and Mark, they have been bought here by Yggdrasil the Ash, they will help you battle them as they are human ghosts after all, the boys will bring the human touch"

The trees began to move forward toward the clutch of humans now among them.

An old gnarly Gum who had been known as Globulas, came to the front of the forest now gathering in strength it spoke

"These, kids, what use will they be, there is nothing of them"

The Gum reached out with its gnarly arm, scratching Mark on the shoulder, the bark armour stood up to the tree, but Mark winced away just the same, Mark had felt the way the three boys felt, no fear, but genuine wonder, Globulas spoke.

"Well, maybe, this armour will be strong, but I don't see it protecting them"

A blue Quandong which was known by the name Elaeo, was standing next to the Moreton Bay Fig, it looked up at the much larger tree beside it and spoke.

"So at least there is three of them, when we have battled for them in the past normally there is only one, and an adult, these three, along with Marlii, I think we can overcome what we need to"

One of the Conifers offered.

"I have no idea why we need to help them out at all, I mean they are full of destruction, just look at what we have done for them, ALL of them, but they will go on hacking down our brothers and sisters, for their own comfort"

Marlii came to the front of the boys standing there looking up to the Moreton Bay Fig and spoke in a solemn tone.

"I know how you feel about us, we do harvest forest for our own gain, our comfort, to burn, to keep us warm, to build our homes, but this is different, these malign ghosts will stop at nothing, and the thing in the center of it is set on destruction, it will not stop until this world is finished, and if we don't take up the mantle to fight these things we may as well give up now"

Ficus Mac closed its eyes, his bark mouth twisted he let out a sigh and spoke.

"We all know what is transpiring, we know that this thing has spread, and continues to spread across the world, its poisonous tendrils have reached ALL across the world, our brothers and sisters all over have been seeing a sickness working through them, no I think we forget that we remain alive after harvesting it how we are treated, that make us what we become, I say we fight again"

That had answered the question that had been on the three boy's lips, Mark spoke for them.

"We have been shitting ourselves, over all of this, we didn't ask to be chosen there was no choice in it for us, we are here because it was destined, we are here because we have seen what this thing is capable of, it's not Desmond Brown, nor is it Michael Longstreet or Joshua, I think we are here to stop those "ghosts" they are a distraction"

Ficus Mac spoke.

"So have you all had your say, Ian what do you have to add, Craig?" Ian just shook his head he had nothing to say.

Craig on the other hand had much to say.

"Let's go get it done, let's go and kick some butt, and this time without the boomsticks" As the light began to change on them, the birdsong saw them into the last night before chaos, deadfall was collected for fires as the nighttime came they had all settled, the forest fell silent all that could be heard was the bird song, which built to a crescendo and then stopped, just as suddenly.

CHAPTER TWENTY-SIX
MARLII AND LEE.

Lee had been in her room later that night, she was beat, and as she pulled back her bed cloths, he heard it faint in her mind.

"Lee"

It was more than a whisper but not much more than spoken softly. It came again.

"Lee" This excited her because she had known Marlii had been there in her dreams, she was waking, was this a waking dream?

And then Marlii was with her.

There was an auric light coming in by the window, but that should not have been it was dark outside, and then the light was in the room, her bedside lamp dimmed in the glow of the aura.

"I am mustering the forest, you must do the same, we must bring our tribal magics together, Nick is set to go in for the final fight"

The auric light had begun to dissipate, it dissipated into Lee, and she was gone.

CHAPTER TWENTY-SEVEN

THE APOCALYPSE

Nick, Margaret and Gerald had been in talks with all the chiefs from the region.

The Boab was not meant to be here, it grew in only two other places on the planet, and this was not one of them it was far too cold in Polk County for the Boab seed to germinate.

An old Cherokee Chief, Arwana, had said to them that tree is anomaly.

"It should not be here, the fact that it is here is a travesty" Gerald spoke.

"It is here because it has to be, it is protecting us from that house, Nick needs to go to the tree, he knows it will be strong" At that moment there was flash of light from Lee's bedroom, Margaret jumped up from where she was seated and went quickly to the room, she came back seconds later.

"She is not there, she has gone" Nick looked at Margaret and back to Gerald and spoke.

"Marlii, you both remember her saying this morning, she dreamt of Marlii, I would say that is where she has gone, I think we will find her with Marlii, she will be safe with her, but I think we can't wait any longer, I have a job to do, so let's all get to it"

While Gerald and Margaret prepared Nick for his journey, Jess was winging her way to the U.S.A. Polk County to be exact.

As they approached the corner of Kent, the house had grown in size, the crowd being forced much further back now the police cordon had been up for a little over two hours, Nick, who had been nervous about going into the house on his own, but it had been decided that was the way it should be, as they approached the sheriff guarding the cordon, Gerald spoke to the Sheriff he allowed them entry.

Nick looked up at the tree, house and the Boab opened its eyes, it shuddered, flowers fell, it spoke.

"Nick, I have been waiting for you, come we must make haste" Nick turned to Margaret and Gerald.

"So, this is it, here we are, and you heard the tree, I've gotta go"

The three of them embraced, and when they broke away Gerald had spoken.

"Are you sure you want to do this on your own?"

Nick answered solemnly. "There is no other way it can only be me, on my own with my note pad and pen, I will do this on my own, and with your lot chanting, keep them chanting, and with him"

He nodded toward the Boab.

He shook Gerald's hand once more and kissed Margaret on the cheek and turned and went. On his approach to the Boab it once again shook it limbs, it lifted one of its roots, Nick disappeared into the tree.

Marlii was in the either, she was not alone Lee was with her, they floated above their worlds looking down they saw the either stretch and fold in on top of itself the swirling colors coming together and bouncing off each other, they both spied the boys and could see that they were preparing for the battle along with the Forest, but there was no sign of Nick, he had gone into the tree, the Boab, but he could not be seen, they must find him, it is imperative that they can see their subjects for the magics to work, they saw the Cherokee along with other first nations people, they had continued to chant for the tree, and Nick, they wandered through the either, searching and searching, but to no avail.

He walked into the entry way of the Desmond Brown Mansion; it was how he had remembered it the last day they were there.

He spoke up.

"Boab, why have I come back to the house, my house, it is not how I left it?" "It is Desmond Brown and his cohorts, don't be fooled"

He continued forward and soon was upon the maw of a cave, there was no light emanating from it, he thumbed the switch on his Eveready dolphin, the beam cutting through the darkness to show the darkness behind it, he had heard noises from inside, he listened, harder, were they human, or were they not, he listened again craning his head and concentrating, they were not animal sounds nor where they human, the cycle of sounds went around in his head for a minute, a guttural sound, a low growl with a series of clicks and taps at the end of it, and it was getting closer, the clicks and taps were coming closer and closer, then the light fell on Michael Longstreet.

"Hello Nick"

Said the voice, that was Michael Longstreet, Desmond Brown as well Joshua Brown.

The forest is alive, trees moving around making weapons, crude weapons, ugly weapons, hewn from themselves, branches formed into clubs, spears, hammers.

The boys walked around and through the forest, watching them work, Globulas shook and shivered producing sap which fell to the ground and instantly became solid, he looked down toward the boys, its bark mouth opened up into a smile, the boys looked down at the sap sitting on the ground and growing hard in front of them.

Globulas spoke to them, its narrow long trunk, leading out with limbs that sprouted leaves, along with small wattle flowers, it was the flowers that held it soul.

"They are bullets, but you have no need of a gun, you simply throw them, very effective, fill your pockets Mark, Ian and Craig, fill them up, as this will be the battle of all battles, I assure you of that"

Craig bent over and began collecting sap bullets stuffing his pocket full with them Ian and Mark were quickly down next to him.

The earth thundered, the trees all coming together, once arranged and into their species, (A human term) among their number was the Moreton Bay Fig, it came to the Eucalypt, and addressed the boys.

"You are becoming prepared, good, join me at the front of the column"

Mark Craig and Ian fell in behind him, they walked to the top of a small hillock, once there all was laid before them, it was an awe-inspiring site, Norfolk Pines stood beside huge Yellow Box, Mountain Ash along with Jarrah's and Oak's, there were Gums, as well there were Acacias, Wattles, deciduous as well as ever greens, all were grouped together, a small track running around and among them, Ficus Mac addressed them all.

"This is it, I won't go into a raging mad speech about what we are, we know what we are, we must care for the three boys who fight this battle with us, it will be an epic battle and one we must win" The Forest Army all began to shake and shudder dropping their leaves and foliage, brandishing their limbs which now had rocks and stones in their grasps, as well their weapons made from their very own limbs, a Yellow Box who went by the moniker Melliodora, its limbs all sharpened to a needle like point, yelled.

"Impale them all, finish this mess for the last time" There was crescendo of noise as the trees again began to yell and call for the battle.

It was at that point, Ficus Mac picked up the three boys, leading the army forest to "The Plug"

Ficus Mac yelled into the forest.

"Oriades Signata, the time has come to remove the plug, come forward and do your deed" From the rear came a Scribbly Gum, the forest parted to let the tree through, he was as scribbly as anyone had ever seen, from the top of his highest branches his limbs were decorated with the pattern from the Scribbly Gum Moth, all the way down to the base of his trunk, his eye took on a serious look and he had furrowed his bark brows and as he approached Ficus Mac, his lips had a cunning smile.

"Ficus Mac, back to the battle"

Oriades shook, his sap rained down along with his green spear shaped leaves, the boys stood and watched the sap as it high sheen came to it as it hardened, Oriades sap dried to a brilliant gold color, the boys couldn't help themselves going to the ground and stuffing the sap in their pockets, they watched as the Scribbly Gum went to the plug, it grabbed the end of the plug and as he pulled, Scribbly Gum Moths erupted from the tree, the insects although only verry small created a mist that enveloped the whole top half of the tree, only to be dissipated as the plug was removed and the rush of air that came from the plug hole was cyclonic.

They were deafened by the roar of the rush of air that had almost managed to blow Ian Mark, and Craig, clean out of the tree, they all hung on for grim death as the cyclone blasted past them.

Then they appeared, the human ghosts, thousand upon thousand came through the portal, that had been capped with everyday refuse, and as soon as they came, they were felled, Oriades took the brunt of the wind, he had known that he would be the resistance, and that was why he had volunteered to remove the cap, the ghosts attacked him en masse, but he fought back, slashing through the ghosts and impaling them on his pointed fingers, three had gone to his face, their own faces twisted in scowls, and yells, their own whitish yellow skin sluiced in a soup of puss and blood, Oriades batted at the one going for his right eye, snagging him on a thorn, he was able to get a hold of that particular soul throwing him into the forest, he hit the limb of the Yellow Box and smashed into a million tiny pieces, the boys had begun to pelt the ghosts, every shot was true, Mark was taking aim, but before he could release, he was taken from behind, Ficus could only do so much, Mark forced his hands to the side, the ghost was just about to put its foul smelling hot breathed mouth on his throat and Mark pitched the one gold piece he had picked up after Oriades had dropped.

It hit the ghost, just above the slanted misshapen right eye, it opened a furrow there where its jellied brain oozed out of the wound, the ghost looked into Marks eyes, its face flowered into a brilliant explosion, the look in its eyes as it felt the explosion take, it was one of wonder.

Mark took the force of the explosion and pushed the ghost away from him, it fell from Ficus, hitting almost every limb on the way down, smashing it, limbs fell and disappeared.

Ian was sitting on a limb a little higher than mark and witnessed this with an almost uninterrupted view, Craig on the other hand was firing of in rapid succession, he had missed it.

The forest raged against the ghosts, the boys held their own, but then the ghosts began to come with fire, catapulting fire into the foliage of the Oaks the evergreens, and the Mountain Ash, they began to burn, but it would take much more than fire to destroy these trees, most had lived through more savage forest fires in the past.

They shook and shivered furiously extinguishing the fires in rapid succession, the smoke haze over the battlefield was acrid with the remains of the ghosts burning more fiercely than a forest fire.

A tall Norfolk Pine simply known as Pinni, came through from the back of the battlelines, he had learned in previous battles the most effective way to pierce a victim and have them slide from the limb without sticking.

The spirits and ghosts kept coming, centuries, eons of displaced ghosts.

Ghost of many faces.

Mark swung down from the limb where Ficus had put placed him and as he swung he pitched three stones one after the other, shattering the ghosts, one he hit in the chest, and it went over in a splattering mess, it exploded in every direction blood and gore decorated the trunks and limbs of the oncoming forest, of the oncoming army, Mark landed on a larger lower branch and when he turned he was face to face with his father, it struck out at him, heaving a huge axe to cleave him, the battle axe stroke went wide of the mark, his swing went down in an arc that carried through into the branch they were standing on, the ghost father tried desperately, to pull the axe free, Ficus was not letting it go.

Mark stood there stunned, he had seen photos of his farther, and the thing before him now dressed in a business suit, but his face held the pallid waxiness of a long dead corpse, the bugs that spilled from his mouth with a putrid green slime attested to that.

Mark took aim and fired his sap into the head of the thing as it was grunting to release the axe from the grip Ficus had on the axe, he hit it directly in the center its forehead, the sap seemed to buzz around in it head, then a fire began to blaze there, it ended with an explosion that ripped down the ghosts front, ripping the suit from its skeletal frame.

He did not stop, he kept pelting his sap bullets at them, until finally he was forced to jump from the tree, where he was able to replenish his bullets, he twisted and feinted, as he harvested enough to get back into the battle.

Ian had stayed where he was put, Ficus and he would be the best of friends once this was over, Ian was harvesting sap directly from his limbs, as the sap rolled of Ficus Ian was taking and pitching it, while it still held a waxy feel, when they found their targets, they were the shiny solid sap bullets that Globulas had showed them.

Then the plug exploded.

The mouth that had somewhat contained the flow of ghost, had ripped open leaving a huge gaping hole between the two worlds, now the multitude had trebled, quadrupled, it had felt that they were to battle the ghosts from time beginning.

Nick stood before the ghost of Michael Longstreet, it shimmered in front of him, changing, giving glimpses of Desmond and Joshua Brown.

Nick spoke.

"What are you, where do you come from?" It chuckled, spilling into a laugh, as it laughed harder Nick remembered Desmond laughing just the same.

"I am old, I am ancient, I have been since the beginning of time, I am immortal" Nick took a step toward the thing purporting to be Michael Longstreet, the torchlight shone directly into his eyes, he had the eyes of Joshua, it disappeared from his sight, he flicked the torch this way and that trying to find the thing, there was silence, he had heard a trickling stream off somewhere in the black inkiness of the cave.

Then there was that sound again, low and guttural, it finished again with a series of clicks and taps, it was hard to pinpoint the direction the sounds were coming from, he listened more intently, the groan came, then the clicks, it was when the tapping began again Nick realized it was coming from just beside him, he turned to see an oozing blob, it was like an overstuffed rubbish bag, just like the ones he had remembered carrying out of a Chinese Restaurant he had worked at just after absconding from Shrives Island.

It was immense, what was making the clicking and tapping sounds had been the things sensor, it slithered toward him, it reared up, clicking clicking, tap tap tap, a proboscis slithered from the end of the thing, it was not human, it was not animal, was it alien?

It regarded Nick in a careful stance, Nick yelled.

"Stop this" It stopped mid click, it came closer to Nick, it trumpeted a note that almost deafened Nick.

A voice came from above.

"Oh you will be tasty" "You and me, I will crush you, I have been warned of you, and I will not let you pass" Nick bought up his note pad, and put his pencil to the paper, and he began to write.

When he had finished, he looked down to see what he had written.

"Cant seem to see the forest, for the trees"

"Like black rose that nobody can hold no one"

He stopped and thought for a moment, it was fooling him.

"I can change this I can write it all over" He went back to his pad and began to write, and a laugh boomed down from above.

"You do not understand do you, you have no idea where your friends are what their fate may be, the perfect split, the three, who were with you just yesterday, they are going to their deaths as we speak, the multitude will soon take them over and they will be finished, and the two girls know nothing" The Desmond Brown thing came to him, it was more ugly than the other thing could be, it was still rotting like a fish, from the head down, it spoke.

"You know you are trapped, give it up and die for me now" He walked up to the Desmond Brown thing and plunged the pencil into the putrid mess that was his right eye.

The Desmond Brown thing shrieked and disappeared, the proboscis was back, it trumpeted again almost deafening him again, it raised itself above him and swallowed him whole.

LEE

Hi, a greeting to you in the tradition of the Cherokee Nation, My name is Lee Thorn, like my mother I have taken my father's name my Cherokee birth name, is Little Pebble, I was rather small when I came along, my father bathed me in waters of Polk County rivers, giving me strength and allowing me to grow, to learn how to become a part of the land, to live with the planet the way we were meant to inhabit, my father a proud Cherokee Chief left the Nation to "Take a Job' with government ironically enough Forestry, he is involved in decisions that "Manage" our woods, like they need protecting, if people just stayed away we all would have thrived, from the time hat De Soto arrived it has never really been the same, our farmlands were taken away from us, that was the first thing, when we began to see the land turn over to the United States Government, the loss of the wild life, now the bears are returning, and in greater numbers, and we need to get along with them, when Mum told me I would be attending school in New York City, I was heartbroken, now I am glad, had I not been in New York the day September eleven, I would have surely become insane, but that whole silly sorry mess is still pending further investigation, those buildings did not fall down like that without human intervention, and I don't trust George Bush, oh and building seven was blocks away from the Twin Towers, but that is why I have been chosen to take my spiritual path, I have followed the tribes ways, and after knowing reservation life, well I would prefer my freedom, just as my father has, this thing found is way by the roots of the Boab, the Boab is known as the Tree of Life, why it grows in two places only in the world unless propagated?, is still a mystery, I believe the Boab Tree finds itself where it needs to be, its root's weave a line all the way back to Yggdrasil, that of the Nordic trees, of Odin and Freja, it is no different to the tales, the stories, that my father has told me, I believe that there is a truth to those stories, just as Marlii who holds the tradition of her father, full of the tribal understanding that a father passes on to his offspring I have had that, my father has allowed me to wear feathers at our last Pow Wow, I wore the plume of a Hawk, my dad said that it is my totem animal, my familiar, but the Boab, why did it find its way to me? I will tell you, the Boab picked Polk County, because I was the closest auric friend to Marlii, I had known for some time that something big was about to happen, but when I saw that tree, house thing, and at the time, the explosion in The Crossing, the Twin Towers, and Polk County, and that is where the Boab's root system is the strongest here, had that house taken "root" as it first seemed it would, well I don't want to think of that, but to know you are facing the killer of all mankind, well, that would be Nick, I hope he has a handle on this, and then there are the three boys, fighting a war that should never been allowed, I am sure the forest will protect them, my

Mom, who is only just understanding that I had a relationship with Marlii, Mom insisted that she had saved my life when that concert crush took two of my closest friends, Marlii had lost a friend in the exact same way, crushed to death under a sea, no an ocean of people, I could not imagine how that would feel, having your breath crushed from your lungs, every breath you take is shorter, and shorter, aghh that would be awful, but I will meld my magic through Marlii's magic, because if we don't do this it is the end of the world as we know it, it's over, kaput, so we win or that thing does, in the tradition of the Cherokee I go forward and offer my magic to Marlii together we will overcome.

CHAPTER TWENTY-EIGHT
PART TWO
THE APOCALYPSE

The forest had kept pounding the ghosts from every time, and any place they came from, one thing was for certain, that portal was their one destination, the boys had not escaped unscathed, they were all going topless, their armour coats flung into the elbow of a branch, their hair was singed to the edges, but their bark trousers would be enough protection for now, the fires had been doused, and the flow of ghost had slowed, those who were coming through were the last vestiges of the real light, and then Desmond Brown was there, he appeared to them full of confidence, and his face was intact, in fact from the tip of his perfectly shined boots to the perfectly positioned cravat, and that top hat at its rakish angle, he held in his right hand a whip, Mark looked directly at it and bounced down from Ficus and stood by his trunk, a cease fire was called, the forest fell quite but cautious, Ficus spoke.

"Why do you do this, this destruction, these ruins, will you not call a truce?"

Desmond floated just above the ground, Mark was joined by Ian and Craig, Mark nudged Ian and whispered.

"Look, in his right hand, I have that whip, the older me" He went into his back pocket and the stick was there, he pulled it out and held it down beside himself, he whispered.

"Sshh, listen, follow my lead"

Then from behind them a man's voice spoke up.

"Desmond Brown, how I have waited for this day to come, heck this hour to be exact"

It was Tim, or as he liked to be known at this point in his existence, Timothy, Mark had recognized his voice straight away, it was his voice, just older, it dawned on Ian and on Craig at the same instant, he approached the boys, he had looked twenty, twenty one years, he was well dressed in a loggers shirt, his trousers were pressed to a razor thin crease, his hair, something about him that was striking was hidden under a stout blue fedora that was topped with cock feathers

"Hello Mark, Ian, Craig" He spread his hands out and spoke.

"I thank the forest for coming to our defense, again"

He looked up at Desmond Brown.

"I know your secrets, four lifetime's some would say, but I got them in one, you do go back some way Desmond Brown, your son, well, not as effective as you"

Desmond began to change to a brilliant hue of magenta red, he huffed.

"You, you think you know my secrets, really, I don't think so"
"Your whip, take a look at it"

He bought up a stick and brandished it toward Timothy, he took a step back from Timothy when he realized he was brandishing a stick.

Mark stood forward holding the Crop in his hands, Desmond shrank back further when he realized that Mark was holding the whip he bellowed down at Mark.

"Give that back to me you little scoundrel"

Mark slashed the whip and yelled through gritted teeth.

"You want it, come get it, but you won't, you are too weak" Memory's flooded through him, he was in his "Older" self, but he was remembering horses, he was a race horse trainer, a rather successful Race Horse trainer, and then there was Cindy, sweet, wonderful Cindy.

Timothy went toward Desmond, he shrieked back, and his face turned to a scowl, the ghosts all contained behind him shrank back along with him, he said.

"Lets fight, sort the chaff out"

Timothy ignored him and turned to Craig and addressed him.

"So you do know, I took a couple of these" He pulled from his pocket a plain paper bag, from it he took two sticks of Dynamite, and went on, holding a stick in each hand.

"You call these boom sticks, how appropriate, here catch" He threw a stick of Dynamite, Craig reached out his arms and caught it in his hand.

Timothy looked up toward Desmond and spoke.

"He is dangerous with that stuff, did you hear about the damage he done in the town that the adults put down to get this, an earthquake, so yea I would be carful if I were you" He turned back to Craig and said.

"Here is number two" He threw the second stick and Craig caught it just as swiftly with the his left hand, it was of that moment

Ian had realized that to have a pollen flower at this moment in time, would be the missing puzzle, and at that moment Ficus blooms began, and two of the flowers dropped at Ian's feet, he picked them up and as he did he looked up at Desmond Brown, and back to Craig and nodded.

Timothy who had seen the exchange, distracted Desmond again.

"So, Desmond, what about your son, he got lynched by an angry mob when it was The Crossing didn't, he, they hung him from the limb of an old Morten Bay Fig just like Ficus here" Ficus Shuddered, Timothy went on.

"There were no Yard Arm available, so they strung him up on the old Ficus Tree"

The three boys began to laugh, laughter from the forest joined them, Timothy said.

"I think they have you by the balls and they are squeezing them, I can see you cringing"

This bought out gales from Ian, which in turn bought out gales from within the forest, from its beginning deep into the forest, from the Conifers to the Gums to the smaller Blue Quandong

The wind that came from this blew against the ghosts, Desmond Brown held on for grim life, and that was when Craig launched the sticks of Dynamite, one from each hand, they turned in an arc in perfect symmetry, which caught the timing of Ian pitching of the flowers, which met the sticks of dynamite in perfect timing.

The flowers turned end over end, seeing the silver glint off one of the petals, Ian had known ignition would be imminent, as the flowers came together with the Dynamite, they were on the arc of decent that would land them both squarely between those brilliantly shined and buffed Riding Boots.

The explosion was ear splitting, and anything within two armlengths was obliterated in a mass of blood flesh along with the occurring bone fragments, the wind which had continued, carried the explosion backward, giving it strength, the original flame that burnt on ignition turned to a brilliant white light, then extinguished back to the brilliant orange sun that sat there suspended before going down.

Mark who had witnessed Desmond Browns last second, remembered watching him look down at that critical moment, and the look on his face as they exploded, Mark did not actually see anything of Desmond to know what had registered because at that moment he felt the first aftershock of the explosion, they all felt the aftershock, Mark remembers his eye bulging, and popping back into place, that was when he felt his eardrums explode, both of them, blood trickled from his nostrils, and from his left ear was an eruption of blood, his hearing which had always been near perfect was, now useless to him.

Ian, who was protected from the blast by Ficus, who stood in front of him, could do nothing, but he bounced into action as soon it was safe, he went to Mark and grabbed him before he hit the ground.

What followed was a huge backward explosion, the flames had a one-way ticket back into the void, the fire hung over the portal, or pit you would now call it, spiraling down into the hole, and danced there for a minute, burned high one more time before burning out in a fierce blue green flame.

Timothy, came out of the forest, he had a bandana around his face, he went to give Ian assistance, Ficus who still had craig in one of his highest boughs, turned back to where Ian, had gone to help Mark, saw Timothy kneeling near him, he spoke down to them.

"It is gone, there is nothing there, just field and meadow" Mark had suffered a concussion, Timothy had called up to the tree, the ground shook beneath them in a shudder that lasted a full minute, trees all throughout the forest shook, when the Earthquake took them the trees shuddered, they huddled on the ground, close to the ground, they had felt safe under their umbrella, the ground shook and shuddered along with the trees, and the boys hung on along with Timothy.

When the ground subsided to a low rumble, Ficus was the first to say something.

"It seems something has happened; I mean more than getting rid of that" Ficus shrugged back toward where the "Plug" had been and went on.

"Ian, you are Ian" Mark, who was regaining a semblance of what had happened had looked up at Ian, it was the older Ian, Mark said.

"Wow, we are older, this flipping about is getting tiresome, the trees were seeing to their battle wounded, Ian Craig and Mark came together under Ficus, Timothy joined them, they met in a huddle, and when they broke they all looked up to Ficus, Timothy spoke on their behalf.

"I don't know how to say a thank you that is worthy, but we do this with sincerity"

At that Timothy led the three "Boys" into a bough.

Ficus shuddered, and continued, when he began to shake backward and forward and from side to side, he began to lose all of his foliage, his bark faced changed, it shuddered and was gone.

Marlii floated with Lee, just above the either, they saw many worlds, all in this galaxy.

They helped the boys with their fight, by adding as much protective layering around them first encasing the boys, and then around the forest as much that was left of their protective magic, they had no sign of Nick, through the veil with which they should have seen him they were looking through a dirty mist, the tried as much as they could, but there was no sign of him.

As Jess was landing at Bangor Airport, Nick had just began to battle the beast a huge maw closed over him and it was cavernous, all he could do was stand there, it was having him one way or the other, once in its mouth, but before he became homogenized, he took his Black Beauty Number 9, and stabbed the thing in its gullet, it let out a shriek, Nick did it again and again until in a tremendous heave the thing ejected him, spitting out onto the ground in the center of the cavern, Nick looked down at himself, was disgusted in what he was carrying with him, he leaned over and puked, he looked up the thing, it shimmered there, it was his father and mother, the memories that folded over in his brain was awash with vibrancy, there was even memory that he should not have, but does with perfect clarity.

It was his teacher in Prep, she had been encouraging, it came forward with its proboscises raised in a gesture it was set to impale him this time, but it stopped short lowering its proboscises.

A voice again from above boomed, and cried, but it fell silent for a moment before bellowing into laughter.

"You really think you can defeat me, well, you cannot, I will take you gobble you up, and then I will be released, it is just a numbers game, and you are the number" Nick looked up into the barren cave, he squinted to see where the voice was coming from, but there was nothing to see or so it seemed, it echoed out from all points, he was convinced that the thing who had him captured at this moment was nothing more than an oversize leech, with an oversize nose, Nick got up from the ground and spoke.

"Tell me who you are, why don't you show yourself"

It bellowed laughter again.

"Because if you see me you will be struck blind, I like you to be able to see the look on your face as I insert you into the pits" At that moment the Leech, overstuffed garbage bag began to retreat, it backed up until the light sone only on its proboscises, it hung there for a moment and disappeared, there was a silence that fell on the cavern, it was eerie, a whisper came to him.

"Nick"

Silence, then lower, quieter.

"Nick" He did not recognize the voice, it was a girls voice.

It was drowned out by the thing as it came back out of the silence.

"You, you lot have destroyed my minion, it is in taters, you will pay and so will the others"

A green light flashed around the cavern, pulsing, then the wind came, cyclonic winds that threatened to take Nick of his feet, he had hold of the note pad, and Black Beauty pencil, he was up off the ground, and then he was spinning, twirling, thrown into what could only be space?

He had known he was seeing his life flash before his eyes, as a baby dressed for a Sunday party, in his teens doing "The Job" on the mine, working in the restaurant, meeting Jessie, signing his first book deal, and then the explosion, he had tempted fate and had bought that house, and that had led to this.

He had known at that point it would go on, it would kill him and continue, beginning with the boys as well as Marlii, heck it would not stop, taking Margaret, Lee and Gerald as well.

"Think"

He began to write, and that settled him, now he was back in the library in the house, his P.C buzzed lightly on the desk, he was sitting in his comfy leather chair, and he was typing furiously onto the computer keyboard.

Little boxes on the hillside.

There's a green one and a pink one and a blue one and a yellow one.

Like black rose that nobody can hold no one.

Every time I get started, you pull me apart.

It was garbled nonsense, but he had kept writing, he had felt its presence, its confusion.

He shifted again, he was back in the cavern, sitting high on an outcrop, he was still sitting at his desk his Apple P.C buzzed its drone echoed into the cavern, once again it was eerily silent, that voice came again, this time not a whisper, a voice, he had realized it was Lee.

Lee had been the closest person to him capable of astral travel, so she was the communication conduit, she spoke again.

"Nick they have won, the Desmond Brown ghost is no more, it is up to you, you have your job to do"

And that was all he was able to hear.

He looked down at the blinking cursor and back up the screen, he had written fifteen pages, he clicked back to the top, those fifteen pages explained what had been happening, being back in the cavern he thought his odds were fifty/fifty of getting out alive.

He read how that thing had arrived here long before any man walked the earth, it has slept, fed, placed its roots, and has grown, and grown, but the Boab had tangled its roots, entwined, itself into its roots, and it grew as "It" festered with its collection.

The Boab could not let it win, and with the help of Nick, well he would succeed.

Nick went back to his writing feverishly, he did not hear it at first, he was so involved, but he heard it, almost whimpering, he stopped typing, and listened.

"Please stop, please listen to me, you can have it all"

Nick continued writing and spoke.

"I have it all, I have no need of anything"

That was when it appeared to him, it came out of the caverns innards, carrying a flaming torch, Nick shone his torch toward him, he looked human, it was an old man, his pallid pale face was framed by wiry old hair that waterfalled into a silver beard, his eyes shone the deep emerald green of someone you can trust, he raised the torch as in a gesture of meeting, as he dropped the torch, Nick could see that the man had a Loincloth wrapped around his privates.

Nick was taken back, but spoke.

"You, you are the killer of all people"

He clicked "PRINT" and got up from his desk, walking around he picked up his pencil, as he waited for the printer to do its job he continued.

"Why not show yourself to me for who you are, you said the sight of you would strike me blind, well, show me"

The old man came forward the torch held out in front of him, he stopped a foot away from Nick's face, his face was pockmarked with zits and pimples, its breath was of rotten flesh, old, gone over meat.

"This is the end, do you remember me saying I like to see you being ingested?"

It was weak, Nick felt the energy running down from his head out of the end of his toes, it was sapping it from him, he had known he had to look into its eye's, he had to see it.

Nick lunged forward grabbing the old man around the throat, his fingers danced around and swam in what was becoming and oozing pulsing soup, it changed.

There was a single movement, in front of him he had his hands around the roots of a single large eye that hung there, its crooked stare waited for Nick to release it, Nick loosened his grip.

The eye spoke.

"You cannot kill me, I am infinite" Nick raised the pencil throwing the papers he took from the printer between stabbing the pencil deep into it, there were sparks, circuitry was whizzing and popping, why? Why was there circuitry there?

Nick yelled.

"There, read that"

The single eye that at that moment was about to take Nick, investigate his mind spun, it whirred around and stopped, Nick removed the pencil and the papers fell to the ground, the eye was bleeding crimson red, it looked at him, but Nick was already in its head, the scenarios rolled in his head backward, from the felling of the Twin Towers, back rolling over he saw the wars as they were a macrocosmic all the way down to a microscopic look all the way down to "Being" in the eyes of a soldier who had nothing but saving the young girl for his own Luciferic concerns, then he was in the eyes of a serial killer, he had known one of them, his name escaped him, his eyes saw him dismembering a corpse, wrapping it in plain brown paper, and sending it off all over the nation, but mostly when he looked he had the eyes of a Politician, the wars were the worst of them, innocent young men who were taught by the Politian's to hate, hate the enemy, he forced his memory a respite and was back at home in Shrives Island, it was his birthday, he was seven, and had woken up to find the brand new bike he had dreamed of, he was thrown back into the nightmare, and at every turn there was a war, the war to end all wars, keep going back, not forward, to know what happens from here is horrific, go back, the wars, The Roman Empire, and back further, back to the stone age, he saw the thing arrive, it was Alien, he came back to himself, the eye was looking at him, trying to look into him, he yelled into it.

"I saw it all, I saw everything, everydeath, you cannot see into me because I am infinite"

He bought the pencil up above his head and bought it back down in a lowering arc, stabbing the eye up through the pupil through the flowering white egg substance to the outside, the Black Beauty number six punched through the top off the eye, blood hung from the tip of the graphite, hung there for just a moment, then went end over end, finishing as a blot on the ground, and again he pulled the pencil up, stabbing it down, yelling.

"I am infinite" Stab.

"I am infinite"

Stab.

Then there was a buzzing in his head, a memory, no an echo, he was seeing with his own eye's the forest, the boys, and Tim?

He saw the victory as it happened, and looked into that eye one final time, he saw its last dying light in there, and bought the pencil down a final time.

"I AM INFINITE"

There was a high whizzing sound and the eye exploded, this time it threw Nick after knocking the wind out of him, he was hit with shrapnel, glass, and metal from the innards of that single orb, he had known he had killed it, he had known he had finished it when he had control, for that infinitesimal moment, when he took that moment to get into its head, look and see, time for you to go was Nick's last coherent thought, and with that, Nick took the blast, to end that thing he would die ten times over.

Nick was spat out of the Boab, as it went into recovery, Gerald had been there with Margaret, she winced as Nick was thrown smoking from the Boab, she watched as he bounced twice before rolling limply onto the ground.

Margaret was the first to get to him.

"Nick, Nick"

She bent down and rolled him slowly over onto his back, he winced and held his mouth in a grimace, he tried to speak.

"Je, Jes" Margaret was handed a blanket, she threw it over him, then the Paramedics were there, and begun to go to work on him.

"No no, leave me, you cannot do anything for me, please" "Sir we could keep you alive, well for a bit any way" Nick looked up to the ambulance man, the look on his face just simply said "Really" he turned back to Margaret, and spoke, this time with more success.

"I have killed it, it is dead, look at the tree, it is shrinking, no sign of the house" He winced, the mortal wound came from the eye, as it passed through him, it began at his midriff, on his left side, continued through, destroying his organs on the way through, when it had popped out on the right side it had left nothing, his shirt hung in limp rags, the powder blue color, darkened with the blood, he only had remaining, the vestige of a ribcage, but he went on.

"It is dead, but so am I, where is Jess?"

Margaret knelt closer and whispered.

"If you can hold on for three minutes, she will be here"

Margaret looked up to Gerald, the question on her face, asked him where they were? Gerald only nodded.

With that a car came around the cross section of what had once been South and Kent, a big burbly eight-cylinder ford, it pulled up close to where Gerald had set aside some land for just an occasion, Jess jumped from the car and bounded across the playing field to where Nick had lay.

She kneeled in close, she whispered.

"Shh, don't say anything"

He looked up at her perplexed and spoke.

"No, you shh and listen, that thing is dead, I am as well"

Jessie held back the tears, until he told her what was next.

"You are pregnant, go take a pregnancy test, the other girls as well" His breath shallowed down to a whimper, the rise of the one good lung just kept on keeping on, and he went on.

"You look after our little girl"

"I would only be poison for her with what I have seen, what I have witnessed, better of dead"

He took a final breath and as his last exhalation occurred, the older Nick was gone, he was a boy, beaten and crushed just as his older forbear, it was then that Jess looked up to the cloudy lightening sky, and that was when she began to scream, Margaret was there to comfort her, as the morning turned to day, Jess finally gave up the body of Nick, now lying lifeless and cold on the ground.

Later that day, Jess was up after a long sleep, she went down to the kitchen, Margaret was up, and on the bench, a package from the local druggist, Margaret said to her.

"Use that before you get coffee, let's see how right he was" "I really don't need that to tell me I am pregnant, I had known last night, but so you don't think I am crazy I will take the test, but not before I get a coffee" Margaret got a cup from the bench and poured a hot brew, Jess was there with the sugar, and lots of cream, she stirred it and took a sip, she said.

"Besides, I'm not ready to pee yet"

She was in the bathroom when the call came from Lee, she was in The Crossing, she was safe, treat it as a holiday, she came out holding up the test, showing two strong bars, she was pregnant and full of hormones.

She had come to Gerald later that night, she found him in his study, she stopped at his door it was ajar, she knocked.

"Come in"

Jess pushed the door open to find Gerald sitting at his desk, he was facing her, he said.

"I was expecting this visit She went in, Gerald pulled a chair over to her patting it, she sat and spoke with a dignity never witnessed before, clear heroic bravery.

"I think we need to leave him here, I mean that Boab is going nowhere, and it will want Nick here I know that, Nick will be free here, if we can send him of in proper traditional ways, I mean bring everyone together, can you, will you do this for me, for Nick" "Well I thought I would need to wait a day at least, but yes I will do it, I would be proud to do it"

Gerald got up and went to Jess gathering her up in a cuddle, she began to weep quietly on his shoulder.

In the days after that fateful day they had all gathered at the big sprawling ranch house, Mark and Ian, along with Craig who had walked out of the silent forest only a week ago along with Timothy, were the first arrive, Cathy and Cindy were tow, Jack and Estelle were picked up from Bangor airport, Gerald put his hand up for that chore, because Lee would be with them, Marlii along with Craig, had travelled in convoy to arrive in time they were all there, Uncle Pete would read as would Rose and Rhonda would sing a number with Lee, and they would celebrate Nick's life.

The dreams for most of them had stopped, and the remaining few who had dreamed were dreaming pleasant thoughts, Nick was laying on a bier by the Boab, he was viewed by everyone in the county, some there to say thank you to the stranger, the man many had only met in a novel or two.

Others were there to gawk at the body, hoping to see the gore that so many had expected, all they got to see was the lifeless body of a hero.

They gathered beside the Boab, chairs were lined up in long rows, they looked just like soldiers awaiting on orders, there Gerald ushered in the guests, among Nick's acquaintances, there were other writers, Artists, Sculptors, and many were present, music played and the perfumes from the floral arrangements was pleasant, as Gerald got up the speak, a silence fell over those present, the Boab came to life.

It shook its limbs, ruffling its foliage and leaves, its face came to life, its eyes fluttered opened, it yawned.

It reached out with its limb, stretching, just as it was coming out of a deep sleep, a Kookaburra song came from the tree, most of the crowd looked up at the tree, that was a different cry than they ever heard before, a Kookaburra's laugh is verry distinctive, and Kookaburra's did not exist in the USA The tree spoke.

"You have come to say goodbye, revere him as a hero, this is good, but time is of the essence, you must say your goodbyes, I must take him, to the Neitherworld, that is where he belongs, to live among the heroes to live among your Gods" The tree's limbs shook and went to the bier Nick lay upon, it said.

"So peaceful, he will keep this peace, he will lay in it an eternity, Chief please say what you want to say" Gerald looked at the crowd arranged before the body, he looked over to Nick where he lay, he finally looked at the tree, and spoke.

"No, anything I can say about this man would pale into insignificance with what you could say, what you witnessed, and the result we now have, no, I think we should all listen to you" "He looked into the face of death, that one single thing, we are all most frightened of, my fears, of Borers, fires, rot, I am scared of all those things, just as you all have what fears you in little boxes, all tied up in string, but there is no way to compare what any of you have seen in your combined lifetimes, with what Nick saw before his mortal death, he should not be dead, with me he will not be, he could never survive here now, he would be horrified, he would be mad, revere him now before he is gone" And with that the branch arms swept down to the corpse, laying on the bier, its branches had surrounded Nick, until he was completely covered, the foliage turned green, the limbs went back to their position, the outline of Nick's body hung high in the tree, the Boab looked down into the crowd, eyeing them all over once, he said.

"He will be gone in minutes, watch my magic, watch me make him disappear"

JESSIE

Yes okay, I get it, I think, I am currently in my last trimester, I have had all the assistance I have needed, my writing retreat will be opening on my due date, fingers crossed it all goes smoothly, hey it will be alright if I am not there, Nick would, no will be happy with everything, with Miranda donating land for me to build on, she personally drew up Nicks plans which she had a photographic memory of, she had almost mastered that house out of Nick's head, getting in there and reading him.

But back to my story, Angie and Rhonda, and those around them are sympathetic, I think we got off extra light, I don't think any one would ever learn what had happened, but when Nick had killed it the pall that hung over the town dissipated into nothing, for the first time in since the early days of The Crossing the place was crisper, fresher, it changed in hours, I suppose how it was back in Polk County, I remember seeing the people looking up into the sky, in awe of the clarity.

Everything is much clearer now.

Nicks books are enjoying a resurgence, because of past stories and history, The Forest is on the best seller list, and will stay there for a little longer, maybe a lot longer, I will visit later today with Miranda and Timothy, I will catch up with Craig and Rhonda, Mark and Cathy as well Ian and Cindy, Nicks parents will be there as will Graeme and Jill along with Angie, I know I will be placed into a corner with Cathy and Cindy, and we will all talk about our pregnancy's.

It has been tough without Nick here, I know I am on my own, well there is plenty of help around, I will miss Nick, his presence is what I miss, but his parents are going to love this Granddaughter.

The one thing I keep remembering about that day was something he said to me, "Better of dead"

He said that to me, after saying what he had seen, what had he seen?

His injuries had been horrific, it was a wonder he had lasted as long as he did, but the many hoodoos he put paid to on that day was inescapable, from that day on people have become more calm, the wars have ceased around the world, greed is being reversed, everything is changing or has changed, we have all changed here at Shrives Island, but we are producing more timber, more Gold than we ever have before, the town has survived, and with the rail head, travel has changed here, it won't be long before we have an airport.

I can feel my baby kick, I have no doubt that we have a ballerina in there, or we may have a ball player of some sort, the girls are going out for ball sports now days, aren't they?

She will be anything she her heart desires, I can say that with some confidence, she will be a success at whatever she puts her hands too, my paintings have changed to a dark pallet since Nick has been gone, not evil dark, just verry dark in my color selection, they have sold so I don't know, if people want them I will keep producing them, most of them are of the Boab, but some I have done have been of Shrives Island, and the House.

I like the ones of the Town and its outskirts, the Mill, there is a café there now, Bobby is doing tours out there, he controls the tours at the mine as well, coordinates it all, everyone has taken a new role in the town, Uncle Pete, well what do you say about that man, his family, still does the best ice cream on the planet, and the whole Grange's soft drink thing, well that was handled perfectly by Uncle and Timothy Grange, and that was a tidy deal, so how do I console myself? I do, I just do it as they say in the Nike add, I am far too busy to lay comatose, rolled up in a fetal position, my husband has left me a legacy, and I will see it through, when Nick first spoke to me about the Twin Towers, I thought he was finally losing his marbles, but that was until my cousin who works in aeronautics told me it was not possible to fly passenger jets at such a low altitude, at such a high speed, that was when I realized he was right, and it all made sense, what was destroyed on 9/11 was innocence, you have to ask yourself, who had purported this on the people, they will ask questions, and they will be appeased with bald faced lies, "They" cannot let the sheeples know, so we will continue, the evil will go on, but we can deal with the human monsters, and this little bundle of joy is going to offer so much, so as I head toward my due date, and the opening of the Writer & Artist retreat, I am hopeful for the future, with a healthy skepticism, I will be hopeful for the future.

CHAPTER TWENTY-NINE

THE CROSSING

The town, had settled back to "Normal" as normal as it could get, the town which was known as The Crossing as a term of endearment had three new baby's, a female with the surname Lester, there were two males one a Harris the other a Luther they had all come into the world exactly nine months after the Twin Towers, all on the same day all coming into the world in the first minute of September the eleventh two thousand and two.

Since that day Shrives Island has gone through a transformation, the Boab, that sprouted from the ground on what was left of the hill, was growing at an inordinate rate, in the first months its root system had overgrown the fountainhead strangling it closed allowing the water to dry up, from that time forward the trunk of the Boab threatened to over inflate with water and explode in the end but the Boab just kept growing, Miranda never took a husband but left many a man in love, Timothy will finally marry, in the next month, Mark along with Cindy have moved their family back to Shrives Island permanently, his winning rate went up in the first six months, training from the Island was cleaner and clearer.

Ian and Cathy had come back to the Island, along with baby, he has decided to go solo, and is in great demand as a session musician, Tin Soldiers have gone on, the replacement of a guitarist/vocalist is easy today, you could have that, his baby came first.

Jess has had guests in her writeaway, as it had been known, the Baby Nicola was the treat of the day for most of the guests, she came in the afternoon, when tea and cake was served, Jess would not see her again until she had been passed around, and she would finally come back to where she found her besties, Taron Harris and Bobbie Luther, were there they sat in the afternoon sunshine that flooded in through the big picture window, where artists and writers spoke to each other about what they were working on, sometimes, the writer or the artist, is sure of their work, so would lend their own ears out to those who had a story to tell, some seeking advice, some willing to give it.

Those three children together is just like watching magic, no one had known why it was like watching magic, it just was.

At the time they had all turned four months old, they had begun to show their abilities, and they let them be, let them improve what they were good at, but they all showed the ability of "Seeing" or "Knowing" it will continue, they are all very bright.

The whole town has been transformed, the hotel, the old hotel along with the houses along the Odistgeeg, Mark, Nick as well as Ian's childhood home that was unindated were rebuilt on the east side of land, under the Boab tree, where they should have originally built, Jess had taken a parcel of land from Miranda's trust fund, where she had built her Writers Retreat made her neighbors not just with Miranda, but Mark Cindy and Taron.

Uncle Pete had stayed right where he was, most traders chose to move into the new marketplace, but Pete was staying where he had been all these years, it made no difference to Pete, he had no worries or needs for customers, there was always a line at Uncle Pete's.

Rose had been verry busy, selling her father's wares to the new cafes out at the Mill, and new marketplace, Angie had become the new waitress, mainly as a distraction to her paintings, she was painting as she had needed today, pocket money was how she had thought of the wages, but her painting slowed back down, from the insane rate she was painting the boxes, she was now finally back to normal, painting "things" that came into her head.

Rhonda had recently moved into the new library, the books arrived and Rhonda showing the true professionalism of an old school librarian had everything cataloged, and was in its home, by the end of that day, it has seen a resurgence since being reopened, the waterfall park is still there, now just above the river line, that now ran through the old motel, most of which was washed away in the first flood, the bar b qs are back, the crowds much more in control than in "The old days".

Moving up to what has been renamed Boab Hill, the tree now sat on a squat small hillock, it was rather large for the time it had been growing here, but people found their way to the tree, the drying riverbed had become a well-worn path up to the base of the Boab, it will be grassed over soon, returning more parkland to the town.

The Mill, of what had not been flooded, kept producing, they had been far enough up stream for the flooding to do much damage.

The flooding had subsided in days, the root systems coming free, had taken care of the floods, Miranda had dealt with the floods, she had sent the water back, however closing down other worlds was a brave move she had decided to go with, she had put herself in jeopardy, while protecting her brother and the three boys, she had recovered and was back to full life, both her and Timothy loved having toddlers around them, they both adored them.

It was to Miranda that Nicola had put a sentence together, the semblance of a sentence.

"Look Randa, Boab growing" The had all stopped, and gawked at her, Jess had no doubt she was observing the order, that was why she had chosen Miranda for that little message, the most unusual point to this point was the fact that Taron and Bobbie were looking out the window, both standing in the corner of the picture window, looking off into the distance, directly toward the Boab.

The Boab was doing what it had always succeeded in doing, even overcoming dark hauntings and ghosting's, it stood and grew, stood and grew.

TIM

Hi, I know you have a lot to ask me, I went missing on returning to my time, I have aged, a couple of decades in a century, what I have seen would curl your hair, I was there when they lynched Joshua Brown, I was there through all the misery of the great war, and the other one, and Vietnam, and the one Iraq, I will stop there, I found the secrets of Desmond and his son, that part of this story began in Polk County in 1880, and when Desmond Brown returned from a voyage in that year he told his son of his wish to move to The Crossing, and so it begins, Desmond did not get to travel in life to Australia, but he did travel in death, attached to the house that will stand again, the history was lost with their travels, Joshua succeeding in at least managing to put enough of a scare into this little town, as much as I would like to explain to you, how Nick pulled us out, pulled us out of the drain, I can't maybe Miranda could explain it, but I have no memory or very vague, I have been to many worlds, I have had my mind ripped from me many times, however we prevailed, the forest and the boys, I had something to do with that, I had known it was a good idea to grab a couple of "Boom Sticks" came in handy in the end, I was hauling them around with me for quite a while, I travelled the Neitherworld and met many who had a story about the Browns, I learned that to be in that place at that time I would be useful, with what I brought with me, I had known that to be rid of Desmond Brown and his cohorts would bring down a barrier that was stopping Nick from getting to where he had to get to, he finished it, and so did the boys, when I walked out of the forest, into Shrives Island, I was taken back, I had to see Miranda, I cannot believe the years she has lived, she has aged, but gracefully, we walked out of that forest, and into Shrives Island, we walked into a first aid van, still busy helping with the aftermath, we were treated, I was treated by Constance, we have been out quiet a lot, she knows my history, she said if you live at The Crossing, you have to be able to suspend belief, I asked her to marry me, now wild horses could not get her to the chapel quickly enough, and we will be happy, oh and I have a piece of Jessies art, it is of the old pub, that was my home, it has taken pride of place over the fireplace, and it will go with me when I move out into my new place, I am building it at the moment, that's the funny thing when it comes to erecting things I am the champ, I have held the knowledge in my head just as my father would have hoped, it is nearly done, past lock up, come to the house warming, that is this weekend, next week is the wedding, I kept the plans pretty close to my father and my ideas for the original ranch house we built way back when, the mod cons are a bonus, but the house is a stunner, rock and stone everywhere, with the most lustrous timbers, and that painting will look just grand over the fireplace in the sitting room, we will be honeymooning in Sydney, you know Luna Park, Taronga Zoo, Manly Corso, I think then back to the safety of The Crossing, we will come back with our tails between our legs, I know, the Boab is growing well, it stopped the last of the water flow, just the other day, that fountainhead did cause problems in the town, but it's not a problem any longer, but I feel the Boab working its magic over us, over those three baby's we were blessed with, the Babies of the Boab, that is how I feel, and most of the people in town are talking again, they speculate on the "Kids" all the time, a newspaper reporter contacted Mark Harris just the other day, Mark told them how far to run, how fast, stay away from the Island they were told, and for a couple of days, I think they made it to Moe, before the locals stopped them there, busted some of their gear and sent them back down the freeway toward Melbourne, I believe the strength of those "Kids" are keeping people away, can you believe that, all that magic controlled by three children about to turn twelve month's old, WOW, Craig and Marlii had still not become pregnant, they had catching up to do and will get pregnant when they are ready, they have spoken about it, what will there child bring, we will need to wait to find out, it will be full of magic, I have no doubt, oh do you remember that doll that was found in that police evidence box, I took it, I used it early on in the peace, it held him for ten minutes, it wasn't his vessel at all, his vessel was that pit he ended up in, I don't know what is next, I hope we live a peaceful life, after all we have been through, long happy lives, not too much to ask.

THE BOAB

Yes, I am here, My name is Yggdrasil of the south, there are many of us, how do you think we imbue our magic through everything, all things, like Oden's tree there is a poem "An Ash I know there stands, Yggdrasill is its name, a tall tree, showered in shining loam.

From there comes the dews that drop in the valleys.

It stands forever green over.

That stands for me as much as it does in Oden's world, call me the hanging tree if you wish, but that story goes on further, to tell you of the meaning of Yggdrasil, and the Gallows, and so it goes, Odin had made his way to Yggdrasil, after looking into the nine worlds, he found his way to Yggdrasil's roots, where he was able to find Mimir's Well, he seeked out Mimir and asked for a drink, the horned god told Odin, that without an eye he would not let him drink, Odin instantly ripped out his eye and dropped it into the well, Mimir dipped his horn into the well rewarding Odin for his sacrifice, a sacrifice that he still had to live through, he had given an eye for the knowledge, and as a compensate he had to stab himself in the side with a spear and hang from Yggdrasil for seven days and nights, this much sacrifice, there are many like him Nick Lester is one, he gave his life at a beat and only he knows he has saved mankind, for now, I have been involved in life here on this planet for eons, and I can say humans are really doing a great job, they are, doing a great job of stuffing it up, and while we are still on this merry go round, I will say it will be more of the same, until one of you silly little people hit the red button, the one that will light enough "Boom Sticks" to wipe out all of mankind, and yes I know, humans will probably rise up out of that primordial ooze, and yes we will be here, call us the lungs of the planet then strip forests bare, makes perfect sense, not, but I am blathering, now, that young Boab, the one that sprung up in Shrives Island, where the house used to be, it has taken over the life force there for the first time in over one hundred years, it has it battles in front of it, but with the peeps there in that town it will overcome anything that is thrown at it, and the Boab that got tangled up literally, with the Desmond Brown Mansion is doing great in its new patch, it has taken Nick and has doubled its size, I would say Nick is still doing good work, I think the Boab is enjoying the stories that Nick is reading to him, telling him of his adventures, as a boy, or reading one of his novels, things go back to normal, that's the way it always is, especially with you humans, back to commerce, living, loving, life, do you know how infinitesimal your lives really are, trees live many human lifetimes, and you pack much into a lifetime, I say slow down, you need to come back to the land, and there you will prosper, mark my words, and of the forest of soldiers, that is one special forest, it was the forest of Shrives Island, and they know each other well, the Mill and the forest have promised to speak to each other, my roots have spread further, and have grown wider, there will be more Boab's around the world, soon in England, we have strengthened, we have grown, having been able to rid ourselves of that evil being, Nick knows what he had battled, me I only got a glimpse, and what I saw for the time I saw it scared the leaves off me, you do know I am hearing from Nicola, Taron and Bobbie they are coming through, I almost had a conversation with Nicola just the other day, from the boys I am getting giggles and laughs, but they are coming through loud and clear, she said my name Yggdrasil, she also said clearly Boab, she is aware, so she is aware of her father, I can imagine it now, sitting with Jess and Nicola, having a conversation about her father, but that is in the future, not too far into the future, I am getting weary, I hope I fall into a great slumber, and sleep and grow, as I said the magic is alive in Shrives Island, and strong, the new custodians will come up to the mark, and the forest is going back to sleep, recover, and be there to stand the next time, when that will be I have no idea, but not soon I hope, we will stop now, I have said all I have to say, I am glad we are parting with all things looking up, the pall that hung over everyone has lifted, it cost them with the death of Nick, but little sacrifice, goes a long way.

EPILOGUE

NICK

Hi, I don't think I need any introduction, my writing precedes me, I am dead, that explosion in the end almost ripped me in two, but I outlived it, I killed it, but before I did it showed me, it showed me of how it was slowly taking control of everything it came into contact with, it aged me going all the way back to where that thing, the eye, came here to this world, its horrid black magic it had within it, was the cause of wars, and will continue, this lust for power will continue as the bad men will continue to run politics, but it was the smaller battles that cause the most grief, the most misery, my daughter is thriving I am watching closely, I am watching The Crossing closely, if I begin at the start of this whole saga we will be here for a couple of days, but if I give you the edited version, well that will be shorter, so how about I go back to where Tim and Miranda came into our lives, I had known from the first day what a miracle I had achieved, may be they sapped a bit of "Magic" from me that cost me, I do know my death was inevitable, having the knowledge going in to fight the eye, that I was never one of the number, it is ironic actually, we thought we were the awesome foursome, with Marlii as a side act when in fact she was the main attraction, but as I was saying, those twins changed our lives, heck they changed everyone for the better I think, but after Craig lost the plot and ended up in hospital, well I thought we were seeing the end, and when he came to me with the plan to blow the place up, it rekindled a memory from way back when, and when it Went off with that town altering explosion, that was when it got mixed up for me until later that morning I turned on the T.V to see the twin towers fall, and after contacting Margaret I had known I would be coming to Polk county, I didn't know that this was where it would end for me, my life as I knew it, but I went in with my eyes opened, I wrote that thing out of existence, my reward was to be given a second chance of eternal life, and through the Boab I will continue to exist, but not in your world, I am tethered to the Neitherworld, but from there I can peak in and have a look, but ultimately I end up back with the tree, I exist in it root system, as I said my daughter is thriving, and so are Mark and Cindy's boy, along with Ian and Cathy's boy, The Crossing will be a better place, well it's time for me to say goodbye, arrivederci, see you round like a rissole, and I know my time was short, but I say short and sweet, and to the point.

The End

www.ingramcontent.com/pod-product-compliance
Lightning Source LLC
Chambersburg PA
CBHW051309190726
48290CB00001B/72